# Heroes at Risk

Moira J. Moore

ACE BOOKS, NEW YORK

**THE BERKLEY PUBLISHING GROUP**
**Published by the Penguin Group**
**Penguin Group (USA) Inc.**
**375 Hudson Street, New York, New York 10014, USA**
Penguin Group (Canada), 90 Eglinton Avenue East, Suite 700, Toronto, Ontario M4P 2Y3, Canada
(a division of Pearson Penguin Canada Inc.)
Penguin Books Ltd., 80 Strand, London WC2R 0RL, England
Penguin Group Ireland, 25 St. Stephen's Green, Dublin 2, Ireland (a division of Penguin Books Ltd.)
Penguin Group (Australia), 250 Camberwell Road, Camberwell, Victoria 3124, Australia
(a division of Pearson Australia Group Pty. Ltd.)
Penguin Books India Pvt. Ltd., 11 Community Centre, Panchsheel Park, New Delhi—110 017, India
Penguin Group (NZ), 67 Apollo Drive, Rosedale, North Shore 0632, New Zealand
(a division of Pearson New Zealand Ltd.)
Penguin Books (South Africa) (Pty.) Ltd., 24 Sturdee Avenue, Rosebank, Johannesburg 2196,
South Africa

Penguin Books Ltd., Registered Offices: 80 Strand, London WC2R 0RL, England

This is a work of fiction. Names, characters, places, and incidents either are the product of the author's imagination or are used fictitiously, and any resemblance to actual persons, living or dead, business establishments, events, or locales is entirely coincidental. The publisher does not have any control over and does not assume any responsibility for author or third-party websites or their content.

HEROES AT RISK

An Ace Book / published by arrangement with the author

PRINTING HISTORY
Ace mass-market edition / September 2009

Copyright © 2009 by Moira J. Moore.
Cover art by Eric Williams.
Cover design by Annette Fiore DeFex.

ISBN: 978-0-441-01776-8

ACE
Ace Books are published by The Berkley Publishing Group,
a division of Penguin Group (USA) Inc.,
375 Hudson Street, New York, New York 10014.
ACE and the "A" design are trademarks of Penguin Group (USA) Inc.

PRINTED IN THE UNITED STATES OF AMERICA

10  9  8  7  6  5  4  3  2  1

*For Seán and Cate, who surprised me*

# Acknowledgments

Thank you to my mother, who is my most dedicated PR agent, to Jack Byrne, my agent, and to Anne Sowards, my editor.

# Chapter One

The residence of the Source and Shield Service was unimpressive in appearance, a plain, large square of a building. Simple in style, drab in material, anyone would look right past it. It was boring and forgettable.

But to me, it was beautiful. I had been away from it for over a year. I couldn't wait to get settled back within it. And it seemed to me that the carriage we had rented was taking its own sweet time to draw up before the building and come to a complete stop. Once it had, Taro and I leapt out with our bags, and I thought about kissing the ground.

"All we need are fires!" Taro announced as he kicked open the front door to the residence.

I looked at him and couldn't help grinning. He was healthy and relaxed, his black eyes practically glowing, his black hair mussed by a hard day of travel. It was good to see him finally back to himself. While he had been steadily improving in body and disposition since we'd returned to the mainland a few months earlier, I realized just then that he still hadn't regained his usual buoyancy. Not until we'd gotten home.

"Aye, we certainly do." I, of course, had no idea what his

words meant. Shintaro Karish was, in many ways, the most stereotypical Source I'd ever met, which meant that at times he was compelled to make incomprehensible statements. I was a Shield, the fairly average Dunleavy Mallorough, which meant I was very sensible, and knew when not to bother twisting my brain trying to figure out the meaning of my Source's words.

Besides, all I needed to know right then was that his words were expressing his joy in being home. A joy I shared. The Triple S residence in High Scape and the Shield Academy in Shidonee's Gap were the only homes I'd ever known. Well, the only ones I remembered. I had spent seventeen years in the Academy, and then had been sent straight to High Scape. In the three years that my official address had been the Triple S residence of High Scape, I'd spent more time away from it than in it. Still, it felt like a proper home, a place I belonged, and a place I had the right to bar others from entering. That was all a home was, really.

"It's probably too much to expect that any of the others are in," Taro commented, and he carried both of our bags into the foyer.

He wouldn't let me carry my own bag, unless I wanted to get into an argument over it, which I rarely did. Sometimes I just grabbed my bag and we got into a tugging match, which made me feel ridiculous, so I would let go. Taro, of course, didn't look ridiculous. Just patient and lordly. He was good at that, damn him.

Seven Pairs were needed to keep High Scape stable. It was one of the hottest sites in the world, constantly barraged with earthquakes and tornadoes and other natural events that would normally tear down the buildings, bury the crops, and decimate the population. Sources were born with the ability to channel the power of these natural disasters and keep the land stable. Shields were born with the ability to make sure Sources weren't killed by the forces that swirled through and around them.

I was a Shield; Taro was my Source. All we were supposed

to do was keep High Scape calm. But when Taro had been abducted by Stevan Creol, I'd found myself playing amateur Runner trying to find him, with an incompetence that made me cringe every time I thought of it. Stevan Creol had been a Source with a lot of anger he didn't keep nearly repressed enough. He had been taught how to prevent disasters while in the Source Academy, just like every other Source, but once he was released from the Academy he discovered how to create natural disasters, something no one had ever thought of doing, because why would they? He had been using that perversion of a skill to try to destroy High Scape as a means of expressing his frustration with his lot in life. During his captivity, Taro had picked up the same skill, because Creol had liked to show off and Taro has eyes. It turned out to be a handy talent, one Taro had already used more times than I liked.

I was the one who had figured out how to kill Creol while he was attacking High Scape. I did it by manipulating his Shields while he channeled. Words couldn't describe how very uncomfortable I was with that. I didn't know whether the fact that no one other than Taro knew about it made me feel better or worse. I had no desire to admit to my actions and face the consequences. We wouldn't be executed or placed in prison—Pairs were considered too valuable to be unrecoverably destroyed—but we could be sent to a cold site for the rest of our lives, where no one needed or respected our talents. It would be a waste, and it would be hell.

Yet shouldn't I be punished for killing someone? How could something like that just pass away, like it had never happened? Was there anything I could do to make up for that?

I thought about it a lot. Good ideas never came to me.

After that mess, we had very little time in High Scape before Empress Constia, unhappy with the quality of her son and heir, had sent Taro and me to the remote southern island of Flatwell to search for the descendants of her exiled sister. It was Taro who was wanted for the job, for my illustrious Source had first managed to catch Her Majesty's eye and then earn her trust. I was just dragged along to make travel more comfortable for Taro, whatever that was supposed to mean.

I was fully justified in resenting the Empress for this folly. We were a Pair, and we had responsibilities. To pull us off our roster for personal use was an abuse of her position. I didn't care why she had felt Taro was the only person she could trust with such a delicate task. She had unlimited wealth and ultimate power; she could have sent anyone. She should have sent someone better suited to the task. She could have paid them enough that they would have done the job and kept her secrets.

What made the whole situation even worse was that the one descendant we found, Aryne, was not to the royal taste. Not properly educated, Her Majesty declared, and lacking that certain quality that every ruler needed. Apparently, being clever and resilient didn't mean much.

Fortunately, we hadn't told Aryne she had the potential to be the future ruler of our world. Even more fortunately, she was a Source. So she'd had a place to go when her great-aunt hadn't wanted her. The Source Academy.

That was one good thing that had come out of that ridiculous trip. Aryne had gotten out of a situation of ignorance and abuse, and was on her way to a much better life. Provided she hadn't run away from the Academy yet.

Now we were finally home. Perhaps, after disappointing just about everyone who had ever expected more from us, we would be left alone to do what we were supposed to do. Be a Pair. Channel and Shield.

Please.

"Do you think our rooms are still ours?" Taro asked.

"Why wouldn't they be?"

"They might have brought in another Pair to replace us."

I stared at him, shocked. I had never thought of that. "They wouldn't do that."

"We've been gone a long time, Lee," he said. "And we've been gone a lot. A volatile place like High Scape, maybe they need a Pair that's not unreliable."

We weren't unreliable. Things outside of our control kept pulling us off the roster. "They'd better not."

That didn't come out quite the way I'd meant.

Taro snickered.

Ben Veritas stepped into the corridor from the kitchen. "Source Karish, Shield Mallorough, welcome home." He reached out to take the bags from Taro, who eased them out of reach. Ben was a regular, neither a Shield nor a Source, of late middle age, retained by the Triple S to clean up after us and make our meals. I found him disturbing, though I wasn't sure why. There had been people at the Academy who prepared our meals and cleaned up after us, usually Shields who had been through the Matching ceremonies for decades and hadn't managed to bond to a Source. They hadn't disturbed me at all. There was just something in Ben's manner, like he was watching us more closely than he should. "You should have sent word ahead of your arrival. I would have had a hot meal ready for you."

"Optimism is despised by nature," said Taro. "Besides, we're going out to eat."

"We are?" I asked. It was the first I'd heard of it.

"We have to celebrate our return. Delicacies excellently prepared and accompanied by chilled goblets of the best wine. Brought to you on trays carried by handsome young men and women. Sometimes there's music."

I was starving. And one of the good things about eating in a tavern was the variety of possible dishes. I wasn't sure I wanted to just sit at home, tired though I was. I wanted to really soak in High Scape again, walk down the streets, hear the familiar accents and turns of phrase, really feel that I was back. I'd missed it.

"I thought I heard you two." Source Kyna Riley came clomping down the stairs. "Shintaro, Dunleavy, welcome home."

"Kyna!" Taro crowed, dropping our bags and throwing his arms open and hugging Riley whether she liked it or not. Fortunately, Riley remembered Taro's exuberance, and she accepted the embrace with only a roll of her eyes. "Tell me all the exciting things that have happened while we were gone."

Ben silently picked up our bags and carried them upstairs.

"How can anything exciting happen in your absence, Shintaro?" she asked, and there was the slightest bitter edge in her tone that informed me that all was not calm on her sea.

"What's going on?" I asked.

"Giles and I have been transferred to Ice Ridge."

"Ice Ridge," I echoed. That had been a cold site, the last time I'd looked.

"A volcano erupted a few months ago and has been giving off little spurts ever since."

"And they're just sending a Pair now?" I used to have high respect for the Triple S council. I now found myself becoming distressingly disenchanted. It wasn't my fault. They kept indulging in behavior that smacked of ludicrous incompetence.

Riley shrugged. "Ice Ridge isn't important to anyone."

Which may have been the cause of her bitterness. A transfer from High Scape to Ice Ridge was taking a big step down in prestige.

"They have the best oranges!" Taro protested.

They did, actually. "Was anyone hurt?" I asked.

"No lives lost, but a lot of structural damage, and they can't rebuild with the ongoing events."

I wondered why we hadn't heard of this during our travels from Erstwhile. I would have thought that was the kind of news that would get around.

"We're not the only ones being transferred," Riley added. "Vera and Lauren left for Blue Rock a few weeks ago."

This was disappointing. Triple S Pairs never stayed in one place for too long, but assignments usually lasted at least a few years. "Do you know who's coming to replace them?"

"No one," said Riley, "as far as I know."

"Why not?"

"High Scape's been a lot calmer for the last year. Not quite cold, but, I don't know, it might be on its way there. I haven't channeled in weeks. So we don't need as many Pairs."

High Scape was known for its frequent turbulence. The population practically prided themselves on it. Certainly, hot spots and cold sites could switch designations, but usually it took decades. What could have caused such an abrupt change? Creol couldn't have been responsible for all of the natural events in High Scape before his death. And I refused to believe that the half year the Reanists had spent sacrificing aristocrats to their gods had actually accomplished the stability they had claimed to seek. That was just ridiculous. "Do you know how many Pairs are going to be transferred?"

"Not yet."

And if they had to send Pairs away, why couldn't they send the annoying ones? Like Beatrice and Benedict? Or Wilberforce and Ladin?

I couldn't help feeling oddly deflated. I'd had an image of what to expect from home. And that had included all the Pairs. Even the ones I didn't like. I hated change.

Riley was looking at me with an expression of puzzlement. "Are you all right, Dunleavy?"

"Of course."

"You look different."

That was probably the remnants of the southern sun. While I never got as brown as Taro, I'd turned a kind of golden beige. It made my hair even more blazingly red than usual, too. Those effects had faded a great deal during our journey home, but there was still a hint of additional color here and there. However, Riley wasn't supposed to know where we'd gone, so I couldn't tell her any of that. "Oh," I said, because I was a witty person.

"There's something different about your voice, too," she added.

"I see," I said. My voice sounded the same to me.

"We don't go until next week," said Riley, clearly giving up that line of conversation as a nonstarter. "And the night before, those of us not on watch are going out to, I don't know, celebrate or say farewell. Will you two go?"

Taro gently took her hand and bowed over it, kissing the back of it. "I am devastated that we will be losing you. If it does not conflict with my duties, I will surely be there to mourn your departure."

I must have been smirking, because the look Riley sent me was slightly hostile. I straightened my mouth. "My apologies, Riley." I had been laughing at Taro and his melodrama, not Riley. "Of course we will be there. I am very sorry to lose you."

"Thank you." Riley nodded. "I'm pleased you were able to get back before we left. I was worried we'd miss each other." She headed off toward the kitchen.

Taro grinned at me then, a particularly wicked grin that I had seen many times before. He grabbed my hand, and the next thing I knew, I was running up the stairs behind him. I ran behind him to his door, through his sitting room, and into his bedroom.

His bedroom. I had always avoided it. I never wanted anyone to expect to find me in his bedroom. I had never had any interest in knowing what was in it.

Well, I had never *wanted* to have any interest in it.

Now I was being dragged into it and I was smiling at the feeling of wickedness it engendered. I was going to have sex with the Stallion of the Triple S in the Stallion's bedroom.

He hated that nickname, so I didn't use it unless I wanted to tease him. But it wasn't one I'd come up with; it was too lurid for my taste. But he was known for sleeping with everything on two legs, though he claimed the numbers of rumor were highly exaggerated.

Taro closed the door and immediately curled his arms around my waist. "You have no idea how many times I imagined you in here," he said, just before he kissed me.

I had lost all common sense, or sense of self-preservation, when it came to Taro. I'd fallen in love with him. With my own Source. One of the most stupid things I could ever have done.

The regulars liked to think of a Pair feeling nothing but everlasting love for each other. That assumption seemed to be supported by the fact that when one partner died, the other followed into death. But in truth, for partners to fall in love with each other was a complication that could have disastrous repercussions. No one had figured out exactly how the bond really worked, but it did affect the emotions of the partners. Sometimes it put them into a form of harmony with each other, sometimes it brought out the worst in each other, and sometimes it created weird possessive and obsessive behavior. Falling in love made the latter all the more likely.

Which was why the instructors at the Shield Academy—and no doubt the Source Academy as well—drilled the lesson into our thick skulls again and again and again. Don't sleep with your Source. Certainly, don't fall in love with your Source. If you become unstable, you won't be trusted to guard any of the prestigious sites, and you don't want to ruin your chances over something so fleeting and so stupid.

It had all sounded very logical to me. It had seemed even more logical after I was bonded to Lord Shintaro Karish, the Stallion of the Triple S, handsome and engaging and full of life. Aggravatingly handsome. Annoyingly engaging. Exhaustingly full of life. It would be dangerous for someone like me to get sexually involved with someone like him, because I was of a nature to take things more seriously, and he was of a nature to cast a wide net over the world in his search for pleasure. I wasn't sure I could remain mature and professional once he moved on to new partners.

I still didn't know if I could remain professional and mature once he was no longer interested in me. But it hadn't taken me that long to come to want him, and he had seemed to want me, too. And although I knew I would end up paying for it in the long run, the damage I had been doing to our relationship by sticking to my principles, principles Taro didn't agree with, could have lasted a lifetime. He had thought I was refusing him because I thought there was something wrong with him. If he had come to believe I thought him in any way inferior, we would have never recovered. It would have poisoned everything.

Besides, I wanted him. In a moment of clear self-indulgence, I had asked myself why I shouldn't have him. And while I was leery of the turmoil I would feel once he made his waning interest clear to me, I didn't at all regret the decision to enjoy him while I could. Maybe not the most sensible decision, but the right one.

So we indulged in a thorough homecoming, bathed together, and then headed out for supper in the most expensive tavern Taro knew of, to his surprised pleasure. "I'll have you thoroughly corrupted yet," he gloated.

"Corrupted?" I wouldn't go that far. Perhaps he'd ruined me for other lovers, but that wasn't his fault. He would be a hard act to follow.

"Before we were banished off to that damned island, you never would have consented to eating in a tavern like this."

Shields and Sources weren't required to pay for anything, as a sort of compensation for the fact that we weren't paid for our services. That didn't mean I felt we should always seek the most expensive of everything. We didn't need it, and I couldn't help feeling regulars would feel ill used if it became a habit. Still: "This is a special occasion."

"Aye, sure. And the reason you agreed to stay at the Imperial when we first got back to Erstwhile?"

I shrugged. I had been very tired of living rough for a year, and not in the mood for an argument.

"Face it: I'm corrupting you," he said. "Soon, you'll be just like me."

"Zaire forfend," I muttered.

I ordered the buffalo broth, a dish unique to High Scape that I hadn't realized I'd missed until I saw it written up on the menu board. And how could I have forgotten it? It teased the nose with heated spice and positively drowned the tongue in thick, savory flavor, the meat so perfectly tender it practically melted in the mouth.

Gods, I'd missed home. I almost couldn't believe I was actually here.

The food was wonderful, but the meal itself was not restful. Taro was well-known in High Scape, despite the frequency and length of his absences. Every few moments, someone would stop to exchange greetings and chat for a bit. Taro would try to draw me into the conversations, but neither I nor his devotee of the moment was interested. I watched him laugh and smile, and I wondered which of these people he had already slept with, and which would succeed me.

I would not act foolish when I was replaced. I would not. I had some pride. In fact, if I had my way, I would know it was coming before he did.

After enjoying a light, creamy dessert—oh, I had missed dessert!—we left the tavern and decided to stroll about High Scape to reacquaint ourselves with our post. It wasn't necessary in order for us to do our jobs well, but I was anxious to see the city.

High Scape was unlike any city or settlement I had ever seen, and so far I'd seen more settlements than I'd expected to by my age. It was divided by three rivers into six sections, called quads by the residents who apparently lacked a clear understanding of basic mathematics. Each quad had its own hospital and Runner Headquarters and government buildings. And each quad had its own character, largely influenced by the level of wealth enjoyed by its residents. The North Quad had the wealthiest residents of High Scape, and that was where we were headed. I rarely went there, having little reason to, and it was interesting to see the perfectly cobbled streets, the large, clean buildings with so much space between them, and the many large and leafy trees. As it got dark, lighters lit street lamps, adding a nice glow to everything.

A loud hissing sound, followed by a sharp pop that seemed to shake the night air, jolted out of nowhere. The shock of it pushed my heart right into my throat. "What the hell was that?" Taro demanded, and he leapt over the short iron fence beside him. He didn't immediately start running, as I had expected him to. "Ech!" he uttered. "Know what this is?"

I took a quick glance over the small field, seeing through the darkening air the scattering of small stone, iron and wooden posts. "It looks like an ash grove." Where the ashes of the dead were buried in copper urns.

Taro shed his hesitancy and started running, presumably in the direction from which he thought the noise had come. To me, it seemed as though it had come from everywhere. I climbed over the fence with the plan of running after him.

But I took only two steps before having to halt. I felt something odd. Some kind of resonance. Or vibration. A quick look around gave no evidence of anything that could create such an uncomfortable sensation. It seemed to skitter underneath my skin. It was horrible.

"Hey!" I heard Taro shout, and I looked up to see him sharply change direction.

"What the hell are you doing?" I called, and I got no answer. Why was my Source racing about in the dark? Chasing around after people was rarely a good idea under any circumstances. To do so in the dark was just begging for a disaster. One of us was sure to trip over one of the grove markers and break a leg.

"Hey!" Taro shouted again. "Stop running! That's an order!"

An order? Taro was no one to be giving orders. But maybe regulars didn't know that.

In the midst of running in the dark and trying not to fall and kill myself, I felt Taro's mental protections, the personal inner shields that guarded his mind when he wasn't channeling, drop down. That meant I had to raise mine around him. Which meant I had to stop running, because I wasn't sure I could run and Shield at the same time, and I wasn't insane enough to try. But really, what the hell was he doing? There were Pairs on duty. It was their job to settle any disasters, and they would resent us for stepping on their toes.

Almost immediately, though, I realized Taro wasn't channeling a natural event. When he channeled normally, he opened himself to the forces causing the disaster, and they rushed through him. In this manner, a Source drained a disaster of its power and diverted the forces in a harmless direction. But this time, he was pulling in selected forces, much fewer than usual, and he was directing them far more precisely than the raw power of a natural disaster normally allowed.

Taro was creating an event, not eliminating it. Damn it. I wished he would keep in mind that that was a skill he'd learned from a madman. It was unnatural to create disasters, and I didn't know why he was doing it right then. There was no good reason for it.

There was nothing I could do, though, except Shield him and keep him from killing himself. I'd yell at him after.

The ground trembled beneath my feet. Another sign that this was an artificial event. If it were real, I wouldn't be able to feel any of the physical manifestations. Taro would be stopping it before it got that far.

I hated earthquakes. I hated any kind of natural event, really. I was never supposed to have to feel any. That was part of what being bonded meant.

At least the tremors weren't very strong. No serious upheaval in the ground. None of the markers fell over. Nor did it last very long. The tremors faded away with nothing, as far as I could tell, being accomplished. I waited, ready to Shield again. Maybe he would try something else.

Moments burned by with nothing happening. It was eerily quiet, and I couldn't see anything. Zaire, this had been a stupid idea.

Then I heard, "Lee?"

And just like that, I was furious. "What the hell was that?" I demanded.

"There were people messing about," he answered as he appeared from the darkness and trotted up beside me.

"Doing what?"

"I don't know, but it probably had something to do with that racket we heard."

"So you decided to run after them? To what purpose? What would you do with them once you caught them?" Other than get beaten black and blue, if they were doing something illegal. Though I had no reason to think they were doing anything illegal. Just because I wouldn't imagine what anyone would be doing in an ash grove at night didn't mean their behavior had to be nefarious. Maybe they were visiting the remains of a family member. I could imagine plenty of scenarios out of novels and plays where some exiled member of a family would feel compelled to visit the ashes of a loved one under the cover of darkness.

It was possible.

"I couldn't do nothing," he insisted.

"Were they hurting another person?"

"I couldn't tell. I couldn't see."

He'd be able to tell. Any such victim would have been left behind, or would have run off in another direction. "I can see you risking our lives to help another person, but who cares about markers in an ash grove?"

"The families of those whose ashes are buried under the markers," he chided, trying to shame me.

He was unsuccessful. It was stupid to risk one's life for stone, no matter what the significance. "What was the point of the earthquake?"

"They weren't stopping."

"And did the earthquake stop them?" I knew damn well it hadn't because, clearly, they weren't there. "Wait, you didn't bury them, did you?" Because he could do that, too, and that disturbed me as much as his other unnatural skills.

"No, I did not," he snapped. "And no, it didn't stop them. Whichever Pair was on duty was trying to channel the earthquake. I didn't want to get into a battle for control over it. That could get messy."

It could get stupid, was what it could get. What was he thinking?

"Did you see what they were doing?" Taro asked.

"I haven't seen anything." I was only taking his word that there had been people in the grove at all. For all I knew, there'd been nothing going on and we'd been running around like idiots for no reason.

"Let's see if we can find what they were doing." Taro seemed enthusiastic about the possibility of finding something weird.

I really didn't care. I didn't like this place. It felt very strange, and I just wanted to leave.

But something small and white, almost glowing in the darkness of the night, caught my eye. Frowning, I stared at it, and as my focus cleared, other white somethings appeared. As I drew closer I was able to see that they were set in a sort of pattern. They were candles, unlit, and they made a circle. There was a line of a very pale powdery substance drawn from candle to candle, barely perceptible in the grass. The circle surrounded a marker. Dead center in the circle, a hole had been dug into the ground, and the marker had been uprooted.

I thought about stepping into the circle for about half an instant. Something about the whole scene made me very, very uncomfortable. Not uncomfortable in the "someone dug up someone's ashes" sort of way, though that was disgusting enough. I felt jittery, like something inside me was screaming to run while something else within me was keeping me rooted to the ground against my will. My heart was pounding, my breath was short, I thought I might have been sweating, and I could tell I was trembling.

It was probably time to give up on that ridiculous dream of mine, that I could ever be the cool, calm, unflappable Shield I had been trained to be.

I sighed.

It was our first damn day back.

# Chapter Two

Risa Demaris was a Runner. It was her task to hunt and catch criminals. It was a task demanding good health and an iron spine, but no family connections or education of distinction. From what I had observed—and Risa's bitter comments—it didn't pay very well, and I now had the experience to understand just what that meant.

Risa was a glorious woman. She was tall and beautifully shaped, strong and lean. Her skin was a gorgeous warm brown and her eyes were stunning. Really, if I was going to envy any woman for her appearance, it would be Risa.

She was wearing the uniform of a Runner right then, the tall black boots, the black trousers, the black tunic, and a black cape. She looked stern and imposing. When she was not on duty, she wore flowing garments of bright orange and yellow and half a dozen pairs of earrings. In either scenario, she stood out in a crowd, and she liked it.

Risa was my friend, one of the few I'd been able to make in High Scape. She had been put to the task of finding Taro when he'd been abducted by Stevan Creol. She hadn't been successful with it. I had, but only because I'd had a follower of Creol leading me every step of the way.

She wasn't visiting us for a social call. The evening before, Taro and I had reported the disturbance in the ash grove to the first Runner we could find, but Risa had come to do a follow-up interview. She said people had been digging up ashes all over the city, which was apparently what Taro and I had stumbled into the night before, and her superiors thought we would be more comfortable being questioned by her, as we knew her.

I didn't think I could possibly be comfortable with any conversation concerning digging up human ashes, regardless of the participants. Why would anyone want to mess around with that sort of thing?

"To start off," Risa said, leaning back into the settee in my suite. "Do either of you recall any new details about last night? Something you've remembered since you spoke with Runner Elliot?"

"I have nothing to remember," I told her. "I didn't see anything."

"Aside from the defiled marker."

"Aye."

"But, Karish, you saw people."

"Yes, but not faces or hair color or anything like that. Except . . ." He trailed off, his eyes narrowing.

Risa leapt on him. Verbally, of course. "You're remembering something."

"Nothing useful. There was just something familiar about the way one of them moved."

"But you have no idea why he seemed familiar."

Taro shook his head and shrugged.

"Well, keep thinking on it." She looked at me. "What about the grass immediately around the marker? Did you notice anything unusual?"

"I didn't get close enough to see."

"Why not?"

"I wasn't going to step inside the circle."

"Why in the world not?"

"It felt strange." I didn't like admitting that. It was fantastical and childish. But it was what had happened.

"It felt strange?" Risa asked with a snicker.

"Yes," I snapped.

She narrowed her eyes at me. "You're different," she accused me. "So are you," she said to Taro. "Why are you so quiet?"

"Silence enhances my beauty," he announced solemnly.

Risa clearly didn't know how to respond to that, so she didn't. She was smart that way. "Did you notice anything unusual about the grass around the marker?" she asked him.

"I didn't step into the circle, either."

"Why not?"

"Lee said it felt strange."

Risa rolled her eyes. "So neither of you touched anything?"

"Correct."

"And you didn't see or hear or smell anything other than what you've already mentioned?"

"No."

"You're sure."

"Yes."

"Then I guess all I can ask is that you let us know if you think of anything else."

Hopefully, we would never have any reason to ever think of it again. It was weird.

"You said this has been going on a lot?" Taro asked.

*Shut up, Taro. This is none of our business. Oh, except—*
"Were any of the other markers for the ashes of aristocrats?" Just in case. Taro had been born into an aristocratic family, and that caused him a stupid amount of problems, even though he'd given up all rights to the family title.

"Aye, but not all of them. There's everything you could think of. Merchants. Gamblers. Actors. Farmers. All sorts of different people."

An interesting selection of victims. If one thought the dead could be victims. Which I didn't, as they were dead.

"Do they have any idea who's doing it?" Taro asked.

"Not yet," Risa said in a curt voice. "Why? Are the two of you going to be supplying desperately needed assistance?"

That wasn't fair. We didn't try to get involved in these things. It just happened. "No," I answered loudly, before Taro could say anything. "It is none of our business. We are a Pair. That's what we do. That's all we're going to do."

Risa looked amused by my words.

Taro raised an eyebrow. "I would think after the last year you'd have a different opinion about that sort of thing."

Flatwell had been a rude shock for us both. It had been terrifying to be in a place where Pairs were neither respected nor supported. We had been expected to pay coin, which we didn't have, for everything we needed. It had been a harsh lesson in the dangers of having only one skill and relying entirely on it.

On the other hand, it was wise to know one's limitations. I was not a Runner. Who was I to get involved in a Runner's business?

"Where did you two go, anyway?" Risa demanded. "And why?"

No one was supposed to know where we'd gone, or why. Showing up after more than a year of absence, it was hard to lie, and I wasn't good at lying. "Triple S business." Which wasn't entirely a lie, as taking Aryne to Shidonee's Gap was Triple S business, and it was also a catchall phrase used to tell regulars to stop asking questions. Handy.

"Huh," said Risa, unimpressed.

"Did you bring your costume back with you?" Taro asked, sounding innocent when he was acting anything but.

I couldn't kill him. I wasn't suicidal. But I could hurt him a lot without experiencing any ill effects myself. Testing the limits of that ability might prove educational.

"Costume?" Risa demanded, eyes alight.

"It's not as interesting as it sounds, Risa."

"I beg to differ," said Taro.

Why was he doing this to me? I couldn't remember aggravating him recently. "Part of the task I was required to perform demanded particular clothing."

"Task, eh?" said Risa. "Some task other than Shielding, I suppose?"

"Bloody barbarians," Taro muttered, suddenly losing his good mood. "Wasn't enough that we were a Pair. They expected us to work."

Risa gaped at him for a moment, then started cackling with laughter, nearly falling off her chair in her enthusiasm.

"It's not funny," Taro objected, and no, he didn't sound at all petulant.

"It's beautiful!" Risa exclaimed. "Finally! You two had to work to earn an honest coin?"

That was all it took to bring Lord Shintaro Karish back. He sat up even straighter in his chair, his shoulders squaring back and the haughty mask slipping over his face. "We spend our lives risking our lives settling natural disasters, and have never gotten a damned coin for it."

I loved the way his *r*'s rolled whenever he was particularly annoyed.

But Risa was not the sort to be intimidated. If pushed, she could tell dozens of stories about lordlings whom she'd picked up in various drunken positions of embarrassment or destruction. "So what did you do?"

"Nothing we can tell you about," I told her.

"You can't tease me with a mention of a costume and then just drop it."

"Just watch us."

"At least tell me why you had to wear it."

"I'm sorry, Risa," I said. "Really. It's just that our time away was difficult, and to come home and come across—" More weird ritual trash. The people we'd known on Flatwell had taken their belief in ritual and superstition to fatal extremes. I hated rituals. They were never a good thing. I sighed. "It's disappointing, really." And frightening. And frustrating.

Risa tried to stare us into confessing. We stared back, silently. Then she shrugged. "All right. For now. But I'm getting some of that horrible white wine you like and pulling the story out of you."

Like hell. I was making a note of it. No more drinking with Risa.

We were able to tell her some of the more ridiculous things that had been going on in the Imperial court, claiming we had heard the stories during our travels. Risa told us of some of the goings-on in High Scape, which included a rash of home fires, a mayor who'd been caught spending too much government money on personal pleasure, and a series of successful jewel thefts. Risa's world was largely shaped by criminal activity, which was perfectly natural given her occupation, but it could make for a depressing conversation.

Risa was always, for some reason, a little less fun when Taro was with us. She seemed less relaxed and more likely to be offended. So it was a bit of a relief when she decided it was time to leave. But that wasn't necessarily an improvement of my overall circumstances, because Taro declared that it was time to go shopping. "For what?" I demanded.

"For whatever takes our interests. We work damn hard at our jobs and deserve whatever compensation we desire."

I looked at him with concern, discomforted by the tone of bitterness in his voice. "I don't need anything," I said.

He rolled his eyes. "That's subject to debate."

And that quickly, the bitterness was gone. Perhaps it had been a momentary aberration. "You can stop it right there." I found myself pointing at him, which was rude. "Only my mother is allowed to nag at me about my clothes." And only because I'd failed to find an effective means of gagging her.

"The point of shopping, my love, is not to go hunting for things you need, but allowing yourself to stumble across things you like and delighting in the discovery."

"How like a flighty lordling you sound."

"Hush, you, and be a good girl. It's not like you have anything better to do."

He was unfortunately right, but that didn't mean I was going to obey him unequivocally. "We are not shopping for clothes."

"Aye, aye. There's plenty else to find, you know. We need to get you some trinkets. You almost never wear any."

I shrugged. It wasn't as though I didn't like jewelry; I just never thought of it much. And when I did, I was uncomfortable with the idea of taking it from merchants. It was expensive, and I didn't need it at all. What few pieces I did have had been gifts from my family, and those would have been properly bought.

But there was no harm in looking.

In my experience, no city did markets as High Scape did them. It wasn't merely a matter of size, though High Scape did have a much greater number of merchants than any other city or settlement I had ever been to. It was also the fact that it was pretty much spread out all over the city, with a concentration in each quad and tendrils of stalls winding through the surrounding streets.

And then there was the sheer variety of goods. Clothing, of course. Clothing already made to fit general standard sizes, at which Taro always turned his nose. Fabric, to be purchased by those forced to make their own clothes. Tailors for those who could afford to have clothes made for them. Consumables, such as chocolate—Taro picked up three bars—and other luxuries, as well as vegetables and fruits and fish and meats and breads and cheeses and ales and wines and other liquors. Paintings and rugs and wall hangings and trinkets and toys. Dyes and cosmetics and perfumes and hair combs. Playing cards and name cards and news circulars and books. Just everything imaginable.

The noise of the market was often deafening, the scents in the air a battle between the sublime and the disgusting, and the streets completely crammed with people, animals and stalls. Sometimes I found it overwhelming. As well, fingering items I didn't need and listening to people bicker just wasn't terribly interesting to me.

Still, shopping with Taro could be fun, for he obviously enjoyed it, and his enthusiasm was a pleasure to observe.

Besides, there was a part of me that still hadn't quite recovered from worrying about every coin and whether we'd have enough to buy food, which had been a constant preoccupation of mine while on Flatwell. I couldn't say I wasn't thinking about how much things cost—I could never return to such a state of perfect ignorance—but knowing I could have it if I wanted it, regardless of price, was an almost dizzying relief.

I was disgusted that I felt that way. I was ashamed of how much I'd hated my time as a regular, how stressful I'd found it, how eager I was to return to the ease of being a Shield. I would ignore such self-assessment, if I could.

"That," he said, nodding at a bolt of blue cloth, "would look brilliant on you."

Aye, it would. "No clothes," I reminded him.

"Blue brings out the green in your eyes and makes your hair look exceptionally red."

And that was a good thing? "No clothes." Especially clothes that had to be made for me. That meant fittings, and fittings were time-consuming, irksome things.

"But you agreed to jewelry."

"I agreed to look at it." And I hadn't even done that. I just hadn't verbally opposed it.

Jewelry itself covered a lot of variety. There were plenty of rings, bracelets, anklets and chokers woven from leather or a variety of fabrics, and some of it was quite pretty. But that, of course, wasn't what Taro had in mind. "Gold," he declared.

"Copper would do, too," I suggested, but only because it made him give me that look of affronted disdain.

"Gold," he repeated.

"You know, if copper were more expensive, you'd be insisting on that over gold."

"There's a reason gold is more expensive."

"The merchants flipped a coin?"

"Because it's more rare, and it's prettier."

"Pretty being so much more valuable than useful."

"That's something that damn island taught us, didn't it?"

Taro never called Flatwell by its name if he could avoid it.

The stalls with the valuable jewelry were easy to spot. They had solid wooden walls on three sides and a guard or two standing at the front. The guards gave us a glance before returning to scanning the rest of the crowd, recognizing us as a Pair by the braids we wore on our left shoulders, and therefore not a threat.

Ah, and there was that disappointed look from the merchant when he realized some of his precious stock might be walking out with no coin in return. I'd almost missed that look.

"And don't even think of hiding your best stock," Taro warned him.

I looked up at him, startled. As the first words out of his mouth, they were a little harsh.

"I wouldn't dream of it," was the merchant's snappish reply.

"In fact, why don't we start with your strong box and move from there?"

The merchant sighed and ducked behind his display. He pulled out one black box, about a foot square, and then a second, unlocking both with keys secured to his belt. He raised the lids and pulled out the drawers.

I knew immediately that this was not the stuff for me. Gem-encrusted necklaces, rings, earrings and bracelets, thick and heavy and glittering. My skin hurt just looking at it.

Taro seemed to be reading my mind, for he tugged on one of my naked earlobes. "The holes are fairly small. You might have to work your way up to earrings such as these."

"Don't be ridiculous, Taro. I've no occasion for earrings such as these." I didn't expect any repetitions of the one party I'd attended in honor of the Crown Prince. Thank Zaire. I enjoyed music and drinking with friends as much as the next person, but there was something rather stiff about the gatherings of the High Landed. Plus I knew they were looking down at me, which was never a comfortable sensation.

The look of relief on the merchant's face was hilarious.

"You have in the past."

"And if I have any luck at all, I never will again." I looked at the merchant. "You can put these away."

He was pushing in the drawers before I'd finished speaking.

Taro growled but didn't press, instead choosing to glance over the rest of the man's inventory.

It wasn't a matter of modesty with me. I truly didn't care for jewelry that was too fussy, no more than I liked fussy clothing or fussy furnishings.

"So, what are these things?" Taro asked, holding up what looked like a gold lump on a gold chain. The chain was too short to be a bracelet, too long to be an earring. "I've seen people wearing them."

So had I, now that I thought about it. A faint memory teased at my mind and faded away. I took the item from him. I found a small pinning loop attached to the chain. The lump, upon closer inspection, was beautiful golden knot work.

"Not like that one, sir," the merchant objected. "Few have the taste required to—"

"Yes, yes," Taro interrupted him with a wave of his hand. "But what is it?"

"Are you visitors here?" the merchant asked in return.

Taro raised a haughty eyebrow. "We are Shield Mallorough and Source Karish."

And before the merchant would make the mistake of admitting the names meant nothing to him, I added, "We returned to the roster only yesterday. We've been at another post."

The merchant nodded in a quick, abrupt gesture, because it wasn't as though he actually cared. "These are called harmony bobs. They have become highly fashionable. They are said to bring good luck."

"Bring good luck?" Taro picked up another bob from the display. "How do they do that?"

The merchant shrugged. "The spells cast on them."

Taro chuckled. "Spells?" he asked incredulously.

"Casting has become popular this season."

How could belief in casting become popular? Like a style of boot. Who believed in casting outside of plays, poetry and novels? And, of course, Flatwell.

"You are to wear it pinned to your clothing, over your heart," the merchant explained. "The beating of your heart is supposed to wake the power in the metal. The bob itself must be given enough length to hang freely, to give it direct exposure to the forces it is supposed to affect."

What a ridiculous idea. "What has brought this on?" I asked.

"I suspect it has something to do with the Riverfront Ravage," said the merchant, and I could hear him capitalizing the words.

The what?

"Excuse me?" Taro asked.

"Some kind of illness. It started a few months ago. No one knows how it started or where it came from. Some people think it's from the trade boats. Some think it's because of all those little flies that seemed to be springing up down there."

How had we not heard of this during our travels?

"What's being done about it?"

The merchant shrugged. "There are healers looking into it, I expect. It's nothing too serious. No one's died or anything. It's pretty common for these kinds of illnesses to flare up in larger cities. It's nothing to worry about."

"Yet they are developing this interest in casting because of it?" Taro gestured at the merchant's display.

"The ignorant get scared," the merchant answered. "I believe people started feeling uncertain about things during the Harsh Summer."

Though I had not heard the title before, I imagined he was referring to the summer before last, when unseasonable weather had a devastating impact on crops and stocks, on all number of livelihoods and lives.

"Many have still not recovered. I imagine there are those who never will. And then this illness comes, and the healers can do nothing. The Pairs can do nothing, the healers can do nothing, the mayor can do nothing. People start looking for other solutions."

How incredibly sad. I couldn't imagine what was worse than feeling utterly helpless, having terrible things happen and knowing there was nothing to be done about it. "But no one has died from this illness?"

"Of course not."

All right, then. It was unpleasant but not fatal. I was really tired of fatal things.

"Does the design have special meaning?" Taro asked of the bobs.

"Yes. A design will determine the nature of the luck you're seeking. In wealth, in health, in love and so on."

"And is there a limit on the number of designs?"

The merchant frowned. "Not that I know of."

"You have several repetitions here."

"Ah, those are partner bobs. Two people, wishing for the same thing, means twice the luck for both."

"Really?" Taro grinned, and I began to feel nervous. "What are these for?" He held up the bob.

"Luck with cards."

"Don't need it." He pointed at a design still on the display. "And that one?"

"Many children."

Taro apparently desired no luck in that area, either, for he moved on to the other bobs. He found none of the harmony bobs appealing, in meaning or style. So we left the merchant stall empty-handed. Which was a relief to the merchant and fine with me. I didn't want matching jewelry.

Except he dragged me directly to another jewelry stall. "You've got to be kidding me, Taro." It was a fashion. Taro in the past had sneered at those who felt compelled to follow fashion. He himself was always stylish, but never fashionable.

"What? They're funny."

"They're childish."

"Too much maturity makes you old before your time."

"No matter how old I get, I'll always be younger than you."

His response was to pinch my ear.

"I'm not wearing one of these harmony bobs, Taro. They're ridiculous." And while I wasn't overly concerned with what I

wore or what others thought of it, that didn't mean I went out
of my way to attract ridicule.

Besides, wearing a piece of jewelry identical to what
Taro wore, it was too suggestive. People who were promised
to each other in marriage wore matching jewelry, or those who
belonged to some kind of organization. Either way, I'd look a
complete fool once Taro went back to his licentious ways.

"So don't wear it if you don't want to. But you're getting
one with me."

I sighed. "Yes, milord."

We went through three more stalls like the first one, and
they didn't have anything that appealed to Taro, either. The
design, the metal, or the meaning put him off.

It was the fifth stall that had what he was looking for. And
I should have predicted that such would be the case, because
this stall looked different from the others. There were no
guards, and the only solid wall was the one at the back. Apparently this merchant wasn't overly concerned about thieves, for
the wares were pinned to slanted boards that faced outward,
rather than inward like at the other stalls.

This merchant, unlike the others we'd so far encountered
that day, didn't seem worried about the loss of revenue to us.
He greeted us with a smile that appeared genuine. He looked
different, too, now that I bothered to really look at him. His
brown hair, surprisingly curly, was worn longer than was the
fashion for men, and his blue eyes fairly beamed out of a face
that was masculine but sensual, his full lips curled as though
he were gently amused at something. Perhaps us. His posture
was relaxed, his clothes loose and colorful and designed for
comfort rather than style. Something about him felt odd. Not
dangerous or unpleasant. Just odd.

He was extremely handsome, an embodiment of all that
was lush. There was something about his face that made me
want to reach out and touch, starting at those amazing cheekbones with a side route to the enticing mouth and along that
beautifully defined jawline. Really, everything about him was
just so inviting. I folded my hands together to keep them still.

I looked to Taro, wondering what he thought of this tooth-some young man. My Source didn't seem to have noticed him yet, focusing instead on the jewelry.

He found a bob he liked almost immediately. A simple silver chain supporting a symbol that looked like a sideways number eight, only slimmer and elongated.

"It's the wrong metal," Taro said regretfully. "Silver doesn't suit you."

"It suits you, though. And you're the one who'll be wearing it." I liked the look of it myself. It was nonfussy, but elegant, and something about the figure implied balance. I liked the idea of balance. It was calming.

"What does this one mean?" Taro asked the merchant.

This was the first time Taro had addressed the merchant directly. I watched his face, waiting for the coy smile, the spark in his eyes. There was nothing, no recognition of the merchant's beauty. What was going on?

"Eternity."

"Eternity? An eternity of what?"

"Maybe it means something like immortality," I suggested.

Taro frowned. "Never understood the appeal of living forever."

"But eternity is not limited to immortality," said the merchant. "It can symbolize the desire for everlasting youth, or love, or the success of one's family, through every generation. It can refer to a search for knowledge that spans all existence, or an understanding of one's connection to everything else. Its meaning can adapt to the desires of the wearer."

That didn't make sense. Objects didn't adapt to their users. They were what they were.

"We'll take these," Taro told the merchant, and he moved to pin the thing on my chest before I could move to stop him.

The merchant was faster. "No, no, my lord," said the merchant, surprising us both with the use of Taro's former title. "There is a way to be doing such things."

That couldn't be good.

"Please." From beneath one display the merchant pulled out

a very short stool, a second one from beneath another. "Sit."

One couldn't properly sit, the stools were so low. It was more like kneeling on the mat, with the stool supporting the buttocks. Taro and I ended up facing each other a short distance away from one another.

He wasn't going to sacrifice a chicken or anything, was he?

He got our names first, my two and Taro's string of them. He lit two candles, setting them down on the mat, one before Taro, one before me. Beside each candle he placed a black feather, a silver ring, a triangle of smoky incense and a bowl of clean water.

"Think of what you wish would last for an eternity," the merchant said. "If both of you desire the same, the power of the symbol will be brought to bear. If you do not, the bobs shall be nothing more than pretty pieces of silver."

That was all they were anyway. "We don't need to put you through all this trouble," I said to him. I didn't add that I had noticed a few curious onlookers pausing outside the stall, wondering what was going on. Taro and I no doubt looked like a couple of right fools.

"If you're not to give me the proper coin," the merchant said coolly, "you might at least observe the appropriate rituals."

That told me.

To make us even more uncomfortable, the merchant started to walk, circling us. "Think of what you wish to be eternal. Don't speak of it, for you will feel guarded in what you say, and may shape each other's wishes. Only if you are identical and sincere in your desire can the casting work."

Ah, so when the casting didn't work, it would be our fault.

But just as a mental exercise, I thought about what I would wish to be eternal. Not my life. I couldn't imagine living forever, continuously watching everyone I knew die and die and die. To have an unlimited thirst for knowledge might be useful, but it might be discomforting, too, to want more and more information and never be satisfied. Like an addiction. I didn't care about having an unlimited amount of possessions, though that might be useful for any children I might have.

Actually, I did know of one thing I would wish to last forever or, at least, as long as I lived. It was a weak and childish kind of wish. I couldn't even form the words in my mind.

The merchant stood beside Taro, a bowl in one hand and a knife in the other. "If you would take the bowl, my lord."

"What are you planning?" I asked sharply.

"Just a few drops of his blood, to be mingled with yours."

"No." I didn't know why that idea offended me so much. It just did.

"Relax, Lee," said Taro. "It's harmless. Unless you think I've got some fearsome disease I've been hiding from you."

"Of course not." If he did, I'd no doubt already gotten it. "It's just barbaric."

"Spoken like someone who has no understanding of the process," said the merchant. He wasn't sarcastic or snide or condescending. Just gently amused. I didn't know that I liked appearing amusing to other people.

Taro took the bowl, in his right hand as the merchant hinted, and held his left over it. The merchant carefully sliced into the fleshy part of Taro's palm. Taro hissed in reaction, but shifted his hand over so the first drops of blood landed in the copper bowl. The merchant pressed the bob into the bloodied palm, curling the hand into a fist.

Then the merchant was beside me, and I rolled my eyes at the childishness of it all. I took the bowl and let the knife cut into my palm. I felt it, but it didn't hurt. One of the benefits of being a Shield, I didn't feel things as much as other people did. I held my hand over the bowl and watched the blood drop down.

I actually felt a little odd. Almost a little faint. Which was stupid. I'd never before been squeamish over the sight of blood. But this was causing some kind of buzzing sensation under my skin, and I didn't like it.

The merchant put the other bob in my hand and balled my hand into a fist. He took the bowl from me, mixing the blood within it with the tip of his knife. He dribbled a drop of blood into the wax of each of the candles, right by the flame, then set the bowl on the floor, an equal distance between Taro and me.

"To the river from the north," the merchant said, much more loudly than he needed to. "To the river from the south. To the river from the east. As they join together, let Dunleavy and Shintaro join together in their will and their desire." Lovely. It had only needed that. He walked around us, continuing to speak in what seemed like a blending of a poem and a speech. "As the waters flow together to a single end, so will the blood of Shintaro and Dunleavy." At times, he would pause beside one of us, picking up the feather, waving it in the smoke of the incense and returning it to the ground. After he had done that with each feather three times, he slid the rings onto them and placed them both on the ground, never lifting them again.

I looked at Taro. He was smirking.

And then the merchant stopped. "My lord, you may pin the bob on Shield Mallorough. Go directly to her; don't step outside the circle. Wash the bob off in the bowl beside her feet. Then dry the bob on the inner wrist of your left hand before pinning it directly over Shield Mallorough's heart."

Taro did as instructed, and with the lightest touch pinned the bob over my left breast. No inappropriate fondling.

"Please return to your post, my lord. Shield Mallorough, if you would do the same for your lord."

That made Taro snicker, again. He was enjoying this far too much. With a straight face I repeated the actions required by the merchant, ending by pinning the bob on Taro's chest. It suited him, I had to admit. Smooth and elegant, just like him.

"And now," the merchant said once I'd returned to my stool, "each of you remove your candle from its setting and stand. Each of you approach the center bowl. Now douse the flame in the blood." We did so, and I, for one, was feeling silly. "Put the candles in the bowl, and stand straight." And we did. "It is done."

The applause startled me. An audience had formed. Lovely. I had no doubt they totally misunderstood the significance of what we had done. Which was to humor the merchant so Taro could get his meaningless matching bobs.

Taro had his hand shaken by many. I was given flowers. And someone pressed a wrapped package into my hand, which I would later discover held a loaf of spice bread, gushing best wishes for a happy future.

Oh, aye, totally misunderstood.

And no, there would be no embarrassing repercussions from this.

# Chapter Three

"All right, that's enough for me," I said to Taro, my voice low because we were still surrounded by well-wishers. "Let's head back to the residence."

"What? Why? We just got out."

"We have what we came for. You wanted to get some jewelry, and we got some jewelry. Let's go home." They were still watching us. What did they expect us to do now? *The show is over, people.*

"Lee, we've been away for over a year. I don't want to be shut up in the residence."

"People are going to be watching us because of that spectacle."

"So? That spectacle wasn't my fault."

"I didn't say it was." Though it was, sort of. If he hadn't insisted on requisitioning harmony bobs, we wouldn't have had to endure that ridiculous ritual. But then, I could have refused, so it was sort of my fault, too.

"And you had no problem being a spectacle on that damned island."

I glared at him. That wasn't fair. "I wasn't a spectacle."

"Oh, no? Leavy the Flame Dancer. You couldn't be anything but."

"My making a spectacle of myself put food on our table," I hissed.

"Which was more than I could do, right?"

"Stop putting words in my mouth." What was wrong with him?

"All I'm saying is that you're letting other people's interest control what you do. Why do you care whether other people stare at you?"

"How can you not care?" Who enjoyed being stared at by strangers, every move made and word spoken judged and possibly communicated to someone else? "Maybe you're used to having strangers speculate about you, but I'm not, and I don't plan to get used to it."

"You're overreacting. I just want to go shopping."

"And I don't. I've done enough shopping."

"Fine." He sketched out a little bow that somehow managed to appear sarcastic. "I need clothes, so I'll be off. I hope you enjoy your afternoon." He turned on his heel and strode off. Most of the crowd either followed him or dispersed.

Having an argument in front of an audience was humiliating. What had gotten Taro so upset? So what if I wanted to go home? Taro knew hundreds of people he could go shopping with, if that was what he wanted. Why did he have to turn it into an argument?

There were still a few people watching me, wondering what entertaining thing I would do next. Repressing the embarrassing urge to smile or wave, I turned away to head back to the residence. I felt like I could sense their eyes boring into the back of my head.

As I passed the jewelry stalls we had examined earlier on, I looked for signs of other such rituals being performed. There was nothing. I even watched a couple purchase a pair of harmony bobs and they were required to do nothing more than hand over the coin and pin the bobs on each other. So that blue-eyed merchant had done all that to Taro and me just for

the hell of it. I felt even more of a fool. No wonder so many
people had been watching. The display had no doubt appeared
positively freakish.

I caught a carriage for the rest of the way back to the Triple S residence. I could have walked the distance easily
enough, but the streets just felt too crowded, and I needed
some space. That was one positive aspect of Flatwell; there
was always space and it had almost always been quiet.

I hated being stared at. I really, really did.

I entered the residence with a sense of relief. Standing in the
foyer were Source Claire Firth and her Shield, Dee Stone. They
were ladies in their fifties who loved to drink and dance and
have sex with a lot of people. They were a delight and a hoot
and I was happy to see them. I'd managed to miss them since
returning the day before. "Firth, Stone, how are you?"

"I am well," Stone answered.

And Firth said, her words treading on Stone's, "Is it true
that you slept with Shintaro last night?"

I stared at her, shocked speechless by the question.

"Hush, Claire," said Stone. She was blushing.

Firth wasn't. "Answer the question, Dunleavy."

I finally found my voice. "I will not." How dare she inter-
rogate me? She had no authority over me.

"Oh, so you're ashamed of it, are you?"

"I've done nothing to be ashamed of." But I did feel odd.
Yes, it was suggested one shouldn't sleep with one's partner.
This reaction, though, was unexpected, especially from one I
considered a friend.

"Haven't you?"

"It is simply none of your business."

"What goes on in our house is our business."

"Now's not the time, Claire," said Stone, grabbing Firth's
arm. "We're going to be late for our watch."

"We'll be discussing this, Dunleavy," said Claire. "All of
us will. And we have every right to. Because it's wrong." And
then she let herself be dragged out by her Shield.

It wasn't wrong. It was merely foolish. And while, if I had

thought about it, I would have expected some ribbing, outright disapproval was a shock.

Oh, what a day.

I went up to my room. My luggage, still packed, was on the floor in the center of the bedchamber. No time like the present to get that done. I pulled out the trousers and shirts I'd worn for most of my travels, the two gowns I'd worn again and again before the Empress in Erstwhile, and the sandals I'd purchased with money I had earned on Flatwell. My one skill, besides Shielding, was dancing the benches. That had been a skill of value to the troupe with whom we had traveled. But bench dancing couldn't be done in ordinary, loose-fitting clothes, not on Flatwell. Oh, no. There had to be drama. There had to be flair.

The costume consisted of two pieces, a brown halter that left the midriff bare, and a scandalously short skirt. Copper beads had been sewn onto the brown material. Not by me—I couldn't sew to save my life—but by the woman whose assistance was the only reason Taro and I had managed to survive at all.

The clothing wasn't the entire costume. There had been cosmetics, too. Shadowing my face, bringing out the color of my eyes, coiling down my arms and legs in temporary tattoos. All of it applied, before every performance, by the same woman who had sewn the beads.

The first time I'd been in that costume, I'd felt exotic and beautiful. Then Taro had seen it. He'd thought it looked ridiculous.

He was right. I had made a spectacle of myself. But it had been necessary to get the coins we needed in order to eat.

I put the costume in my wardrobe, far in the back. I should get rid of it—I certainly wouldn't be wearing it again—but I wasn't ready to do that quite yet.

I craved a bath, but lacked the patience to wait for water to be heated and brought up. I poured some water into the wash basin and disrobed entirely. With the cloth, I scrubbed the grime of the market from my skin.

I was so happy to be home.

Once I was bathed and I had put on a fresh dress, I picked up the bundle of discarded clothes. At the moment before putting them in the laundry bag, I remembered the bob. I took it off and, after depositing the clothes in the bag, I put the bob in my jewelry box. I went to the door of my suite, preparing to go down to the kitchen for some coffee.

And I couldn't make myself go through the door. I didn't know what it was; I just felt restless and uncomfortable. I felt as though I was forgetting something important.

I felt better when I took a step back, and better again when I went another step back. I felt best of all when I went back to my bedchamber and stood over my jewelry box.

It was stupid. It was all the power of suggestion. That merchant had performed that ritual, and now I had spells and casting on my mind. It was making me act all ridiculous.

Still, I opened the jewelry box and picked up the harmony bob, holding it at eye level. It was a pretty little thing.

And I had to admit, I wanted to wear it. I would have had no problem wearing it if Taro weren't wearing the same thing. Why did we have to get matching bobs? What was Taro thinking?

I was so adverse to the idea of putting the bob in the jewelry box that it shocked me. But I was not going to pin it on my dress for all the world to see.

Feeling like a complete idiot, I stripped down to my chemise and pinned the bob to that. I felt better. I dressed again, and when I went to the door of my suite again, I was able to pass through it with no difficulties.

It made absolutely no sense, but I wasn't going to think about it. I would wear the bob and I wouldn't think about it. And when I went to bed that night, the merchant's influence would have dissipated and everything would be normal. I really, really wanted everything to be normal.

# Chapter Four

Stomp, stomp, stomp, stomp, stomp. Stop. Grumble, growl or sigh. Turn. Stomp, stomp, stomp, stomp, stomp. Stop. Grumble, growl or sigh. Turn. Do it again.

The Stall was a very small building. One small room, in fact. Built just outside the general sprawl of High Scape, its official name, according to the Triple S, was the Observation Post of High Scape, where the Pair on duty waited while they watched for natural disasters to channel. It had been nicknamed the paranoia stall by one of our predecessors, so everyone called it the Stall.

It was a very boring place to be. That was the intention. The Pair on duty was not to be distracted by anything interesting.

High Scape was unusual in having multiple Pairs. Most sites that required Pairs had only one, and that Pair was not set to any kind of schedule. A Source and Shield didn't have to be together when they channeled, though it made it easier when they were. In most cases a Source and Shield went about their separate business. The Source would feel the onset of an event and lower his or her natural protections in preparation for channeling. The Shield would feel the Source's protection going down and would erect his or her Shields. This could be accomplished over a distance.

But High Scape was the largest city in the world and, until recently, had been one of the most turbulent, with events at least once a day, and often once a shift. It was filled with constant distractions, both day and night. The Triple S had deemed it wise to arrange to have a Pair on official duty at all times, and while on duty, to have them in the Stall.

One of the consequences of having fewer than the usual seven Pairs was that our watches in the Stall were much longer. I had been told that the shifts had lengthened from seven hours to nine when Taro and I were sent to the Southern Islands, and then to eleven when the circuit Pair had left. They had stayed at eleven once Taro and I returned, as Riley and Sabatos would soon be leaving.

For some reason, eleven hours felt so much longer than seven. It felt as if it were twice as long, not just four hours more. The books we'd brought had all been read; the games had been played too many times. All we had to keep ourselves from going mad with boredom was each other. There were times when that wasn't enough.

Don't get me wrong; Taro could be a very entertaining fellow. I really thought the flaw was with me. I wasn't the best conversationalist, and I couldn't listen to someone else for more than a few hours before getting tired of reacting to everything he said. I was used to having my attention absorbed by reading and writing, not people.

And if I felt that way, I could only imagine how Taro felt. He wasn't a person who read, or could sit still in quiet contemplation. He needed people and activity, and the long, eventless shifts tested what little patience he had.

And he tested mine. "Stop pacing," I snapped.

"I'm bored!"

"So? Is that any reason to torment me?"

"It's ridiculous for them to expect us to just sit here and do nothing for eleven hours. There is no reason why we couldn't just stay together in more interesting surroundings. This is a stupid waste of time."

That was true. Why didn't they trust us to stay together at the residence? "We could play cards."

"I'm sick of cards."

Taro loved playing cards, even when I was his only opponent and there were no real stakes. We had whiled away many a slow hour losing our firstborn to each other. He was just being difficult.

When I thought about it, I couldn't believe Taro had never developed any solitary pursuits, with the upbringing he had. What did he do all those hours he was locked alone in his room as a child? "Then please find yourself something to do that isn't so distracting." Because I couldn't settle down as long as he didn't settle down.

"Let's practice the weather," Taro announced, suddenly seating himself at the table.

"Practice the weather?"

"Aye, see what you can do with it."

I was shocked as I realized he wanted to experiment with my uncertain ability to tamper with the weather, an ability we'd discovered during the Harsh Summer. The regulars hadn't been able to understand why Pairs who could calm tsunami and earthquakes and volcanoes were helpless against things like blizzards and temperature. I'd thought they'd had a point, at the time, so I'd bullied Taro into experimenting, seeing if he could do anything. After all, he could create natural events when he wished, not just channel them. There had been reason to think he might be able to tamper with the weather, too.

Except he couldn't. He would open himself up to the forces, let them swarm through him, but was unable to glean the sensations that were caught up in the movement of the weather. It was as though all of his attention was absorbed in the grander sweeps of the forces, making him blind to the more subtle shifts of weather.

I wasn't. I could see them, hear them, feel them. More

astounding, I could give those sensations a nudge, which resulted in a change in the weather.

Unfortunately, the changes were largely unpredictable, and ended up being negative at least as often as they were positive. So I was leery of the whole thing. There was no one to act as a mentor for me, and I had no way of knowing what the long-term implications of changing the weather might be.

So, of course, I was caught in a circle. I didn't want to experiment because I couldn't predict the results, but I would never be able to learn how to predict the results if I didn't experiment.

There were worse conundrums. I didn't like the idea of doing it unless it was absolutely necessary, anyway. I didn't want to do it just to see what I could do. That seemed disrespectful somehow.

"I'm not playing with that sort of thing just so you have something to do."

"I'm bored."

I rolled my eyes.

"Don't do that!" he snapped. "I hate it when you do that."

"Don't do what?" What was wrong now?

"Dismiss me," he interrupted. "I hate it when you dismiss me."

His leaping about in tangents was not a good sign, but if I stayed calm, I could possibly steer him back into making sense. "I'm not dismissing you. But it's not my fault you're bored. You knew what it would be like. Why didn't you bring something to entertain you?"

"I brought you."

Cute. "I was thinking along the lines of racing circulars. Or letters to write. Or read." I knew that the man was practically bombarded by letters from various admirers.

"You're acting like you did before," he accused me.

How bizarre. People had been telling me I looked different, that I was acting differently. Here was Taro, telling me I was acting as I had before. But perhaps I was misunderstanding him. "Before what?"

"Before we went to that damn island."

Why was that a bad thing? What was wrong with the way I had been then? "What do you mean?"

"Why did you leave your things in your room?"

Sometimes his conversational leaps just took too much energy to follow. I wished he'd pick a topic and stick with it for a while. "Because we have separate rooms. We've always had separate rooms."

"We always shared a room on that damn island."

"That's not entirely true. And when we did share, it was often a matter of saving space or money."

His eyes widened in shock before narrowing into a glare. "I see," he said coolly.

Clearly, it had been a bad idea to mention that. I should have said I'd wanted to share space for pure sentimentality. But damn it, it was the truth. "I assumed that once life got back to normal—"

"What does back to normal mean to you?" he demanded.

What, he was going to make me say it? "Well, coming back here, getting back on the roster." I wasn't going to mention the fact that now we were home, Taro would wish to return to his more philandering ways. Because I wasn't stupid. Comments to that effect had always infuriated him.

Taro wasn't stupid, either. Sometimes he could hear what wasn't being said. "You are assuming a great deal," were the chilly controlled words that came out of his mouth. "But then, you always have."

The anger in him seemed to spark off some anger of my own. "Seems to me I'm not the only one making assumptions."

"Really?"

When Taro got angry, he had a whole repertoire of responses. He snapped and snarled. He shouted. He became rigidly polite. But I really hated that soft voice with the almost hidden edge.

"And what assumptions am I making?" he asked.

"Well, you obviously assumed we'd be sharing quarters once we got back here." Why should he be making all the decisions about how we did things? He was going to be the one to decide when it was over. It was only fair that I would be able to have some influence over the rest of the relationship.

"And you think that expectation presumptuous, given the circumstances."

Yes, but I knew better than to say so. "Just illogical. Why settle for less space when we can have more?" It made perfect sense to me. We'd spent so long in cramped quarters. Didn't he enjoy being able to stretch out more?

Didn't he enjoy having his own space again? Somewhere that was purely his when he wanted to be away from me, when he wanted privacy to do whatever kinds of things he did that needed privacy?

Sure, it meant a little more inconvenience on the sex side of things. He could no longer just roll over and find me there. But the trip down the hall wasn't too taxing. And it would make things so much easier when the relationship was over. No awkward moving-out scene.

Taro opened his mouth, no doubt ready to say something cutting. Then he frowned. "Something's happening."

Wonderful. He'd shifted moods again. I was still stuck in anger, because I was a normal person, and once I felt something, I felt it for a while. "No need to go overboard on the specifics, Taro, my love." No, that wasn't sarcastic at all.

He scowled at me briefly. "An earthquake, but not in High Scape."

"Oh." It was assumed that Sources could only feel events that were in their vicinity, but no one really knew what "vicinity" really meant, when it came to actual measurements. "Can you tell if there's anyone doing anything about it?"

"There doesn't seem to be."

"So, do you want to do something about it?" It was possible that the reason no one was doing anything was that the earthquake was hitting an empty area, but it was also possible that someone wasn't doing their job, or that this was an area that didn't normally experience events and so didn't have a Pair to protect it.

"I'd really like to."

That, I thought, was an odd thing for him to say, and it made me curious. Were there events that Sources preferred to channel over others? What made a particular event more appealing? I couldn't believe I'd never thought to ask.

But it wasn't time to ask right then.

I felt that little spurt of excitement I always felt when I knew I was going to Shield. This was what I was good at. It was what I was born to do. And there was something so cleansing about it. It was almost like a good, challenging, physically exhausting but satisfying bench-dancing competition, except it was for the mind.

His barriers lowered, I raised my Shields around him. I felt his mind open to the forces, only not to the forces around him, which was what he usually did. It was more like he was reaching out, trying to find and pull in the forces that were setting off an earthquake, somewhere far away. This was the moment, when it was too late, that I wondered if his channeling an event so far away was such a good idea. What if it drained him too quickly?

There was a bit of a wait before he found the forces he was looking for, and then he drew them in, channeling them through his own body. My task was not only to prevent all the other forces that were swirling about from rushing in and crushing him, but also to make sure the blood didn't burst from his veins, his heart didn't beat itself to explosion, and his brain didn't tear itself apart, literally, under the strain of world forces being funneled through a vessel that really hadn't been designed to do the job it was doing.

This took great concentration on my part, as well as a firm knowledge of how Taro's mind worked, how thoughts traveled over his mind, how his blood moved. That, as far as we knew, was the reason for the bond, to enable me to feel all of that information within him. I could do it with other Sources, but not as well as I did with him.

The flickering of color behind my eyes was my next hint that this was going to be an unusual channeling. Sometimes, I got images when I Shielded. This was not common. In fact, I'd never heard or read of another Shield seeing images when they Shielded. That didn't necessarily mean they never had. I hadn't gone out of my way to tell anyone, and perhaps all other Shields who had seen images had been similarly embarrassed. If I was the only one to see such things, I was clearly a freak. Both of these possibilities were a reason, as a rule, to keep the experience to myself.

The images never really made any particular sense, and this time was no different. What was different was that the sensations were not limited to the visual. A dark, clouded sky. High, rocky cliffs. Some kind of eagle or hawk screaming. Fast, rushing gray water laced with whitecaps that made me feel cold. The smell of rotting greens, and a taste of salt.

The assault on my senses was confusing, distracting. And the forces Taro was channeling seemed to be rushing through him particularly fast and particularly hard. I felt like I was scrambling to keep everything under control. It wasn't the first time that had happened to me, nor was it the first time it had frightened me. I didn't know why it was happening. Was it because the source of the event was so far away?

At least there wasn't any pain this time.

As the channeling continued, the screaming of the birds became continuous, and louder, pressing against the insides of my ears. My nose and mouth felt coated with salt. And the waves kept reaching higher and higher until thoughts of drowning trickled through my mind.

The rushing of the water nearly obscured the rushing of Taro's blood, which strained against the sides of its carriers in an unusual bid to break free. His heart was racing, pulling against the confinement of its own form. And the fluids moving over his brain seemed to be, what, curdling? Something vile. Something not good. I pushed against the entrancing images in my mind in an almost desperate bid to prevent Taro killing himself.

I had lost awareness of everything around me. I couldn't see the table in front of me, couldn't feel the floor beneath my feet. Usually I didn't so thoroughly lose all sense of what was going on around me. Should this worry me?

And then, finally, it was over. Taro was re-erecting his own protections and I breathed in a deep sigh of relief. "What the hell was that?" I demanded. Without thinking, I put my hands on my legs to see if my dress was wet.

"What do you mean? What is wrong?"

"Far too hard and fast."

He grinned. "Not to your taste, then?"

I didn't roll my eyes. Men. "What happened?"

"Nothing happened. Why?"

It had all seemed normal to him? Really? "I saw strange things," I admitted.

"I see," he said, appearing serious. At least he believed me. Probably because I'd told him of the other times I'd seen images while channeling, and it had always been a bad sign. "What did you see?"

"Cold water and high cliffs. Lots of screaming white birds. The air tasted like salt. It was very gray."

"Hm," he said. "That sounds familiar."

"Really? I can remember no place like it."

"I can't remember if I've actually seen such a place. It just seems familiar." He shrugged. "Oh well."

In my mind, he was dismissing it too easily. "Don't do it again."

He arched a brow. "Excuse me?"

I was reluctant to talk about what I had seen within him as he channeled. The images, the potential for danger, had been too gruesome. "Your heart was going far too fast. For a moment, I thought it was going to rip right out of your chest." That was a nightmare of mine, watching his body literally burst apart because I'd failed to Shield him properly.

"You can handle it," he said with utmost flattering and foolish confidence.

"I'm serious, Taro. I almost lost control there." It was hard enough admitting my failings without having him disregard my warnings so lightly.

"Almost means nothing. You did your job and that's all that counts. You always do your job."

It seemed to me that as time went by, Taro was becoming a little careless, a little too quick to believe that I could follow wherever he went, with no warning. I wasn't sure what to do about that. A part of me believed that it was only natural for him to become more confident in his abilities as he acquired more experience. The other part wondered why I wasn't acquiring the same confidence.

Our watch dragged by. The episode of channeling seemed to have calmed Taro down considerably, and it had washed my anger away. Still, we bickered as we usually did when we were stuck somewhere with nothing to do. It occurred to me that Taro and I never really talked about anything of any substance, except for our work. We either bickered or bantered. I wondered if that was a problem.

Eventually Source Chris LaMonte and Shield Fehvor Hammad showed up for their watch. A little more eventually than I'd been expecting. Source LaMonte was a pompous, aggravating stiff who thought too much of his advanced experience, but his sense of duty was infallible. The very idea of him being late for anything was shocking.

"My apologies," was his greeting, which shocked me even more. "But there's madness in the streets. Empress Constia has died."

My mouth fell open as I stared at him. "She what?"

"Apparently the word reached the deputy mayor last night. The Empress died nearly three weeks ago. Some sort of wasting sickness."

Taro, who had risen upon the opening of the door, fell back into his seat. "Zaire," he muttered.

It shouldn't have been a surprise. Rumors of Her Majesty's poor health had been circulating for the past couple of years, and she hadn't looked all that well the last time I saw her. And even if she weren't ill, well, she'd been in her sixties. At that age, people started dying for no reason.

It was just that I wasn't ready for her to die. I didn't like who would be taking her place on the throne. Even though she was married, no one assumed that her husband, Prince Albert, would be taking over her title when she died. Spouses usually didn't if there were children to inherit, and given Prince Albert's complete absence from public life, I, for one, wasn't sure he was still alive.

The only surviving child of the Empress was Crown Prince Gifford, and his mother had been so thrilled with him she'd sent us out to Flatwell to look for possible options for heirs. Prince Gifford, who'd conspired with Taro's mother, for some bizarre unknown reason, to get Taro's title back after he'd abjured it. Which was illegal, but it wasn't like the Prince was the one who would have suffered the consequences. That would have been Taro. And me, by extension. That little plot had been easy enough to circumvent, but it had caused a lot of sleepless nights.

Gifford's interest had resulted in my enduring a lot of exposure to Taro's mother, which I could have lived without. I'd never met someone I'd so very badly wanted to hit, and considering she had usually ignored me, her ability to raise my ire so quickly and so thoroughly revealed real talent.

I didn't know a lot about Gifford, but my limited exposure had shown me a man of exceptional arrogance, and little concern for the law. And he was to be our new ruler. Zaire save us.

# Chapter Five

"So, Dunleavy, how's married life treating you?"

Oh, no, that wasn't the first time I'd heard that in the week since that ridiculous harmony bob ceremony. Instead of answering, because it was a stupid question, I took a sip of wine. As I let the wine roll over my tongue, I wondered why wine always tasted so much better in taverns than it did at home, even when it was the same kind of wine.

"Ya done it now," said Shield Giles Sabatos. "She's fuming."

I was not fuming. I was calm. I was serene. It was merely that the comment was so lacking in originality, it deserved no reaction at all.

The misunderstanding of the bob ceremony was far worse than I'd predicted. Those who had seen us indulge in it had thought we were getting married, of all things. Married! Why in the world would we be getting married? We had neither titles nor property. But the gossip about the married Pair had spread everywhere. Including to the other Pairs of High Scape. Who abused us mercilessly.

Harshly, actually. I was surprised by some of the things they'd been saying, about a lack of proper control and a weak understanding of professionalism and ethics. Especially Source Claire Firth and her partner, Shield Dee Stone. I was a little relieved they weren't able to join us for Riley and Sabatos's farewell dinner.

Taro's only comment about it was that he hoped the gossip reached his mother. She'd have an apoplectic fit.

I hated it. It was stupid, irritating, humiliating and no one's business. Of all the things to be right about, all the things I'd been worried about when I'd first experienced the dizzying disappointment of being bonded to Taro, this had to be it. People who didn't even know me, talking about me, about my private life. It was awful.

It was baffling. Where were people's priorities? The Empress had just died, but while those who could afford it wore the dark purple of mourning, few were speaking about her, and it seemed to me there was too little being said about the man who was going to be ruling our lives. More than enough was being said about me, though, and about Taro. I couldn't believe it.

Really, we weren't that interesting.

"This is not a matter for levity," LaMonte scolded, and I had to silently rebuke myself for being on the same side as he on any issue. "Really, what were the two of you thinking, to make such a spectacle of yourselves?"

"But being a spectacle is what I do best, Chris," said Taro.

I didn't answer. I couldn't think of anything to say that wasn't embarrassing. I hadn't objected to the little ritual because Taro had wanted to do it, and the merchant had been gorgeous. I wasn't admitting that.

"At least Dunleavy has the good sense not to wear the trinket," LaMonte continued, ignoring Taro's response. I didn't blame him. "I've yet to see you without it, Shintaro. I imagine you enjoy the attention it brings you."

It was true. Taro did wear the thing all the time. Even I'd noticed it. I hated seeing it on him. The symbol of eternity seemed to be mocking me, a grotesque reminder of how fragile the more emotional side of our relationship was, how it would be ended at any time, with no warning. Despite this, my only words to him on the subject had been that I thought he was too much of a gambler to believe in luck. He'd said a little good luck never hurt anyone, and I guess I had to agree with that.

Besides, I tried to avoid being a hypocrite. I was wearing mine, too. It was stupid but I just couldn't leave it off. I wore it every day. But I didn't let Taro know. Every night I took it off in my bedchamber before joining him in his.

I had to recognize in myself the unworthy trait of cowardice.

"This is our last night in High Scape," Riley announced. "And yet we are speaking of Dunleavy and Shintaro. How unusual."

"Not at all," said Taro. "We are the most interesting people here."

"Here" was the rather reclusive Silver Penny, one of the few taverns that hadn't become a dangerous place to eat during the Harsh Summer. At least, the servers had continued to treat us well, so I chose to believe they hadn't spit in the food, or done anything even more disgusting that I didn't want to contemplate. We were supposed to be eating and drinking and talking of old times. Except we didn't have many old times in common. Taro and I had been bonded for only around three years, and were the Pair who had been in High Scape the longest. Of those three years, over half of our time had been spent either absent or otherwise off the roster. And the other Pairs had never worked together before coming to High Scape.

Besides, we all lived together. We talked to one another all the time.

"One would think," Sabatos said in response to Taro. "But you've been characteristically closemouthed about what you were up to while you were away."

See? It wasn't our fault that the conversation stayed on us. They kept asking questions they should have known better than to ask. "Why don't you tell us what you've learned about Ice Ridge?" I asked.

Sabatos shrugged. "The name is the result of someone's twisted sense of humor. It's hot and humid and far from any-where civilized."

It sounded like Flatwell.

"The only ridges are those belonging to the volcano. And every spring they sacrifice a virgin to it."

Hammad's eyes widened. "You're not serious."

"Well, not literally, because it's been totally inactive until recently. But aye, they dress up some old spinster crone and carry her up and around the top in a litter, and cut off some of her hair and throw it around. Then they bring her down and there's a big feast and dancing. It's supposed to bring good luck."

Of all the idiocy. Were there really so many superstitious people in the world? How had I missed them?

"At least it sounds interesting," Riley muttered. "The vol-cano may keep things active enough to keep me from falling asleep on watch. Or getting pregnant."

Hell, I hadn't thought of that. Channeling prevented preg-nancy. I had gone about a year with very few events, and had managed to avoid getting pregnant. If High Scape was settling down to the point where I rarely channeled, or didn't channel at all, I did risk quickening. Not that I didn't want children, I did. Just not yet. I didn't know anything about kids yet.

I'd have to see how regular women avoided having children.

"Something strange is going on, though," said Shield Elata Benedict.

"Strange how?" Riley asked.

Benedict shrugged. "I don't know. It's just a feeling."

Source Derek Beatrice, Benedict's partner, snorted in derision.

Benedict ignored him. "All this new dabbling in superstition and casting. I know Karish is wearing that bob as a joke, but there are people who are really starting to believe in this stuff."

"A fad," LaMonte said in a dismissive tone. "I doubt it will last the winter."

"I'm not talking about those ridiculous metal cages some women are weaving into their hair," Benedict objected. "Aye, those'll go out of style, and none too soon. This is different. People are really starting to do things out of the belief it will bring them good luck. And not just the peasants, either. Lord Noirden sacrificed a cow on his front lawn this morning."

My wine almost went down the wrong way at that. Riley sputtered and coughed. "He what?"

"He did it personally, and of course he didn't know what he was doing. The poor animal was moaning and practically squealing as the idiot was sawing at its neck"—Sabatos grimaced and dropped his knife and fork on his plate before pushing the remains of his meal away—"and there was blood everywhere. Once the poor thing was finally dead, he poured oil all over it and set it on fire. There was a merry little blaze going before the Runners showed up, and once they got there, they didn't really know what to do. Apparently no one knows whether it's illegal to sacrifice an animal on your own property, because no one's done it before."

"I thought the casting was being attempted only by people with that riverfront illness," I said.

"Who told you that?"

What did that matter? "So it's more widespread than that?"

"Clearly, if Noirden was trying it. His son has a bleeding disease and probably won't live to be a man. It's said the healers can't do anything."

"Did he end up getting arrested?" Hammad asked.

"I don't think so. And if he did, he'd just buy his way out of it."

"I wonder if that'll become illegal after this," Taro mused, whirling his wine in his goblet. "Sacrificing animals, I mean."

"The Runners have a hard enough time trying to catch people who murder other people. I don't think they can afford to add murdering animals to the list of crimes," said Sabatos.

"Who was he sacrificing the cow to, anyway?" Beatrice demanded.

"No one seems to know."

"And where did he get the ritual? He didn't just make it up, did he?"

"He got it out of a book."

"A book about what?" I asked.

"Now you've got her started," Taro groaned.

"How could anyone not be interested in a book about how to murder animals for the purposes of healing someone? It's insane." Who would write such a book? Who would print it? How would Noirden even learn about it?

"I don't know anything about the book," Benedict told me. "The Runners confiscated it."

Maybe Risa would be able to tell me. She wasn't supposed to give me details about investigations, especially those that had nothing to do with me or Taro, but surely it wouldn't hurt to tell me the title of a book. I wanted to read the book that taught people to kill animals as some kind of ritual. I thought the writer was brilliant to be able to pander to this fashion so quickly. Cruel, and possibly lacking any normal sense of responsibility, but definitely brilliant.

None of this made any sense. A whole bunch of people couldn't just start believing in spell casting, all out of nowhere, no matter what difficulties they were experiencing. How did all of this start? The lunacy of it kept me distracted through the rest of the evening.

Taro and I were the first to leave. We had an early watch in the Stall the next morning, and it would take us a good hour and a half to walk to the Triple S residence from the tavern. Not that the distance was so great. It was just that Taro would need the time to chat with the dozens of people who would want a word with him when they saw him.

However, the first person to stop us was not one of Taro's many admirers. It was someone far worse. Someone much more able to create the sharpest discomfort within me.

It was Doran Laidley. Doran was a lord who, he said, had

no money. There was an estate, which he claimed was really nothing more than an ugly stone house on a miserable plot of land with a handful of tenant families barely eking out an existence on the barren soil. Doran joked that the family kept a roof over their heads by marrying money, though he confessed himself unable to understand why anyone would be willing to pay for such a tired old title.

Doran Laidley. With whom I had been shamelessly flirting before Taro and I had been sent to Flatwell. With whom I'd been contemplating doing considerably more than flirt, because he had a pleasing face and shining green eyes and a comfortable manner. To whom I had given a too polite brush-off because I wasn't sure how long I'd be gone or if I'd ever really be coming back.

Doran, whom I'd forgotten all about almost as soon as I'd stepped beyond the city borders of High Scape and hadn't thought of once since our return. I couldn't believe it.

He looked startled to see us, and then he grinned with genuine cheer. "Lee! Taro! How wonderful to see you! When did you get back?"

Taro slung an arm around my shoulders. "A few weeks ago," he answered in an attempt at a casual tone that he didn't quite pull off.

"Just one week, actually," I added quickly. I would not have Doran believing I'd been back for ages without seeing him. "I do apologize for not contacting you immediately, Doran. Things have been strange here, since we got back."

"Yes, there have been a lot of changes since you've been away," Doran agreed. "Have you heard about—"

"Our apologies, Laidley," Taro interrupted with civility so cool it was almost rude. "But we're on our way home. We have an early watch tomorrow."

"Oh," Doran said, clearly taken aback by Taro's manner. And I couldn't remember Taro ever calling Doran by his family name, not once since they'd first been introduced. "Yes, of course. Will you have time to meet me tomorrow, Lee?"

"No," Taro answered, curtly, before I could.

I gouged him in the ribs with my elbow. "Take your lordly temperament on ahead. I'll catch up." And I stepped out from under his arm when he seemed disinclined to remove it.

"It is inappropriate to leave you alone on the street at this time of night," Taro objected.

"I didn't turn into a child over the last half hour." Really, he was acting like a prat. "I won't be long."

He glared at me.

I raised an eyebrow at him. What was his problem?

He stormed away, muttering under his breath.

I turned from watching him to see a pensive look on Doran's face. "Your relationship with him changed while you were away," he commented.

I didn't know what to say to that. On the one hand, it was no one's business. On the other hand, one might say it was Doran's business, due to the nature of the relationship we'd had before I'd left. And if I had another hand, I could worry about how I was going to explain to Doran that the current stage in my relationship with Taro was only temporary without sounding addled or desperate for reassurance. So I said nothing.

"When can we meet?" he asked.

"I'm not sure," I answered. "It's not the best time. We just got back, and we're scrambling hard to catch up." Oh, such lies. Could he tell I was lying? He appeared only politely interested. "May I contact you in a few days?"

"Of course." He kissed my cheek. "I'm looking forward to it."

I wasn't. It was going to be awkward. If he suspected there had been a change between Taro and me, why couldn't he just accept that and fade away?

Zaire. How self-centered was that?

I caught up to Taro, expecting him to be in the same bad mood in which he had left. He didn't appear to be, though. He grinned when he saw me, slung his arm over my shoulder and strode on with a relaxed gait. I didn't know why he had gotten so upset; I didn't know why he was now so calm. It was frustrating to be unable to read him.

# Chapter Six

High Scape had a lot of celebrations. Days where government and most businesses closed and people watched performances and played games and drank too much and ended up getting arrested for being really stupid in public. The reasons High Scape found for closing down varied from the profound to the trivial. There would be something massive for Crown Prince Gifford's coronation, Zaire help us all. Every year there was a celebration to mark the day we guessed our ancestors first arrived on the world from who knew where. There was a marking for the changing of the seasons. There were annual celebrations for the existence of the sun and the moon each, a festival in praise of balance, and days marking battles that had occurred back when cities still fought one another.

And there were others that I hadn't had a chance to learn about yet, due to my many absences from High Scape. For the last few days, I had seen evidence of another citywide occasion, extra scrubbing of public statues, wreaths and colorful drapes decorating the buildings. I ran through my mental list of holidays and couldn't think of anything that fell at that precise time of year. I had meant to ask someone what they were celebrating this time, but I kept forgetting.

So I got up late on a day on which I had no watch at all in the Stall, and the only other person in the Triple S residence was Ben. He was in the kitchen, which, as usual, was my first destination in the morning, and he poured me a hot cup of coffee. I breathed in the delicious aroma. My plan for the morning was to drink coffee and read, and maybe write a letter to Aryne.

"How are you settling back in, Shield Mallorough?"

Damn it. He'd asked a question of me. That meant I couldn't take the coffee to the parlor and consume it in sweet silence. "It's nice to be back," I said.

"You must have enjoyed your trip away," he said, wiping at a countertop that looked perfectly clean to me. "When you returned, you seemed much more relaxed than I remember seeing you before."

What was he talking about? I was always relaxed.

"Pairs are so very fortunate, that they may travel so much." He sounded wistful.

Recognizing I was going to be there for a while, I perched on one of the stools at the table and sipped at the coffee. "Is traveling so difficult for people to arrange?"

"Most can't spare the coin. Or the time away from making their living."

Yes, that made sense. I felt stupid for not thinking of that. "I would have rather stayed here." I didn't care how much he thought the trip to Flatwell had relaxed me: it had been awful.

We sat in silence a short while, both of us watching him wipe his cloth over the counter. Then he bit his lip and asked, "What do you think makes a Source or a Shield?"

That was odd. From what I understood, Ben had been working around members of the Triple S for most of his life. He should know the answer to such questions as well as anyone did. "They channel forces."

"No, no, excuse me. I mean, what decides a person is going to be a Source or a Shield?"

I frowned, still not sure I understood quite what he meant.

"Before they're born," he added.

Oh lords. Philosophy. "Circumstances," I said. "Life. That was just the way things fell together."

"Really? That's it?"

It was far too soon after waking—I'd had only one cup of coffee—to be having a discussion like this. "What are you suggesting?"

He smiled sheepishly. "Nothing, Shield Mallorough. Sometimes it just strikes me as odd, how different life can be for different people."

Yes, life was unfair. I was lucky enough to have been born a Shield, which was, I knew, a privileged position. If I hadn't been a Shield, I still would have been the daughter of wealthy merchants, also a fairly privileged position. I didn't know why I was so fortunate. I only knew I was uncomfortable when I was reminded how much harder other people had it. People like Ben. "Aye, it is strange."

"Hm," he said. Then he folded the cloth in a neat little square. "Are you going to the parade today?"

Ah, a parade. So that was the big event. I wasn't a great admirer of parades. Waiting around for hours while various people drove by. They tended to be crowded and extremely noisy. "I'm not sure. What's it for?"

He looked shocked. "To celebrate the appointment of a new mayor."

"When did that happen?"

"Word of it was announced a few days ago."

Oh. I supposed I should have known that. I had to get back in the habit of reading the news circulars. "I'm surprised they were able to throw together a parade so quickly." And surely it was hugely inappropriate? The Empress had just died.

"Aye, it does take a while to organize. The parade has been planned for weeks, since the corruption of the last mayor was announced. I am told the city had been assured the name of the new mayor would be given in time for the parade."

I drained my mug and Ben immediately reached for the

coffee warming on the stove. I found it bizarre that a parade was planned without knowing the identity of the new mayor, with the Empress—or whoever—making sure the name was provided in time. Almost as though the parade were more important than the mayor it was designed to celebrate. And what if the people didn't like the person appointed?

Actually, maybe that was why they did it. It would be too late to cancel the parade if the new mayor was despised by the populace, and that was probably a good thing. It would be embarrassing for everyone if a mayor were appointed and everyone refused to celebrate. By picking the day in advance, all the participants and merchants would already be committed.

"So, are you going to the parade?" Ben asked again.

I guess I'd better be. Ben certainly seemed enthusiastic about it. If I didn't know better, I would think he was trying to get me out of the house. "Certainly. I love a good parade."

"I'll wrap something up for you to eat."

"I can get something while I'm out," I said quickly.

"Festival stall food," he sniffed.

Hey, I'd always liked it. "Have you seen Taro?"

"He left with a friend very early this morning."

Taro and his bizarre early-morning habits. I refused to ask how good-looking said friend was. I really didn't want to know.

I left the residence carrying a small bundle of fresh bread, cold cooked bacon, and cheese—good, wholesome food that wouldn't stand a chance against the more savory fare that would be available closer to the parade route. Of course, it was a bit of a hike to Center Street, the popular choice for parades, and most of the carriages usually available for hire would either be somehow involved with the parade itself or sticking to the streets with the residences of those who could afford rates that had been tripled in honor of the day.

So that meant walking, which meant I'd be starving by the time I got to any stalls. I dug into the little package Ben had made. Cold bacon and cheese could be really tasty when one was starving.

I'd never seen the appointment of a mayor before. I had seen parades. With this in mind, I asked for directions and made my way to Ivy Point, more popularly known as Confusion Square, where the parade would end. That was the first place where royal proclamations and other political speeches were given in High Scape, and it was apparently where the mayor would be appointed. It was a large empty space, basically, where Center Street ended and dozens of other, smaller streets branched off in crazy directions. Instead of the usual cobblestones, the street of the Square had large slabs of stones in circling shades of light gray. There was a huge memorial in the middle of the northern half of the Square, a ridiculously tall statue of Emperor Benik in a ridiculously heroic pose. And there was ivy everywhere, crawling up the walls of the buildings lining the Square. That was why it was named Ivy Point, but people still called it Confusion Square back from the days when a handful of merchants had fought for control over who could sell in the area, with the result that on any given day no one knew what would be available for sale, if they would be risking their lives trying to buy it or if they'd even be allowed in the Square at all.

When I reached the Square, I saw that many others had had the same idea as I, and a small selection of merchants had set up stalls. I'd been uncertain as to whether it was appropriate to wear mourning purple to the celebration of a new mayor, but I saw many others were also wearing the color to some degree or another. So I wouldn't stand out.

It looked like everyone was wearing harmony bobs.

A platform had been constructed beside the memorial, and on the platform, a canopy with cushioned chairs. That was where the important people would sit, when it was time to swear in the new mayor. Runners kept a huge swath of Center Street clear where it entered the Square and stretched up right to the memorial. That was where the parade would end, the participants splitting off before the platform and disappearing into the crowd or down the smaller streets as they chose.

I was aware, from the chatter going on around me, that the

parade had started before I'd risen for the day, but none of the entrants had reached the Square yet. I browsed through the stalls. Most of the fare seemed of a cheap variety, the kind of things a merchant would be less devastated to lose if the Runners chose to enforce the laws and confiscate their goods. I found a stall selling books, thin with jagged paper and loose bindings.

After perusing the titles for a while, I asked the merchant, "Have you any books about spell casting?"

Her eyebrows shot up. "Of course not," she said quickly.

That was a strange response. "What do you mean by that?"

"Look, I've answered your question. Do you see something you want?"

"No."

"Then please leave."

Well, that was weird.

The first participants in the parade showed up, a troop of Imperial soldiers wearing copper breastplates and blue capes, marching to the beat of the troop drummers and horn blowers coming in behind them. They were impressive. They were dangerous. At least, to me.

Marching music was bad. It made me want to march somewhere and do something martial. I was such an idiot. Of course I knew parades had music. I'd just, somehow, forgotten the impact such music would have on me. Because I was an idiot.

Music could have a really bad effect on Shields, worse than alcohol, and probably down there with drugs if it were the right kind of music and the wrong kind of Shield. I'd nearly started a tavern brawl once because of the music being played in it. One entry in my endless list of embarrassments was how particularly sensitive to music I appeared to be.

I noticed people giving me uneasy looks. The white braid sewn into my left shoulder practically glowed against the dark purple material of my dress. And a Source, who would be known by a black braid over the left shoulder, was nowhere in sight. My Source was supposed to keep me under control. That was aggravating, but necessary.

I had a method for getting through musical assault. Not a great method, and it didn't always work, but it was better than nothing. I made my way to the platform, to the side away from everyone else and, an added plus, the farthest from the marching band, and I wrapped my arms around one of the support beams. Hold on to something and don't let go. And when the music stopped, I would go home.

But the music didn't stop. It seemed that the military musicians had taken up a position on the other side of the Square and planned on serenading each entrant in the parade. Just lovely.

At least there were plenty of Runners around. They'd stop me if I tried to attack anyone, which was the sort of behavior this kind of music could inspire in me. Violence was far less embarrassing than the other possibilities.

I pressed my forehead against the wooden beam, trying to focus on the grains of wood digging into my skin. They didn't hurt, and normally I wouldn't even feel them. But I concentrated on the rough grains biting so slightly into my flesh. It almost felt good.

I closed my eyes. Images popped into my head. Images of running. With a sword. Charging toward the enemy. Rising up to the crest of a hill and ready to leap into the fray below. It didn't matter that I wouldn't know what to do with a sword if I had one, and leaping into the fray would no doubt result in my tripping and falling on my face.

When someone tapped me on the shoulder, I swear I almost jumped right out of my skin.

"My apologies." The man, middle-aged and almost rigidly slim, bowed low. He wore the plain tunic and trousers of a servant. "But Trader Fines has learned of your difficulties, and offers a place on the platform as a means of collecting yourself."

I stared at him, my mind blank. He was going to make me talk, damn it. I tried to think about something other than the music. "I thank him." Hey, I could still form words. "But it would be better if I stayed out of everyone's way." The top of the platform was just as open to noise as under it, with the added disadvantage of exposing me to everyone's easy view.

"There is no one to look after you here," said the man. "We may be able to assist you and allow you to preserve your dignity."

There was no dignity in losing control in front of an audience. I would know.

"Trader Fines will be able to attend to you, give you something on which to put your attention and prevent you from harming yourself or anyone else. Surely that is better than cowering down here."

I wasn't cowering, prat. I was being discreet.

"Please. Trader Fines fears what havoc your parents might wreak on his trade relations, should they learn he left their daughter in distress and without her Source out on the street."

Trader Fines. I knew no Trader Fines. That didn't mean my parents didn't know him. And if he lived in High Scape, it wouldn't be ridiculous to believe he knew who Trader and Holder Mallorough's daughter was.

It was better than accepting aid from someone who didn't know me at all. But would accepting his assistance put my parents into some kind of debt? Surely not.

Was it normal for complete strangers to assist each other in this way? We had been assisted on Flatwell, but with the expectation that we would bring our benefactors money. Would Fines expect something in return from me? But there was nothing I, as a Shield, could do for him.

It was really hard to think. "I can't let go," I confessed.

"Your pardon?"

"I have to hold on and not let go." I closed my eyes again.

"Then perhaps I can be of assistance." I opened my eyes when the man touched my wrist. He pulled gently, but my fingernails were dug as deeply into the wood as I could force them. "Please," he said softly.

I looked at the hand in question, and with great effort forced myself to unclench my fingers. Once my hand was free, the man took it, tsked at the blood under my nails and wrapped it around his forearm. It was hard work to avoid sinking my nails into him, but it gave me focus and a distraction from the music bombarding me.

He slowly escorted me around to the front of the platform, and then up the steps. At the top, I realized that people had arrived and taken some of the seats. A quick glance at the Square showed me that it was much more full, and that there were a lot more parade participants mingling about. How long had I been standing under the platform, anyway?

I recognized two of the people on the platform as attendees at the disastrous party held by Lord Yellows, who had been using the party as a means to get all of the local aristocracy, as well as the visiting Prince Gifford, into one place so his fellow Reanists could sacrifice them all at once. The two, along with everyone else on the platform, turned to look at who was joining them, and the two sacrifice survivors surprised me by nodding greetings at me. I nodded back.

The servant led me to a man who remained seated as he watched me approach. His black hair had a single wide stretch of white so perfectly linear and white that I wondered if he'd dyed it so for effect. His eyes were dark brown and his skin was the color of copper coins. His face seemed free of lines, but there was an edge to his features that made me think he was much older than he looked.

I really didn't know much about fashion, certainly not as it pertained to men, but even I could tell the cloth was of the finest quality. He was wearing the dark purple for mourning, and a cloak that looked similar in cut to what I'd seen many other men wear.

He was wearing a harmony bob. That made me respect him less, even though I knew this made me a hypocrite. I had a sentimental reason for wearing mine. What was his excuse?

He rose when I was about a foot away from him. "Trader Fines," said my escort. "May I present Shield Dunleavy Mallorough. Shield Mallorough, this is Trader Richard Fines."

He bowed. I always tried to avoid bowing, because it seemed too subservient. It was bad enough that I had to do it for royalty. But when the other person did it first, well, I had to hunker into a curtsy. So I did. "A joy to meet you," I said.

"A joy shared is twice blessed," he responded, which was a greeting I had never heard before. "I understand you are experiencing some difficulty."

"Yes, I hadn't expected the music to be so . . . loud." I realized my nails were digging into the servant's arm after all. The poor man hadn't made a sound.

I was afraid to let go of him.

"Please be seated."

"No. Thank you. I need to go." But I couldn't move. Not by myself. I was surprised I was able to string words into coherent sentences. So stupid, to have come to the parade alone. Or at all.

"Nonsense. I will take care of you. To my understanding, it is merely a matter of having you give your attention to something else, correct?"

Ah, not entirely. It depended on the Shield, and how badly music affected him or her. Music affected me very badly.

But I couldn't move on my own, and for a moment the music welled up, sweeping through my mind.

Perhaps Fines continued to speak. I didn't hear him. I found myself pressed into his chair, my hands transferred from the poor servant to the arms of the chair. And once I was seated, I felt frozen in place. This had become my new anchor.

I was able to notice that Fines had ousted the person from the chair next to mine and seated himself.

A few—or a great many, I couldn't be sure—moments later, the music changed to something a little softer. Still a little rambunctious for my taste, but it was easier to keep still, and I could actually listen to what this Fines person was telling me.

"Your father outbid me on the shipment of buttersilk," said Fines, and it sounded like he was at the end of a story.

"Oh." What did one say in response to that? Good for him? I'm sorry? I wasn't really listening?

Fines appeared pleased by my response. Perhaps he hadn't been expecting one, which wouldn't be surprising, considering my behavior. "What with the frost destroying so many trees in the Beatrum Triangle the year before last, buttersilk is scarce."

I didn't know the location of the Beatrum Triangle, I didn't know there had been frost there, and I didn't know what buttersilk was. Should I tell him that?

"Your mother will make an absolute fortune."

"I'm pleased to hear it." Because I had to say something. And I was always happy to know my family was doing well.

"Your family has quite able traders and holders. It's rare to see so much talent in one family. Usually that sort of ambition skips a few."

"Does it?" The servant offered me a goblet of something. I shook my head.

"Do you have any skill with trade?"

"None at all."

"Well, it would be wasted in a Shield, wouldn't it?"

It would. Completely. And yet I found his comment insulting nonetheless. As if a Shield could do nothing but Shield. It was true that I could do nothing but Shield, but that didn't mean no Shields had any other skills. I was offended on their behalf.

Zaire, I wasn't even making sense to myself. It had to be the music.

"And I understand that you are an exceptionally skilled Shield."

I wouldn't have said "exceptionally." I was good, I knew that, but there were a whole lot of Shields out there that I had never met. "That sort of thing is really very difficult to quantify. It's more a matter of the talent of the Source than that of the Shield." After all, if the Source couldn't channel well, the skill of the Shield didn't really matter much.

"And Source Karish is a highly skilled Source."

"Yes." I felt I should do more in this conversation than answer questions, even though I hadn't asked to be part of it.

"I gather from your place on the platform that you have a part in the appointment ceremony?"

"Actually, Mayor Izen been already been appointed. There was a ceremony held at city hall last week. I am merely introducing him to the people. He is a good friend of mine, and he is well suited to his new role. I am honored and pleased to be part of his introduction."

I wanted to ask why he was given what I assumed was a significant honor, introducing the mayor to High Scape, but I had a feeling I should already know. The thing was, he was just a merchant. With all the aristocrats who lived in High Scape, I was surprised to find a merchant so singled out. "Have you done this before?"

"Oh, no," he chuckled. "I think I was chosen because I have a seat on the Imperial Council. I just received it, because of the bill. You know the one, introducing a quota for merchant seats on the council?"

Ah, yes. I'd even met one of the people who wrote it.

Fines must, I thought, have an awful lot of money.

I was getting cynical in my old age.

"As well, I was part of the campaign for Mayor Izen to get this post."

"Really?" I said. "What does such a campaign involve?" I had no idea how a monarch chose a mayor.

He winked. "Now, that would be telling."

That would be telling me what? What couldn't he tell me? Had there been something nefarious about the campaign?

I was being completely ridiculous. Of course there had been nothing nefarious going on. Fines was just amusing himself by playing with me.

It was so hard to think.

The Square was becoming uncomfortably packed as more and more jugglers, dignitaries, acrobats and musicians decided to wait around for the introduction of the mayor. At least the musicians stopped playing once they entered the Square. The cacophony of competing musicians would have driven me insane.

Fines talked on. About local politics, of which I knew little, about trade, of which I knew nothing, and about scandal, of which I knew more than I liked. And time passed. The rest of the chairs on the platform filled. More and more people crammed into Confusion Square.

And then, finally, a carriage was drawing up before the platform, a heavyset man with a chain draped over his shoulders and chest stepping down from the carriage and lumbering up to the platform. The new mayor, I assumed. The music, thank Zaire, finally stopped. I breathed a sigh of relief, unclenched my fingernails and worried at the sliver that had worked itself into my left index finger.

And I realized, really realized, that I was on the platform upon which the mayor would be introduced to everyone. The platform everyone was watching. What the hell was I doing on the platform?

My hair clashed horribly with my dress.

Fines rose to his feet and assisted the man I presumed to be the new mayor up the last few stairs. The two men walked to the center of the platform, near the front, and waited for the crowd to quiet down. It took a while, but the silence, when it finally came, was soothing to my abused ears.

Everyone heard the single person who, hidden by the crowd, booed.

I pressed my lips together to keep from smiling.

Ignoring the malcontent, Fines called out, "Good citizens of High Scape! Welcome to this glorious day of renewal." He paused, and a lot of people obligingly applauded. "Although it is a time when many of us carry sorrow in our hearts—" Did we really? How could people mourn the death of someone they had never met? "We must always seek solace in new triumphs, and recognize that change brings with it opportunity as well as loss."

I hated change. Change brought anxiety and uncertainty. I didn't think I knew anyone who actually liked change. At best, they accepted it with a sort of grim resolution. At worst, they denied the reality of that change to the detriment of themselves and everyone around them.

Did Fines like change?

"Today is our opportunity to welcome to the helm of our great city an able man of discipline, compassion and wisdom."

I could swear I heard someone snicker.

"There were many who could have done the job of acting as mayor of High Scape. There were even more who wanted the position."

Really? I wondered why. There was a goodly amount of money to it, I supposed, and prestige. But the mayor probably learned a whole lot more about the inner workings of the city than I would ever want to know. I imagined there were a lot of long meetings while people debated endlessly about building bridges or water ducts. It certainly wasn't how I'd want to spend my time.

"But few would be able to bring to the role the dedication and honor of the man it is my privilege to introduce to you." Fines put a hand on Izen's shoulder, squeezing it slightly. "I give you Yuri Izen, mayor of High Scape."

The applause was thunderous. I was made aware once more that I had no idea who Izen was and whether anyone in High Scape, aside from the person who had booed, really knew anything about him. Maybe the only thing they liked about him was that his introduction provided an excuse to take a day off and drink beer.

My studies at the Shield Academy had never given much attention to local politics. We had been encouraged to meet regulars, of course, and to understand that it was important to protect them, but not to get too attached, and certainly not to get involved in anything that could make the blood boil as politics could. It was not our place to interfere. We would always be moving on soon.

"Dear people of High Scape!" Mayor Izen shouted. He didn't have a voice for public speaking. It cracked on every word. "I stand before you fully aware of my responsibilities as the mayor of the greatest city in the world." There was more loud applause at that, and I wondered if Izen had visited every city in the world, that he could make that claim. "We have been put through some difficult times in the past, but we made it through. We are facing some challenges now, and we'll face and defeat those, too. Because we are the strongest, smartest, bravest people in the world." More applause, and I wondered if the spectators believed what they were hearing. How could they think they were better than other people in other cities? It was silly. "I was born in this city. I grew up here. My parents were both on the city council and they instilled in me the knowledge that service to others is the greatest employment a person can have. I bring to my role as mayor this knowledge, as well as great pride in this city, and the willingness to do whatever it takes to assist in the prosperity of High Scape."

The new mayor droned on with more rhetoric about what a wonderful leader he was going to be. The audience applauded dutifully where the mayor paused. I wondered how much longer he would be.

With the music silenced, my mind cleared. I looked at Fines, who was standing behind Izen. I couldn't see his face, but he was standing very straight. I imagined he looked proud. I wondered why he had wanted Izen to be the mayor. How did he benefit from it? While I didn't know much about such things, I did know that little was done in political circles without favors changing hands.

Ah, it had nothing to do with me. None of my business.

Izen finally stopped talking. I noticed wagons with barrels of what I assumed was beer being pulled into the Square. So did a great many of the spectators, it looked like, for many didn't bother applauding Izen's last words as they headed for the beer.

Despite the defection, Fines spoke again. "Please remain with us," he called, "as we celebrate this great man's rise to our highest office."

Really, people didn't need the encouragement.

I rose from my seat. I wanted to get out of there in case any of the music started up again.

Fines was suddenly by my side. "Shield Mallorough, will you not remain with us for the afternoon? There are people I would like you to meet."

Why would he want me to meet anyone? "I apologize, but being exposed to such rousing music for as long as I was can be very draining. It would be irresponsible for me to remain here without my Source. Truly, I shouldn't have come at all."

"I am glad you did come, though I am, of course, regretful that you experienced such difficulty. It gave us a chance to meet."

I didn't know how to address that. "Thank you for your kindness." And I made my escape.

I was tired from my interaction with the music, I had been telling the truth about that. All the muscles of my body felt loose and watery from being held so tensely for so long. There were still no carriages available for rent. I was thoroughly exhausted by the time I dragged myself over the threshold of the Triple S entrance. I went straight to bed.

The next day, I learned that Izen had been murdered in his sleep.

# Chapter Seven

A bench-dancing competition that didn't conflict with one of my lengthened watches at the Stall, one that I was free to enter. For the first time since we'd gotten back. Finally.

And it was a proper bench-dancing competition. Never mind that it was one of the smaller ones, one that no one of exceptional skill would enter. It was enough for me that it would be a regulation match, with two benches and four bars, and the only musical accompaniment would be the drums. The kind of match I'd been trained to expect when I was in the Academy, the kind I hadn't been able to enjoy since before Taro and I were sent to Flatwell.

There were no costumes, because no one cared what anyone looked like. My hair was tightly bound, though much of it was likely to escape at some point. My trousers and shirt were loose and comfortable and covered me from throat to wrist to ankle. I wore no cosmetics, no flashy baubles. I'd used nothing more than my plain name, no adjectives included, when I'd signed up.

There was a Runner among the gathering spectators, his solid-black uniform standing out against the varying clothing of the others. I thought it odd that one would waste time watching a bench-dancing competition while he was on duty. But perhaps he was looking for suspicious behavior. Since the mayor had been killed, Runners seemed to have multiplied, and they interfered with the most innocuous of activities.

I wouldn't let his presence distract me. Finally, my muscles would be used as they were meant to be used. A good, proper working out. I was going to enjoy it.

And no one would be tossing coins on the ground for me to scoop up after my performance. That had been so demeaning.

I was excited, to my disgust. I tried to calm down. Not just look calm, but be calm. Deep breaths, sedate thoughts. It didn't help. I was excited. I stretched a little harder than was good for me, ground my bare feet into the chalk box a little too enthusiastically, and I found it difficult to stay still once I was standing on the bench. I practically shivered once the drums started rolling.

But the drums weren't the only instrument that sounded through the air. I heard the winding tones of a double-reed recorder, felt it low in the pit of my stomach. That wasn't traditional. Why were they playing that? I shook my head in an attempt to shake off its influence.

And then the bars started moving. I nearly lost right then as a strange battle developed between my mind and my body. My mind expected me to dance the proper way, the way I had always been trained. My body, however, remembered a different way of dancing, the way that had been drilled into me over endless practices and performances on Flatwell. A way with a slower pace and lower bars, where legs and arms curled and coiled unnecessarily, for the show of it rather than the need of it.

The first couple of steps were taken in such confusion that I almost slipped from the benches for no reason at all.

I was not going to do that again. I struggled to get myself under control.

*Remember what you were taught.*

*Get your arms back where they belong.*

There were two benches. Two dancers stood facing each other, one on either end of the benches, with a foot on each bench. Four bars were held and moved by people called stalkers, two at each end of the benches. They brought the bars up and over the benches, banging them together, and it was the task of the dancers to leap over the bars without getting their feet or ankles caught, or resting two feet on a bench at the same time, or falling off. It was dangerous, with a real possibility of permanent injury.

Ignore the flashes of gold, the memory of the slithering tones of the sandpipe, the dark, hot, tropical air. This was not a performance before the ignorant; I was not striving for the coins needed to keep Taro and me in clothing and food. This was a competition—that was all—and what was at stake was my pride.

Listen to the drums. The drums that are actually present, not the ones you remember. Let the solid beats mingle with that of the heart, warming it and the blood it sent racing. Let it fill your chest and mind and drive your thighs and feet.

Ignore the recorder. The recorder shouldn't be there. It was fighting the drums. The drums were a steady beat. The recorder was sinuous and entrancing. Why did they have a recorder? Did they know what that could do to a Shield? Were they trying to drive Shields out of the competitions?

It was insidious. It coiled around my spin and slid into my mind, clouding my eyes. And suddenly, I was transported. The hot, moist air, the flickering torches, the desperation of knowing my survival relied on how well I danced.

I was there. My arms curling. My hips swaying. My heart pounding so hard I could feel it in my throat. I lost sight of my opponent. I forgot he was even there.

I didn't know I had missed this.

The recorder sounded so good with the drums. Why had no one thought to mix those two before? Why hadn't bench dancing changed at all during my life? It was glorious to add the recorder, to add the hips and the arms, to add color. Why had it taken people so long to realize that?

And then, just as suddenly as it had started, it ended. My brain full of the echoes of the music, I half stumbled to the ground, panting. As my eyes cleared, I realized people were staring at me. My opponent, the stalkers handling the bars, the other competitors, the adjudicators, all of them looking at me like I'd lost my mind. As I clearly had.

Oh my gods. What the hell had I been doing?

One of the adjudicators cleared her throat. "Shield Mallorough is disqualified for . . ." There was a pause as she clearly strove for appropriate words. ". . . unsanctioned maneuvers."

I was pretty sure that wasn't anywhere in the rules, but I was too humiliated to object.

I slunk to the competitors' bench to wipe my feet and strap on my boots.

"You're in fine form," a voice said from behind me, "but I'm still happy I didn't wager on you."

Of course I didn't need to look up to know who it was. "You're making a habit of this, Doran." And wasn't that annoying? I'd told him I would contact him when I had time, I didn't contact him at all, and he caught me at a bench-dancing competition. He could be forgiven for wondering why I had time to dance but no time to send him a note.

Plus he'd seen me act like an idiot.

"I like to watch you dance," he said, sitting beside me on the bench, but with his back to the competition. "Was there something different about it today?"

He was being kind, or he was subtly teasing me. Either way, it just made me more embarrassed. "I thought bench dancing wasn't your sport."

"It isn't. I like to watch you dance."

I shot him a glance. "I hardly look my best on such occasions."

"It's not about your hair being perfect, or wearing a gown of the latest fashion. It's like you let the real you come shining out when you dance."

What the hell did that mean? "I'm always the real me." I didn't play games.

"No. You're always so worried about keeping your face blank and your voice moderate and your eyes . . ."

Dead? I'd been accused of having dead eyes before.

". . . unrevealing. It's admirable, of course, and I assume it's necessary for your work. But when you dance, it's like you forget all that. You become what you really are, at the core. Full of fire and drive."

"I hate to break it to you, Doran, but the reserve you so generously described"—the prat—"is the real me."

"It was imposed upon you by your training," he insisted. "Just like healers are supposed to give only good news and not react when things go wrong. Just like barristers are always supposed to look like they expect everything that happens even when they've been shocked six ways from rest day."

I cocked my head to one side. I didn't know anything about healers or barristers but I could ask, "Do you assume all Shields are alike?"

"Well, I—" He cut off his words, abruptly.

He did. He really did. How very disappointing. How could any sensible person think that every member of a profession had the same personality? That just defied logic.

"You're the only Shield I've ever met," was how he tried to save himself.

That was easily fixed. I could introduce him to the other Shields of High Scape. I wouldn't, though. I wouldn't encourage his entrance into that part of my life. The fact that he had nothing to do with the Triple S was one of the things I liked about him. I needed people that kept me in touch with the world outside of the Triple S.

On the other hand, ignorance could be tiresome. "Don't assume you know the whole from meeting the one," I said.

"Yes, ma'am," he answered, not chastened at all. "Do you have a watch today?"

"Not until late this evening."

"So you have time for a picnic with me in Gray's Park?"

I had time. I just didn't know if I had the inclination. I liked him. A lot. And if Taro and I hadn't started sleeping together on Flatwell, I would have no problem accepting his invitation. But things were different, and I had to tell him that, and that was something I would like to put off for a while. "I need to wash up and change," I warned him, hoping it would discourage him, for the day, at least.

"That's perfect," he said. "It will give me time to gather our meal. I'll pick you up at your boardinghouse, shall I?"

Oh, aye, that was a brilliant idea. Someone else might be there, and I didn't know which would be worse, Taro or someone who would fill Taro's head with all the wrong ideas.

And the fact that I was worried irritated the hell out of me. I had every right to see a friend anytime I wished to, damn it.

I wouldn't hide that I was seeing Doran. In fact, I would make sure to tell Taro about it, because I knew Taro wouldn't see Doran as just another friend of mine, and sneaking around would only make it worse.

Of course, maybe I was being presumptuous. It was possible Taro really wouldn't care. It was possible he would even be relieved.

Since returning to High Scape, I'd felt a little buried in Taro. He was my Source, the most important relationship I would ever have. But that shouldn't make him everything, and it felt to me that that was what he had become. We spent most nights sleeping together, me changing in my bedchamber before joining him in his, we usually ate together, and then there were the endless watches. It wasn't healthy for me, and it would leave me at a total loss once Taro tired of me.

I wanted Doran to remain a part of my life. That would depend on how he handled my news regarding Taro, and my decision that anything between Doran and me would have to be nothing more than friendship. But only in my nightmares would any part of that discussion take place in Taro's presence. "I'd prefer to meet you at the park. I'm sure to finish before you do, and I'd rather wait at the park, where there's something to look at, than wait around at the residence looking like I'm being stood up. You have no idea how the others would torment me."

Doran probably didn't believe my reasons, because he wasn't stupid, but being a proper gentleman, he agreed to the lady's wishes. He bowed and left.

It turned out that none of the others was at the Triple S residence, not unusual at that time of day. So I quickly bathed and dressed in the same kind of clothes I normally wore when I wasn't doing anything in particular, a comfortable long skirt of sturdy cotton, a loose cotton shirt of a creamy color, and my hair left free. I was going to be comfortable, physically if not emotionally.

If I had any discipline left at all, I wouldn't worry about being emotionally comfortable.

I practiced what I was going to say to Doran as I walked the streets toward the park. I lectured myself on the importance of being calm and not falling into any behavior that may seem leading or suggestive with him. I told myself that I was an idiot for meeting him at all. I then argued with myself that I was allowed to have friends, whether Taro approved of them or not. And I wasn't betraying Taro because I wasn't sleeping with Doran.

If we had never gone to Flatwell, Doran and I would have continued on the path we'd started, into something steady and possibly permanent. I knew, without a doubt, that nothing would have happened between Taro and me had we not been so far from home and so very miserable about it. This thing I had with Taro, it was just a fancy, and like all fancies, it was insubstantial and would fade in the hard light of reality.

When that happened, I would need as many friends as I could find, people to be with so I could be away from Taro when I needed to be, when he was off somewhere with his new lovers. I knew my limitations. I wouldn't be able to maintain an emotional balance after Taro had tired of me without Risa to listen to me complain about him, and Doran to distract me from it all. Provided, of course, he was willing to fulfill that function.

Of course, if I had any self-respect at all, I would break it off with Taro immediately, instead of waiting for him to do it.

But I didn't want to do it. I couldn't. I wanted to enjoy this wonderful thing I had with him, for as long as it lasted. Once it was over, I knew I'd have nothing like it again.

At the same time, I couldn't dive into it wholeheartedly. It would end. If I put all my belief into it, once it ended, I wouldn't be able to bear it.

I had to be careful.

Engrossed in my internal argument, I could perhaps be forgiven for missing the early signs that something unusual was going on around me. The purple smoke, the hissing sound, and the windows cracking in the building I was passing all escaped my notice.

But then the roof blew off. I noticed that.

My internal argument halted. I stared at the trembling building. Made of wood to allow give in case of natural events. The slats of the roof blown high and dropping down, deadly little missiles falling down on the heads of people not quick enough to dodge out of the way.

Then the windows blew out, and the purple smoke became mixed with black. It was only then that I heard the screaming.

I happened to be closest to the building. I could feel the painful heat of fire. I was stupid enough to run to the front door, screaming as my palm was scalded by the handle.

I was pulled away by firm hands on my shoulders, and a long leg kicked out and forced the door open. Smoke poured out and the heat was searing.

"Hell," muttered the stranger beside me. He took a few steps back. "You're a Shield, right? Can you do anything about this?"

"No, because I'm a Shield, not a member of the fire brigade." Normally, I would have stopped my response after the first word, but my hand hurt, and it was bloody hot. I was not at my best.

There were screams coming from within the house. Damn it.

I was not a member of the fire brigade. I'd never aspired to be. But the fire brigade was not there. My eyes blinking with tears, I ducked low and through the door, because I was a complete idiot. I crouched. Near the floor the smoke was lighter and it was easier to see.

I didn't waste much time looking at the furniture. My eyes were drawn to a woman dragging two young children toward a set of stairs that was across the room from the door. In other words, away from the way out. Stupid woman.

I looked up. There was a hole in the ceiling, clean through the second floor. I could see the sky through what remained of the roof. What could do this?

Gods, the heat was unbelievable. I felt as though my skin was blistering off my face, my eyes boiling in their sockets. But I couldn't leave while those people were in there.

The older child was close to the woman in size. She pulled away to make for the door. The woman astonished me by grabbing the collar of the child's dress and yanking her back. I wanted to shout at her for that bit of stupidity, but the air felt too dry to talk.

This caused the woman to look up and notice me. She released the smaller child to throw a hand out at me. "No!" she shouted. "Stop!"

What the—? I looked to the floor at my feet, searching for the gaping hole of fire I'd obviously missed the first time around.

What I saw was a circle of white powder on the bare wooden floor, symbols that I didn't recognize drawn within the circle, a knife with a white handle, a knife with a black handle, and a small silver bowl with a red liquid within. Oddly enough, nothing within the circle had been disturbed.

It was nearly the size of the floor, and the room couldn't be crossed without crossing the circle as well.

I stared at the woman, stunned. She was trying to cast a spell? And when her house caught on fire, she was more concerned about preserving her precious little circle than the lives of her children? Look at her, herding them up the stairs, with flames reaching down from above. Heartless bitch.

Some people should not be allowed to breed.

I swept at the circle with the length of my foot, the first step to crossing the room.

And immediately, the flames and the smoke, both the purple and the black, were gone. The noise dove into thick silence. Even the smell disappeared.

The damage remained, though. The shattered windows, the holes in the ceiling, the scorches on the walls. I couldn't quite understand what was going on, but before there was chaos, and suddenly the only sound was the crying of the two girls.

I felt so annoyed, so restless and jittery, that I wanted to charge across the room and slap that woman.

The man who'd kicked in the door stepped inside. "You've been casting!" he gasped, pointing at the floor.

It didn't make sense. There were no candles within the circle. If there had been, that would have explained how the fire had started. Though not how it had ended so abruptly.

There had to be some explanation other than my breaking the circle. There absolutely had to be. Just because I couldn't think of one didn't mean one didn't exist.

Damn, my hand was killing me.

"Get out of my house!" the woman shrieked. She was a pretty thing, I noticed almost absently. Very fair skin, wide blue eyes, true blond hair. "You have no right to be here!"

"Your house was on fire," I pointed out, just in case she had failed to notice it herself.

"And now it's not."

All right, so not unobservant. Just really, really stupid.

"Get out!" she shouted, and there were tears in her eyes. "This is my house! Get out! All of you, get out!"

All of us? Oh. Others were looking in through the broken windows and the door.

I looked at the two girls, about six and twelve, I guessed, with the white blond hair and blue eyes of the woman I assumed was their mother. They wore shapeless white dresses, possibly pristine prior to the fire, and their feet were bare. They looked confused and frightened, and although their mother clutched them close, they didn't appear reassured by her presence. At least they weren't idiots.

"Get out!" the woman screamed again, her voice cracking.

I didn't know what else to do. It was her house. I didn't really want to have to help her clean up the place. And now that the fire was out, however creepily that had been accomplished, whatever was going on in the house was none of my business.

The man who'd come in with me had a different opinion. "I'm getting the Runners!" he threatened before charging back out of the house.

"Go ahead!" the woman shouted after him. "You!" I found her staring at me. "Out!"

Why was I standing around here? If anyone needed saving, and I had a feeling all three of them did for different reasons, they didn't want to be relying on me.

Well, maybe the girls did. They didn't look like they were comfortable with their mother. But there was nothing I could do about that, either.

I walked out of the house. There was a crowd outside, waiting for the Runners to show up, no doubt. There was still no sign of the fire brigade. I wondered if they would be showing up at all.

An older man tsked and touched the back of my right hand. "Best have that looked at, lass," he said.

There was a truly ugly burn in the palm of my hand and along the insides of my fingers. It stung, and I didn't want it getting infected.

Still, I couldn't help lingering a little, looking at the mess that had been made of the house. Really, how had she managed that? And then the scowling woman slammed the door shut.

I did leave once I heard the Runners approaching. I didn't want to get caught up in their investigation. I made my way to the closest hospital, waited forever and met with a healer who slathered my palm and fingers with salve and wrapped my hand to uselessness. I was instructed to wash my hand daily and change the bandages every time I washed.

Life would be just too unusual if there wasn't something wrong with me. And it gave me something to think about other than the fact that that woman appeared to have created a fire by casting a spell. Spells weren't real. There had to be some other explanation.

# Chapter Eight

I'd forgotten about Doran and our picnic. The whole thing with the fire had driven all such mundane ideas out of my head.

I was reminded of them with painful immediacy when I returned to the Triple S residence. Because Doran was in the kitchen, which was, as usual, the first place I went. I needed some water to clear out my throat. Doran was seated at the long wooden table, picnic paraphernalia piled on the chair beside him.

Taro was at the other end of the kitchen, leaning back against one of the counters, a mug of something in his hand. Oh, lovely.

Not that they appeared to be arguing, or sitting in stony silence, or anything else so adolescent. I seemed to have interrupted a polite conversation, Doran with his own mug of what smelled like tea resting on the table. The two men looked comfortable and casual, and would have fooled any stranger.

I wasn't a stranger. Doran was wary, but hiding it well. Taro was furious, and the only way to tell was by looking at his eyes. I was pretty sure it wasn't Doran that he was angry with. I probably held that honor.

Yes, this was going to be a treat.

But Doran noticed my hand and jumped to his feet, crossing to the door. "What happened?" he demanded, and I backed a step away before he could touch my hand.

"I passed a building that was on fire, and there were people inside screaming, so I—" Did something really stupid.

"Decided to join the fire brigade?" Taro asked coolly. He didn't move.

"It's just a burn. Not a bad one. No harm done."

"Your face is very red."

"That will fade."

"So you're all right?"

"Aye."

"And up for talking, are you?"

Well, I'd rather skip the conversation I feared was coming. I really didn't feel like dealing with the two of them at once. Should I take the coward's way out and claim I was shocked and tired and needed to lie down?

And suddenly, I was irritated. An ambush, that was what it was. How dare Taro try to call me to the carpet? I was doing nothing wrong. "Certainly."

"I was concerned when you didn't meet me at the park," said Doran.

I'd already explained that. "I was at the hospital for a while." I waved my hand. "I do apologize for making you wait. And I don't know that I'm up for a picnic right now. I'm not really hungry."

"Of course," said Doran. "I understand. Perhaps tomorrow?"

I wanted to put him off, tell him I'd discuss it with him another time. But that was cowardly, too. And the firm line of Doran's mouth indicated he knew of the temptation, and he probably wasn't going to let me give into it. Not quietly, anyway. Well, fine, then. "Yes, I can do that."

He smiled only slightly. There was something almost smug in the expression, something I had never seen in him before. I didn't care for it. "The third hour of the decline?"

"The third hour."

"Excellent. I'll pick you up here." Another challenge.

"That would be lovely." Challenge accepted.

He nodded. "I'll see you tomorrow, then." He looked at Taro. "It was a pleasure speaking with you again, Shintaro."

"Aye, it was, Doran," Taro responded.

Never had I seen the men so chilly with each other.

I saw Doran out, well aware that the more difficult man was the one still in the kitchen. He was going to get all emotional. It was important that I stayed calm. Because there was no doubt he was misunderstanding all of this.

Doran was no rival for Taro's affections. Doran had never inspired in me the depth of feeling I had for Taro, and I didn't believe he ever would. It wouldn't be fair of me to pretend otherwise, and I didn't want to play with people.

I needed to make sure both men understood that. It would have been so much easier if I could have met with Doran as expected, had been given the opportunity to make everything clear. Now everything I said was going to sound weak or insincere, because Doran had shown up with clear expectations, and Taro had known nothing about it. Damn it.

Taro was pacing in the kitchen, all pretense of courtesy gone. "What the hell are you playing at?" he demanded.

*Oh, let's dive right into the irrational part of the discussion, shall we?* "I think we should go somewhere more private." I did not want to be providing the evening's entertainment for the other Pairs.

"As loud as I'll be getting, there'll be no privacy no matter where we go."

Wonderful. "I see."

"Don't you dare!" he snapped, pointing a finger at me. "Don't you even think of pretending you're the mature, stable one when you're the one stepping out!"

"I am not stepping out."

"Picnicking with Doran? I beg to differ."

"Differ all you like. I have every right to see my friends."

"He's not a friend! He's in love with you!"

I nearly laughed. "Don't be ridiculous. You don't believe that any more than I do."

He didn't deny that, but he glowered at me, and I waited for another explosion.

But there was no explosion. He pulled in a deep breath through his nose. Then he closed his eyes and pinched the bridge of his nose. He let the breath out through his mouth. He dropped his hand and opened his eyes.

The glower was still there, but his shoulders were a little lower.

"You can't claim he is a friend like any other."

His voice was almost calm, but the 'risto in his accent was coming on thick. Never a good sign. At least, not when it was directed at me. I enjoyed it when he used it on others.

"He is now." Or he would be, once I was able to explain everything to him.

"You would go on a picnic with Risa?"

"Sure." Though I couldn't see Risa enjoying a picnic. It seemed a little tame for her.

He snorted in derision. No doubt he agreed.

"Have you slept with him?"

My mouth dropped open. It had been doing that a lot lately. "Of course not!"

"Before we went to that damned island?"

"That's none of your business!" So much for staying calm.

"So you did sleep with him!"

"No, I did not!" I snapped. "I don't—" I cut myself off before I said something really, really stupid.

The way Taro's eyes narrowed, though, told me I was too late. "You. Don't. What."

It was interesting how much words relied on tone. Technically, his words should have constituted a question. The flat tone made it a dare. He was daring me to finish.

Sleep with people at the drop of a hat. That had been the

end of my aborted sentence. That would have sounded like an accusation, which wouldn't have been my intention. And I knew Taro didn't sleep with absolutely everyone he met. I really did. But sometimes the habit of speaking as though I thought he did snuck back up on me. "I don't see how that matters now, anyway."

"It matters a lot. It matters that you were slithering off to see him!"

"I wasn't slithering."

"What do you call going off to see him without telling me?"

"He asked me to go to the picnic this morning at the bench-dancing match. I came here to change, and you weren't here. If you had been, I would have told you." I would have. "If we'd had a picnic and I came back, I would have told you then."

"Why are you seeing him, anyway?"

"I like his company."

His hard-fought-for calm was slipping. His hands rose to clutch at his hair. "I can't believe you! You say it like there's nothing wrong with it!"

"There is nothing wrong with it!" I searched my mind for an explanation as to why there was nothing wrong with it. It was sometimes difficult to explain the obvious. "Where were you today, when I came back from the match?"

"Racing track!" he growled.

"All alone, I assume," I said sarcastically.

"With friends."

"So what's the difference?"

"None of them want to sleep with me!"

I snickered. I couldn't help it.

"Oh, my mistake," he said with heavy sarcasm. "I'd forgotten. That's the only reason anyone would want to spend any time with me, right? To see if they have a chance."

"No!" I was horrified. "That's not what I meant—"

"Because all I am is a face and a penis, right?"

After all the times I had told him he was smart and talented and generous and kind, and he had the nerve to say that to me?

"I didn't say that and I don't believe that."

"Doran is not just a friend and he's interested in more than just sleeping with you."

Damn. I'd kind of thought we'd gotten away from Doran. "It doesn't matter what Doran's interested in. I'm only spending time with him because I enjoy his company."

"Does he know that?"

"He would if I'd had a chance to meet with him today."

"You were going to tell him you never wanted to see him again at a nice romantic picnic?" Taro asked skeptically.

"I have no intention of telling him I don't want to see him again. I will tell him that any expectations he might have had before I went to Flatwell will have to be put aside."

"Oh, I'm sure he'll be delighted to accommodate you." He rolled his eyes. "You're such a child."

How very obnoxious of him. "Then, if he can't accept that, yes, I won't be seeing him anymore."

"I can tell you right now that he won't agree to—whatever you're expecting to do. Not if he's any kind of man at all. So what you will do is forget all these unnecessary steps you're talking about and you will send him a note canceling your plans for tomorrow and that will be the end of it."

"You will go to hell!" How dare he try to tell me what to do? This was between Doran and me.

"Or do you like having him dangling? Hm? Maybe you like having two men acting like idiots over you."

"Of course not!"

Well, maybe a little.

No, of course not.

"After all, it can't be a common thing for someone like you."

"Someone like me?" I echoed without thought. Definitely without thought. It wasn't as though I actually wanted him to elaborate.

"Someone so rigid. With your blank eyes and your flat

voice. So determined to show the world that she doesn't give a damn what we think and she doesn't need us and we can all go to hell!"

"This is interesting," I mused. "You perceive that I am insulting you, so you have permission to verbally abuse me."

"I notice you're not actually denying what I'm saying."

"Would there be a point?"

He made another grab for his hair. What was his problem? I was, for the most part, refusing to rise to all of the insults he was throwing my way. I was answering all of his questions honestly. I was doing my best to prevent this discussion from degenerating into something really nasty.

And he was being ridiculous. I would wager my last coin while stuck on Flatwell that he hadn't acted this way with any of his other lovers. And, aye, I could see why I was different, in that I was his Shield and the Pair bond always made things a little weird. Still, he neither expected nor wanted the relationships with his other lovers to be exclusive. So why did he have to act like a domineering lord of the manor from a bad melodrama with me?

Perhaps I could end all the posturing if I pointed out what should be obvious, even to him. We simply were not suited for the long term. He was Karish, and as much as he tried to deny it, he was unique. He was dazzling and exciting, such characteristics unusually coupled with generosity and genuine kindness. He deserved someone who matched him.

That was not me. I was quiet and steady and serious, interesting only in my connection to him.

But I dared not say that to him. Much as he accused me of purposely misunderstanding him, he just as often did the same with me. If I gave him my description of him, he would accuse me of thinking him nothing more than a pretty shell. If I gave him my description of me, he'd either agree with me, or think he needed to reassure me. Neither reaction would assist in this situation.

"Please make yourself comfortable," I heard Veritas say,

because he was speaking much more loudly than he usually did. "I will see if they are in."

I wondered how many arguments Veritas had overheard in his years of working at the Triple S residence. He'd probably heard things much stranger and more damaging than what Taro and I had been shouting at each other. That didn't make me feel any better about the fact that I knew he'd no doubt been listening to us.

Ben showed up at the kitchen door. "That Runner woman is here to see you, Shield Mallorough."

Interruptions were wonderful things. "Thank you, Ben."

"What happened to your hand, Shield?"

I'd forgotten about it. "A burn."

"What kind of burn, if I may know?"

What difference did it make? "Metal. Heated metal."

"A healer has seen to it?"

"Aye."

"And has given you a poultice for it?"

"He spread something on it."

"But gave you no more for the following days?"

"Ah, no." Should he have?

Ben tsked. "Come see me tomorrow morning, after you have washed but before you leave for the day. I will refresh the treatment."

"You have healing skills? I didn't know that."

"There is much you don't know of me, if you'll beg my pardon, Shield Mallorough."

I thought that was an odd thing for him to say. It was almost as though he was accusing me of something. I didn't think that was like him.

His words did make me wonder that Taro hadn't touched me once since I'd come to the residence. Not only was that not like him, in general, but he knew if he touched me, it would ease any discomfort I might be feeling. That was sometimes one of the characteristics of the bond between a Source and Shield. We were lucky enough to have it.

I could ask Taro to touch me, I supposed. After that ridiculous argument, though, I wasn't going to ask him for any favors.

"Thank you, Ben." I headed to the door.

"I shall bring you some wine, shall I?" he offered.

"Thank you. That would be lovely." I said nothing to Taro. I had no desire to spark off the argument again. I was aware, however, that he wasn't following me from the kitchen.

Risa was lounging on one of the settees, examining a small statuette that had been left by some long-gone resident of the house. It was the naked form of a youth, stretching one hand up over his head as though reaching for something. It was a pretty piece, but I'd never understood what it was supposed to mean.

"Good evening, Risa," I said. "I am pleased to see you here."

"Well, I'm not here for pleasure, I'm afraid," she answered. "Business."

Oh, that was never good. "What kind of business?"

She gestured at my wrapped hand. "Of course, the fire isn't in my docket. But it seems everyone at Headquarters thinks I'm the one to look into things when you're involved. And you do end up involved in an awful lot of crimes."

"I don't commit crimes," I huffed. Then I froze. Because I'd killed Creol. That was murder. I couldn't believe I'd actually forgotten that.

Risa didn't seem to notice that part of my reaction. "No, but you do always seem to be in the vicinity when crimes are committed," she said.

That was an exaggeration. All sorts of crimes were committed in High Scape and I was nowhere nearby. "What do you want to know?"

"Just tell me everything."

"Oh, is that all?" I did as she ordered, describing my knowledge of the fire with as much detail as I could. During that time, Taro left the house without pausing to say where he was going, and Ben served us red wine. "But is that really a crime?

Accidentally setting fire to your house?" Criminally stupid, maybe.

"No, that's not what the strike is. Pretending to cast spells is a crime."

"I don't think she thought she was pretending."

Risa laughed. "The only alternative is that she was actually casting a spell. A spell that worked. Are you saying it worked? Do you want me to quote you on that?"

"No, thanks all the same, but just out of curiosity, what is the difference in the punishment?"

"The difference?"

"Between pretending to cast a spell and actually casting a spell."

Risa's expression suggested she thought I was suffering some form of delusion. "There's no such thing as truly casting spells."

"Well, no, of course not, but it doesn't seem to make sense that pretending to cast is illegal while actually casting isn't."

"Of course it makes sense. One is possible and the other isn't."

I understood her point, but there was a fundamental lack of logic involved that disturbed me. "So why is pretending to cast illegal?"

"People use it to steal."

"How?"

"You know, selling love potions and things like that."

"How is that different from medicine men who sell physicks that don't work?"

Risa scowled. "I don't write the laws, Dunleavy."

Did that mean we couldn't discuss the inconsistencies? Apparently so.

"Speaking of fake spells, have you heard what those freaks digging up ash groves are doing with the ashes?"

"No, and I don't really care to." I didn't want to imagine doing anything with the ashes. Just the act of digging them up was disgusting.

She gave me a toothy grin. "They mix them into a bowl of the liquid of their choice and rub the mixture on their skin in preparation for casting a spell."

My throat closed up in protest and I put down my glass of red wine. "You can't be serious."

"We've learned that the victims are all people who were considered particularly fortunate by those who knew them. These spell freaks dig up the ashes and try to absorb the luck of the dead person through their skin."

"That's revolting." My stomach twinged just at the thought of it.

"Or they sell them."

"They sell the ashes?"

"There's quite a market developing. People dig up the ashes and sell them to a slew of customers who are desperate for luck. There's even talk that they're running out of people to dig up."

"This is insane." And also none of my business. "Are you supposed to be telling me this?"

"I'm not giving you any specifics of any particular investigation." Risa shrugged. "But if it disturbs you, we can talk of other things. Why did Shintaro go storming out of here?"

I could be so stupid. I kind of set myself up for that. "Storming?"

"He didn't tell you where he was going."

"He doesn't always."

"Of course he does."

How in the world could she claim to know that? "You don't live here, Risa."

"So? Seeing habits isn't hard for someone with my job."

I sighed, because she was right. "We had an argument."

"About what?"

"Do you honestly expect me to tell you?"

"That's what friends do."

Not since I left the Academy. I'd never found talking about such things helped me feel any better, nor did they improve the situation in general. Besides, Taro would kill me. "So if I were really your friend, I would feel obligated to tell you, is that it?"

"No, that's not it. Sometimes you can be terribly stupid, Dunleavy."

Oh. So if I were truly her friend, I would want to tell her. Really? She wanted to play that game? "How much debt are you in right now?" See? I could ask highly inappropriate questions, too.

"You have a nasty habit of attacking people when they ask questions you don't want to answer."

"Isn't that what you're doing now?"

"How about this, then? I'll answer your question after you answer mine."

Perfectly fair, yet that wasn't going to happen. Really, Taro would see it as a betrayal, were I to talk about our affairs with Risa or anyone else, and I wouldn't blame him. I assumed he didn't talk about us with others and if I was wrong and I found out he did, I'd have to kill him.

Of course, once he was done with me, things would be different.

I felt like I'd offended every person I'd encountered that day. It was all catching up with me, the craziness and the people I'd infuriated for no good reason. I didn't want to add Risa to the list, not that day. "So both of us will have to survive having our curiosity unsatisfied," I said. "Want more wine?"

She grinned and I felt relieved. "Sounds great," she said. "But if you're not going to tell me about Karish, the least you can do is show me the costume you had to wear while you were away."

I rolled my eyes. "Are you crazy? Believe it or not, I don't go out of my way to humiliate myself." That always happened by accident.

After Taro's reaction to the costume, I wasn't going to show it to any other Northerner. Ever.

"So you still have it."

"No," I lied.

"I could go to your room and find it."

She wasn't seriously suggesting she would go rifling through my things. "You don't know which room is mine."

She actually pouted. "You won't wear it for me?"

"No."

"Do you wear it for Taro?"

What an odd question. "No."

She grinned. "You've just given me another reason to get you drunk."

And she'd given me another reason to kill Taro. He was the one who'd told her about the costume in the first place. It should have been *me* who stormed out on *him*.

# Chapter Nine

Alone in my sitting room, wearing a light night shift, I sat cross-legged on the floor. I had pushed the furniture close to the walls to give myself plenty of space. I had lit two candles and set them on the floor before me. It was late, everyone in the residence asleep. It was quiet, not a sound coming in from the streets. I stared at the taller candle, letting the golden glow fill my eyes and wrap around my mind.

I didn't usually rely on such artificial relaxation techniques. I couldn't remember doing it even once since leaving the Shield Academy. It seemed to me that it must be unhealthy to try to put the mind asleep while it still had thoughts to work over. But I couldn't sleep, and I really, really wanted to. My mind was spinning so hard with so many thoughts, it was stiffening my muscles, shallowing my breathing and creating imaginary explosions in my ears. The thoughts in my mind were not resolving into any conclusions, just circling uselessly. It made sleep impossible, and it made me anxious.

The shambles of my mind made it clear how very sloppy I had gotten since leaving the Academy. As time went by, I seemed to have less and less control over myself and my emotions and how I expressed them. That was dangerous. A Shield without self-control was useless.

So, out of desperation, I had dragged out some old half-forgotten lessons about finding peace, and the tools to be used when simple deep breathing wasn't enough. So, two candles. One tall and unobstructed. The second low, to accommodate the small metal arch that covered it. On that arch rested a small bowl filled with water and a few drops of dark bark essence. Staring at the flame of the tall candle, breathing in the soothing scent and blowing it out slowly, I followed the thoughts of serenity.

> *The candle brings light.*
> *Lights shows truth.*
> *Truth brings knowledge.*
> *Knowledge crafts balance.*
> *Balance brings peace.*
> *Peace crafts clarity.*
> *Clarity is light.*
> *The candle brings light.*

A simple sequence of words, yet I couldn't keep them straight. I kept remembering other words that didn't belong. Colors flashed behind my eyes, soiling the golden glow of the candle. The explosions increased within my ears, and my heart wouldn't slow down.

So, eventually, I gave up and stared at the candle and got angry at the fact that everyone else was able to sleep.

I heard the door to the corridor open with just the faintest of creaks. I looked up.

It was Taro, of course. His hair was loose, his earlobe was bare, and he was wearing a nightshirt that covered more skin than mine. He slipped into the room and leaned back against the door after closing it. "Are you all right?"

"Of course."

"You're sitting on the floor in the middle of the night."

"Is there a better time to sit on the floor?"

He tsked and crossed the room so he could sit on the floor

on the other side of the candles. He had in one hand some crumpled paper, and I wondered if he'd received another letter from his mother. That always put him in a precarious mood. "What's wrong?"

"Nothing serious." I didn't want to talk about it. It was all so childish and embarrassing.

"I will decide what is serious," he declared.

"Will you?"

"Indeed."

That made me smile, for a moment. "Do you ever get the feeling that the Academies don't really prepare us for the real world?" Though perhaps I was speaking too broadly. The Source Academy might be a very different experience, as Sources spent a great deal of time outside the limits of their Academy in order to practice channeling different kinds of events in different environments. While still closely guarded to avoid spontaneous bonding, it was a lot more experience and exposure than that granted to Shields.

"Yes," was his answer. And that surprised me. I'd really thought it was just me. "I think they think they're being thorough. They tell us of things like illness and crime, the dangers of Shields in the grip of music, the friction that can accidentally happen with regulars."

"Aye," I said. "That's pretty much what they taught us. I guess there isn't a lot more that we can expect from them. But they don't tell us much about what it feels like when other Shields and Sources, people you live and work with, die. Or when the city you're living in suffers some kind of devastation that Sources and Shields can do nothing about."

"Those aren't trivial concerns," said Taro.

But those were concerns from a while ago. "The Empress dies. People are digging up ashes because they believe in luck. And spells. A woman burned her house down because she thought she could cast a spell and have it actually accomplish something. It's like people are going crazy. Again."

"Or still," Taro suggested.

"Still?"

He shrugged. "It's not like they were sane while we were gone and only got crazy after we came back."

Now, there was an idea. Maybe we had brought the craziness with us. "I think I like that idea better than the possibility that they're just getting progressively crazier with no end in sight."

"There's always an end," he said.

"Aye, but some ends are better than others."

"We're not going to get into a philosophical discussion, are we?"

"I certainly hope not."

"Air is better blown to water," Taro added.

"Exactly," I said, though I didn't really know what that meant. I assumed it was something relevant.

"How can a school prepare you for murderers and madmen?" Taro asked. "Friends who would betray you to your death. People in authority who use their power to perform the most unnatural acts. People hating you because you can't do things you aren't supposed to be doing anyway. That's a lot to expect of a school."

"Maybe if we hadn't gone to the Academies, a more normal upbringing would have better prepared us for the real world."

He snickered. "Depends what you call normal, love."

True enough. If some smart and plucky servant hadn't recognized him as a Source—and then promptly gotten fired—Taro might have spent the rest of his life locked up somewhere, by parents who thought he was embarrassingly mad. And that was assuming some event didn't occur and he didn't kill himself trying to channel it without a Shield.

If I'd been a regular, I would have been sent to a boarding school that, from what my brothers told me, was far more rigid than the Shield Academy. That probably wouldn't be considered too normal an upbringing by the average regular, either.

"Speaking of which," said Taro. "I received today a letter."

That was never good.

"From Her Gracious Duchess of Westsea."

It took me a moment to remember who that was. Not Taro's mother, the woman I always associated with that title. The current Duchess of Westsea was a cousin of Taro's, and the woman to whom he'd given the means to acquire the title so he could avoid taking it himself. "Does she write to you often?" I didn't really like the idea of his maintaining contact with that world. It might manage to lure him back.

"This is only the second letter, the first being to thank me for helping her get the title and offering her services should I need anything. This one is giving me details about how things are going. Did you have any idea that there are all sorts of fishers belonging to the estate?"

I'd never thought about it, but it made sense. "It is on the water."

"Aye, but how can there be both fishers and farmers on one estate?"

"What can I say? It's a crazy world." I found it more surprising that he hadn't known that about his own land, though perhaps I shouldn't have. He'd rarely been allowed out of his room before he was sent to the Academy. His parents had never visited him at the Academy. Perhaps they hadn't written much, either, or hadn't bothered to give much detail when they had.

He tapped me on the forehead with the paper as a mild reproof. Then he unfolded it. "It was a lengthy missive, but I'll just read the interesting bits." He squinted his eyes in the dim light, and I almost scolded him for it. He'd wrinkle his lovely skin. "'I have to confess, cousin,'" he read. "'You have a reputation in our family for being a lack wit, or at least half mad.'"

I clenched my teeth to keep from voicing my outrage. How dare they? And what the hell did they know, the thick-skulled provincials?

"'But have you met your mother? She's truly insane. And sometimes I think I mean that literally. She will not stay in the dowager house. She invades the manor at any time of day or night, rousing the servants for mulled wine or chilled ale, waking everyone. She tried to give orders to my gardener about the ash on the east corner of the main plot. They have begun to rot, you see, and will collapse if they aren't cut down. And yes, they are beautiful and have stood there for generations, but are virtually dead and will be a danger if they're left to collapse on their own. So I ordered them cut down, and your mother saw one of the gardeners beginning to work at the first tree, because apparently she has nothing to do all day but watch what's going on on my land, and she descended upon the poor man, denigrating his intelligence and his appearance and his lineage, and then she tried to fire him. My gardener. Fortunately, I'd been pretty close myself, seeing if there were any other changes that needed to be made to the garden, and one of the under gardeners fetched me over. When her imperious Dowager Duchess saw me coming, she changed her target and told me my lineage was nothing more than a graft onto hers and my upbringing had clearly been deficient if I thought I could stride into a position that was never meant to be mine and make changes to a place that would be mine only temporarily.'"

"'Temporarily'?" I interrupted. "What does that mean?"

"Well, when you think about it, every titleholder has the title and the seat only temporarily. They don't die with the holder. That's the nature of it. The title's been in my direct line for a few generations, though. Perhaps Her Grace feels that the recent transference to another line is only an anomaly."

"But there is no one else in your line. Unless you've got some other siblings you haven't told me about." Or maybe some children.

He shrugged and resumed reading the letter. "'While she was talking, I took the axe from poor Forrester and swung at the trunk of the nearest tree. The blade kind of bounced off the bark, which was really embarrassing. But it did shut the woman up, at least for a few moments.'"

"I like this person," I commented.

Taro smiled and continued to read. "'She started up again, though, once I gave the axe back to Forrester and he started chopping the proper way, but we all kept working. Or watching Forrester work, as a more accurate depiction of events.

And then your mother, overcome by our brutal attack on her delicate nerves, fainted. It appeared a painful collapse. I think she was expecting someone to catch her.'"

I snickered.

"'Her useless little companion pulled out a handkerchief and fluttered it around her mistress's face, and then she looked at the gardeners, outraged. She demanded they carry your mother back to her home. I told her we were all busy and she would have to fetch one of the dowager's servants to take her home. The little companion actually tried to throw some of her own orders around, warning us that the mistress would be most displeased. When that didn't work, she walked off with a loud huff, and it was clear that your mother was miming her entire episode, with the sour expression she pulled at being left there to lie on the ground.'" Taro paused to laugh. "'We kept cutting, and eventually a couple of handsome young men—whose functions within your mother's household I've never been able to ascertain—came and carried her away.

"'The fun wasn't over, though. A few weeks later, my housekeeper came to me and told me she had just had a lengthy audience with your mother, who had given her instructions for the menu, the music and the decorations for the ball I was apparently having.

"'I confronted your mother, who had not only sent out dozens of invitations to this ball in my home and in my name, but had also received all the responses. Which were all positive. And all humor aside, it was a little disquieting to talk to her about it. She really thought it was perfectly acceptable to plan this huge undertaking in my name without telling me about it. Because she believed I was too stupid or too badly raised to know what was required of me as the Duchess of Westsea, or how to go about it. She didn't care that she was insulting me grossly, or that she was engaging in behavior to which she flatly had no right. It was baffling. And frustrating. I've never so badly wanted to hit a woman in my life.

"'So now I wonder if I should revoke the gratitude I expressed to you in my last letter. It seems to me you've enjoyed a lucky escape, and I wonder if I've been had.'"

"Zaire," I breathed. "She's blunt, isn't she?"

"She has to be, if she's dealing with Her Grace."

Actually, it seemed she did have the knack for handling Taro's mother, though it was difficult to be sure from a letter. Maybe she could give Taro lessons. Though, truly, I was hoping we could spend the rest of our lives without seeing the Dowager Duchess ever again.

"She has something to say about our favorite royal, too." Taro flipped to another part of the letter. "'Our Emperor-to-be has sent notice of a new tax against everyone with servants. Can you believe it? I am to pay three sovereigns a year for every adult in my employ. It is sheer robbery, in my opinion, and I have informed him that as he has not yet ascended to the throne, he lacks the authority to tax me, and he can just wait until he has the right before his gets his grubby little hands on my money.'"

I put my hand over my mouth, as it had gaped open in shock. "And she says your mother is mad?" I mumbled through my fingers.

"She certainly doesn't seem worried about making enemies." He folded the letter up. "I think she will be good for Flown Raven. I'm pleased I chose her."

I really wished I had been there when the Dowager Duchess had feigned a faint and no one had bothered to catch her.

Taro reached around the candles and caught the fingers of my right hand, turning it over. "I never really let you explain what this was about."

I didn't want to go back to our discussion of earlier that day. I didn't want another argument. I didn't think I could bear it well, not right then. "This woman set her house on fire trying to cast some kind of spell. She had two young children with her."

"And you rushed in to rescue them," he commented in a soft voice, one corner of his mouth curled into a small smile.

He was just gorgeous in the candlelight.

I shrugged. I didn't know if I was thinking of rescuing anyone. I didn't think I was thinking at all, really.

"And just out of curiosity, what would you have done if I had gone rushing into a burning building?" he asked.

The very idea made my chest tight. "Slapped you up the back of the head," I admitted.

He leaned forward so he could reach around with his free hand and give me a gentle tap on the back of the head.

"But you're different," I said solemnly. "You're so much more fragile than I." I was joking, but only a little. It was sort of true. As a Shield, I was resistant to things like extreme temperature, and pain was much less acute to me than it would be to Taro.

"Fragile!" he roared. He placed the candles to one side and grabbed one of my ankles, jerking me to him so I collapsed onto my back. My admonishment to stay quiet was obscured by giggles as he pulled me beneath him. "I'll show you fragile."

He felt so good. Strange and safe and sure and exciting and so many other things. I loved pushing my hands through his hair. I loved the low tones of his voice whispering against my ear. I loved the taste of his skin.

I loved being forgiven when I acted like an idiot.

# Chapter Ten

The next morning, Ben had prepared a white, milky glop to put on my palm, and he appeared to be waiting in the kitchen for me to show up so he could apply it. It did take a bit of the sting out of the burn, and Ben seemed so pleased about being able to do it. I was happy to be able to do something that made him feel appreciated.

Taro was already out, helping a friend change residences. Apparently, the fellow was falling behind on his rent and skipping out. While I couldn't approve of anyone slithering out on their financial obligations, it wasn't unlike an action Taro and I had been considering not too long ago back on Flatwell, and the rent Taro's friend was expected to pay for that hovel was criminal.

Taro's absence meant I got to go book hunting, something that would have bored Taro into incoherence.

All this casting craziness, it had nothing to do with me, and there was nothing I could do about any of it. Screaming at people to start making sense was surprisingly ineffective. But I felt driven to find out where these people were getting their crazy ideas. If nothing else, it had to make for interesting reading.

So I headed out to the nearest print shop, and I asked for materials about spells, and the printer looked appalled. "Of course we don't sell such filth here!" she exclaimed.

"Filth?" I echoed. "How is it filth?"

"Encouraging people to believe in casting. It's unnatural."

I didn't disagree. Believing in casting was unnatural. Still, that didn't mean books about it could be classified as filth. "You print a circular with a mystery series. The descriptions of the deaths are horrible. Really graphic." I didn't like serials, as a rule, preferring to read a full book in a sitting or two. I'd started the serial to which I was referring because I'd thought the writing was unusually good, but the gruesome nature of the murders had put me off.

"That's fiction."

"So's casting."

She looked irritated by the reminder. "That may be, but selling materials purporting to instruct the reader in how to perform spells is illegal."

"Really? Since when?"

"Since always."

"Really?" That was surprising. On the one hand, it kind of made sense, in that if it were illegal to pretend to cast spells, it had to be illegal to print materials teaching someone how to pretend to cast spells. On the other hand, really, where was the harm? "But people are getting it from somewhere."

"Not from this shop, they aren't," the woman declared. "And you should be ashamed of yourself for looking for it. You should set a better example."

"A better example?" I frowned. "Of what? To whom?"

She stared at me as though she thought I'd said something outrageous. "You're a Shield! You are to be a good example of honor and decency for all."

"I see." That was the first I'd heard of it. "Thank you for your time."

I left the shop feeling puzzled and a little disturbed. I didn't like the idea that printed material about casting was illegal. I could sort of see the sense of it, if idiots tried whatever was in a book and ended up setting their houses on fire. But I wasn't an idiot. And I wasn't going to try any spells. I just wanted to know what was being written and read. And I didn't like being told I couldn't see it.

Of course, I knew that just because something was deemed illegal didn't mean it wasn't being done. People were getting the books from somewhere, and book stalls and printing shops were the logical places to look. My search required a lot of stops, a lot of walking and a few carriage rides. I would wait until the shops were empty of customers, which sometimes took some time, and then I'd have to convince the printer that I was no kind of authority and that I had neither the ability nor the desire to entrap anyone. Only once that was accomplished— and it wasn't always—would I be allowed to see the hidden cache of banned goods.

The end result was a collection of pamphlets and small, cheaply bound books with no indication of the contents embossed on the covers. I was given a cloth bag to carry my bounty, so no one could guess that what I was carrying wasn't anything other than respectable literature. I supposed I should have been feeling guilty or nervous or something, since I was doing something illicit. But it didn't feel illicit, and in my opinion it shouldn't have been illicit. I was tempted to sit down on a bench by the road and start reading one of the pamphlets, just to see what would happen.

But I didn't have time to sit and read and scandalize everyone who walked by. It had taken me much longer than I'd expected to find the books. I had to go home and bathe and change for my meeting, my picnic, with Doran.

I was glad that Taro knew about the picnic in advance. And he was apparently fine with it, having gotten over his initial reactionary snit. And so he should be. Nothing Doran did would have any impact on my relationship with Taro, which was more than could be said of Taro's friends.

When Doran came to the residence, he was not carrying the same sort of supplies he had had the previous day. He said he'd left everything at the park, and I wondered if that was a wise decision. Surely there was a good chance of something being stolen.

"I confess, I half expected you to find yourself suddenly unavailable today," he said as he insisted in helping me into the carriage he had borrowed for the occasion.

"Really," I said coolly. "And why is that?"

"Your Taro seemed a little upset with you last night."

He had better not expect me to complain to him about Taro, because that was never, ever going to happen. "He can get nervous if I'm away too long and he has no idea where I am. Things have happened in the past." Though they had usually happened to Taro.

"I hope there was no unpleasantness after I left."

I studied him for a moment. If he had expressed any hope that there was unpleasantness, I would have been unimpressed with him. But his face showed only polite concern. "No, no unpleasantness." And it wasn't really a lie. Not when one took the long view. We had had a little, insignificant spat, and made up for it gloriously.

"That's good," he said, and he seemed sincere.

I wondered if he would feel the same way after I told him what I had to say.

Stepping down from the carriage, I saw a vision that put Taro right out of my mind. Under a large tree with a wide, solid trunk and leafy branches stretching out into a glorious sun-spattered umbrella, the ubiquitous picnic blanket stretched out on the ground in loose white waves. Where it sheered off from my experience was the small white table set up on the blanket, with two white cane chairs. There were two servants, one male, one female, and they either ruined or complemented the look of the scene by being dressed entirely in black; I couldn't tell which. They were moving a little before they noticed our arrival, at which point they stilled into silent attendance.

"Where did you get them?" I asked, nodding toward the servants.

"Borrowed them from my mother."

We sat at the table, the servants waving serviettes into our laps. From side bars they produced covered plates, revealing slices of cheese and skinned grapes.

"Is it really that bad?" Doran asked.

"Excuse me?"

"You look tense, like you're expecting something to be dropped on your head without notice."

I forced my shoulders down, and I knew I was blushing. I could feel it, damn it. "I'm sorry. I just wasn't expecting anything like this."

"Don't you like it?"

"It's lovely." It was conspicuous. It made sure that everyone who entered the park or passed on the road would get a good look at us. But it was definitely lovely.

The cheese was great. Strong and chewy.

"I had some difficulty choosing the menu for today," Doran commented.

"Oh?"

"I was thinking of a light spinach salad," he said.

"Oh." Not my favorite but it would have been fine.

"Followed by a light serving of sliced roast goat."

"Goat meat?" I couldn't help wrinkling my nose at that. The only time I'd ever had goat meat had been at that horrible dinner party at the Yellows estate. "Oh my gods. Are you serious?" That would have been in such bad taste.

He chuckled. "The meal we were enjoying the night we met."

"Or not enjoying, to be precise." It had been a ritualistic meal meant to prepare us to meet whatever gods the Reanists believed in. Meant to make us slow and stupid and easier to sacrifice. And Doran had thought that meal might be something appropriate to serve to me? "You can be a twisted sort of fellow, can't you?"

He grinned. "My dear, sometimes the best results can come from the worst circumstances."

"I suppose." I knew what he was implying, but I didn't want to encourage that line of thinking.

"But given how unpleasant those circumstances ultimately ended up being, I decided to spare you."

"Thank you. I appreciate it." Ugh. Could this conversation be any less witty? What was wrong with me? What was wrong with us? We were usually so much more relaxed than this.

"Dunleavy!" I heard a voice call out, and I looked to the right. The woman I saw, leading two young children by the hand, was a prostitute I'd met through Risa. Doran rose to his feet.

"Zeva." I smiled. "Good afternoon." The woman was gorgeous, curvaceous and blond, her hair tightly pinned back and coiled at the back of her head. "Who are your friends?"

The young woman smiled down at her charges, wearing a warm, gentle expression that I couldn't recall seeing on her before. "This is my daughter, Amber." The little girl dipped into a cute little curtsy. "And my son, Viker." The little boy, he was maybe four, bowed. "Say good afternoon to Shield Mallorough."

"Good afternoon, Shield Mallorough," they said in perfect unison, and it would have been a little creepy if it weren't for the fact that Viker had trouble pronouncing my name.

"And who's your friend?" Zeva asked, an eyebrow raised.

"This is Lord Doran Laidley," I said, avoiding his proper title in favor of his actual name. He could correct me if he didn't like it. "Doran, this is Zeva Smith."

Doran took her hand and bowed over it. "It is a pleasure to meet you," he said.

"It certainly could be," she smirked. Then her eyes widened in alarm and she looked at me. "Dunleavy, I'm—"

I waved away any impending apology. For some reason, the idea that Zeva might flirt with Doran didn't disturb me. He deserved more fun than I could give him.

"I'll wager everyone wishes they had husbands as understanding as yours," Zeva said impishly, quickly over her discomfort. "Allowing you romantic picnics with other handsome men."

Oh lords, spare me.

Doran narrowed his eyes at me. "Really, Lee? You've gotten married in the last couple of days?"

I wasn't sure what he meant by those words, or by the odd tone in his voice. He seemed annoyed. Did he think I had gotten married and just hadn't bothered to tell him? "You'll have to ask Zeva, I suppose. I didn't have a husband the last time I looked."

Zeva pretended to pout. "You're not wearing it."

"Not wearing what?" Doran demanded.

I sipped at the apple wine that had been poured into the goblet before me. It was nice. Sweet.

"I'm surprised you haven't heard, my lord," said Zeva. "Dozens saw it."

I looked at her more closely. Was she trying to cause trouble? She appeared to be teasing, but I didn't know her very well.

I decided to stop any further insinuation or misunderstanding. "Taro had his eye on a matched set of those harmony bobs, and the merchant made us go through a ritual that was supposed to trigger their power. It was in no way a wedding. We are not married and won't ever be married. And"—just to be thorough—"Taro was there when Doran invited me to this picnic."

Zeva cackled. "You've got him well under heel, then. Good work, Dunleavy."

Strangely enough, I didn't find the suggestion that I was somehow oppressing my Source at all flattering.

Really, this picnic wasn't turning out to be nearly as pleasant as I'd expected.

The boy tugged on Zeva's hand, and she leaned down so he could whisper into her ear. "I'm afraid we must be going," she said. "It was pleasant to meet you, Lord Laidley. Nice seeing you again, Dunleavy."

"You, too," I lied.

"She likes to stir things up, doesn't she?" Doran commented once she was out of earshot.

"Apparently." Not a trait I'd noticed in her before.

"I don't think I've once seen you wear a harmony bob."

I shrugged. "It was a whim of Taro's."

"Hm," said Doran.

All right. It was time to get the unpleasantness started. "You were right when you said things had changed between Taro and me," I confessed. "We do have a different sort of relationship now."

"Do you plan to marry him?" Doran asked.

"What? No!" Why would I do that?

"Have children with him?"

"Definitely not." It wasn't likely, within a Pair, both of us channeling. Channeling and Shielding tended to prevent conception. And even if it were possible, Zaire, what a bad combination. With our luck any children would have my looks and his mood swings.

"So it's not a permanent liaison," he said.

I knew the answer to that, but I wasn't prepared to say it out loud. To anyone.

Doran nodded, though, as if I had spoken. "I understand that Taro was almost grown before he was sent to the Source Academy."

"He was eleven." And what did that have to do with anything?

"No doubt he was taught something of the courtship rites."

As far as I knew, Taro didn't learn anything from his family except how to sit excruciatingly straight and use his cutlery. Apparently, he could barely read when he'd left his family. And at the age of eleven, that was just shocking. "The what?"

"The way we do things."

"Who's we? What things?" It suddenly felt like we were speaking in a different language. And maybe we were. The language of the aristocrats, which I had never learned.

"Nothing is settled between you. There has been no promise made, correct?"

I wasn't sure where this was going, but it didn't seem a positive place. "That's really none of your business." Aye, yes, blunt, but if he had any manners, he wouldn't be pursuing this line of questioning.

"Sometimes being open and honest can really save a lot of time," said Doran.

And when had I started appearing closed and dishonest?

It wasn't about being honest, anyway. It was just that I didn't want to talk to anyone about this thing between Taro and me. I didn't want to add to the gossip. What rule said I had to talk about it, anyway?

Was Doran entitled to know about this? Did the relationship we had before I left for Flatwell give him that right? Really, I had no idea.

"I like Taro very much," said Doran. "I mean no disrespect to him in what I am about to say. But he is not the sort to make that sort of commitment, is he?"

I was suddenly amused. Doran's aristocratic upbringing was showing. What normal person talked about commitment in reference to sexual relationships? And even if normal people did think that way, Taro and I were bonded. An expression of commitment was redundant. Where could he go?

Doran's eyebrows rose. "My dear, where did you pick up that smirk?"

Smirk? I did not smirk. Smirking was something children and obnoxious men did. I was far too mature for such an expression.

"He hasn't spoken of commitments, has he?" Doran persisted.

"Of course not." I wanted to add that I wouldn't welcome any such discussion, but I had a feeling Doran would interpret such words as evidence that I really did want a commitment, I was merely too proud to admit it.

Which was stupid. If I wanted a commitment, I would ask for one.

"I really don't care for this subject of discussion," I said coolly.

And suddenly, his posture relaxed, and he smiled. "Can't blame a man for trying."

I certainly could, even when I didn't know exactly what he had been trying.

"Lydia would like to see you," he said, mentioning a friend of his, whom I had met and liked.

She was another person I hadn't thought of since leaving for Flatwell. What was wrong with me? "How did the wedding go?"

He grinned. "It was a total disaster. Her fiancé's father forced himself into the planning and turned it into an overly elaborate nightmare." He took a sip of wine. He didn't appear about to expound.

"You can't just leave it there," I chided. "Details."

Details there were many, from people being given the wrong location for the ceremony in the invitations, to the celebrant showing up dead drunk, to no fewer than seven chairs collapsing under guests during dinner. It was clearly a day of endless calamity and Doran described it with heartless glee. I couldn't help laughing, badly though I felt for Lydia.

It felt good to laugh.

The list of problems was so long that Doran wasn't able to reach the end of it before a Runner appeared beside the table, without warning. I'd forgotten we were in a public place. I felt embarrassed for having laughed so much while being observed. Was that why the Runner was approaching us? Were we not supposed to laugh so much in public?

"My apologies, my lord, Shield," the Runner said. "Due to the illness in the riverfront spreading to other parts of the city, the deputy mayor has outlawed the use of the parks. Any unnecessary public gatherings are prohibited."

I was shocked. "I had no idea the illness was so severe."

"Well," said the Runner, "there is no reason why you would, is there?"

What was that supposed to mean? Was that an insult? "So this illness is contagious?"

"No, not at all," the Runner answered rather quickly.

"If it's not contagious, what does it matter whether people gather in public or not?"

"It is a preventative measure."

"In case it might be contagious?"

He looked impatient. "It is not contagious, ma'am. I know nothing more about it."

That sounded cagey, to me. Maybe I was always too suspicious, but this seemed odd.

"How long is this ban expected to last?" Doran asked.

"I don't have that information," the Runner said in a rather snippy tone. "Please gather your things. I have other areas to clear."

I wanted to object, or to think about it, or ask more questions. This had all come out of nowhere. But I didn't know what to say.

"I'm sorry, Lee," said Doran, which was the cue for the servants to start packing up.

"Not at all," I answered without thought. What was the nature of this illness? Where had it spread? What were the healers doing about it?

Why hadn't I learned more about it? How could I be so ignorant of what was going on in the city in which I lived?

"Well, that was disappointing," Doran commented once we were back in his carriage.

"It was very pleasant, aside from the interruptions."

"So you wouldn't mind doing it again?"

We couldn't do it again, because they were closing all of the parks, but that wasn't what he meant. "Not at all."

"We can remain friends?" he asked.

Relief seemed to loosen every muscle in my body. He understood. I smiled. "I would like that." I couldn't believe he would be willing to do that. And yet, why not? I'd always known he was an exceptional person.

"We can still see each other?"

"Of course."

"Shintaro won't mind?"

"He had better not, not after I explain things to him." Taro spent all sorts of time with all sorts of people, and although he had neatly avoided admitting it during our last argument, he

knew as well as I did that a lot of people he ran with were in
lust, if not love, with him. I'd never suggested he stop associat-
ing with his friends, and he had never offered.

It didn't seem right that he should be able to spend time
with people who admired him while I wasn't to have the same
right. At the same time, it didn't really disturb me that Taro
was meeting with his friends, while it clearly disturbed Taro, a
lot, that I met with Doran.

Did my insisting on doing something that I knew made
Taro upset make me mean-spirited?

Would pandering to his feelings, while not insisting he observe the same behavior, make me weak?

Would insisting that if I couldn't see Doran, he couldn't
keep his menagerie be just plain childish?

I would have to think about that.

But in the meantime, I got to enjoy the company of a good
and entertaining friend. There was no harm in that. Taro would
just have to accept it.

# Chapter Eleven

Taro was waiting for me when I returned to the residence. He was lingering in the parlor and jumped out as soon as I was through the front door. "What did you tell him?" he demanded.

I was annoyed to be assaulted so quickly. I looked through the correspondence deposited on the table in the foyer, surprised to find a letter from Trader Fines addressed to me. I was tempted to read it right then, an indication that I didn't appreciate his behavior, but that was just a little too rude.

"I made it clear that you and I were—" What? I hated all the descriptors that immediately leapt to mind. They were either too saccharine or too coarse. "Together."

"And?" he prodded.

"That any plans he might have had for the two of us were to be put out of his head, because they weren't going to happen."

"And?"

I just looked at him. And what? I had had nothing more to say.

"And you're not going to see him again?"

"I didn't say that." And I wouldn't say that. "I'm not going to talk about this anymore, Taro. I'm not going to be told who my friends are."

"He's not a friend, Lee! He loves you!"

I grimaced at the melodrama. "That's an exaggeration, Taro." Doran had never said so, and had given me no reason to believe that was the way he felt. And I respected him for it. He really didn't know me well enough to fall in love with me. "I told him that any kind of romantic relationship between us was over. He argued about it for a bit, and then he accepted it and asked if we could be friends. And I was happy to agree. I'm not like you, Taro. I don't have a lot of friends."

"You can't be this naive! No one wants to go from lovers to friends."

"We were never lovers," I reminded him in a sharp tone. "And are you saying you don't stay friends with the people you've had as lovers?"

"Not usually," he muttered.

"Really?" I said, my surprise evident in my voice. That was a bad sign for us.

We were still standing in the front foyer, which meant we were in the way when Stone and Firth came clattering in. "Hells, not another argument," were the first words out of Firth's mouth.

"We don't argue that much," Taro objected.

"You argue constantly," Firth snapped. "And it is much more bitter than it was before you left." She poked me in the chest. Hard. "This is one of the many reasons why partners should never sleep with each other. It was incredibly foolish for you to let things go that far."

I stared at her. Why was I, of the two of us, responsible for letting things go anywhere? And where was this censure coming from? All the Pairs had thought we were sleeping together, I was sure, from the moment they'd come to High Scape, and there hadn't been a hint of disapproval. Annoyance and a lot of eye rolling, certainly, but not actual disapproval.

And Firth was always going on about sleeping with everything on two legs in her long, adventure-filled life. She tormented Taro every time she saw him, about how delicious she found him. What had all that been about, if it didn't demonstrate a certain flexibility in her morals?

And yes, sexual relations between partners was discouraged by the official policy of the Triple S. We were lectured about it the whole time we were in school. But while it was considered an extremely bad idea, it wasn't illegal or even really immoral. I'd met a Pair who were married to each other, for Zaire's sake, so how wrong could it really be?

"Ignore her," Stone said to me. "She's just upset that Prince Albert died."

Hold on, the Empress's husband had died? When?

"Don't tell her to ignore me," Firth snapped. "What they're doing is disgusting."

Disgusting. *Disgusting?* Seriously, where the hell was this coming from?

"We've talked about this," Stone said to Firth.

"No, you lectured me about it. And where did you get the idea that you could lecture me, I wonder? You've been spending too much time with this one." Firth nodded at me with a sniff, before turning on her heel and striding away from us, ascending the stairs with an uncharacteristic heavy tread.

"She's actually disgusted by us?" I asked Stone.

Stone shrugged. "I believe so," she said. Which surprised me. I had been expecting her to discount Firth's accusations as an aberration.

"But why is she only getting upset about it now?" Unless she had always disapproved of us and had been able to hide it better before.

Stone frowned, looking puzzled. "She's disapproved of it since she realized the nature of your relationship," she said. "This is fairly new, is it not? At least, you weren't sleeping together before you went on your trip."

There were too many surprises happening in a single conversation. I had really thought the other Pairs had thought Taro and I had been sleeping together all along. They'd certainly acted as though that was what they believed.

"I'd felt like she'd been avoiding us," Taro commented. "But I'd thought it was just me."

"But she's always talked as though she enjoyed . . ." Sleeping with a lot of different people. I wasn't comfortable saying that about someone so much older than I. I wasn't sure why.

Stone rescued me. "She likes to talk," she said. "And she likes to tease. But her morals are actually very firm."

"Meaning what, exactly?" I asked. "She really thinks what we're doing is immoral?" That was a stupid question. I knew it as soon as it left my mouth. I just couldn't believe she actually thought what we were doing was wrong.

"Yes," Stone answered, with no hesitation.

"And do you think we're immoral?"

It took her a little longer to respond that time. "Not immoral, precisely," she said finally. "Just incredibly foolish. I have to say I expected better of you."

And again, I was fairly sure the use of the word "you" was meant to refer only to me, not to Taro and me collectively. And seriously, what was that about? Why was I the only one to blame?

"If you will excuse me," said Stone, moving away.

"Dee," said Taro.

Stone kept moving. "I don't care to continue this conversation."

"No, I just want to know how Prince Albert died."

Stone hesitated and turned back. "They say he died in his sleep. Apparently, he has been bedridden for close to fifteen years, and demented for most of them."

Demented? I'd heard no such rumors, and I would have, wouldn't I? If this had been going on for fifteen years? I had spent time at Erstwhile, staying right in the palace. People living in the palace, or spending their days at the court, they would have been aware of something like that, and spoken of it. Wouldn't they?

"Thank you," said Taro. Stone nodded and went upstairs, presumably following her Source.

I couldn't believe they had the gall to think there was something immoral about us. "Why am I to blame?" I muttered.

"Oh?" Taro arched an eyebrow. "So you feel what we're doing is blameworthy?"

"No, no. Bad choice of words. But why am I the only one considered responsible?"

"Because you're the only one considered able to be responsible," Taro said bitterly. "I'm just a Source, after all. Little better than a child."

"That can't be it. Firth is a Source and she holds me responsible, too."

"She wouldn't be the only Source to think that way. Sometimes we're our own worst enemies."

That didn't make sense, to think one's own kind was inferior to another. And what did that mean, in Firth's case? That Taro was incapable of making his own decisions, and that I was abusing a position of authority in the pursuit of sex?

I felt a little sick. I'd never been despised before. Not by someone who knew me. I'd never been thought of as something vile and reprehensible. It was a disquieting position to be in.

"Who is your letter from?" Taro asked in a welcome change of subject.

I had forgotten about the folded paper I held in my left hand. "Trader Fines."

"The man who guided you during the parade?" Taro's expression was flat. I had told him of my experiences at the parade, and he had read me a fine lecture about my idiocy in attending alone.

He'd been right, but it was so aggravating to be limited that way. Talk about feeling like a child. "Aye."

"What does he want?"

We moved to the parlor as I opened the letter. It was addressed only to me, though the invitation within was for both Taro and me. It spoke at length of Fines's laxity in not inviting me sooner—revealing that he hadn't been aware of my absence from High Scape, though there was no reason why he should have been—but his holdings had enjoyed a sudden expansion that had left him and his staff scrambling. He owed me no explanation. I hadn't known he existed before the day of the parade. "Trader Fines wants us to come to dinner."

"You're not going to refuse," he said, because he knew me quite well.

"Why shouldn't I? It's likely to be deadly boring."

"You said he said he knew your parents."

"Aye, as business rivals. Not friends."

"That you know of. And I wager that you haven't even written to your parents to find out."

I didn't respond to that challenge, because he was right. I hadn't even thought to do that. Why would I? "It doesn't matter what kind of relationship he has with my parents. That has nothing to do with me."

"They're your family."

"Those ties are severed once you enter the Academy." He raised his eyebrows at me to inform me that my opinion was stupid. "That's what the rules say," I insisted. While any child sent to a Triple S Academy could retain his place in his family, all obligations that would normally bind him were considered eliminated.

"I know for a fact that doesn't actually happen."

"Your case is different. No one expected your highly titled brother to die without producing an heir. And most families wouldn't have expected a Triple S member to take on the obligation of a title. No one's going to expect me to play nice with merchants because of my family." They'd better not. I didn't know the first thing about trade, and it wasn't fair for anyone to expect me to play the game.

"All right, then go to thank him for the kindness he showed you during the parade."

"Won't that be just acquiring another debt to him?"

"Not if you play it right."

"I don't play things, Taro."

He winked. "That's what you have me for."

"Fine. I'll send an acceptance." Clearly, I had no willpower at all.

And then I felt Taro's inner protections fall.

Really, I should stop expecting not to have to Shield merely because we weren't on duty. Time was, Taro would warn me when he was going to channel in unusual circumstances. It was odd for him to desert that courtesy. I'd have to talk to him about this, after he finished channeling whatever he was channeling.

It wasn't long before I knew what he was doing. It was an event from that place of cliffs and water. Or at least, it was the place that inspired those images in my mind, and filled my nose with the scent of salt, and my mouth with the impression of water. As with the first time, Taro let the forces rush through him too quickly, pushing the workings of his body and his mind too hard. The anger that behavior inspired in me made it a little bit easier to Shield him in the slightly chaotic circumstances.

And when the forces dissipated and Taro's inner protections were resumed, I glared at my idiot of a Source. "I asked you not to channel like that again," I snapped.

"No, you ordered me not to," he responded in a cool tone. "When did you develop the delusion that you can give me orders?"

When I saw him acting like an idiot. "We are both put at risk when you—"

But he turned on his heel and walked out of the room, his lack of interest in any further conversation clear. Arrogant prat.

# Chapter Twelve

I curled up on the settee in my sitting room with the bag of books and pamphlets I'd gotten from the printers. Taro and I didn't have a watch at the Stall that day, and I was finding it more and more important to learn something about this spell casting everyone was talking about. Really, where did it come from? How long would it take to go away?

I picked up a book at random and upon reading the very first page noticed with shock and discomfort that it had first been written a good seventy years before. So much for the theory that this belief in spells had been created by the effects of the Harsh Summer or the Riverfront Ravage. People had believed in magic for at least seventy years? What had happened seventy years ago, to get that belief started?

I found it amusing that the first chapter of the book was dedicated to the discipline and hard work needed to achieve results. Because wasn't casting all about trying to gain things one couldn't acquire because one lacked the discipline or the will to do the hard work? If casting required all of this effort, wouldn't it be easier just to get things the natural way?

I found it less amusing that many of the methods described

in the book for getting into the proper frame of mind to cast spells were similar to the methods taught to Shields to stay focused and calm. It was enough to make me wonder if a Shield had written the book.

Of course, that was ridiculous. Being a Shield had nothing to do with casting spells. It had nothing to do with magic of any kind.

Being a Shield, or a Source, was a talent one was born with, like being able to sing or having skills with one's hands. There was no magic. We didn't create forces that weren't already there. Even Taro's ability to heal and my ability to influence the weather—both skills that were not, as far as I knew, the usual skills associated with Sources and Shields—were still just the manipulation of forces that were already there. From what I could determine, casting spells was about creating something from nothing. Which was what made it impossible.

We had encountered people who claimed what Taro and I did was magic. It was not. I knew that. So, that there were similarities between what a spell caster did to prepare and what a Shield did to remain calm was disquieting, but not particularly significant.

I almost got drawn into a description of the history of the use and development of spells. The book I was reading claimed the tradition of using spells was brought to the world by our ancestors, when they'd relocated here from some other world several hundred years ago. That the knowledge had been lost and then rediscovered. But that was ridiculous. From all we had learned of the Landing, the ancestors had had enormous and complicated machinery at their disposal, machines that let them fly between worlds and communicate over great distances. Such people would have had no use for spells, no reason to dream up such beliefs.

Of course, the machinery hadn't worked on our world, for some reason. But that had merely caused most of the ancestors to leave this world. The failure of the machines was no motive to suddenly start believing in spells. It didn't make sense.

It was something I wanted to look into further, but later.

Right then, I wanted to read more about what kinds of spells people were going to attempt, killing cows and setting houses on fire. Actually, spells about the ashes, those were what I wanted to know about first. The bit with the ashes was what I found most disturbing.

I didn't know exactly what I was looking for, though. Was there going to be a spell mixed in with all the others that dealt with ashes? Was there a separate section dealing strictly with supplies, of which ashes would be one? I didn't know, and the book I was examining didn't have any kind of index, so I skimmed through the pages. Within the one book, there was an astounding array of subjects, or goals, for the spells. Love spells, of course, a popular subject for plays. Raising people from the dead, which I kind of expected, grief being what it was. I wasn't surprised to find spells that gave one a talent, or attempted to direct another person's will. I was shocked, however, to find spells allowing the caster to inflict an illness or death on another person, or to render them unable to have children. That was horrible. What kind of twisted mind came up with such things?

I was almost tempted to wonder if having such books criminalized wasn't such an awful thing, after all. I didn't want anyone encouraged to try such terrible things, even knowing they wouldn't work. When the spells failed, having sparked a person's imagination, said person might then move on to more reliable methods of accomplishing the same things.

As I continued to read, I was surprised by the degree of complexity some of the spells required. While some needed nothing more than facing the right direction, closing one's eyes and reciting a few words, others took months in preparation, lists of ingredients several pages long, multiple participants and several sonnets' worth of incantations.

Who had the time to make this stuff up?

What made people think any of it worked? Even though some of the rhetoric describing how spells functioned was intelligently written and appeared almost logical, it was still casting. When had a spell ever worked for anyone? Even the books didn't point to any example for whom a single spell had worked.

It was in the next book, a thicker volume with heavy gray paper, that I found what I was looking for, a lengthy chapter dedicated to the procurement and use of human ashes. And even the procurement was much more complicated than I would have expected. The ashes were to be harvested—and wasn't that a horrible word for it?—during the night of the new moon. I couldn't remember if the night we'd interrupted a harvesting had had a new moon. I never noticed such things. A copper bowl was considered best for holding the ashes, an ivory spade the best for digging them out. That particular item had to cost more than most could afford. The list of instructions for the making of the candles that circled the ash grove marker was more than three pages long.

The book confirmed that the best source of ashes was someone who had enjoyed good fortune during their life. There was no definition of good fortune. I supposed that could be a subjective determination, but I had no doubt Taro would be considered fortunate. If he were dead, I'd have to be guarding his ashes, if I were able, which I wouldn't be, because I would be dead, too.

There were a lot of uses for the ashes. Often they were an ingredient in other spells. Sometimes they were put in a vial and worn around the neck—which was just disgusting—to increase the user's general good fortune or the talent of the user when they lacked the skill to perform one of the more specific spells. There was even a recommendation to wear the ashes on a daily basis to improve health and mind. And then there was, of course, the practice of mixing the ashes into a paste and rubbing it into the skin.

Just reading about it made my stomach gurgle and created the sensation of something thick and slimy coating my mouth and throat.

A quick, loud knock on my door made me jump. The door opened and Taro stuck his head in. "Come to my suite," he ordered and he closed the door.

Sir, yes, sir. I tossed the book aside and went to Taro's suite. He gestured at me kind of frantically until I closed the door behind me.

A young man I'd never before seen was standing in Taro's sitting room, leaning against a settee. He was pale and sweaty, and his dark and ragged clothes were dirty and rank. He looked at me with more intensity than I found comfortable. "Good day," I said, hoping that would be enough to prompt someone to give me an explanation.

"Good day, Shield," he responded in a low voice that cracked unpleasantly.

"Lee, this is Lan Kafar," Taro said. "Lan, please go through there." He pointed at the door to his bedchamber. "Lie down. We'll join you in a moment." And Kafar did as directed.

We were going to join him? What the hell? "What the—"

"He's ill," said Taro. "He's from the riverfront."

"And you brought him here?" I demanded in a low voice.

"He just showed up demanding to see me. He remembers those rumors about me healing people during the Harsh Summer. He says the healers won't go to the riverfront anymore, and the hospitals turned him away."

"Because it's contagious!" No matter what that Runner had said, I was sure it was contagious. Why else would they be closing the parks? Why would the hospitals refuse to treat people? And were they really? Were they allowed to do that? I couldn't believe that. It was appalling if it was true.

"He kept saying I was a healer, over and over, and getting louder and louder. People on the street were noticing."

"So you close the door."

"Dunleavy!" he said, clearly appalled. I didn't think he had ever addressed me by my formal name before. "He's ill and he can't get treatment."

"No one's dying from this illness." And if every single member of the Triple S residence caught it, that could leave everyone in High Scape vulnerable to natural disasters. A whole lot of people would be dying then.

"That's not what he's saying."

"So he's claiming people are dying from this and you've brought him into the residence and exposed us all to it?" Seriously, what was he thinking?

"The more time we stand here talking about it, the more of a chance the illness has to spread."

Was that true? Was that how it worked? I had no idea. "You don't even know if you can do anything for him."

"And I won't know until I try."

I couldn't believe how careless and selfish he was being. Aye, it was horrible to be ill, and if it was true that the healers were refusing to help, I was appalled and felt nothing but sympathy for the man in Taro's bedchamber. But to expose us all to this illness to perform a task he had no duty to perform would bring us the ire of all the other Pairs, and so it should.

"I'm going to try," said Taro, having clearly lost patience with trying to persuade me. "You can join me if you choose." He headed to the bedchamber.

I was tempted to threaten him with a refusal to Shield him—really, this was something that required the both of us, and he shouldn't be making unilateral decisions—but I always tried to avoid making empty threats. As if I would ever refuse to Shield him, even when he was being ridiculous.

When I entered the bedchamber, Taro was instructing the man to lie out on the bed, and I winced as the man did so. All of that bedding would have to be burned. Taro sat on the edge of the bed. "I'm not a healer," he said to Kafar. "I can't be sure I can do anything."

"Neither can anyone else," the man croaked.

"I'll do my best. That's all I can promise."

The man nodded. Taro put a hand on his shoulder.

Taro had learned he could ease the pain of others while he was at the Source Academy. Since we met, I'd had reason to believe he could actually heal some people. These were not abilities I'd heard of a Source having before meeting Taro, but I was coming to suspect there were elements to Source abilities that were largely unexplored. It made me wonder what else Sources might be able to do.

Taro had always kept his additional abilities as much a secret as possible. He claimed that if the Triple S council suspected he could do odd things, they would order him back to the Source Academy for tests and he would never be seen again. He refused to say more than that. And while I couldn't believe the Triple S would do something nefarious with Sources who fell outside the mold, I also didn't believe Taro was lying. It was frustrating, though, that he wouldn't say more.

He couldn't heal everyone; we knew that much. He seemed able to ease everyone's pain, but he hadn't been able to save a woman enduring a difficult childbirth, and he couldn't mend broken bones. He could heal frostbite for some reason, which was what he was doing during the Harsh Summer. That was what created the rumors that caused his secret to grow legs and skitter away from him.

Really, I was surprised there hadn't been any repercussions before this.

Shielding while Taro attempted to heal someone was a much more gentle experience than regular channeling. The forces were weaker, and Taro used a light touch, so light it almost felt like he wasn't doing anything at all. His blood and mind worked at their usual pace, and he was in almost no danger. Sometimes I suspected I was superfluous during such occasions.

"The illness is not contagious," Taro announced.

I saw Kafar's eyes widen. I wondered if he was feeling something in this process. I'd never thought of that before. "Everyone says it's contagious," he said. "Often every person in a household is struck."

"That may be," Taro answered as he continued to channel, "and I can't explain why I know this, but this doesn't feel like a proper illness."

"What is a proper illness supposed to feel like?" I asked.

"Something other than what I'm feeling here," he retorted.

"Can you fix it?" Kafar demanded.

"I'm not finished yet."

So we let him continue. Shielding while he healed was a

little boring, but it was a nice change from what we'd been doing recently.

In time, Taro ceased channeling and I withdrew my Shields. He removed his hand from Kafar's shoulder. "I'm sorry," he said with soft sincerity. "I can't help you."

"Keep trying," the man ordered. "You barely tried."

"I'm not a healer," Taro reminded him. "I told you when I let you in that there would likely be little I could do."

"Why don't you want to help me?" It was more a complaint than a question. "You're a Source. You're supposed to want to help people."

Why, that ungrateful little plonker. He comes to our house, a stranger demanding services that we have no obligation to provide, and after an attempt to provide those services is made, he starts throwing around accusations? How dare he? "He has no training in this and he's doing this to be kind," I said, making no attempt to dull the sharpness in my tone. "He is an honorable man and a Source, and you accuse him of lying."

To my shock, the indignation seemed to drain right out of him, and his eyes lowered. "I am sorry, Source," he mumbled as he sat up on the bed. "This was my last hope."

Really? He didn't look to be in that bad a shape. He was of a decent weight and he seemed able to move easily. Of course, I wasn't a healer. I didn't know.

"You are certain this isn't contagious?" Kafar asked Taro.

"Completely."

I was very uncomfortable with Taro's claim, but no one was asking me, and it wasn't like I actually knew anything about any of this.

"My sister lives on Gray Fields Row," Kafar said, naming an area outside of the riverfront area. "She said I can move in with her for a while and help her with her shop if I can prove this thing doesn't carry. I can say you said it's not contagious?"

Sounded to me like his sister really didn't want him anywhere near her. How could anyone prove the absence of a contagion?

"Aye," said Taro. "I can't promise she won't get ill, but she won't get it from you."

"And I'll get better?"

"I can't answer that. I really don't know."

"Have you tried all of the hospitals?" I asked.

Kafar glared at me. "Now you are calling me a liar?"

For all I knew, he'd merely been told the hospitals were refusing to treat people, and he hadn't investigated it personally. Or he'd tried only one hospital. Perhaps the others weren't following the same policy. But I didn't try to defend myself. Clearly he wasn't in the mood for logic.

"We'll see you down," Taro said as a means to hint the man out of the room.

Kafar didn't object to being herded down the stairs and out the front door. I fought the urge to order the man not to tell anyone else about Taro's talent. I supposed Taro's failure would take care of that.

"How do you know this thing isn't contagious?" I asked Taro.

He shrugged. "The illness doesn't feel natural to the body."

"I would think illness is never natural."

"Aye, it is. It is unpleasant. It involves a breakdown of the natural workings of the body. But a natural illness is a natural reaction to a breakdown within the body."

"I don't understand," I confessed.

He scratched the back of his head. "To be honest, neither do I. All I can tell you is that there is something off about what that man is carrying. It's not natural, so it can't spread from person to person."

Huh. I still didn't know what that meant. However, Taro wasn't in the habit of claiming abilities or accomplishments he didn't actually have. If he said Kafar wasn't contagious, then he wasn't contagious.

But I still thought Taro should burn his bedding.

# Chapter Thirteen

Like most of the wealthy, Trader Fines lived in the North Quad on the outer edge of the city limits. He surprised me by having a house made of wood, more sensible than stone in a place where earthquakes could be prevalent. The house wasn't particularly large, either, being only two stories and squarish in frame. It was set far back from the road and was shielded from public view by trees as opposed to wall and gate.

It was kind of ugly, from the outside at least. But most buildings in High Scape were, in my opinion.

I had no interest in being there. I'd felt terrible all day, my stomach gurgling unpleasantly. Our watch at the Stall had been nothing more than a long test of endurance with my head in my arms on the table. Not sleeping, of course, just tired and queasy. There were no events, which in a way was a good thing, because it might have given me a nasty headache to try Shielding while feeling under the weather, but it was also a bad thing, because there was little to distract me from my discomfort.

I'd worried that I'd picked up something from our uninvited guest from the riverfront. Taro was certain that wasn't the problem. That didn't reassure me at all. He wouldn't know.

He wasn't able to do with me whatever he did with the people he healed, as I was his Shield. I couldn't Shield him while he tried to heal me; it just didn't work.

After our watch, I had gone to a hospital to see what was wrong. I had no difficulty getting a healer to see me, though perhaps that was because I was a Shield and didn't live in the riverfront area. She said I was suffering from too much bile and that would wear away in time if I drank enough water. It was nothing serious.

Still, the last thing I wanted to do after a long, uncomfortable watch at the Stall was eat a formal dinner with strangers. Taro had insisted that we go. It would be terribly rude, he said, after having accepted, not to show up for any reason other than a genuine calamity. I wondered what it said about me that I didn't care at all about being rude, especially to someone like Fines, who was probably too used to having people fawning all over him. But I had to admit Taro had a point.

I dressed nicely, but not too nicely, because this was a merchant's dinner, and not an aristocrat's ball. I was a little pale, but that was easily obscured with face powder and a light-colored lip ointment. I pinned up some of my hair with a wooden hair comb and let the rest hang loose, and in my ears I put small hoop earrings of yellow gold. These were both items that Taro had picked up in the market, on a whim, and their understated elegance appealed to me. My gown was of a simple cut, with long loose sleeves and a relatively modest neckline, light green in color with cream-colored piping, so that my white Shield braid had a chance of blending in with the ensemble.

Taro was dressed in his most severe style. All in black, his shirt buttoned up to the throat and down to the wrist, his hair tied tightly back at the nape of his neck. The only brightness about him was the harmony bob he wore on his chest and the small emerald stud he wore in his ear.

His choice of outfit told me he viewed the evening with extreme discomfort. He felt he was going to be out of his element, and perhaps an object of ridicule or abuse. Which just made me wonder all the more why the hell we were even going.

We took a carriage. Even were I in top form, the walk would have been a bit of a challenge, and I wanted to arrive at the home feeling as fresh as possible. We were met at the merchant's door by an older woman who curtsied before taking our wraps, which custom required we wear though the weather didn't demand. This process distracted me, at first, from the mural in the small room that acted as the foyer. The entire wall facing the entrance was painted dark green, and rising from the floor was some kind of sun, painted in silver, with its rays spreading out in stark lines and stopping only when it reached a corner of the wall.

It was quite ugly. And it gave me bad memories of eating dinner in the house of another rich man who also had atrocious taste in decorating and had served a positively vile meal, and had then tried to sacrifice us to his bloodthirsty gods. "Trader Fines doesn't believe in anything, does he?" I whispered to Taro.

"Not that I've heard of," Taro whispered back.

Not that that really meant anything. Neither of us had known Lord Yellows was a Reanist.

The servant led us around a corner to the left, through a short series of three doors and into a parlor. "Sir, Source Karish and Shield Mallorough have arrived," she announced with another curtsy.

The parlor, thankfully, was much more tastefully decorated than the foyer, not too fussy but with enough color and enough knickknacks to appeal to the eye without being overwhelming. I did, however, notice small and less vibrant replicas of the silver and green sunrise above each window. They clearly weren't meant to be as obvious as the image in the foyer, but they seemed of serious significance to Fines.

That didn't mean there was anything sinister about them. I knew that. Yet their existence made me uncomfortable, and I wondered if I really wanted to know what they represented.

"Dunleavy, Shintaro." Fines, who had been standing near the unlit fireplace, saluted us with a drink. "Delighted you could join us. What can I get you to drink?" Taro was given a glass of wine, and I took advantage of the lovely light sweet juice chilling near the liquor stand. "Please sit, and I'll introduce you to Dean Gamut, the finest actor in High Scape, maybe in the civilized world."

That actor was a middle-aged man, a head of abundant black hair with the gray dyed out of it, his skin ruddy and rough, his neck thick along with his body. I'd seen him on the stage a few times, and he was brilliant. He usually looked more handsome on the stage, but for me it was really his deep voice that took my breath away, and he was an exceptional actor, sliding from laughter to lust to rage and every subtle shade in between with dignity and grace.

"Ayana Cree, the foremost healer in High Scape. She has her own practice. She doesn't work through any of the hospitals."

That surprised me, and it must have shown when I looked at the older lady, sharply thin with beautifully styled iron gray hair and dark brown eyes that appeared strangely warm in her stern face. "It allows me more control," she said in a low voice. "My choice of treatments, medicines, suppliers and staff."

"I would think that an expensive undertaking, Healer Cree," said Taro.

"It is, but my patients are willing to pay for the superior quality of their care."

Ah. Medicine for the wealthy. I shouldn't have been surprised that such a thing existed. I wondered if she would treat people from the riverfront if they could scrape together enough money to pay the fees.

The woman was staring at me in a way I did not like. "Are you quite well, Shield Mallorough?"

The actor laughed then, and the explosive sound was too big for the room. "You don't want her as a patient, healer," he boomed out. "Her sort are notoriously bad payers." He laughed again. The laughter seemed to physically bounce off the walls.

From the look the healer was giving the actor, she found him about as hilarious as I did. "What injury have you done to your hand, Shield Mallorough?"

Oh, that. "I burned it on heated metal." Zaire, did that make me sound stupid.

"Is that dressing being changed daily?"

"Yes, Healer Cree." Ben was insistent about it.

"With a vinegar and soda salt compound?"

"I have no idea." Well, I was pretty sure there was no vinegar involved, and for that I was properly thankful. That would hurt.

"Find out."

I was tempted to salute.

Fines resumed the introductions. "This is Grace Ahmad, high master of the Construction Guild of High Scape."

High Master Ahmad was an elderly lady, her brown skin heavily lined, hands gnarled by arthritis and resting on the head of a sturdy cane. There was something solid and settled about her, and she merely nodded in return to our greeting.

"Is Morgan going to be here?" the actor demanded. "Or is he only late?"

"He promised he was coming," Fines said with a look of amusement. "You know as well as I how much that is worth." He then looked a little alarmed. "Not that he is not a man of his word," he said to me, quickly. "It is only that he gets caught up in things"—the actor snickered—"and sometimes it makes him forgetful."

There was an exchange of glances that made me curious. It led me to believe there might be something off about this Morgan. I wondered how rude it would be to ask.

"So, Dean," said Fines. "That play of yours."

The actor grimaced and groaned. "I am not, alas, in charge of the repertoire."

"Or the script," Ahmad added. Her voice was crinkly. "But surely you have some influence over the selection?"

"One would think," Gamut sniffed. "I have warned Beezly—"

"The owner of the theater," Fines clarified for the benefit of Taro and me.

"That contracts were made to be broken and I would have no difficulty leaving a house so ready to debase my talents. There are other theaters."

So perhaps I should forgo attending his play. I had been planning to go. I was likely to see any play that had Gamut in it. But now, even if the play would be something I would normally enjoy, knowing that Gamut despised it would make it impossible for me to see him in character.

"Have you ever thought to put your hand to writing yourself, Dean?" Fines asked.

"Writers," Gamut snorted. "Such temperamental creatures where they have no right to be. Always flying into hysterics if you change so much as a single precious word."

"I believe I have heard some expression," said Healer Cree, "that if it hasn't been written on the page, it cannot be acted on the stage."

"Aye, aye, I am not saying playwrights are not without their uses, but it is the players who breathe life into their words, and give shape to their characters. Players are what give a playwright's work meaning, for if scripts are not made into plays, they may as well never be written at all. It's not as though anyone reads scripts."

I did.

The same servant who had greeted us entered the room, a middle-aged man, very lean and with a shocking white mane of hair, trailing in behind her. "Morgan Williams," she announced before curtsying and vacating.

Interesting. Apparently he had no honorific of any kind. I couldn't remember ever meeting an adult with no title. It implied that he had no occupation at all.

"Morgan!" Fines greeted him. "What can I get you to drink?"

I found it interesting that Fines was serving everyone, and that there were no servants remaining in the room. I had never spent much time among people of my family's or Taro's fam-

ily's class, but what little exposure I had taught me they used
servants if they could afford it. Fines could clearly afford it.

We were introduced to Morgan Williams, and as he was introduced to us we were told, "He owns the Mercury Brothels."

"Really?" Taro asked with sincere interest. I raised an eyebrow at him and resisted the urge to ask him if he'd ever visited one of those brothels. These people were strangers and I
wasn't comfortable teasing Taro in front of them.

"You've heard of them, then?" Williams asked with a slight
emphasis on the word "heard."

"Aye. I've been told it's unusual for one person to own
more than one brothel."

"I should hope that's not all you've heard about them," Williams said a little huffily. "We also accommodate a wider variety of tastes. Except, of course, anything involving animals or
children. We don't deal in perversion," he sniffed.

I bit back a smile. There were those who believed that paying for sex was a perversion all its own.

Another servant stepped into the room and then stepped out
without saying anything.

"Supper is ready," Trader Fines announced.

We followed Fines through a corridor to the dining room,
which was considerably longer than the table it held. It appeared
to me that most of the leaves of the table had been removed to
allow our small number to sit around the table in comfortable
proximity to one another. The table was almost completely obscured by an array of dishes, most of them covered, and by each
chair there was a wine stand holding a dark bottle. "I would beg
your indulgence in the informality," Fines said as he closed the
door. "We prefer to entertain without servants always getting in
our way."

"Ears are too big," Gamut muttered, and the silence that
followed seemed oddly tense.

"So, everyone, please take a seat," Fines invited, surprising
me by seating himself at the side of the table instead of one of
the ends. "We don't follow any rules for seating. I find that a
little pompous in a private home."

Well, all right, then. I took an end seat, just to make a point. There was a small brown clay pot at my place, and one at each place of the others. Everyone except Taro and I took the lid off the pot, dipped out some of the substance, and rubbed it vigorously on their hands. "Please try it," Fines prompted with a smile. "Ayana created it, to cleanse the hands before eating, and it's relaxing."

I lifted the lid from the pot. The contents, an off-white translucent paste, had a pleasant, clean scent. It spread smoothly onto the skin with no noticeable grease. It was nice.

"Ayana," Fines said to the healer, who had sat at the head of the table. "I believe you have the main course before you, but I propose that everyone dip into whatever dish is placed in front of you and pass it to the right until everyone has had access to everything."

The next several moments were spent in silence, following Fines's suggestion. It was an odd way to have a meal served, but it had to be fashionable or otherwise common, because the other guests easily handled the platters that were small and light enough to be held with one hand, with utensils and portions easily manipulated from platter to plate.

The soup wasn't even in a tureen, but in a silver jug for pouring into the small bowls unusually placed to the upper left of the dining plates.

All of the food was piping hot, though, and delicious. Unusually delicious. I couldn't remember ever eating anything that tasted quite that good. It was really astonishing. And soothing on my stomach.

"Please try the wine," Fines prompted, though Gamut and Ahmad were already filling their goblets. I joined them. The wine was red, not my favorite, but it was lighter than most reds I'd had before, and I enjoyed it.

"This is excellent wine, Trader Fines," said Taro.

"Richard, please. And I'm pleased you enjoy the wine. It's one of my best sellers."

"The best wine on the market," Williams drawled, sounding impatient about it, like it was something he had heard too many times before. But Fines saluted him with his goblet as though it were a genuine compliment.

"And you're my most reliable customer," he said.

Williams shrugged. "My clientele like it, and they can afford it."

I was curious about his bordellos, and I had a thousand questions to ask. I'd heard of bordellos, of course—some of the best plays took place in them—but I'd never given the reality of them much thought. But then, I'd never sat down with someone who owned one. Would it be rude to ask him how he got into the business in the first place? That had to be a fascinating story.

"So tell me, Dunleavy," said the healer, who had the food on her plate in discrete little piles, no one item touching another. "Which theory do you prefer for explaining how Shields and Sources become Shields and Sources?"

Damn it, why did I always get that question? Taro was right there. Why didn't she ask him? "I feel it's just one of those things. Just like being born with any other kind of talent."

"There are those who believe talent is inherited."

"Yes," I said, because that was one I'd heard often enough.

"So that is a theory you agree with?"

What did it matter? Shields and Sources were born, and that was good, and why not leave it at that? I was no expert on the subject. What would I know about it? She was the doctor. "I don't agree with it, necessarily. I don't disagree with it, either. I really don't know." And I never really thought about it.

"Are there others in your family who have this talent?" she asked.

"A cousin on my mother's side is a Shield," I told her. "He is the only one I know of."

"Taro?"

He plastered on one of the fakest smiles I'd ever seen him use. "Just me," he said. "For I, Madam Healer, am unique and far outside the ken of the Karish ranks."

"Hm," said Gamut, perhaps in recognition of the only other person at the table who was as melodramatic as he.

"I'm serious," said the healer. "Where does this ability come from, if it is not a matter of breeding?"

"It's just happenstance," I said.

"Or luck?" Ahmad suggested.

I would have felt fine about agreeing that it was merely a matter of luck a few months earlier, before people were buying harmony bobs and killing cows with their bare hands in a futile quest for luck. Now I was afraid to use the word, afraid of the meaning listeners might take from it. "Happenstance," I repeated.

"Do you think there's any way to influence happenstance?"

Wasn't happenstance beyond the reach of any influence? Wasn't that the nature of happenstance? "I can't imagine how."

"Well, let's take that Yellows's fiasco a couple of years ago," Ahmad said. "You two were there, were you not?"

"We were so honored," Taro answered with a bitter twist to his words.

"And are the rumors true? That the dinner was just an elaborate ritual for their gods?"

"More like a big trap for aristocrats," said Taro. "With very bad wine."

"Do you believe what the Reanists believe? That killing aristocrats calms the world?"

"Of course not," Taro scoffed.

"So there were still events happening even while aristocrats were being abducted and killed?"

I was glad that I wasn't being asked that question. Because the truth was, no events threatened over the months that the Reanists were abducting and killing aristocrats. That didn't mean one had anything to do with the other, but try convincing some regulars of that.

"If the Pairs are doing their jobs properly, there never are events," Taro answered smoothly.

"And you, Dunleavy? Do you believe there might be any magical potential in killing aristocrats?"

Aside from ridding ourselves of some deadwood? "I don't believe in magic," I said. I wanted to say there was no such thing as magic, but I had the feeling that in doing so I might offend our hosts, and possibly some of their other guests. "And I've been given no reason to believe that if magic does exist, the blood of aristocrats is any different from the blood of anyone else."

Gamut was snickering.

"I find it entertaining," said Ahmad, "when a Shield claims not to believe in magic."

Claims? "I don't understand," I said, my voice nice and flat.

"What do you think you do, if not magic?"

Ah. We'd encountered this argument before. "It is a talent we are born with. From what I have learned of the magic people are currently exploring, it involves the casting of spells; it is something one studies in order to become proficient at it. We don't cast spells. There are no specific ingredients or words that we use. We just do it. It's natural to us."

"But perhaps there are many forms of magic," said Fines. "People who are born magical, and people who must study to acquire magical skills. Just think of it, we're sitting down with two magical beings."

What a ridiculous thing to say. I almost winced.

"Have you noticed," Cree asked, "that the incidents of spells that have worked have all occurred in specific locations about the city?"

"Spells have worked?" I retorted, and I knew I sounded sarcastic, but I couldn't help it. She was a healer. Wasn't she supposed to be smart?

"There has been some dispute about it," Cree admitted. "But the people performing the spells have claimed they work."

Huh. "And they all live in the same place?"

"You should read the news circulars more often."

Aye, I knew that.

"Speaking about rituals and their supernatural results," Williams interjected. "Ahmad, it took only eight months to have that crater at Center and Dove streets fixed. How was that accomplished?"

Ahmad shot him a crusty look.

The conversation moved on to other things, and after dinner we moved back to the parlor and drank more alcohol. That was where Gamut started telling stories about his early days in the theater, about humiliating costumes and missed lines and sets that collapsed midperformance. He had a brilliant knack for description and a way with accents, and he had me laughing so hard it made my back hurt.

It was a pleasant evening, but I didn't know why Taro and I had been invited. These were all tradespeople of one sort or another. And they were all older than us. What interest could they have in us?

I never liked to be the first to leave a gathering—I was always afraid the host would think I was anxious to get away—but all of a sudden my stomach started to slosh, and no one else was making any signs of moving, so Taro and I were the first to say our thanks and farewells. Fines sent out a servant to flag down a carriage for us.

"None of them had their partners there," Taro said once we were one our way.

He was right. I hadn't really noticed or thought about that. But, "I've been to a lot of parties where people didn't bring their partners." Though, granted, it wasn't the rule.

"People in positions like that always have partners, usually even marrying them. To handle things while they work, like buyers or other contacts. Except Dean, I guess, but even he would bring someone. They all would, to a social event. But they didn't even talk about having spouses or partners, or offer excuses as to why they weren't there tonight."

"Are you saying it wasn't a social gathering?" I asked. "What else could it be? Why else would they meet? They could be a group of friends who had grown up knowing each other, which would explain why partners and spouses weren't welcome."

Taro shrugged. "Maybe it was. I don't know. I'm just saying it felt strange."

I decided I didn't care. It wasn't likely that I'd ever encounter Fines or any of the others again.

# Chapter Fourteen

I was taking Cree's advice and reading news circulars. I used to read them regularly, but I had fallen out of the habit while on Flatwell. Which was unfortunate, because there were all sorts of interesting things in news circulars. Like a long editorial ranting about the transfer of so many Triple S Pairs with no replacements, accusing the Triple S council of negligence in its duty to an important city like High Scape. I wondered whether it would be appropriate to tell the writer that High Scape hadn't been threatened with a single event for weeks, if not longer. For all I knew, such information would cause that same writer to complain that the remaining Pairs were a waste of resources.

"Shield Mallorough."

The sudden voice made me jerk in my chair, and I glared at Ben, who was standing in the doorway of the parlor.

He didn't appear to notice. "You're up early."

"I slept poorly." Lately, I was always sleeping poorly. It was getting annoying. "Have you been away? I feel like I haven't seen you for a few days."

"Is that why you've taken your wrap off your hand?" he chided, carefully taking my right hand in his.

The burns were still discolored and tacky. I'd had no idea burns took so long to heal. "That seemed safer than using something harmful out of ignorance."

"It is safer to leave the wrap on. The plaster remains viable for several days. I'll use a stronger plaster today. Hopefully that will address any damage you might have done."

Hey, he was the one who left without telling me how to take care of my hand.

"You're not having coffee?" Ben asked.

"I didn't feel like making any when I got up." Which was bizarre, but so was getting up early.

"I'll put some on for you."

"Oh, no. That's not necessary. But thank you."

He nodded and left the parlor. I continued to read and came across the information that the ashes of the mayor for a day had been stolen. It was ridiculous how many ashes were going missing. People were getting obsessed.

As Ben rewrapped my hand, Taro came in for some breakfast, and then we headed out to the Stall for our watch. Almost as soon as we were on the streets, we saw the new notices pasted on flat surfaces all over the place. The paste was so fresh and smelled so strong I couldn't stand to get close enough to read the notice. "What are they about?" I asked Taro.

"New punishments for people pretending to engage in the practice of casting spells," he said.

"Really?" I didn't even know what the old punishments were. "What are they?"

"Lashes," he said with distaste.

"Excuse me?"

"A public whipping. A single lash for each book of spells owned." He shot me a look. "Five for performing any alleged spell or ritual. An additional lash if it's a love spell. An additional ten if the spell harms someone else's property. Twenty lashes for each instance of collecting, possessing, selling or consuming human ashes."

I didn't know why the idea of digging up ashes for the purposes of selling them disgusted me more than digging them up for personal use. It just did. Not as much, though, as the idea that someone would get tortured with twenty lashes just for doing it. After all, ashes were merely the remains of dead people. Dead people weren't capable of caring. Yes, the practice was disgusting and stupid, but so was torture, and torture was perpetrated against live people.

"I didn't know there were standard punishments for crimes." I'd always thought it was up to each individual judge. "Who decided these?"

"His Imperial Majesty Emperor Gifford."

"Can he do that?" He wasn't an emperor yet.

Taro shrugged. "Who's going to tell him he can't? You might think about getting rid of those books."

I stared at him. "What did you say?"

He tapped the notice with the tip of his finger. "A lash for each book. How many books would you say you have? About twenty-five?"

"No one is going to tell me what I can and cannot read."

"Would you be saying that if you weren't fairly confident that as a Shield you are excluded from the force of this decree?"

"Yes." But I would also be getting rid of the books, coward that I was. I wasn't going to be tortured for reading about something I wasn't all that interested in.

Taro seemed to stiffen, and I felt his inner shields shift. "We're not on duty yet, Taro," I said sharply.

"No one's doing anything. It's not here." The words were rushed out of his mouth, and then his shields were down. I had to put up mine and there was no point in talking any further because he was committed and there was nothing more to be done but follow along.

But damn it, I was tired. Besides, the natural events had to be allowed to happen somewhere. If nothing was allowed to happen anywhere, well, the world would just explode, wouldn't it?

Taro was just showing off, damn him.

Again, it was an event from the place of crashing waves

and jagged cliffs. What was it about this place that Taro kept feeling the events taking place there? He wasn't feeling events from anywhere else.

Then something strange happened. An unpleasant sliding sensation that hit me right in the stomach. I felt myself stumble. "Taro."

Water heaving and swirling brought a stinging to my nostrils and dizzying tension to the bridge of my nose.

And Taro was channeling too much, all at once. It frightened me. The racing of his heart was mixing in with the cacophony exploding in my ears. "Taro, slow down."

I was vaguely aware of falling against a wall. A stench assaulted my nose, which didn't help with the nausea.

And the forces rushed through Taro, much like the gushing water pressing against the backs of my eyes.

I felt a rippling in my Shields. Were they slipping?

My gods. That couldn't happen. That didn't happen. "Taro!"

Couldn't he hear me? The panic in my voice was obvious to anyone who cared to listen, I was sure. Why wouldn't he answer me?

But maybe he couldn't hear. He was letting too much rush through him, and I had no idea how aware he might be of what was going on around him. Or of me. Maybe when his blood was rushing about that hard, he couldn't really hear anything.

Yet I would have thought he would notice that there was something happening to my Shields.

The rippling became more intense. "Taro!" I shrieked. "Slow down!"

He couldn't stop once he'd started. I knew that. We were in trouble.

But the forces lessened in their volume. By slowing the channeling of the forces, Taro lessened the demands on his blood and his organs. That released some of the pressure from my Shields. Unfortunately, the more the forces lessened, the more my Shields seemed to weaken. That made no sense.

I couldn't let my Shields fall. It would kill Taro. It would kill me. But the sliding turned into spinning, and there were moments when I wasn't sure whether I was standing up or falling or lying down. I curled my arms around my stomach, because letting them hang loose made them whip around.

I couldn't believe my Shields were failing. They never failed. I'd been in far more trying situations without a doubt that my Shields would hold. What the hell was going on?

The forces smoothed out; the flow lessened and lessened again. Still, I had to push hard, my arms tight against my stomach, my knees hard against my forehead. The images faded from my mind, the screaming birds were silenced, and all I could feel was the tension in my muscles as I fought to keep my Shields up.

I managed to say out loud, "We need another Shield here!"

"No, we don't!" Taro snapped. "We're all right!"

"We're not."

"It's almost over. You can hold on."

"I can't. We need another Shield."

"No one's here. And another Shield can't Shield me. Hang on. We're almost done."

But he lied, and the channeling went on and on and on. The pain in my nose tightened and spread over my forehead and into my temples. I ground my fingernails into my arms and just held on.

It took too long. It should never take so long. Our bodies weren't made for doing this for such an extended period. Why was Taro doing this?

The forces lessened a little more, and in time, a little more, and then, finally, they disappeared. Taro's own protections drew up around his mind, and I let my Shields fall. Finally. Thank gods.

Taro knelt beside me, his face unusually serious. "What happened?"

"I couldn't keep my Shields up." And that was so hard to admit—that I'd almost failed my Source.

"You did keep them up," he reminded me.

"Only because you slowed down," I said. He didn't respond to that. "This is too dangerous. I needed you to slow down because I couldn't keep my Shields up. That's a serious problem." I had never, ever thought I would be in danger of letting my Shields drop. There were Shields who had failed in that way. It almost always meant the death of the Pair. Once a Source began channeling, it was supposed to be impossible for him or her to stop, even when the Shield's protections failed. The forces would kill the Source, and the Source's death would kill the Shield.

That was why Taro and I had to be brutally honest about what was happening.

"So what are you saying?" Taro asked. "That you can't Shield? Do you want us taken off the roster?"

"Of course not," I snapped. Nothing so drastic was needed. "You're channeling events you're not supposed to channel. Stop doing that."

"I'm not going to stop doing that," he snapped back. "I'm supposed to channel these events."

"The only events you're supposed to channel are those that are occurring within High Scape."

"I know, I know, but something feels familiar about these events. I feel I should channel them. That something terrible will happen if I don't."

Now, that was alarming. "Familiar how?" I demanded. "Like when Creol was sending events to High Scape?" Channeling those events had been painful, and I had gotten images while Shielding. But there couldn't possibly be another bitter, crazy Source out there.

"No, nothing like that."

"Then how is it familiar?" I persisted.

"I don't know! There's just something about it that I've felt before."

I resisted the urge to ask, again, what he meant. There was no point in going around and around about it. "All right, fine. But these events aren't threatening High Scape, right?"

"Correct."

"So I need you to stop channeling them."

"There might be people there," he protested.

"We don't know that there are, and I could barely hold out this time."

"It's my fault, Lee," Taro said in a soothing, yet annoying, tone. "I channeled when you weren't expecting it, in a manner you've asked me in the past not to channel. There's no need to panic."

"I am not panicking," I said through my teeth. "I am being responsible."

"Aren't you always," he mocked. He kissed my forehead. "Come on, we're going to be late."

Why wouldn't he listen to me? He was risking our lives to channel events that, for all we knew, were taking place out in the middle of nowhere. Why was he being so stubborn about this?

Because he was always stubborn, especially when it came to the use of his abilities. But it wasn't his abilities at issue. He was apparently having no difficulty channeling. I was the one having problems. He needed to listen to me when it came to how my Shielding was functioning.

How was I going to convince him of that?

# Chapter Fifteen

"I'm not going to let this go, Dunleavy," Risa said just before taking another long swallow from her roofer's black, a heavy dark beer that I thought tasted terrible. She'd brought it with her, and the windows in the room would all have to be left open for hours to get rid of the heavy yeasty odor. It was making me nauseous.

"Let what go?" I knew exactly what she was talking about. I wasn't going to help her along.

"Costume," she drawled.

I rolled my eyes.

"Dunleavy, I will nag at you and nag at you until you tell me," she warned me.

Fine. "It really wasn't that interesting, Risa. I danced the benches against spectators who paid for the privilege." It was the truth, if not the whole truth.

"And the costume?" she prodded.

All right. Something less truthful than the short-skirted, midriff-baring embarrassment in scraps that I'd been forced to wear, but strange enough that Risa would believe I'd be made uncomfortable by it. "These strange trousers that came only to my knees. And a blouse that wasn't too bad, except it was covered in all this golden glitter, and they put glitter in my hair and on my face."

"Oh," said Risa, and she sounded disappointed. "That doesn't sound too bad."

Really? I'd like to see her wearing something like that. "It was bad enough."

"And you had me thinking there was something interesting going on."

"Come now, Risa. When have you ever known me to be involved in anything interesting?"

And I knew right then that I'd overplayed my hand, because that was a stupid thing for me to say, and the look Risa gave me told me she thought the same.

"I'll just get Shintaro alone and ask him," she promised. Or threatened.

I shrugged as though I didn't care. And I didn't. While Taro was happy enough to tease me when he had an audience—and often when we didn't—he knew how much I'd hated the whole Leavy the Flame Dancer experience, and I knew he wouldn't betray me.

"You look like hell," Risa said, because she could be ridiculously blunt if she wanted to be.

"Thank you so much," I said without heat. I'd been hearing similar comments, though less blunt, so often that I couldn't get angry at every one of them. I'd be exhausted. "Did I invite you over? I really can't remember."

I sipped on the revolting tea Ben had brewed for me. It tasted foul, but it did ease the ache in my head a little, which was the point of it.

"I came over to see why you're begging off of drinks all the time. Can see for myself, now. What's wrong with you?"

"Just tired and whatnot."

She eased back on the chair. "Nothing catching, I hope?"

"No. It's too much bile or something like that."

"Are you sure that's all it is? You look really bad."

"The healer said it was nothing to worry about." And I was beyond being bored with talking about my health.

"Where do you get your water?"

Wasn't that a bizarre leap? And one I wasn't able to follow. "What?"

"The water that's used in this house. Where does it come from?"

"There's a well out back."

"Is it connected to one of the rivers?"

"Aren't they all?"

"No, though a lot of them are."

"Well, I have no idea. I've never thought about it."

"They think that's where the Riverfront Ravage is coming from. It's something in the water. That's why the illness is showing up in other parts of the city. Because their wells are fed by the rivers."

"Holy hell." That would be a nightmare. What would people do without water? "What's wrong with the water?"

"They haven't been able to figure that out yet."

"Brilliant."

"Is anyone else here ill?"

"I'm not ill," I said. "I'm just tired. And I have too much bile. I think if I had the symptoms, the healer would have at least mentioned the riverfront illness."

"You look really pale."

"I'm always pale."

"Really, you don't look well."

"Risa." Her insistence on talking about it was making me think about it, and that just made me feel worse. "Leave it alone. Please."

"All right, all right."

"Thank you."

"Anyway, I didn't come to talk about any of that. We found out who killed that mayor."

"Oh?" I didn't really care. I was upset about the fact that he'd been murdered, but I didn't really care about who'd done

it. There was no reason for Risa to think I should know anything about it.

"It was one of his servants. A woman named Sara Copper."

"I see." Still had nothing to do with me.

"She's your Ben's daughter."

That shocked the hell out of me. "Ben Veritas's daughter?"

"Aye."

"My gods. Does he know?" He hadn't said anything while
he wrapped my hand early this morning, and I hadn't seen him
since. If he did know, it would explain his absence today. Though
none of his earlier absences. He'd been gone a lot recently.

"Probably not. She was arrested just this morning."

Oh. "And you're telling me first? Why?"

"She killed him," Risa continued in a lowered voice, "so
she could sell his ashes."

"She killed him for his ashes?" I echoed dumbly. Yes, he'd
been murdered. Yes, his ashes had been stolen. I hadn't thought
both crimes had been committed by the same person.

"Aye."

"I thought they were digging the ashes out of groves."

"Maybe they're running out of likely sources in the ash
groves," said Risa. "Now that more and more people are
doing it."

"She didn't want to wait for someone to die? She murdered
him? That's insane."

"Murderers aren't known for being rational."

"I'd think that would depend on the murderer." Was it possible? Were people really getting that crazy? Because this was
a whole different issue. Digging up ashes, while disgusting
and disrespectful, didn't really hurt anyone.

But killing people. Killing people deemed to be particularly
lucky. Just so their ashes could be consumed by or sold to de-
lusional layabouts who wanted spells to fix whatever they
thought was wrong with their lives. "She said she killed him
for his ashes?" Zaire, this was Ben's daughter. Poor man.

"Zaire, no. She's not admitting anything. But she was one
of the servants who went missing from the mayor's house."

"That's hardly conclusive evidence," I objected. "There are all sorts of reasons why she would run. Fear of being blamed for his murder would be a big one." I would do the same, in her shoes.

"There is more evidence than that. I can't tell you what it is. I shouldn't really be telling you this, but I thought it was important you people knew the kind of man who's living with you and working for you," said Risa.

"What kind of man? You mean Ben?"

"Of course I mean Ben. His daughter is a murderer."

"So? That doesn't mean he's a threat to us. It's not like it's the sort of thing that runs in a family."

"You'd be amazed how much crime does run in the family, Dunleavy."

That was, I thought, a horrible and dangerous assumption to make. "How old is this woman?"

"Twenty-five or so."

"Was she raised by Ben?"

Risa shrugged.

"He lives here. He's worked for the Triple S for years. Decades, maybe." I realized, to my shame, that I didn't know for sure. "I'm pretty sure if his daughter is into this sort of thing, it's off her own bat."

"Oh, she did it all right."

"You can't know that unless she confessed."

"No, there will have to be a trial. But she did it. There's no doubt. And after she's convicted, she'll get as many lashes as the charges demand. If she survives that, she'll be hanged." I grimaced. "She's a murderer, Dunleavy. Don't waste your sympathies on her."

"It's barbaric," I insisted. "And it says something about us, all of us, that we'll inflict that kind of pain on her before killing her. And that there are those of us who'll enjoy watching it."

"Not you, of course," Risa sniffed. "You're above that sort of thing."

Well, yes. Did that make me arrogant? "It is not to my

taste." And I didn't understand how it could be to anyone else's. "So you are here to tell Ben about his daughter?"

"No, that's not my place."

It wasn't her place to tell me, either. "Who will tell him?"

"Some member of the family, I guess."

Wonderful. I knew something that was none of my business, and no one was going to tell Ben? That wasn't right. "I'm out of tea," I said, carefully rising to my feet. "Please excuse me while I get some more." I walked from the room before she could utter more than a couple of words in objection. But Ben wasn't in the kitchen, or in the hall, and I didn't want to alert Risa to the fact that I was looking for him by calling out for him.

And perhaps it wasn't kind to spring Ben on Risa and force her to tell him what she'd told me. Who was I to tell her what to do? Damn it. I filled my cup from the pot of tea brewing on the stove, wrinkling my nose at the strong smell and returning to the parlor.

"What was that about?" Risa demanded.

"I just felt a little unwell," I lied. "The tea really helps."

"Ah," said the Runner, swirling her ale in her mug. "You don't need to be delicate about such things around me."

I did when I was lying. "Wait a moment," I said as a few things clicked together in a mind that had apparently gone to sleep at some time. "You think she killed him to get his ashes?"

"That's what I said."

"And the ashes need to come from someone lucky."

"Apparently."

Damn it to hell. Why was it that every time there were weird killers about, the characteristics of the potential victims matched Taro? It was getting ridiculous.

And Taro didn't know. He was out with friends, doing who knew what. One woman had killed a man for his ashes, and had gotten caught, but if one person would try something like that, someone else was sure to try it, too. People were stupid like that.

My stomach clenched with dread and sharp panic. I had to find him and tell him. I didn't know where he was, damn it.

"What's wrong now?" Risa asked.

Damn it, why was my face so easy to read now? "Nothing," I said. "Just worried about Taro."

She rolled her eyes. "Why?"

"It's what I do." I didn't want to tell her why. She would tell me I was overreacting, which would be annoying, or she would agree I had something to worry about, which I really didn't need to hear.

I wasn't much of a hostess after that. I became increasingly worried about Taro. Because what if the mayor had been murdered because he was lucky and they wanted his ashes, but Ben's daughter wasn't the actual murderer? There might be some homicidal idiot wandering about, cocky because he or she had gotten away with murder.

And the people Taro banged around with, crowds of people. He probably didn't know them all well. He probably wouldn't notice or care if someone new joined the throng. Someone who could lure him away to somewhere more remote. He wouldn't know enough to beware of strangers.

Risa finally, finally left. I was tired and nauseous, but my growing panic gave me the fortitude necessary to leave the residence. I had to find Taro.

# Chapter Sixteen

My first step out of the residence was an unpleasant education for me. The sunlight speared into my eyes and the odor churned a stomach already too delicate. And the noise, it set my ears to ringing.

I hadn't been out since the day before, for the watch at the Stall. And I hadn't expected to need to be out that day until our late-evening watch, something I had looked forward to, getting some solid, uninterrupted sleep. I would be able to get a handle on this illness and start getting better if I could just be still and quiet for a while. That was why I had picked at Taro until he had stormed away in a huff, else he would have hung around the residence asking me if I needed anything every half hour or so.

But then Risa had arrived, refusing to be put off. So that was the end of my peaceful day.

This was also the first time I'd been out of the residence without Taro in a good long while. I'd had no idea I'd come to rely so completely on his supporting arm. After only a few steps I was unusually tired. But there was nothing to be done about it. Taro had to know someone had killed someone they'd deemed lucky, just so they could have his ashes after he'd been cremated. He needed to know he had to be on guard.

Realizing I wouldn't get far by foot, I tried to flag down a carriage. The first three carriages that approached me, all without passengers, refused to stop, the nasty buggars. My hand went to my left shoulder, and yes, the braid was still there.

The fourth carriage stopped when I raised my hand, but the driver narrowed his eyes at me. "Here, now, you've not got some plague, have you?"

"No, just a headache." Was that why the others had refused to stop? Did I really look that bad? I knew I was a little pale, and my difficulty sleeping had darkened the shadows under my eyes, and I hadn't bothered with cosmetics that morning, but I didn't think my fatigue was beaming out to strangers seeing me from a distance.

The driver studied me for a bit, chewing on something hidden in his mouth with slow, long slides of the jaw. He grunted. "Right, then. Where to?"

"The Lyre Loft," I said, naming Taro's current favorite watering hole.

I was gasping for breath after the ordeal of climbing into the carriage, and sweating unpleasantly. The shocks and swaying of the carriage were causing my nausea to bubble up, almost enough to make me disgrace myself right then. But I had to find Taro. He had no idea he was wandering around out there with someone looking to kill him.

It wasn't a long ride, and though I could have used some more time sitting down, I was relieved to exit. I almost tripped getting out, and the driver whistled and whipped the carriage off barely after I had my two feet on the street. Prat.

The Lyre Loft was one of the nicer drinking and gambling establishments in High Scape, though it avoided ascending into exclusivity. Anyone could go there, but anyone who appeared too obnoxious was encouraged, usually successfully, to leave. It was a little larger than the usual tavern, and cleaner, with furnishings of light red wood and small alcoves along the walls that allowed enough privacy for intimate conversation but not so much privacy that people were tempted to try activities less appropriate.

There weren't that many people there, it being early in the afternoon. Perhaps that was why the two fiddle players in the corner were so nerve-piercingly bad. They were practicing. No one else seemed to notice the flat notes or that the two players kept falling out of tempo with each other. I wouldn't have thought it possible for only two players to fall out of unison so regularly, as though each thought he was playing alone.

Taro was not among the patrons. Damn it.

Jek, one of the regular workers at the tavern, came in from the back room carrying a box of bottles. I headed toward him, and when he noticed me, he immediately called out, "Tasa! Vinori! Cut the music!"

The music wasn't having any kind of impact on my Shield sensibilities. Because it was so bad? Was that a possibility? It didn't make sense that only well-played music could influence my behavior, did it?

The grating wails halted, and when the fiddlers looked up and saw me, they lowered their instruments and started talking to each other. It wasn't necessary for them to stop, but the silence was blissful, so I didn't correct their misapprehension. "Thank you, Jek."

He nodded. "Are you all right, Dunleavy?"

I didn't know if he was referring to the music or the fact that I apparently looked awful. It didn't matter. "Yes, quite. Has Taro been in today?"

"Afraid not."

I sighed. Damn it. This was his favorite place. Aside from the racetrack. The chances of finding him at the track, even if he was there, were slim. And the thought of going there, with the noise and the crowds and, oh my gods, the smell, made me queasy, pressure building around my eyes as the bar in front of me seemed to slide back a few feet.

"Are you all right?" Jek asked again.

I nodded by means of lowering my head, slightly and just once, and swallowed so I could say in a low voice, "Thank you for your help." Though I wasn't sure whether he'd really done anything helpful. "If you see Taro, please let him know I'm looking for him. Please tell him it's important." And what was so important? Oh. Aye. Someone was trying to kill him.

And suddenly, Jek was standing right in front of me. How had he managed to walk right through the bar like that? It was made of wood, wasn't it? I tapped it with my knuckles just to make sure.

"You're looking really bad," Jek was saying, and then he went on to talk about carriage and home and I didn't really listen.

"Thank you," I said, and I made my way carefully to the entrance, keeping myself tall and upright, walking with dignity.

Jek said something else from behind me, but I wasn't sure he was speaking to me, and it didn't matter anyway. I needed to find Taro.

Why wouldn't the door stay still?

Without quite knowing how I'd accomplished it, I was back outside. All right, that was good. Now I just needed to get to the racetrack. If Taro wasn't at the Lyre Loft, then he must be at the racetrack.

I called for a carriage, and a sound must have come out, because suddenly there was a carriage standing there in front of me. It took two tries to get my foot on the footplate and whoever was standing directly behind me was surely Zaire-sent, for I wasn't sure I could have climbed into the carriage without his help.

It was only once I was seated in the carriage—if one could call it seated, my head down at one end of the cushion and my rear end pressed against the opposite wall of the carriage—that I realized I couldn't remember giving the driver directions. But I must have, because the carriage was moving.

A lot, damn it. I pressed a hand to my stomach, trying to prevent anything in it from escaping. I was not going to throw up in a carriage.

I wondered if there was any kind of spell to make me feel better. I'd have to look into it. Not that I actually believed in any of that stuff, but hey, it couldn't hurt to try. As long as I didn't have to eat or drink anything disgusting.

Oh, I shouldn't have thought about drinking disgusting concoctions. I groaned and curled more tightly around my stomach.

The carriage came to such a jolting halt that I landed on my knees on the floor. I experienced no surprise at this, because that was just the sort of day I was having. I tried to crawl back onto the cushion. I hadn't accomplished that by the time the door behind me had opened. Then there seemed to be hands all over me.

"Hey," I said in protest. And that was all I said. I couldn't really think of anything else to say as I was pulled out of the carriage and set unsteadily on my feet.

I stared up at the ugly gray building before me, stretching for the full length of a long block and with almost no windows. "This isn't the racetrack," I said stupidly.

"No, ma'am. If you'd please lie down here."

"I need to go to the racetrack." Why were people trying to keep me from finding Taro? I turned against the hands on my arms and shoulders to get back into the carriage. But the carriage was no longer there. "Hey!"

"Please come in, Shield Mallorough. We're going to take care of you."

"No!" I shook at the hands grabbing me, slapping at everything that connected. "I have to find Taro! They're going to kill him!"

"I'm sure Source Karish is quite all right. Just lie down here and we'll get you comfortable."

"No!" I pushed and shoved and shimmied with all my strength. Unfortunately, I didn't have much. "Let me go, gods damn it! Help!"

"Hush," a stern voice said. "You're making a spectacle of yourself." And despite my best efforts, I felt myself being lifted off my feet and laid across some surface.

And then straps were tightened over my chest, my feet and my waist, tying my arms, tying everything down.

I just started screaming. What were these people doing? Who were they?

There was the sharp incline of stairs, and then there was darkness. My screams seemed to echo. Something soft and sweet smelling covered my mouth and nose, and that really alarmed me. I tried to jerk my head to the side, but the softness just followed, and a palm on my forehead forced me to still-ness.

With the second breath, warmth spread from my face down my arms, torso and legs, forcing muscles to relax whether I wanted them to or not. With the third breath, the whirling thoughts in my brain slowed right down. Whether I took a fourth breath or not would always be a little unclear to me.

The next thing I knew was silence, and it took me a few moments to determine whether I was asleep or not. Then my stomach gurgled into almost unmanageable nausea, and I knew I was awake. I put a hand over my eyes as I fought not to throw up.

"You had me worried there," I heard Taro say, and I uncov-ered my eyes. The ceiling above me was stone, as was the wall out of the right corners of my eyes. I looked to my left, real-izing I was in the only bed of a stone cell, and that Taro was seated in a chair beside the bed, a racing circular on his knee. "I don't think they meant for you to sleep this long."

They. Hospital. The taste in my mouth was foul beyond the telling of it. I looked at the hand I'd put on my face. At least they'd untied me.

I was so tired.

"Would you like some water?"

There was a small table on the left side of the bed. On it rested the candle that was the only source of illumination in the room, a mug and a single flower—a blue lily—in a slim glass vase. Water sounded divine, so I shifted up on the bed to sit up. It was hard work.

"No, I'll get it," Taro said quickly.

I was sure he would, but I hated the idea of him propping up my head while I tried to drink lying down, so I continued to press myself upright. By the time my back was against the wall, I was shaking and sweating and dreading the effort it would take to lie back down again. Taro, having sighed loudly over my stubbornness, waited until I held out a hand for the mug.

I didn't object when he continued to hold on to the mug after I'd gripped the handle and brought it to my lips. My hand was shaking badly, and I might have dropped the mug without his assistance.

The water tasted awful, though that may have been due to the taste already in my mouth. It did feel good going down, clearing out the sticky sensation in my throat. There were a few tense moments, however, where it was in danger of coming back up.

"What happened?" Taro asked after I'd sipped down most of the mug. "You look terrible."

I would have stuck my tongue out at him if it wouldn't have taken so much energy.

What did happen? I had to think about that.

"They said you were in hysterics," Taro continued.

I was not. Not until they started grabbing me and yanking me and tying me down, and wouldn't that make anyone upset? "Where is this?" I demanded.

"Just a private room at the hospital," he said. "I had you moved from the public ward when I got here."

I wasn't entirely reassured. "Why's it made of stone?" Cells were made of stone, weren't they?

"It's quieter. They also prefer these rooms if they feel someone needs to be quarantined. But they don't seem to think you're contagious."

Of course I wasn't contagious. I was just . . . tired. Gods, I was so tired. But my mind was slowly clearing. "Someone's trying to kill you," I said, but the words seemed to come from nowhere. I remembered believing that someone was trying to kill him, but I wasn't quite sure why.

His eyebrows rose. "Again?"

All right. Try to remember. That morning, I woke up too

early, an annoying habit I'd developed recently. Spent the morning not eating the breakfast I had put together. Ben freshened the poultice on my hand. Risa had shown up and told me about Ben's daughter. Ah, there it was. "Ben's daughter was arrested for killing the mayor," I told him. And while the shock widened his eyes, I added, "Risa thinks she killed him for the ashes."

"That's kind of extreme, isn't it?"

I shrugged. "That's what she said. That the mayor was killed because he was thought to be lucky."

Taro whistled. "Poor Ben."

"So I was worried that you might be considered a good target for the same kind of attack. Because, you know . . ." I trailed off to allow him to come to the proper conclusion on his own.

He frowned. "Because what? Because I'm lucky? You think I'm lucky?"

From his tone, it appeared that he had taken some sort of offense. I hadn't expected that. "You don't?"

He stiffened. "Do you know me at all?"

I was an idiot. Having been with him for the past few years, I could understand why he wouldn't think himself a particularly fortunate person. "Look at your life from the point of view of someone who is desperate enough to use a spell to fix whatever problems they have in their lives. To them, you lead a charmed life. The son and brother of a wealthy duke, and all that means to people who don't know any better. You're a Source. You're terribly handsome."

"You always make beauty seem such a bad thing," he murmured.

"I didn't mean 'terribly' in the negative sense of the word."

"There's a positive sense?"

There was no point in turning that into an argument. "Do you admit that people who don't know you well might think you're lucky?"

He shrugged.

"I just didn't feel comfortable having you out and about

without knowing someone had been killed because they were thought lucky."

"But you couldn't wait until I got home?"

"Apparently not." Thinking back, I couldn't remember why I was so sure he had to know immediately. Even if he were a potential target, he'd been out with friends, in daylight, and he rarely spent the entire day out. Why didn't I think it could wait until he got home?

"That doesn't explain why you were hysterical."

"I wasn't hysterical," I objected. "I was upset." And why was that, again? Oh, right. "I got in the carriage expecting to go to the racetrack and ended up here. I didn't know where I was at the time." I didn't think I'd ever been to this hospital before. "People pulled me out of the carriage and were pulling me this way and that. They tied me down—"

"They tied you?"

"Aye. I was angry." But I remembered screaming, and not making much sense. How humiliating. Why had I been unable to express, calmly, rationally, why I couldn't stay? All I'd had to say was that yes, I was a little unwell, but it was nothing serious, and it was vital that I find Taro. My Source. They would have left me alone. Instead, I'd shrieked and struck out like a madwoman. What was wrong with me?

After a brisk knock, the door opened and a healer walked into the tiny room, his bald head scraping the ceiling. He had oddly sunken eyes, and while I usually enjoyed prominent cheekbones, his appeared more like squarish blocks of bone pressing right up through his pale skin. His shoulders were freakishly broad, too broad for his body, so his long arms hung down as though they were attached just to the underside of his shoulders, and not the rest of his body. His hands were huge, with prominent knuckles. His loose trousers hid the shape of his legs, but they were long in proportion to his body.

I couldn't recall ever being so disturbed by someone's appearance before. It was as though he'd been too carelessly thrown together and no one had taken the time to sand down all the edges.

"You're looking better," he said. His voice was as deep as his height would suggest, and oddly slurred, as though he'd been drinking. He'd better not have been. "Sort of."

"And you are?" Taro asked coolly.

"Healer Pearson," he answered in an absent tone as he unwrapped my right hand. "This isn't healing as it should be. Is this dressing changed daily?"

"Aye," I said.

"With what kind of compound?"

"I have no idea," I admitted.

"That seems careless." He left my hand unwrapped. "All right, now." He fixed me with a stern eye that seemed too small its socket. "Time for some honesty. Were you drunk when arrived here?" He pressed two thick fingers against my throat as he waited for my answer.

"Of course not."

"Had you taken any nonmedicinal drugs?"

"No."

"Any medicinal drugs?"

"Just this." I raised my right hand. "But I have been under the weather lately. Nausea and headache, mostly."

"That wouldn't explain your hysteria when you got here."

"I wasn't hysterical," I objected snappishly. "People were yanking me this way and that and tying me down and they wouldn't listen to me."

"Because you were incoherent. Are you sure you weren't drunk?"

Prat, calling me a liar. "Yes." I let the sibilant stretch out.

From the bag he'd carried in with him, he picked out some short strips of cream-colored cloth. One he briefly placed over my temple, another on my tongue, and a third over the burn on my palm. "You can rest here while I test these," he said, placing each strip into its own small bowl.

"How long will that take?" I asked. "We have watch tonight."

For the first time, the healer appeared surprised. "You're still on the roster?"

"Of course." Why shouldn't we be? Whatever this illness was, it didn't seem to be too serious.

I remembered then the difficulty I'd had Shielding Taro recently. Was that because of me, rather than because of the nature of the events or how he was channeling? Hell, I could be so stupid.

"How disappointingly irresponsible of you," he said. "You're off the roster now."

"You may not be aware of how few Pairs we have in High Scape right now," said Taro. "We're stretched quite thin. I don't think we can afford to lose another Pair."

"You will take yourselves off the roster, or I will take you off myself. And if I do it, it will take you much longer to get back on it."

I found this healer off-putting, and I felt inclined to do the opposite of whatever he was ordering regardless of how much sense he made. It really irked that this stranger, a regular, could have any impact on my ability to perform my duties, regardless of how right he might be. But it alarmed me that he thought an upset stomach and some headaches were serious enough to necessitate such a drastic step.

"All right," I said.

"Good decision. I'll be a couple of hours with these."

The room felt much larger once he left.

# Chapter Seventeen

Taro folded the racing circular, then he unfolded it and flattened it on his thigh. Then he folded it again, along different lines, and then he unfolded it again.

I watched him for a little while in silence. Now that the creepy healer had left, I was content to lie still and try to will my stomach into settling down. There was something almost soothing about Taro's movements, and I could watch him for a while without getting bored.

In time, though, it flittered into my sluggish mind that Taro had to be agitated if he was fiddling like that. "What's wrong?"

He looked up at me with an expression of shock. "What's wrong?" he demanded. "Are you serious?"

"Oh." I was so stupid. "Are you worried that this is something fatal?" Because if it were, he'd be dying, too, and I remembered what it was like to be in that position. Walking around, feeling fine, no way of knowing whether I'd suddenly die from one breath to the next. It nearly made me crazy.

"Aren't you?"

"I don't think it's anything that serious." Maybe it was

ridiculous to be of that opinion, but I couldn't help believing
that if I were dying, I would know it, or at least be worrying
about it somewhere in the back of my mind. But I wasn't. I'd
never heard of anyone dying just because they were tired all
the time.

"Jek saw you at the Loft. He said you were a complete
wreck."

"I was not." My manners had been perfectly correct. And
Jek could mind his own damned business.

"Tell me the truth!" he practically shouted.

I blinked in shock. What had just happened? "Excuse me?"

"You've been trying to hide how ill you've been," he
accused me.

"I have not. I'm not going to complain every time I get a
headache. You'd find that pretty tiresome after a while."

"You collapsed today!"

"I did not." I took a deep breath and continued in my most
soothing tone. "For some reason, today I felt particularly bad.
But this has been the first time I've felt light-headed. And I'm
here now, and they'll—"

"It should have never gotten this far. You should have told
me what was going on immediately. Why are you always hiding things from me?"

"I'm not hiding things from you," I said in my most soothing tone. "Please calm down."

"Stop pretending you're the rational one!" he shouted.

I stared at him. What was going on with him?

"Why are you doing this?" he demanded.

"Doing what?" Getting ill? Totally wasn't deliberate.

"Playing these games."

"What games?" Why did he have to pick this moment to go
crazy?

Oh, and there went the hands, right into the hair. "What
games?" he bellowed. "You're making time with Laidley. And
you don't want to go about town with me, and you won't let
me go out with you."

Why in the world was he dragging all this up again?

I wasn't making time with Doran. I hadn't seen him since our picnic, which Taro knew all about. "I haven't been with Doran that you haven't known about it." And I resented having to tell him that. "What is wrong with you?"

"On Flatwell and the whole trip back here you were all over me."

I wouldn't have described myself that way.

"And then we're back in High Scape, and suddenly it's a whole new set of rules. And you're the only one who gets to decide what the rules are."

Rules? There were no rules. Certainly none that I had made up.

"Are you embarrassed by me?"

There was a long, stunned silence after that question. I felt like I was scrambling to come up with a response. "No, of course not." He didn't really think that I could possibly find him embarrassing, did he?

"Then what? What is it?"

I sighed. "There is no 'it.'" But that wasn't true. Zaire, I didn't want this conversation now. Or ever, really, but especially not right now. I was too tired and my head was still cloudy. Yet I couldn't deny that my behavior had changed, and I couldn't let Taro continue to think there was something wrong with him. That just wasn't fair. "I believe that now we are back . . . home . . . you will no longer wish me to have the role I had during our travels." There. It was out. Something I'd hoped I'd never have to say. It was humiliating to say. That should be enough.

But, of course, it was not. "Role?" he said, and from his tone, I had somehow made things worse. "Role? That was all just some act?"

"No!" All right. I was going to have to tell him the whole thing, flat out, and it would end things. I wasn't ready for this. "You're used to variety, Taro."

"What the hell do you know what I'm used to?" he demanded. "You've never bothered to find out."

What could he mean by that? I'd been living with him for three years. What further investigation was required? "There's nothing wrong with enjoying multiple partners," I said, and I meant it. It wasn't for me, but I could understand why it would be appealing for others. "As long as everyone knows the circumstances and they are willing. But I'm not willing to be part of a crowd. It's just not who I am."

He twisted the racing circular into a crumpled stick and tossed it aside, resuming his preferred manner of expressing anger and frustration: pacing. The room really didn't have the space for it, allowing him only three strides each way. He looked a little silly, really, constantly stepping and turning. "I'm to tell you everything while you tell me nothing, is that it?"

"I'm not asking you to tell me anything." To be honest, I'd rather not hear him be brutally honest. I wouldn't be able to keep my expression serene in the face of his true opinion, I was sure.

"So you can so nobly claim," he scoffed, "but then you can make all these ridiculous assumptions, and you can be all smug about how reasonable you are."

"Why are you yelling at me?" I asked plaintively.

"It's the only way I can ever get you to listen to me."

"That's not true," I muttered.

"I've not slept with anyone since I met you."

I was sure my shock was written clearly all over my face. Shock that he had just said that, so bluntly. Shock that he could have endured such abstinence, and for no reason.

He swore suddenly. "No, that's not exactly true," he amended.

Hah. I knew it. Though if he'd slept with someone else since we'd started sleeping together, I'd have to kill him.

Or just curl up and die myself.

"A couple of times, in our first few months in High Scape," he admitted through clenched teeth. Then he kicked the door.

I wondered if he'd hurt himself. "There's nothing wrong with that." But, only two? I couldn't believe it. Not that I thought he was lying. Perhaps, as at first he hadn't remembered those first two incidents, he wasn't remembering others. Though I really couldn't imagine being unable to remember everyone I'd slept with.

I had no intention of interrogating him about it. It was none of my business. And I really didn't need to hear a list of his conquests.

"I know there's nothing wrong with that!" he snapped. "Listen to me! Not dozens! Not hundreds!"

Not even I had been thinking in terms of hundreds.

"Two!"

"I understand," I said.

"And that doesn't change the way you think at all?" he pressed.

Oh. That was what he wanted.

Well, to be honest, even if he were forgetting some encounters, that was a lot fewer than I ever would have guessed. "How about before we bonded?"

"You really think you have any right to ask about what I did before we bonded?"

"No, not really. I guess I'm just trying to understand."

"What's to understand? I just told you!"

Gods, he was confusing. "Are you trying to tell me that you did not enjoy a variety of lovers before we met?"

He opened his mouth several times to give me an answer that he clearly changed his mind about, because he finally pressed his lips together without saying anything.

"Are you trying to claim that somehow meeting me changed all that?"

"No!" was his immediate answer, much to my private disappointment. "Damn it, Lee, that was three years ago!"

"What does that have to do with anything?" Three years wasn't that long a time, once one was an adult.

"When people are bonded, it is time to put aside childish things," he said.

"I don't know that many would call sex a childish pursuit."

"Will you stop with the word games!" he roared.

"I'm not playing games," I insisted. "I'm just saying that no one expects you to change your personality once you bond."

Unexpectedly, he laughed. It wasn't a happy sound.

Just as unexpectedly, the door swung open. It was not Healer Pearson but a young woman wearing the colors of the cleaning staff, poking her head and shoulders just beyond the door without actually stepping into the room. "Will you be quiet?" she hissed at Taro.

He sniffed. "I was assured we could not be heard beyond the walls of this room," he said with a pronounced roll to his *r*'s.

"Not when you make such efforts to shout at the top of your voice." Without waiting for any further response, she was back out of the room, closing the door behind her with a soft, but firm, rebuking snick.

Taro scooped the circular up from the floor and sat back on the chair, untwisting the paper and flattening it on his thigh. He stared down at it as though he hadn't already read the whole thing while waiting for me to wake up. So I guessed the argument was over, without having really accomplished anything. But that was the usual nature of arguments, wasn't it?

Two people? That couldn't really be possible, could it? And why would he restrict himself that way? He'd made it clear that it had nothing to do with me, and I believed him. There had been no reason to change his habits so completely from before we'd bonded to after we'd bonded. Unless he was claiming that he'd barely slept with anyone before we'd bonded, a question he'd avoided.

So perhaps he didn't require the kind of variety I'd suspected. At least, not all the time. Then again, it had been a chaotic three years. Maybe things just needed to settle down into a regular schedule for more than a week or so in order for him to resume his former activities.

I didn't know what to think and my head still hurt. I had a

feeling things would get worse if I continued to talk, so I let myself fall asleep instead. I woke when Healer Pearson came back in, jerking into consciousness at the sound of his abrupt knock. "Well, it's nothing contagious," he announced.

We knew that. "But what is it?" I asked.

"Niyacin powder. It's a common means of fighting infection, but there are those who have a strong reaction to it. Reactions can be anything from light nausea to death."

There had been too many bizarre surprises that day. "Death?"

"Aye."

"But I wouldn't have died."

"I wouldn't say that. It looks like the effects have been building up over time. It's possible that you would have died if this had continued."

My gods. This was unbelievable.

And he was so cavalier about it. The tone he'd used was appropriate for announcing it was raining. What was it about healers that they could be so cold? "I see."

It didn't seem possible. A few headaches, some fatigue, nausea now and then. How could such innocuous symptoms add up to possible death? It was just too melodramatic. "Are you sure?"

He stiffened. "I would thank you not to question my competence."

I was not going to apologize for asking legitimate questions. "I'm not doing that."

"Would you like to hear the treatment or is there a traveling man you'd like to consult?"

"I'd like to hear your treatment for comparison purposes," I snapped back.

He glared at me. "Drink as much mint and anise tea as you can," he said. "For the next two weeks, the only reason you should be without a cup of tea in your hand is because you're asleep."

"And what will that do?"

The question seemed to irritate him. "It will flush the adulteration out."

"Really." It sounded a little fantastic to me. I was on my way to dying, and tea was going to fix it?

"My, Shield Mallorough, I wasn't aware you were a healer as well as everything else you do," he commented with crude sarcasm. "How do you find the time?"

I didn't bother to hide the rolling of my eyes, as he was being a prat and I didn't have to worry about managing his feelings. I was sick. I could get away with it.

"You need to eat as much beef as you can, as rare as you can tolerate, to build up the healthy elements in your blood. And I want you to bathe in hot water at least twice a day, to clear away the toxins as they rise from your skin."

The path to recovery sounded exhausting.

"And while there appears to be no infection about your hand, you're to have your bandage changed at least three times a day to make sure it stays completely clean. I don't want it complicating matters. Make sure there is salt and mercury in the poultice."

Salt and mercury. That wasn't what Healer Cree had said. But then, she hadn't actually examined my hand.

"You're to have lots of sleep and no excitement. And don't expect to be back to normal anytime soon. Something like this can take months to clean out of the body."

"Months!" I said, shocked. I was going to feel like this for months longer? I would go mad. "What about bench dancing? Can I do that?"

"Do you feel like bench dancing?"

"No." The very idea of it just made me want to curl up and sleep.

"There's your answer."

"But wouldn't it be good for me? To sweat out the illness or something?"

He snorted derisively. "How positively barbaric."

All right, then.

"Take her home," Pearson said to Taro. "And be quick about it. We need this room."

He left then. Really, he should assume a more sedate pace. Watching him move about could make a person dizzy.

# Chapter Eighteen

We took a carriage home, and Taro was all for bundling me up to bed, but there were a few things I felt I had to do before shutting myself away for the day.

Ben was back from his errands, cooking soup in the kitchen. I watched him from the doorway for a moment. He was so involved in what he was doing, chopping vegetables with fluid precision. He had no idea what was coming.

I cleared my throat. "Ben."

He looked up at me. "Shield," he said. Then he seemed to take a closer look at me. "You don't look well, Shield Mallorough."

"That's one of the things I have to talk to you about."

He put down his knife. "Is there something wrong?"

"Can you leave this for a while? I'd like you to come up to my room for a bit."

"Of course." He covered the pot and followed me up to my sitting room.

Once we were settled, I asked, "Have you been using niyacin powder in the poultices for my hand?"

He blinked in surprise. "Yes, of course. It's a common medicine to prevent infection."

"Well, it turns out I have a negative reaction to it. I turns out it could kill me." I hated saying that. It sounded so ridiculous. And it sounded like I was accusing him of something. I wasn't. I didn't blame him.

"My lords, I had no idea." He leaned back from his proper position at the edge of the settee. "I will, of course, stop using it immediately."

"Thank you. I'm looking forward to feeling better soon." And quickly getting back on the roster.

"Please accept my apologies, Shield. I had no idea—"

I raised a hand to stop him. "The healer said the powder is often used. You had no way to know I'd react that badly to it."

"That's very gracious of you."

"No, no, not at all." No stalling now. It was time to get it over with. "I'm afraid I have some bad news for you."

"I see," he said calmly.

An odd reaction to a warning of bad news, I thought. Was it possible he already knew? It was his daughter, after all. "I have been told that Sara has been arrested for the murder of Yuri Izen."

His eyes widened, and then he stood abruptly, turning his back on me.

The silence stretched, and I had to resist the stupid urge to ask him if he understood. Of course he understood. He wasn't an idiot.

So instead I said, "I am very sorry."

He turned back around. It was hard to read his expression. He seemed annoyed more than anything else. "I have to admit I was worried she might have had something to do with it."

"You what?" I squeaked.

"She was a servant of his. She left his house immediately after his death was discovered. And while we didn't see each other often, I was always able to find her when I wanted to. I haven't been able to contact her since she left the mayor's home. I'd hoped it was only a coincidence."

"I see." He hadn't told me that. Had he told anyone? Was it realistic to think he should? She was family, and he would have had no way to confirm whether she had anything to do with Izen's death if he hadn't been able to speak with her. For all he knew, she really had nothing to do with the mayor's death but had feared suspicion and had run in an ill-advised attempt to avoid it.

Except they thought she'd stolen his ashes, too. There had to be a reason for that belief. "To your knowledge, did she believe that using the ashes of lucky people would bring her good fortune?"

He appeared even more surprised than when I'd told him his daughter had been arrested. That was odd.

"You know of such things?" he asked in a voice lowered nearly to a whisper.

"Of course. Everyone knows." Didn't they?

"People of your," Ben stammered, "of your stature shouldn't be bothered with such things."

"What things?" I asked, deciding that to question him on what he meant about my stature would take us off on a tangent.

"Foolish things," he muttered.

"You feel believing in casting is foolish?" Thank Zaire. I thought absolutely everyone in the city was going mad.

He wiped his mouth and avoided answering that question. "Has she confessed?"

"I've been told she hasn't." I found it curious that he immediately assumed she was guilty. And was prepared to admit that to me.

"So there will be a trial?"

"There damn well better be." With a possibility of a finding of not guilty. To hear Risa speak of a trial followed by a sentence, as though the trial were nothing more than a show for the sake of procedure, had chilled me.

"Good." He nodded, and he kept nodding. "Good. Good. Thank you for your time, Shield Mallorough."

I didn't try to keep the poor man with me. I doubted he

would want to discuss such a personal tragedy with me any more than he had already. And there was nothing I could say to comfort him. Soothing lies never did anyone any good, and it wasn't as though I actually knew anything about how a trial or anything else in this matter would work.

I had another distasteful task to perform. One I wasn't sure I should be performing. Risa had told me about Ben's daughter because she felt we, the people who lived with him, had a right to know. I didn't know if I agreed with that. This information fell purely in the category of Ben's personal business.

On the other hand, this did involve murder. Perhaps something this serious transcended personal business. And Ben might need more time to himself, might want to spend more time with his daughter. If everyone knew why, they would be more understanding. I hoped.

If there was anyone who was the arbiter of correct behavior, at least in his own mind, it was Chris LaMonte. He was the oldest of all the Sources and Shields in High Scape, and he thought that gave him some sort of authority. There was no real hierarchy among Pairs, and if there were, Taro and I would be considered the senior Pair in High Scape because we had been there the longest.

I wanted someone else's opinion on what I should do with the information I had, and it seemed to me that LaMonte would be the best person to ask. He thought a lot about what kind of conduct was appropriate in what kind of circumstances.

I went to his suite, considering it the first logical place to look for him. He surprised me by opening the door. That was unexpectedly easy.

"Dunleavy," he said in greeting. Then he squinted at me. "You look like the moon."

I was pretty sure that was a Source way of saying I looked terrible. "Thanks. Can I talk to you?"

His eyebrows flew up in surprise. I didn't blame him. I never really wanted to talk to LaMonte. He was so arrogant.

"Please come in," he said, standing aside and letting me into a sitting room that was surprisingly dark. Dark brown walls, black furniture, deep red carpeting. Very depressing. "Please have a seat."

"Thank you." Once we were seated, I went straight to the point. "I learned today that Ben's daughter has been arrested for the murder of the new mayor. They think she stole his ashes, as well."

LaMonte was clearly shocked. "Who told you that?"

"Risa. The Runner."

"She shouldn't be telling you things like that."

I kind of agreed with him, but when he said so in that chiding, pompous tone, it made me want to find a good reason to disagree. "She felt we had a right to know because we live with him."

"That may have been so had Ben been the one suspected of murder, but his daughter has nothing to do with us. His family business is his own."

"So you don't feel we should tell the others?"

"Certainly not. I am ashamed of you for telling me."

All right, all right, I got the point. I was completely in the wrong.

"I hope I can rely on you not to treat Ben any differently because of this."

"Of course not." It was nice to know he thought so highly of me.

"Then we need say no more on the subject."

Fine with me. Gods, he was so annoying. I was so glad I'd asked. Damned waste of time. And it was past time I was in bed.

# Chapter Nineteen

Abrupt though his manner had been, Healer Pearson appeared to know what he was talking about, as after a day or so I began to feel a great deal better. I hadn't realized how tired I had felt, how constant the nausea had gotten, how much my head had hurt.

I didn't suggest we return to the roster. I wanted to, now that I was feeling a little better, but I didn't want Pearson to feel forced to take us off. If he did, he would then send a report to the Triple S council to inform them why the removal was necessary. While the removal was quick, I had no doubt that resuming our duties would be a much longer process, because we would have to convince Pearson I was well again, wait for him to write another report and send it to the council, then wait for the council to actually read it, make a decision and send word back that we could work. That could take ages.

I sipped on a cup of tea the healer had recommended. I had to give him this, he recommended good tea. It smelled nice and was soothing on the stomach.

"You have a letter from Morgan Williams," Taro called from the foyer.

I was in the kitchen. It was so childish to shout from the kitchen to the foyer. I did it anyway. "Who's Williams?"

"The chap who owns the bordellos."

Oh, that was right.

Firth, who had been silently buttering some toast as a prelude to escaping my presence, raised her eyebrows at me in an expression of disapproval. "You are keeping company with the owner of a bordello now, are you?"

My first impulse was to exult over the quality of his services. Since that would be a lie in which I could be too easily caught, I said, "I am."

Taro entered the kitchen at this time, handing me the correspondence.

"Do you really think that's appropriate?" Firth demanded.

"Why wouldn't it be?" Taro asked.

"He lives off the profits of people selling their bodies for money!"

"It's perfectly legal."

"Unfortunately, a great many immoral acts are perfectly legal. That does not mean those acts should be condoned or executed."

This was not a discussion worth having. I opened the envelope and found within it an invitation to dinner. This created a sort of conflict within me. The dinner at Fines's home had been interesting enough, but I'd felt very out of place there. However, it would clearly irritate Firth if Taro and I accepted the invitation, and given how much Firth was aggravating me, I thought it was time to return the favor. I handed the letter to Taro. "I'd like to go."

He read it quickly and smirked. "Should be interesting."

Firth huffed. "If you aren't going to have any respect for yourselves, you might show some consideration for the rest of us. What you two do reflects badly on all of us."

"What the two of us do also reflects very well on all of you," Taro retorted, and I thought it timely that Firth be reminded of all the exceptional things Taro had done.

Firth clearly disagreed. "Arrogance does not become you."

"On the contrary, it's one of my most endearing qualities. Ask anyone."

"Dunleavy," Firth said to me, attempting to cut Taro out of the conversation, going so far as to put her back to him. Which was really odd, as he was standing right there. "You have never been foolish. You know this is an inappropriate course of action. Why are you pursuing this?"

Really, I had to frown at her, she was overreacting so very much. "It's dinner," I said. "I was introduced to this man by respectable people and found him amiable. I'm not going to let people who have never met him shape my opinion of him."

Firth stared at me. "What happened to you while you were away? You were so decent before you left."

"And you weren't nearly so judgmental." I'd really liked her before we'd left. She'd made me laugh. She'd been able to make Taro blush. Anyone who could do that was someone to admire. This new—or old but previously unrevealed—side to her nature was really disappointing.

"I'm only saying what all the others are thinking."

Was she? That was even more disappointing. It still wasn't going to change my mind. "I'll send an acceptance when we get back," I told Taro, for Firth's benefit.

Firth left. Success.

Taro took the mug from my hand, sniffed at its contents and gave it back.

Then I smelled the mug. The tea smelled normal.

"Aside from annoying Firth," he said "which is a motive I can commend given her behavior, you don't really want to accept Williams's invitation, do you?"

"There's no reason not to."

"Really," he said with flat skepticism.

"What are you trying to say?"

"Just that you aren't the sort to approve of someone like Williams."

I found that insulting. "And you're the sort who would approve?"

"I'm not saying I approve, just that I don't disapprove."

"But you feel I do disapprove." Because I, apparently, was judgmental and rigid and would therefore look down on people because of issues that were none of my business.

"I'm just saying I thought you'd be uncomfortable with the idea."

"All out of nowhere, without my having said anything about anything to make you think that way."

"I'm not trying to start an argument."

"Is there some reason why you don't want me to accept this invitation?"

He held up his hands in a mocking gesture of surrender. "Far be it from me to have reasons." He backed out of the kitchen.

I wasn't sure what that meant, but it was probably insulting to someone.

Really, I didn't know what was wrong with him lately. He was so touchy. He was almost never in a good mood. I hated to even think this, it was so shallow, but he hadn't been much fun lately.

"Not one more step!" I heard LaMonte roar, and I ran from the kitchen to the front door, from where I'd heard the shout. LaMonte shouting was such an unanticipated event that I envisioned something catastrophic occurring.

At first, all I saw was LaMonte glaring at a strange woman standing in the threshold of the residence. Then I saw the crowd of strangers behind her. I thought of the time a furious, frustrated crowd had nearly torn down the residence during the Harsh Summer. Then, they had felt the Pairs weren't doing enough to calm the violent, unseasonable weather. What had them so enraged this time?

"Kafar told us," the woman claimed with the air of someone who was repeating herself. She was wearing a dark dress that hung close to her arms and legs, and a dark leather apron. I could smell her from where I stood. Not necessarily a bad smell, just kind of astringent. "Why won't you heal us?"

Oh, hell. That was right. Kafar. The man Taro had completely failed to heal, because Taro couldn't do that sort of thing. I should have expected that to come back on us in some way.

"Sources are not healers, you ridiculous woman," LaMonte said, and I had a feeling he was repeating himself, too. He held his head high so it was easier to peer down his nose at the interloper, who was about his height. "Clear off before the Runners come and arrest you."

"You have to heal us! It's your duty!"

"It's our duty to protect the city. That is all."

That was, I thought, a rather warped way to interpret our obligations. What was the point of preserving a city if one didn't preserve the people who lived there? Not that we could do anything for individuals.

It was quite a crowd, several dozens of men, women and even children, all wearing dark, practical clothing. They covered the driveway and were obstructing traffic on the street. This couldn't end well. I stood beside LaMonte. "Source Karish wasn't able to help Kafar," I told the woman.

"Hush, Dunleavy," LaMonte hissed. "I'm handling this."

Don't hush me. "Source Karish can't help you."

The woman squinted at me. She was pale and sweating, and the lines about her eyes made me wonder if she had a headache. "You his Shield?"

"Aye."

"Fetch him."

Really, how dare she give me orders?

But I could see that all the people behind her were as pale and shiny as she, and at least a handful of them looked an alarming shade of green. One man was holding a young boy, about five years old, I guessed, in his arms. The child was exhausted, his head lying against the man's shoulder, too tired to fuss about his discomfort. The sight of him made me ashamed of my impatience.

It did not, unfortunately, change reality. "I am truly sorry, but Source Karish wasn't able to do anything for Kafar."

"Kafar is healed," she announced. "He told us. He sent us here."

There had to be a saying somewhere about how being kind could swing back to punch you in the face.

"He was reckless to make such a claim," LaMonte interjected. "You have no right to be here. Leave."

Not the best way to get the goal accomplished, I thought.

And as if in confirmation of that opinion, the woman looked back at her supporters, and almost as one they all took a step forward. I could almost feel the air they pushed before them. Their rigid determination sent a shiver down my spine. "All right!" I said quickly. "I'll find Source Karish. Please stay calm."

"What are you doing?" LaMonte demanded in a sharp whisper.

"Preventing a riot," I whispered back.

I found Taro in his suite, reading a letter. It appeared to be a good letter. He was smiling and his eyes were sparkling. I wished I didn't have to be the one to drive that expression off his face. "We've got a problem."

"I love my cousin," he declared with a grin. "She's driving Her Grace insane."

I was in full support of anything that tormented Taro's mother, and I wanted to hear all about it, but it would have to be later. "I'm serious. Kafar told a whole bunch of people you healed him, and they're all here." I was surprised he hadn't heard the noise in the street, even if his suite was on the other side of the building.

He folded up the letter. "I didn't heal him. I told him that."

"Apparently he's better and he's telling people you're responsible. That crowd expects you to treat them. And there was a point when I thought they were going to push their way in whether we liked it or not."

"We?"

"LaMonte and I."

"Chris. Oh, that's just lovely." He sighed as he rubbed his face. "What should we do?"

"We?" I squeaked. "I have no idea."

"Of course you do."

"I really, really don't." All the options were bad. I didn't know if we could get them to leave if we refused to try to help them, and they might turn into a mob. We could wait until Runners could be fetched to send them away, but the crowd would only return and we'd find ourselves in the same spot. Or Taro could pretend to try to heal them, and if they, like Kafar, thought they had actually been healed, we could find ourselves with a new, even bigger crowd. There was just no winning.

Taro swore and jumped up. I followed him downstairs, where Firth and Beatrice had joined LaMonte at the front door. Lovely. All my favorite people, all in the same place.

"Explain this, Dunleavy," Firth ordered.

I contemplated the various hand gestures that might be appropriate in the circumstances. "LaMonte knows."

"No, LaMonte doesn't know," the man in question stated. "LaMonte hasn't been graced with adequate explanations himself."

Taro ignored all of us. He could be good at that. "Who's in charge here?"

It was almost entertaining the way the crowd eased back from the woman who'd been doing all the talking. She didn't seem surprised by their actions. "Kafar said you healed him," she said.

"He's mistaken."

"He's better."

"That's wonderful, but it's not because of anything I did. However," he added quickly, for she had opened her mouth to object. "I will do what I did with him. I will do my best for you, and for everyone here, on the condition that not one of you mentions this to anyone else."

"Pure idiocy," LaMonte muttered.

I kind of agreed with him. I hated it when that happened.

"Do you accept those conditions?" Taro asked.

"Aye," the woman answered.

"And the others?"

"They'll hold to it. I'll make sure."

He suddenly seemed to gain in height as he said, "You'd better. You'll be held responsible if they don't."

I was impressed by his delivery. He sounded sure, serious and authoritative. One would almost assume he had the means to punish people who failed to do as he wished.

"Get everyone lined up in an orderly fashion. For gods' sake, get them out of the street. Send them in one at a time."

"So you can do what, exactly?" LaMonte demanded.

"Demonstrate that I'm unable to heal them."

"One at a time?" Firth felt compelled to toss in a coin, too. "That'll take all day."

At least.

"It will cause great disruption for all of us," Firth complained. "Can you never think of anyone other than yourselves?"

I thought the fact that Taro wasn't telling everyone to clear off demonstrated great thought for others.

"I take it, then, Claire, that you won't be assisting in serving refreshments while they wait?" Taro asked.

Firth glared at him and stomped off. Beatrice wandered off after her. I had the feeling he really didn't care one way or the other.

"You can't use our residence for this purpose," said LaMonte. "I forbid it."

Taro laughed.

I wondered whether LaMonte's deep red flush was due to anger or to humiliation.

"I really don't think we have the option of saying no, LaMonte." For what I believed was the first time in our acquaintance, I was trying to soothe LaMonte. The world had to be ending. "They don't look like they're prepared to leave quietly. It could have gotten messy."

LaMonte snorted, but he didn't actually dispute my common sense. He wasn't prepared to help, though, either, and I was disappointed when he walked off. It would have been nice to have some assistance in dealing with all these people.

"Who first?" Taro asked the woman.

And thus began what turned into a very long, hard day. Taro took them to the private dining room, as we hoped that would be less disturbing to the other Pairs than to have dozens and

dozens of strangers traipsing up and down the stairs all day.
Not that everyone in the house didn't find a reason and a
chance to complain anyway.

Every person was asked to sit in a chair. Taro put a palm on
his or her shoulder. He didn't spend nearly as long with any of
them as he had spent with Kafar, but he did make an honest
effort at channeling. After, of course, explaining that he couldn't
heal them, and he was merely humoring them.

No one seemed to believe him, which I found odd. They
were trusting him to heal them, yet they thought he was a liar.

As a whole, they were a quiet, timid group. Even the bold
spokeswoman seemed to lower her voice and her eyes once she
was in the residence, moving from place to place only as instructed and asking no further questions. The one exception was
a pretty young man who flirted with Taro with disturbing skill.
He was also clearly terrified. I would have thought less of Taro
had he not flirted back, a manner of making him feel better.

It was difficult working with these people. They were so
desperate, so hopeful that Taro was providing some miracle
cure. But he wasn't. He wasn't able to do anything.

I wanted to ask them about this illness, about which I was
receiving so many conflicting reports. Were people dying of it,
or were they not? Was it contagious or was it not? Did they
know of the suspicions that it was a problem with the water?
And even if it were, what could they do about it? People had
to use water. But even I wasn't so tactless as to treat them to
an inquisition while they were pursuing a fool's path to a fake
cure.

Why weren't the healers handling this, anyway?

Dare I ask Cree?

There were so many of them—that was the frightening
thing. And I was under no illusion that these were all the ill
people in the riverfront areas. These were just the most desperate of what was probably a much larger group.

The sun was dipping down by the time we escorted the last
visitor to the front door. I had a blistering headache. It was an

easy form of Shielding, but I'd never done it for hours at a stretch.

It was a relief to finally close the front door of the residence. I was tired and desperately wanted to lie down. But the sight that greeted us in the foyer stopped me cold.

On the table was a vase, an odd-looking vase of an earthy reddish brown color and a rectangular shape. In the vase were flowers with which I was unfamiliar, their blossoms an eye-piercing yellow. There was a small, dark, round cake balanced right in there among the blossoms, which was just bizarre. And hanging from the rim of the vase, a pair of earrings, short lengths of gold with small pearls at the end.

There was a small card leaning against the base of the vase, the script informing us that this floral thing was for me and from Doran. There was no other information on the card. "What the hell is this?"

"An expression of intent," Taro said with a scowl.

"Intent to what?"

"Don't be stupid," he snapped.

"I've never heard of anything like this."

"An intent to engage in negotiations for a contract of marriage," he explained, almost spitting out the words.

Marriage? Was Doran insane? Why would he do that? Even if we had ever had a relationship close enough to suggest marriage, I had no property and no powerful connections. It was unnecessary and ridiculous.

"Flowers signify personal affection," Taro continued. "The color of the vase represents stability, the earrings represent financial security and the cake represents fertility."

There was so much wrong with all of that. "Why would he send me something like this?"

"Excellent question," Taro said shortly.

"Don't you dare," I warned him. "I told him that I wasn't interested in anything like that."

"Are you sure?"

"Of course I'm damn well sure."

Taro didn't answer. He just stormed off. I had no interest in calling him back, as he was acting like an idiot.

So was Doran. Really, the flower arrangement was quite hideous. Why did he send it? I didn't believe for a moment that he was suggesting marriage or anything like it, because that was just insane. So what was he playing at?

"If you don't want to start negotiations, you send it back."

I looked up. Benedict was leaning against the wall near the entrance to the kitchen, a cup of what smelled like tea in her hand. "Throwing it away isn't sufficient?" I'd planned on sending the vase and the earrings back, of course, but that seemed troublesome for the cake and the flowers.

She shook her head. "You have to send it back in its entirety. Anything less denotes acceptance of the gesture."

That struck me as a deceitful way to handle things, and I was disappointed in Doran for engaging in that kind of behavior. He knew many of these little customs were outside my circle of knowledge. What if I had been alone when the flowers had arrived, and I'd thought the arrangement was nothing significant? I would have taken the arrangement to my suite, and no one would have seen it to warn me of its meaning. I would have sent back the earrings, possibly the vase, and kept the flowers, thereby accidentally committing myself to something.

I sighed and grabbed the ugly arrangement, leaving the residence to find the nearest messenger port. Really, men did the stupidest things sometimes.

# Chapter Twenty

I slept in my own bed that night, as Taro had been acting like a plonker. And I had a vicious headache. And while it was sometimes nice to wake up snuggled up to someone, it was also nice to stretch out and have the whole bed to oneself.

I slept late for the first time in a long while. I woke with no nausea. That was lovely. And I had an appetite; I was really hungry. I went down to the kitchen and enjoyed a hearty breakfast of eggs and sausage. It was wonderful.

Then Taro strode in. He was scowling. "Where's Laidley's gesture of affection?"

I rolled my eyes. "I sent it all back. Thanks for telling me what would happen had I failed to do so."

"It's not my place to interfere."

"It's not your place to cause trouble."

"No, that would be Laidley."

Was he really willing to have me promised to Doran, or whatever would have happened, just because he was annoyed with me? Why was he annoyed with me, anyway? Doran was the one who was playing games.

"I don't want to talk about Laidley."

"Then why'd you bring him up?"

He sort of growled, then took a deep breath before saying, "There's something strange about this illness."

"So you've said."

"Kafar was ill when he came here. I could feel it. There was nothing I could do for him. He was still ill when he left."

"Are you sure?"

He nodded. "I could feel it."

"Sometimes you're not sure how much you've done for someone."

"Not this time. There really was nothing I could do for him."

"All right." What was this about?

"But he moved in with his sister. And he got better."

"Maybe he just got over it. If they don't die, they eventually have to get better. It's possible he's not even truly better. He might just feel better for some reason and think he's healed."

"Perhaps, but the most logical explanation is that he actually is better."

I had to give him that. "Aye, that's true."

"So maybe there's something in the riverfront that's making people sick."

"Risa thinks it's the water."

"It can't be the water. The water goes everywhere. The illness would be more widespread."

"It has spread beyond the riverfront area."

"But not everywhere the water goes. And most of the illness is restricted to the riverfront."

"If it's not the water, what else could it be?"

"I have no idea. But the logical assumption is that there is some unnatural element in the riverfront that's causing this. Maybe it's something only they are eating. Maybe it's something only they use to build their houses. But it's something that's in the riverfront and nowhere else."

All right, I could go with that theory for the purposes of discussion. "Do you want to tell Risa about this?"

He shook his head. "I don't want to have to explain to her about why I think this is unnatural. She won't believe me."

"Why not? You're a Source. She'll believe you can do anything you say you can do."

"I'm not worried about her believing me. I just don't want someone else learning about this little trick I have. Besides, this sort of thing isn't really the responsibility of the Runners. It's an illness, not a crime."

"But they must be investigating it, if Risa thinks it's the water."

"I don't know where she got that idea. The rumors are that the Runners aren't really doing much about this. They can't. They're too busy with other things, and the riverfront illness doesn't fall within their sphere of authority."

"Whose authority does it fall into?"

He shrugged. "I have no idea. No one's, it seems like. Or maybe the healers, but they're not going down there."

"That's alarming." Was that possible? How could something so serious not have a group of people meant to deal with it?

"I think we should go to the riverfront and see what we can find out."

I nearly choked on my tea. "What in the world makes you think we could find something the others can't?"

"Why wouldn't we be able to see something? We're reasonably intelligent people."

"Why would you even want to do this? You're the man who got so furious when people expected us to do something about the weather during the Harsh Summer. You resented the fact that they expected us to do something beyond our responsibilities."

He sniffed. "I resented the way they expressed their expectations. They were obnoxious."

That was true. Obnoxious and violent. But this was bizarre. This wasn't our task. I'd made a promise to myself not to get involved in things that were not my business. It rarely worked out.

"We're not doing anything else, Lee. We're off the roster."

That was true, too. If we couldn't be useful one way, we might as well try to be useful in another. Not that I thought we would find anything, but it would do no harm to humor Taro. "When did you want to go?"

"Might as well go now."

I sighed and finished off my tea.

We left the residence. It was a bright, mild day. A market day, which meant most people would be haunting the merchant stalls.

The riverfront technically referred to the banks of all three rivers, along their entire length through the city. In reality, it was concentrated in the center of the city, where the three rivers met and crossed. The riverfront of the wealthy quad was kept empty, but the other five quads were filled with dye makers, trash collectors and manure mongers. It was a very fragrant area. And loud. And dirty. The buildings were narrow and dark and a lot of the windows were broken or gone altogether.

"So what are we looking for?" I asked Taro.

"I have no idea. Just something that jumps out as being strange."

I wasn't familiar with the area. How would I know what was strange? It seemed to me we were going to waste an afternoon just wandering around. "This all looks unusual to me."

"You're such a snob, Lee."

"So you spend a lot of time here, do you, Taro?"

"There's nothing here that I want."

"How convenient for you."

People were staring at us. I imagined they didn't see Sources and Shields around there very often.

They looked awful. Pale with dark circles under their eyes, green and greasy. Those who moved did so slowly. Many were just sitting or lying in doorways.

"Let's ask someone," Taro suggested, leading me to a thin woman with lanky brown hair, sitting in a rocking chair in front of her hovel. "Excuse me, ma'am," Taro said politely. "I'm Source Karish. This is—"

"You're the Source what's been healing people," she said.

So much for them keeping that quiet. I'd known that was too much to ask.

"Actually, I haven't been. I can't heal people."

"Healed Kafar, didn't you?"

"No, actually, I didn't. I believe he got better because he moved away from the riverfront."

I suddenly wondered if it was the best idea in the world to imply that the place in which she lived was somehow causing the illness.

But she didn't seem to leap to that conclusion. "So you're not going to heal any more of us?"

How many times did he have to say it? He couldn't heal people of this illness. At least, he didn't think so. I still wasn't sure.

He chose not to answer that question. "Have you noticed anything unusual about? Something other than the illness itself?"

She positively cackled with laughter. "Everything about the riverfront is unusual."

Aye, she was going to be a lot of help.

But Taro gave it one more try. "There's nothing you've seen that you can tell me?"

"What are you, a Runner?"

"Have Runners been here?"

"Runners never come here."

"Really?" I said. That surprised me.

"Nothing here they think is worth protecting."

How odd.

We worked our way down the riverbank, stopping to talk to whoever looked open to conversation. No one knew of anything strange happening. A few of them asked Taro to heal them, and were quite bitter when Taro said no. I was glad I didn't have to convince him to refuse. I could just imagine everyone in the riverfront hearing that he was there and the two of us getting mired in a futile attempt to see to everyone.

A little boy, about eight, I guessed, ran up to us. He was too skinny, he was barefoot, and his clothes were too tight. "You a Source?" he demanded of Taro.

"Aye, I am."

"I want to be a Source," the boy announced. "What do I have to do?"

"I'm sorry, son. You have to be born a Source. There's nothing you can do to make yourself a Source."

The boy scowled.

He was only eight. In theory, he could be a Source, and no one had figured it out yet. Taro had been eleven before his family realized he was a Source. We couldn't know whether this boy was a Source unless we spent more time with him. It was usually the families who discovered it.

"You been asking all sorts of questions," the boy said. "I can answer them, if you take me with you and make me a Source."

"We can't take you with us, and we can't make you a Source," Taro told him. "But I can give you this." He took the emerald stud out of his ear and held it out for the boy's inspection.

I thought he was being careless to offer a bribe, of any kind. The boy could easily make something up, and we wouldn't know the difference. I didn't know how to communicate that to Taro without outright calling the boy a liar to his face.

The boy grabbed for the earring. Taro held it out of reach. "What have you got to say?"

"A woman comes at night sometimes. Real late. She's dressed too nice to be someone from around here."

"What does she look like?"

"I don't know. She wears a hood, and it's dark."

"What does she do?"

The boy shrugged. "Don't know. But she does it at the hub."

"What's the hub?"

The boy snickered. He thought the question stupid. "Where the rivers cross."

"When was the last time you saw her?"

"I don't know. A week, maybe."

Taro gave him the earring. "Thank you."

The boy crowed in delight and dashed off.

"A woman who comes in the middle of the night," I said. "That could be for anything. And would he even be up that late?"

"No harm in looking around the hub, though."

"No, if you want to."

There were bridges all over the city, spanning the rivers at various points. The bridge spanning where the rivers met was massive, wide enough to allow two wagons to cross at a time. The bridge was made of wood, and there were chunks rotted out of it.

Walls about shoulder high were built along the rivers, for about twenty cubits each way. Open drains were built low into the walls to allow some of the water to escape for residential use. The grass in the area was beaten down and dead.

And I felt jittery. It reminded me forcibly of how I'd felt in the ash grove. "Ashes."

"What?"

"I think someone's been using ashes here. I think I have a reaction against human ashes."

"That seems odd. Why would you have a reaction?"

"I react to niyacin powder. That's not common."

"That's true. So you're saying someone was trying to cast spells here."

"Or dumping something in the water. At the drains, not the rivers themselves, which is why only some people are getting ill."

"You're saying someone is making them ill on purpose."

As soon as he said that, I wanted to scramble away from the idea. "I don't know. Maybe it's just a side effect. Because why would anyone want to make a bunch of strangers ill?"

Taro nodded, though he didn't look entirely convinced. "You know what the next logical step is."

"Tell the Runners."

"No." Now he looked impatient. "We come back tonight and see if the woman comes."

I sighed. "Really, why are you so enthusiastic about this?"

"I told you. We have nothing else to do. Why don't you want to do this?"

"Because I'm really bad at this sort of thing. I'll make a fool of myself."

"You just don't want to go through the discomfort of waiting around here all night."

There was a kernel of truth to that, but Taro was right. I had nothing better to do.

"We need to get long black cloaks. We want to stay hidden."

That meant shopping.

So we found nice long black cloaks, and then we went back to the residence for a nap. Luckily our watches at the Stall had gotten us used to strange sleeping patterns. Once the sun was down, we headed out with our melodramatic black cloaks draped over our arms.

The riverfront was quieter at night, which surprised me. I was ashamed to realize I had expected people to be walking around drunk and fighting and causing chaos. Simply because they were poor and lived in a grim environment. What was wrong with me?

We put on our cloaks, though really, who were we kidding? If a lone woman had been noticed simply because she was dressed too nicely, we would stand out by a league. But I pulled the hood as far over my face as I could and held my hands within the sleeves. We huddled into the shadowed corner of the walls, and we waited.

And waited.

And waited.

If spending a watch in the Stall was boring, crouching in silence all night was brutal. Despite my nap, I found myself nodding off, my eyes heavy and blurred.

This was so stupid. If someone did come, what were we going to do? Stop her or merely watch? Go back with the news to the Runners? The latter was the smart thing, but while Risa didn't seem disturbed by my previous foray into the responsi-

bilities of Runners, it seemed to annoy the others. They probably wouldn't take us seriously.

But it turned out that I needn't have worried about that. No
one showed up, and when the sun started to rise we stood with
stiff joints. "That was horrible," I complained.

"Aye, and unfortunately, we'll have to do it again."

"You can't be serious."

"We didn't catch her."

"How long do you expect to do this?"

"Until we do catch her."

I suppressed a groan. There was nothing I could reasonably
do but follow along. But in all the rumors I had heard about
Lord Shintaro Karish before I met him, no one mentioned an
insane dedication to the duties of others.

# Chapter Twenty-one

To my surprise, the location of Williams's home was in the Upper Eastern Quad. It was a good enough area in High Scape, home to midlevel merchants and minor politicians. It was not, however, where I would expect someone as successful as Williams to live. Though perhaps it was an unreasonable assumption, on my part, to think a man who owned bordellos would live in the same area as a merchant as successful as Fines.

The house was nice enough, large, made of a decent wood, with a lot of windows. It was hidden from the road with trees and hedges. The driveway didn't take us to the front of the house, as most driveways did, but instead curved around to the back. We didn't exit the carriage right away, unsure as to whether being delivered to the back of the house wasn't a mistake.

"Are you getting out or what?" a voice demanded from above us. The carriage driver, sounding irritable. So we left the carriage, which was jolted into movement as soon as we cleared it.

Not getting paid for services could certainly put people in a sour mood.

The door in the back of the house opened and a young man stepped out, smiling in greeting. He was extremely handsome, slim with a strong jaw, golden blond hair and bright blue eyes. He was dressed in blue, a strange style of clothing that was loose in cut but of a material that seemed to cling to his very attractive form.

"Source Karish? Shield Mallorough?" he asked, his voice deep and smooth. He probably had a gorgeous singing voice.

"Yes," Taro answered.

"My name is Akira," he said. "Please come in. The others are waiting."

He gestured at the back door. We were actually expected to enter the house through the back door. Had anyone asked me whether I'd be offended to enter a residence through the back, I would have said no, of course not, I wasn't so petty as to be disturbed by such things. But I was. I was ashamed of myself. It was ridiculous. Yet to be asked to enter through the back was bizarre.

I was surprised, upon stepping through the door, to be greeted by a huge foyer, with a grand staircase curving up to the second floor. To my knowledge, the back entrances to residences were usually small and utilitarian, as guests never saw them. There seemed to be a lot of furniture scattered about, lots of comfortable-looking chairs and settees. There were chaise lounges, which I could never recall seeing in the public areas of a residence before. And up against the wall, was that a stage? What would anyone want with a stage in their home?

Akira relieved us of our wraps and, shockingly enough, our footwear. While I had been required to remove my footwear while indoors on Flatwell, it had never stopped feeling unnatural and I'd never heard of anyone doing it anywhere else. For a moment, I wondered if Akira was playing a game with us, but then he removed his own footwear. So I guessed it was just a weird custom of the house.

It was odd to see a grown man in a formal situation with bare feet. He had nice feet.

I did not have a great deal of familiarity with private homes.

I wasn't sure whether there were rules as to how a house should be organized. But something about the huge space, with the furniture that merely lined the walls and created no conversation areas, struck me as unhomelike.

The smell of perfume was overwhelming. And if I found it so, poor Taro had to be almost gagging.

We were taken to the largest and strangest dining room I'd ever seen. The table with its chairs was set up on one side of the room, by the windows, which were covered by heavy drapes. The other half of the room was left virtually empty except for more chairs and settees and chaise lounges pushed against the wall.

The other guests were identical to those when we had dined at Fines's, and again, there were no spouses or other partners. Williams was serving drinks, as there were no servants in the room. "How strange you should arrive at just this time," Fines said once Taro and I were settled. "We were just wondering what our dear Prince Gifford has been doing to show his authority over the Triple S."

I felt that question came out of nowhere, and I was a little confused by it. I looked to Taro, who grinned. "Our beloved monarch is causing some difficulty, is he?"

Gamut snorted. "It has been suggested to my theater manager that it might be in the best interests of the community if our program were examined by some government agent before being performed for the public."

"I thought that was happening already," I said. "Some plays are outlawed."

"Aye, and I agree with some of their choices. Some pieces are nothing but excrement from curtain rise to curtain fall, with no technical merit whatsoever. What the Prince seems to be proposing now is different. Everything we would seek to put onstage would first need the approval of the Emperor's agent, and that is insulting. To us and the audience. Not to mention tiresome, unnecessary and expensive."

"Why would it be expensive?" I asked.

"We'd need to give the agent coin to get the plays approved, of course."

I frowned. "Surely the agent would be paid by the government, not private citizens."

Healer Cree managed to convey, with her placid expression and unfathomable eyes, her belief that I was an idiot. "He is speaking of bribes, Dunleavy."

"Bribes," I echoed, because sometimes I was an idiot.

"One needs bribes to encourage government agents to act in one's favor."

"You mean you need to give extra coin to get these people to do their jobs?" I demanded, appalled. Sometimes I really just didn't want to learn anything more about people. Or the world. It was so often disappointing.

Gamut chuckled. "She's so cute."

I was not cute.

"She has no reason to know such things, Dean," Ahmad chided him before she addressed me. "Whenever the services of a government agent are needed, it is expected that the agent will receive a gift. That is the way things are done."

"And this is legal?"

"Oh, no. Quite the opposite. But there would be no point in attempting to fight it. After all, the only people to report it to are other government agents."

"Everyone's in on it," Williams added. "Including anyone who enforces the laws. The Runners. The judges."

"Not the Runners," I objected. Not Risa. Nothing could make me believe that she required bribes to do her job. She was an honorable person.

"How about you, Grace?" Fines asked. "Has the Crown Prince pulled any of his stunts with you?"

There was a curious tone to his voice, and something seemed forced about the question. I felt I was missing something.

Ahmad snorted. "It has been suggested that all members of the guild should hire services and buy supplies only from sources approved by a government overseer."

"That doesn't seem wholly unreasonable," said Fines. "Especially when you're doing work on government projects."

"None of it's reasonable," she snapped. "But yes, it would be tolerable if it were limited to such circumstances. However, I understand the plan is to restrict us in this way for all works performed by the guild."

"At least they don't plan on eliminating your guild altogether." Williams poked at a chunk of fruit floating in his wine, then licked the wine off his finger. "There have been rumors of plans to close down all bordellos and make them illegal. Which is pure stupidity. Without the protection of the bordellos, the prostitutes are in more physical danger from their clients and the patrons are at greater risk of becoming diseased."

"Why in the world would he outlaw bordellos?" Taro asked.

"Apparently His Royal Highness finds the practice of prostitution distasteful."

"He can't seriously believe," Taro said, "it's equitable to destroy the livelihoods of so many just because he finds it distasteful?"

"Ah, but he will be the Emperor, and what he considers distasteful is well within his power to change. And he will."

Well, aye, that was disturbing, that the Prince would have the ability to destroy something so harmless for no good reason. What would be the point beyond demonstrating his power merely for the sake of it? Not that the Empress hadn't thrown her weight around just because she could, but I'd had more respect for her judgment. The Prince had yet to do a single thing that I hadn't thought was stupid.

"Ayana?" Fines prompted, and it did feel like a prompt.

Cree shrugged. "There has been a suggestion there should be regular inspections of my medications and accounts. The justification is to make sure my methods are sound and my rates are fair."

To be honest, I didn't think that was a horrible idea. The idea of healers being able to sell and do anything without being accountable to anyone was chilling. Those crazy elixirs could do a lot of damage, and the idea of someone without competence setting bones and cutting into delicate tissue made me squirm.

"And I am to be told who I may employ and who I may not," said Fines. "If any of my people are not considered appropriate according to age and training, I will be fined."

I wondered if my family were facing similar restrictions. They hadn't written to me about it. They didn't tend to get into that level of detail with me when it came to trade.

"Many are already suffering new restrictions or fines at the hands of the Prince," Fines added.

"But the Prince hasn't the authority to do those things yet," I said. It took time to make all the preparations needed to have a title change hands, and even more time when it involved the throne.

"He will when he ascends the throne, and he'll remember those who have opposed him. It would be idiotic for anyone to refuse his edicts merely because he temporarily lacks the authority to make them."

I wondered what that would mean for Taro's cousin and her refusal to pay additional taxes.

"Have you not received any such regulations from the Prince?" Williams asked.

Of course not. That was a stupid question. "The Triple S is a self-regulating institution, and it always has been. The monarch has no authority over us."

"And what will the Triple S do should a monarch choose to exercise some authority?"

"I doubt it would ever come up." The Empress had sent Taro and me to Flatwell, which was an unusual exercise of a monarch's authority, but that wasn't the day-to-day interference the others were discussing.

The door opened and in streamed about half a dozen of the handsomest people I'd ever seen in one place, pushing carts and carrying decanters. Three men and three women, all young, their brushed and shining hair left loose, which was unusual for staff who were serving food. They were dressed in a fashion similar to Akira, with loose trousers and the shirts that flowed closely under breasts and against flat stomachs, in colors that perfectly suited the wearer. And they all had bare feet.

This was a weird place.

The food smelled good, though.

"Please seat yourselves," Williams invited once the servants had left. Once again, Taro and I found ourselves sitting across the table from each other. Though there was no reason why we should always sit together. We weren't children in need of proximity for moral support.

There were the same little clay pots on the table, and we all rubbed the translucent paste within on our hands. I rather liked that little ritual. Maybe it was something I could do at home.

The food was delivered in the same manner as it had been at Fines's. Everyone served themselves from the dishes and then passed them along. Each of us had our own decanters of wine. And as had been the case at Fines's house, everything tasted absolutely delicious.

"An appalling waste of life," Ahmad was saying, and I realized I had missed some conversation while contemplating the quality of the food.

"His actions did result in the death of two jockeys and five horses," said Fines.

What was this? I looked at Taro.

"A ditch appeared in the middle of the track during a race," he told me. "No one could stop in time. Five horses broke their legs and had to be put down right there. Two jockeys were trampled after they fell off their horses. There were many non-fatal injuries as well."

"The ditch just appeared out of nowhere?"

"That's what it looked like."

"How could that happen?"

"It's most likely that someone dug it, early in the morning before there were any staff at the track, and camouflaged it in some way, and no one noticed it until one of the horses actually stepped in it."

"Now, Shintaro," Fines chided him. "I expected better from you."

"Excuse me?" was Taro's frosty response.

"I take it you weren't at the track that day."

"I was, actually."

He'd witnessed this event and hadn't told me? Why not? It had clearly been a horrible experience. I'd need to talk about it if I'd seen all that. "When was this?"

My question was ignored.

"You weren't questioned by the Runners?"

"I was."

"But they didn't mention to you that they found the paraphernalia for casting near the track."

"They did."

I could tell that Taro's short answers were annoying Fines. I could sympathize with the trader, because they were annoying me, too. It wasn't like Taro to be so reticent. Nor so impolite. "They think the ditch was created by a spell?" I asked. Why would anyone do that?

Ahmad snorted. "They don't know what to think. They claim a spell couldn't have created the ditch, yet they have convicted and hanged a man for the creation of a ditch resulting in multiple deaths, as well as for possession of implements designed for the purpose of casting spells."

"So they believe he created the ditch, and they believe he was trying to use a spell, or pretending to use a spell, but not that he created the ditch with a spell." I didn't believe it, either. I just thought there was a piece of information missing in what I was being told.

"Isn't it ridiculous?" Ahmad said in apparent agreement.

"But you don't believe a spell was involved, Shintaro?" Fines asked.

Taro was committing the sin of playing with his food, pushing morsels of meat about his plate as he thought about what to say. "It seems an odd thing to do, if one had the ability to do such things."

"Oh? What would you do if you had the power to do anything you wanted?"

"I'm afraid I'd have to give that matter more thought."

"Oh, come now. Don't tell me you haven't been contemplating the possibilities since people have begun exploring casting so openly?"

Taro swirled the wine in his goblet. "The sky is obscured by boundaries."

Heh. No one understood that.

"This appears to be a similar wine to what Trader Fines served," Taro said, in an attempt to divert everyone's attention. And it worked, to my surprise. Williams complained, in a good-natured way, about how much the wine cost, especially considering how many wealthy clients he exposed the vintage to, which was why, Fines explained, he sold the wine to Williams at such a reduced rate. This somehow led to a lengthy discussion between Gamut and Ahmad about someone Ahmad knew who would best be able to make repairs to the theater in which Gamut worked. And then a further discussion of services Cree supplied to Williams's prostitutes.

I liked those topics of conversation much better, even though I couldn't contribute to them.

After dessert had been consumed and cleared away, Williams took his wine and sat in one of the chairs in the other half of the room. The others followed, so Taro and I did, too. Conversation felt awkward due to the organization of the seating.

And then the door opened and seven servants walked in. Five carried basins and towels, one was pushing another cart, and one had a flute of some kind. A light scent of citrus filled the air, carried on a thin waft of cedar, and it relaxed me in spite of myself.

"Dunleavy, Shintaro, you may not be aware of this," said Williams, "but many of my patrons enjoy having their feet bathed. It is a service we provide."

Oh, damn it to hell. This wasn't Williams's home. It was one of his bordellos. Could I be any more stupid?

Was this why we had bare feet?

Suddenly, it felt as though my mind were spinning with questions. Was this appropriate? Were they prostitutes? Not that I had anything against prostitutes, but should I be accepting services from them? Was this what anyone had in mind when they talked about Sources and Shields being allowed to requisition goods and services for free? What should I be doing? They never talked about this at the Academy.

I looked at Taro. He was looking back at me, wearing the tiniest smile, obviously aware of my discomfort and entertained by it. He had no intention of indicating which way we should go with this. Bastard.

Everyone else, I could tell, was observing me as well, with various degrees of subtlety. What was this, a test?

Fine. This was something being provided by my host. Something that was not harmful. It was bizarre, but to refuse might offend my host. So, fine, I was going to have my feet bathed. I could accept that attention with a little grace.

The man with the flute sat in a corner of the room with fluid confidence. The piece he played was unfamiliar to me, but it was lovely, the lower sliding notes curling deep in my belly. Moving, but not dangerous.

Akira knelt at my feet, setting a basin on the floor. With gentle hands he placed my feet in the basin. Then he poured warm, scented water over my feet, and when he judged that enough water was in the basin, he poured oil into the palms of his hands. He rubbed his hands together and grasped my shin to rest my wet foot against his thigh, unconcerned with the soaking the thin material he was wearing was suffering.

And then he started rubbing the bottom of my foot.

I had had my feet rubbed before, primarily by Taro, back on Flatwell when the constant bench dancing wrenched my ankles and made the soles of my feet sting. That had felt nice. But this was different. More skilled, for one thing. And the results were different. Especially at one moment when he pressed his thumb hard against the sole of my foot. It sent an oddly pleasant jolt right through me, making me sit up straighter in my seat.

Akira looked up at me and smirked. Clearly, my reaction

had been anticipated. He was playing a game with me. I looked at the others, who were all enjoying their foot baths with varying displays of enjoyment. No one appeared shocked.

They were all playing a game.

Except for Taro. His attendant was a broad-shouldered youth with closely cropped hair, and his hands looked big on Taro's slender feet. Taro appeared relaxed, and there was a slight smile playing about his lips.

The fact that that disappointed me was entirely illogical. Of course he would enjoy the skills of other people. Just as I would enjoy the skills of Akira, if he weren't being paid to do this, and I didn't suspect this was all some ploy to make me feel foolish, or something.

It was all just bizarre, and I worried about what the next step would be.

"Have you ever enjoyed the services of a bordello, Dunleavy?"

There it was.

"No, I haven't," I answered Williams.

"Why not?"

I didn't know. Was it something most people contemplated? "I've just never thought of it."

"You should think of it. You're welcome at any of my establishments at any time."

Um, thank you? I glanced at Taro before I could help it.

Williams caught the look, of course. "Certainly, the two of you can come together. We provide excellent services for couples."

"Thank you." Seriously? A couple would come and share a prostitute? Or would they each hire one? I really had no idea.

Well, I was certainly getting an education from these people.

"Would the two of you like to spend the night and savor some of our services?"

"No, thank you," I said quickly.

Taro chuckled, no doubt delighting in my discomfort.

"My people can make you feel quite fine. Anyone here can attest to that."

Seriously, that was information I neither needed nor wanted. "I am sure that's true, but I'm really not interested. Sorry."

"Perhaps another time."

"Perhaps."

No one asked Taro anything. He was always the lucky one.

Once everyone's feet were determined sufficiently clean, they were gently dried, and Ahmad left. That meant we could leave, too, and we did. I was relieved. Because that had been odd, and I felt there was some kind of agenda going on. And that thought made me feel ridiculous. Because what would such a group want with us?

# Chapter Twenty-two

"Where do you and Source Karish go so long at night?" Ben asked me as I enjoyed tea and a huge chunk of fresh bread. "If you don't mind me asking."

"I'm afraid I can't answer that, Ben." I had slept late that day after another fruitless wait at the hub. We weren't telling anyone what we were doing, mostly because they would think we were insane.

"I suppose I shouldn't have asked."

"There's nothing wrong with curiosity." But his curiosity made me uncomfortable, so I searched for a change of subject. "This bread is incredible. I don't think you've made it before." It was heavy and dark and rich with nuts.

"I don't make it often. It is a laborious recipe."

"Oh." I felt guilty about the fact that I was on my third piece. I was always so hungry after a night at the hub, and the bread had been the only readily available thing to eat.

Ben smiled. "I made it to be eaten, Shield. Please have as much as you like."

I watched Ben clean up some of the crumbs I had spilled on

the counter. I wanted to tell him to stop. I could clean up my own crumbs. "How is Sara, Ben?"

He stilled for a moment, but quickly resumed his wiping. "She is hopeful that she will be vindicated at the trial."

"Has new evidence come to light?"

"She isn't telling me much about it. She's afraid what might happen if the information got into the wrong hands."

"I see. I understand." I didn't really, as I didn't know what kind of information and whose were the wrong hands, but he clearly didn't want to talk about it, and I could respect that.

"But you're kind to ask."

"No, not at all." But I was very uncomfortable. I shoved another piece of bread into my mouth.

I went back up to my room to read the last of the spell books. I would be getting rid of them soon. I didn't like how obsessed people were getting with the idea of casting. While I really didn't think I'd be punished for having the books, I couldn't help feeling leery about the sheer lack of logic people were displaying about spells, and I didn't want to get caught up in anything crazy. So the books would be gone.

After I read them. Because some of them were entertaining. In fact, some of them were hysterical. There were points where I wondered if the writer was insane. Or had been smoking something creative.

There was just so much about the practice of casting that was ridiculous. Wearing wool when it was hot and silk when it was cold. Honey gathered under a full moon—neat trick, that—or blood gathered from a sheep slaughtered at the mark of noon. Powerful locations included the peak of a mountain, the crossing of two or more rivers and the east end of a ravine. Some spells needed a particular timbre of voice, soprano or alto or tenor or bass. And the tools needed, all made out of materials that, if not expensive, needed to be constructed in ridiculously complex fashions.

Seriously, who had the money to cast spells? Who had the time?

But aye, an entertaining read.

Then Ben knocked on my door, telling me Doran had come to see me.

Damn it, I hadn't seen Doran since before he'd sent me that yellow-flowered monstrosity. I had sent it back to him. I'd also sent a note telling him not to be an idiot.

I knew I needed to have it out with him, but I really didn't want to. I just wanted him to accept the words in my messages and just go away. That was cowardly of me, but I felt Doran was being too pushy.

I didn't want what was sure to be an unpleasant conversation overheard by everyone in the house. I asked Ben to show Doran to my sitting room, and I quickly hid the book I'd been reading in my bedroom.

"Lee, dearest, I'm so glad to finally be able to see you," Doran said upon his entrance. He made no effort to make the emphasis on the word "finally" at all subtle.

I had to admit, there was something that irked me about the belief that a person who showed up unexpectedly should be able to see you, just because you happened to be there when they arrived. "I am very sorry," I said, as an apology was expected. "Things have been busy here."

"But you're up for anything now, aren't you?"

"I wouldn't go that far." I didn't know that I would ever be up for the conversation we had to have.

He grinned. "Want to go dancing?"

What was he doing? He had sent me all that stuff, and I had sent it all back. Why was he pretending nothing had changed?

He was going to make me say it. That was ungentlemanly of him. "Doran, we have to talk."

"We are talking."

"Doran, I'm being serious."

He sobered. "You look a little pale."

"I'm always pale."

"I don't think you should make final decisions when you're not at your best."

"This is a decision I've made. Are you really going to make me say it?"

"You don't have to say anything. I understand what's going on. Shintaro is handsome and a Source and he's full of flair. But he's not the sort to last. And if I have to wait, I will."

"You can't mean that." No man with any pride would.

"Don't tell me what I feel."

"I'm sorry, but you can't mean you're prepared to wait until Taro's done with me and you're going to step in. That doesn't make any sense."

"I don't think of you in such base terms, but yes, I'm prepared to wait."

This was unbelievable. There was no way I could inspire such insanity in a man. What was I supposed to say to this?

There was a knock on the door. "Lee?"

Ah, hell, Taro. What was the best thing to do? I wanted to get this conversation out of the way before I talked to Taro. On the other hand, had Ben told Taro Doran was there? "I can't talk to you right now, Taro."

"Why not?"

"Because I'm here," Doran answered.

Taro, of course, charged in. "What are you doing here?" he demanded.

"You're not suggesting you have a right to control who Lee sees, are you?" Doran asked, attempting to sound innocent.

"Her name is Dunleavy!" Taro snapped back. "And if you had any honor, you would have taken the hints she's given to you to leave her alone."

"And yet, she agreed to see me today."

Only because he'd left me no choice.

"Lee has manners. You apparently have no sense of what's proper."

"What do you know about what's proper?" Doran scoffed.

"I know you come sniffing around like a vagrant hoping for a spare crumb instead of declaring your true intentions as an honorable gentleman would."

I couldn't quite figure out whom Taro was insulting more

with that simile, Doran or me. And hadn't that yellow-flower monstrosity been all about declaring unwanted intentions?

Doran was laughing with disbelief. "You're not seriously expecting me to announce a challenge."

A challenge?

"Not at all. Such requires a certain elevation of character that you clearly lack."

Doran flushed. "You are hardly in a position to criticize someone else's character."

"And you are? Who are you? What do you do? Spend all your days playing and gambling while your mother and your sisters handle all of your responsibilities. You do nothing for anyone else. Just another useless lordling whose existence is irrelevant."

Doran emitted another false laugh. "You mean what you would have been, if you hadn't been born a Source?"

Ouch. That was a telling blow. Because it was true. I adored Taro, and he took his responsibilities as a Source seriously, but I had a hard time believing that if those responsibilities hadn't been imposed upon him by an accident of birth, he would have chosen to be industrious in some other way. Would he have ever developed the gumption to break out of the seclusion in which his family had held him? Though, if he weren't a Source, and didn't express himself in the nonsensical manner Sources sometimes employed, his parents wouldn't have thought him mad, and probably wouldn't have locked him in his room until he was eleven. Instead, they would have raised him to be the second son he was, with an older brother who died from his philandering, and apparently a father and a mother who had much the same habits. Would Taro have been able to fashion himself into something different? I couldn't help but doubt it.

"And everyone knows it's the Shield who does all the work in any Pair." Just like that, Doran had swung from forced humor to unreasonable anger. "Shields make plans and study maps and learn about things and write reports. Sources just flit around and open themselves to whatever disasters might occur.

And from what I've been hearing, there's been little of that around here lately."

"That's not fair," I objected, wondering how he'd heard that. The regulars should never know whether events were happening or not, not if the Pairs were doing their jobs properly. Someone had to have been telling him that, and it hadn't been me.

"No, it's not," Doran agreed, taking a different meaning from my words than I'd intended. "But it is correct, isn't it?"

"No," I asserted, my voice weaker than I liked. All the tension in the air was giving me a headache.

"As though your opinion mattered," Taro sneered. "What would you know of Sources and Shields? Nothing but what we choose to let you know."

"I know you're not lovers," said Doran. "Or, you're not supposed to be. That's considered something of a perversion among your kind, isn't it?"

Nausea erupted in my stomach. It was breathtakingly painful.

"It happens all the time," said Taro, bending the truth a little. "And you regulars love all those romance novels and plays that drone on about the love between Source and Shield being unlike any other."

When had Taro been reading romance novels?

"That's fiction," Doran jeered. "Though I can understand if the distinction eludes you. There are other sources of information, you know, books that speak of what the bond is truly like, and what it's supposed to be, and that bringing any sexual element into it is rare, because it is so very wrong. Base. A perversion of something meant to be pure."

"Perversion." That word again. I wanted to object to its use, but I couldn't spare the air to speak. Horrible cramps were developing in my stomach, and it was all I could do not to curl into a ball and moan.

"I have to admit, I'm a little disappointed that Lee would allow herself to be lured into such perversion."

Hey! Who the hell gave him the right to be disappointed in me?

"But she can't be blamed. She was so young when she met you."

I wasn't that young. Twenty-one. Most were hard at labor and parenthood long before that age.

"I can imagine how someone like you would appear to someone so sheltered and immature. The noble bloodline and the flashy looks. And no doubt she was taught to worship Sources at that school of hers."

These words sounded so familiar. Who had said them? Or was it just a common assumption made by all who met me? Did I really appear that weak? Was I that weak?

Apparently. I was sleeping with the man, after all.

"I am confident," Doran continued, "that exposure to someone normal will assist her in seeing how wrong her infatuation with you is, and she will end it. She is, at her core, a sensible woman."

I was seeing something, all right. A whole new side to Doran that I really didn't like. I didn't understand it. I thought Doran really liked Taro. He saw him as a sort of rival, and he couldn't be thrilled with that, but everything Doran had ever said about Taro had implied admiration and respect. Where had all this disdain been hiding?

"And you think you are the someone normal she'll be using as a comparison?" Taro asked with an unpleasant smile. "She is interested in you only for your similarities to me, because she considers you a safer version of me."

That was not true. The two men were hugely different. Doran was less moody, less complicated, and I could be fairly confident that with him, I wasn't merely one among many.

"Please," Doran sneered. "What she appreciates about me is how I am different from you. I'm stable and reliable."

"How romantic." Taro snickered.

"Deride it all you like, but it doesn't change this basic, fundamental truth. You're the sort a woman plays around with. I'm the sort she marries."

What a pile of bull. How dare he say something like that? How dare he? And what did he know about it, anyway? And when did he turn into a bastard?

I wasn't marrying anyone. The mere mention of marriage was stupid, and I didn't believe for an instant that Doran was actually interested in marrying me. This was a game he was playing, only I couldn't decipher the point of it.

Taro didn't seem at all moved by Doran's insult. There was no real reason why he should be, I supposed. He knew Doran was no threat to him. Yet he didn't seem anxious to end the argument. "If you are the sort one marries, surely you have an understanding of procedure, duty and tradition."

"I'm not going to issue a challenge over Lee," said Doran. "It's barbaric and stupid."

"No more than trying to slither your way in between us without properly declaring your intentions."

"I did declare my intentions," said Doran. "To Lee."

Taro looked at me, and I would have crawled under the settee to avoid his gaze if it wouldn't have taken too much effort. "I said properly declaring your intentions."

"To you?" Doran snorted. "Why do you keep trying to draw me into a lineage challenge? Do you think yourself at an advantage, because you're higher born than I? From what I've heard, your parents kept you in a box in a cellar until they shipped you off to the Academy."

"Get out." The words were out of my mouth before I'd formed any intention of saying them. They were spoken too softly, though, for either man to hear me.

"You would be the sort to listen to rumor," Taro sneered.

"No rumor," said Doran. "Straight from a member of your own family, who was only too willing to tell me how everyone thought you a mad idiot, and that some still weren't convinced they weren't at least half right."

"Get out!" This time I'd pulled in a deep breath before I spoke, the words coming out in a shout that broke the air of the genteel restraint the men had been exhibiting.

Other than silence, I couldn't say what Taro's reaction was.

I was looking at Doran, who was watching me in shock.

"Get out now," I ordered.

He seemed surprised by my words. How was that possible? How could he think I would just sit by and watch him denigrate my Source in such a foul manner? "Lee?"

"That's Shield Mallorough to you. Leave." I was infuriated when he didn't obey. This was my room in my home.

"Lee, I know it's appalling of us to argue in front of you, but you mustn't overreact."

"Get out now!" I shouted again, and the effort it took caused my stomach to crush in on itself so hard I couldn't help a little yip of pain, pressing a hand to my stomach as I curled up on the settee.

Taro knelt on the floor beside the settee, putting a hand on my arm. The pain eased immediately, and I could breathe again. "You may leave now," he said to Doran.

"I can help."

"Stop being selfish," Taro snapped back. "We will take care of her."

"As you've done so well so far."

"Get out. And send Ben up on your way out. Tell him she has a fever."

I was aware of Doran hesitating before I closed my eyes and concentrated on trying to breathe without causing more pain. I heard the door open and close, and I assumed Doran left.

"You're on fire," Taro said. "I'm taking your gown off, and I'm going to put you in some cool water in the tub, all right?"

It sounded good to me, especially as, now that he'd mentioned it, my skin felt hot and blistery. Cool water sounded wonderful.

Taro unlaced my gown with light hands. I couldn't help him, for once he'd removed his touch from my skin, the crippling pain jolted back into my stomach.

The door burst open. Ben carried in two buckets. "Why isn't she in the tub yet?" he demanded with uncharacteristic heat. "Put her in the tub."

Choosing not to bother with removing my chemise, Taro

lifted me from the settee and carried me to my water closet, where Ben was pouring the water into the tub. Showing off his upper body strength, Taro lowered me into the tub with no apparent difficulty.

I admit it, I squeaked at the first touch of the water. "That's freezing!"

"I assure you it's not, Shield Mallorough. It merely feels that way, because of your fever. Please have a care of your hand. The poultice can't get wet."

Aye, aye, aye, the useless poultice, mustn't get it wet. Made bathing difficult. Made everything difficult. And right then, I was pretty sure my burned hand was the least of my worries.

"No, no, no, have to get out," I groaned.

"We need to get the fever down, Lee."

"Going to vomit."

The next thing I knew, Taro was propping me up and I was throwing up into a basin Ben thrust beneath my face, and it was so humiliating. Painful, too, twisted around so I could aim for the basin, my knees and ankles smacking against the sides of the tub with the force of my retching.

"You have to fetch a healer," Taro ordered Ben. "Tell them who you work for. Tell them they're in danger of losing a Pair."

I thought that was overstating the case a little, but I was too busy throwing up to say so.

"Aye. Don't let her get too cold. And make sure she drinks something."

"Send in one of the others, if they're about. I'm going to need some help."

Lovely. I was going to have an audience.

Then I was throwing up again, and dignity lost its priority.

# Chapter Twenty-three

Hell. I was in some version of hell. I could swear I could believe in it. Was there anything worse than sitting in a freezing tub, so close to naked the distinction was irrelevant, throwing up the lining of an empty stomach with my head trying to explode with every heave?

I supposed it would have been worse if Taro weren't right there, if having him touching me didn't ease the pain somewhat. I couldn't imagine how bad it would feel if he weren't there. Or if I'd been a regular, without the nice buffer from sensation that being a Shield offered.

It wasn't long before I just couldn't bear to be in the tub anymore. It was too confining and it was making me crazy. With the help of Benedict, who was apparently the only other member in the residence, Taro got me out of the tub and out of my wet chemise and into my bed. Naked, because cloth felt unbearably abrasive against my skin. That meant I couldn't bear to have the covers over me, either.

It was a good thing I had no pride at all.

Instead of soaking me, they tried draping clothes drenched in ice water over my ankles, wrists, throat and forehead. That felt awful. And I just disrupted the whole setup every time I threw up, which seemed to happen every other heartbeat or so.

Taro, taking Ben's advice, forced water down my throat. I threw that up, too. That time, there was blood.

That threw Taro, who had been staying surprisingly calm, into some kind of panic. "Tell me what to do!" he shouted at Benedict.

"I know nothing of healing!" she shouted back.

"You have to know something!"

"She's your Shield!"

"And you're far older than us! Surely you've learned something other than how to bait Derek all those years!"

"You're asking for a tanning, boy."

I hoped they weren't going to start some stupid loud argument. My head wouldn't be able to stand it. I curled onto my side, wishing my stomach into steadiness. I didn't know how much longer my throat could tolerate the constant throwing up. It felt like it had been torn bloody.

"Come on, Lee. Don't do this!"

My head hurt so much, but I opened my eyes just a little. Taro was sitting beside me on the bed, tilting my world crazily, and I lifted my left hand to rest it against his arm. "Be all right," I tried to say, though it came out in a croak.

"Damn it, Lee." He squeezed my hand.

"You say that a lot."

"You deserve it. You're always doing stupid things."

I was sure there was something wrong with that, I was sure I was usually a sensible person, but I couldn't remember why I thought so.

"That stupid healer," Taro muttered. "I knew he was an idiot. I should have insisted that someone else see you, when all the huge brainless wonder thought you should do was drink tea. Wouldn't admit he hadn't a clue. Ignorance and arrogance is such a bad combination. I've never heard of such quackery. Except for that lug on that damned island. Remember him, Lee? That monster who was using Aryne. Surely one of his vile potions would have been better than nothing at all."

I felt so bad for Taro. He had to be so worried. I had no doubt I looked awful, and he was thinking that I was about to die and take him along. I knew what that felt like, that uncertainty, that helpless fear. "S'all right," I said again.

"It's not all right, damn it. Why didn't you tell me you were still wearing that damned bob?"

What a bizarre question. He must have seen the bob when he undressed me. It didn't have anything to do with what was going on.

I was so, so tired. Apparently too tired for the cramps to work as painfully as they had been before, which was a glorious relief. The headache was there, but no longer so piercing that my skull was in danger of flying apart from the force of it. That was nice. And hey, it had been, what, thirty heartbeats since I'd last thrown up? Paradise.

And then I lost track of things for a while. Taro was a constant, of course, draping careful fingertips over my temples and down the side of my face. There seemed to be a lot of slamming doors, and at times I became more aware of myself when a fresh strip of ice water was draped over my skin. I didn't understand what was being said around me for a while. But then Ben was there, and there seemed to be shouting.

I hated shouting. It was nasty and totally unnecessary. "Taro?" I said.

"I'm sorry, Lee." He squeezed my hand, too hard this time, and it hurt. "Ben couldn't get a healer to come to the residence. Apparently a bridge collapsed over the Silver River and there are a lot of victims. We're supposed to bring you to them, but you won't be considered a priority once we get there."

Oh, Zaire, lying around in a hospital like this, waiting for hours until someone could look in on someone with something as insignificant as a fever? What was the point?

Silver River. Because of the color of the water, much lighter than that of the other rivers, and because it was favored by merchants, wide and just deep enough to manage boats and barges but not deep enough to encourage currents that might capsize vessels and destroy precious cargo. I'd never really looked at it before, though there were poems that painted beautiful images of moonlight dappling the little ripples. It was too bad I'd never gone to look at it.

My parents would like that river.

"I'm going to find you a healer, Lee."

And that was when I realized he planned to leave me. "No," I said, and I tried to hold on to him. But my grip was weak to the point of uselessness.

"You have to have a healer, Lee. I don't know what else to do for you, and I've got to get a healer who's not working at the hospitals. I think I have the best chance of finding one."

That was true. Taro could convince anyone of anything.

"Ben and Elata are here. They'll look after you."

But they couldn't ease my pain as he could. "Don't go." I couldn't bear to have him go.

I felt a light touch on my temple. "I love you," he whispered. And then he was rising from the bed, shaking off my weak grip. The door slammed again.

The pain in my stomach leapt into something unbearable, and I screamed, twisting against the hands that held me to the bed. It was too much. I couldn't breathe. I couldn't find peace. I just screamed and screamed until I could scream no more, could bear the pain no more.

When I opened my eyes, I could tell from the light in the room that I had slept. I felt damp and grimy, my whole body heavy in a way that was almost pleasant. I felt numb, and my tongue was thick and unwieldy in my mouth.

Ben was sitting in a chair beside my bed. Benedict wasn't anywhere in sight.

"She had to go for her watch," Ben told me.

I swallowed a few times, and even then I could barely whisper out, "Taro?"

Ben shook his head. "He is still looking for a healer. I fear he won't find one, though. That bridge killed and injured dozens upon dozens of people. And it's caused disruption and stoppage along many streets. Even if there were a healer to spare, one who had chosen not to go to a hospital during such a disaster but was willing to come here, it would be extremely difficult for Taro to get him here."

Oh. That was too bad.

Wait. Wait a moment. Wasn't Ben supposed to be trying to reassure me, and telling me that, of course, Taro would be able to convince a healer to come to the residence, even if he knew it wasn't true?

But maybe he didn't know the part he was supposed to play. He wasn't part of a Pair. If he had a companion of any kind, I had never heard of them. So maybe he didn't know how these events went. Poor man. He was supposed to tell me I was overreacting.

"It won't be long now," Ben was saying. "I know this has been hard on you, but the end is supposed to be painless."

The end? What end? What was he talking about?

"It's really an honor to be chosen, you know."

Why did that sound familiar? Who'd said that to me? So many people I couldn't properly count. I just knew that whenever someone told me something was an honor, it usually really wasn't. "Reanist," I said.

He sniffed. "Of course not. Gods. What nonsense."

That was true. And I wasn't an aristocrat. Pure merchant class, all the way back to my great-grandmother, at least.

Damn it. Why couldn't I think? "Water?" I asked.

"I don't think that would be a good idea, Shield Mallorough. I've given you some blue root to ease your pain." He had? Really? I had no memory of that at all. "Mixing water with it, that's likely to start the stomach cramps again. You don't want that, do you? Not with Source Karish gone. You'd feel them fully, without him here to blunt them for you."

Aye, that made sense. I let my eyes drift closed.

Ben kept talking, though. "It's really not that common, you know, for partners to be able to ease each other's pain the way you and Source Karish are able. It happens, of course, obviously, but it's rather rare. Only truly fortunate Pairs are able to enjoy such benefits from their partnerships."

Wait, wait, wait. How did he know we were able to ease

each other's pain? It wasn't something we really talked about.

"Source Karish is a rather remarkable person, isn't he?" said Ben. "Of the finest family, so handsome, so personable, and so very talented. One would have expected him to have an equally talented partner."

Where was Taro? Why was he taking so long? If he would just come back, I could curl around him, and just touching him would make me feel so much better. Perhaps better enough to sleep. I just needed some sleep.

"It's so strange how things turn out sometimes," Ben said. "I'd hoped, so much, that one of my children would be a Source or a Shield and have the kind of life you enjoy."

Would he please just shut up? I'd never be able to get back to sleep with him nattering on.

"Sources and Shields are better off even than the aristocracy, in a way. No matter how wealthy or how highly placed an aristocrat is, a change in fortune can have him disgraced and digging out his dinner from someone else's land. But a member of the Triple S, no matter what they do, they'll always have a roof over their head, clothes on their back, food on their table."

Sleep, or the potential for it, was slipping farther away as the pain in my head grew more prominent.

"But none of them had any talent. In anything, really."

Who never had any talent? If he insisted on going on and on and on about nothing, he could at least make sense as he went about it.

My skin was heating up. Those strips of cloth dipped in ice now seemed a wonderful idea. I could see the bowl they'd been using earlier, sitting on the vanity. It probably wasn't so cold anymore, but even warm water would be soothing. "Water?" I asked.

"I said no, dear. It'll make you feel worse."

"No." He didn't understand. Why couldn't I speak properly?

"It won't be long now, I promise." He put a hand on my left arm, brushing my skin. It burned.

"Don't," I said.

There was a clatter of hooves in the street, which happened often enough, but it made Ben rise to his feet and leave the suite for a few moments. When he came back, he announced, "Source Karish is back."

He sounded surprised.

Thank Zaire. He was back. I would be able to sleep.

# Chapter Twenty-four

Karish came into the room carrying a huge trunk, a heavy one from the way he was using a leg to balance it as he walked. And behind him was Healer Cree.

She halted when she saw Ben. "Who is this?" she demanded in a frosty tone.

"He runs the house." Taro grunted as he set the trunk on the floor.

"I want him out of the house."

"He lives here," Taro objected.

"It is a condition of my assistance."

"It is of no moment, Source Karish," said Ben, backing toward the door.

"Tell everyone else to stay out of the house as well," said Cree. "Their presence will disturb my work."

"Of course."

Cree watched him leave. I heard the door to the suite being closed, and Cree waited a few moments beyond that before stepping to the trunk and opening it. The first thing she took out of it was a bundle of wooden sticks that unfolded into a small, short table. I hadn't seen folding furniture since we'd left Flatwell.

Taro sat beside me on the bed, taking my left hand in his, and my headache eased. "Healer Cree is going to take care of you, Lee," he said. "But you have to remember that she's a different sort of healer from what you've seen before. She's going to do things differently."

Sure. Fine. Whatever.

Only Cree put immediate lie to that statement by pulling out strips similar to what Healer Pearson used. Like him, she put a strip each to my tongue, my temple, the burn on my right hand. With a small knife, she made a tiny cut in my arm, and she laid a strip against that, too.

"It took Pearson hours to examine his strips," said Taro. "She may not have hours."

Really, if he had to exaggerate about such a thing, couldn't he do it out of my hearing?

Cree glared at him. "We discussed this before I agreed to come," she reminded him. "You are to trust me, yes?"

Taro nodded.

"Besides, Pearson is incompetent, and too arrogant to know it. Don't insult me by comparing me to him." From a small pocket in the lid of the trunk she pulled out four glass vials with flat bottoms. From within the trunk she pulled out a bottle. She put a strip palm in each vial, then uncorked the bottle and poured clear yellow liquid into the vials. After corking the bottle and putting it on the table, she picked up each vial and swirled the contents at the bottom. In each case, the liquid clouded from yellow to a dull, smoky brown.

Cree sucked in a quick breath. She put down the last vial and stepped closer to the bed. "Move," she ordered Taro, and Taro moved. Cree sat on the bed and stared at me, putting a careful fingertip below each eye and gently pulling the skin down slightly. Then she had me open my mouth and move my tongue around, which under the current circumstances felt as easy as pushing a tree over with my pinky. She raised my left hand from the bed, sniffed it, then licked it, which was just disgusting. She peered at the fingernails of both hands. "Who wraps your hand for you?" she asked me, glancing at Taro.

"Ben," I whispered.

"Where does he get the poultice?"

"Makes it."

"Where does he get the ingredients?"

"Don't know."

"How long has he worked here?"

"Years," said Taro. "Years before we came here."

"Hm." Cree went back to her table, picking up the knife she'd used to cut my arm. "She's reacting to the niyacin powder."

"No, no, Ben stopped using it," I said. "I felt better."

"I can't say anything to that. Reactions aren't always predictable, and they aren't always progressive. You can feel fine one day and awful the next. But there are huge amounts on your palm and in your mouth. I'd say you've consumed it, very recently. What have you eaten today?"

"Just bread."

"Where did you get the bread?"

"Ben made it. But there was no way he would have put niyacin powder in it." Even I knew that wasn't an ingredient for bread.

"Are you sure?"

"You're saying Ben poisoned her deliberately." Taro looked appalled. And furious. "That's a disgusting thing to say! He's been nothing but good to us."

"I am not making accusations. It is not my job to determine who is responsible. It's my job to identify the problem and fix it."

"Can you?"

"We'll see."

I frowned at that. "I might die?"

Her eyebrows rose. "You're not terribly intelligent, are you?"

"Stop that," Taro snapped. "Just make her better."

"Of course, it's as simple as that," Cree murmured sarcastically. "I must see how far the poison has traveled." Apparently that meant nicking the skin low on my stomach, the bottoms of both of my feet and on my forehead near the hairline, collecting samples of the blood on more strips. It also meant being examined more intimately than I'd ever been examined by anyone before, and that included anyone I'd ever slept with. It should have hurt. It should have been humiliating. But I really didn't feel anything. I was too tired and too numb.

"This is very serious," Cree said once she had fiddled with more vials to her satisfaction. "It must have been a massive dose."

I couldn't bear to watch Taro. He was pacing and it was making me dizzy. "But there is something you can do, yes?" he asked.

There was no answer.

I was going to die. Poor Taro. It really wasn't fair.

"Dunleavy," said Cree.

"Mm."

"Open your eyes."

Did I have to? I was so tired.

"Open your eyes!" Cree ordered.

I sighed and looked at her. She was standing beside my bed, staring down at me with eyes that seemed darker and larger than I remembered. "If nothing is done for you, you won't live through the night," she said.

"All right," I said.

She huffed. "All right. Stupid girl. As though I were offering you a cup of coffee you're too polite to refuse. I might be able to help you, but medicine won't be enough."

"All right," I said, because she had paused and clearly expected me to say something.

"What do you mean, no medicine?" Taro barked out.

"We discussed this before we came here, Source Karish."

"But I didn't think you weren't going to use any medicine at all."

"Adding any kind of medicine to the mix will nullify the spell."

The spell. Oh lords. I tried to giggle, but all that came out was a wheezing sound.

"Dunleavy, you'll have to trust me. I know your beliefs, but you're beyond the help of common medicine."

Spells. Sure. Why not? Go ahead.

"Your life is in my hands. Just as, when we are finished, my life will be in yours. I will expect you to honor that."

"All right." It seemed the thing to say.

"Source Karish?"

"I have no interest in reporting you to the Runners. I think those laws are ridiculous."

Oh. That was what she was worried about. Perhaps I should show her my books. They were around somewhere.

"That is because you don't believe spells truly work," said Cree. "We shall see how you feel after."

"If you heal her, all I'll feel is ecstatic."

"And if I fail to heal her?"

"I won't be around to feel anything."

She nodded. "Point taken." She removed from the trunk a square black bag and filled it with bottles and jars, candles and what looked like alarmingly long needles. "Does this place have a cellar?"

"Yes," said Taro.

"How big is it?"

"A bit larger than this room here."

"Is there much in it that would obstruct movement?"

"A big table in the middle of the room. Very solid."

She swore. "Can you drag it out?"

"I don't think so. The stairs would be far too narrow. I'm pretty sure it was built in the cellar."

"I don't suppose you know how to wield an axe?" she asked without much hope.

"I do."

"Really?" she asked with surprise.

"You'd be astonished at the breadth of my knowledge."

Once upon a time, that comment would have been made flirtatiously. The dignified healer's reaction would have been interesting to see.

"Then chop that table into pieces, as small as possible. Wait, what is the cellar floor made from?"

"It's just packed dirt."

"Perfect. Chop the table into kindling. I want to be able to light it easily. Make four piles of wood, one in each corner of the cellar. I'm assuming the cellar has four corners?"

"There's no place for smoke to escape," Taro said dubiously.

"You mentioned a stairway. That will have to do. Start chopping. Press anything else you find down there close to the walls, and take down anything that's hanging from the ceiling. And be quick about it. We haven't much time. Oh, take this with you." She gave him the black bag. "Come back up when you're done, but leave the bag down there."

Taro stared at me a moment, clutching the black bag, indecision clear upon his face.

"Move, man!" Cree ordered.

Taro left.

"All right, my dear," said Cree, who was, of all the strangest things, taking off her clothes. "I need something of yours that's of great sentimental value. I imagine that's the closest thing to magic that you have."

Things of sentimental value? I wasn't really the sentimental sort. A leather hair tie I'd made as a child, about the only thing I'd ever made with my hands that wasn't hideous. The history treatise given to me by my favorite professor. There was the bookmarker Lamer made for me, braided out of incredibly soft blue fabric, just before we left the Academy. The gold hoops Taro had given me. Would one of those do?

She wasn't going to destroy it in one of her spells, was she?

Though right then, I couldn't say exactly where any of those items were.

"Wait a moment," Cree said, stepping out of her skirt. And yes, it looked like she was getting completely naked. That couldn't be good. "I feel something in here."

Possibly a draft.

"Here it is." She scooped up my chemise, which had been left in a puddle on the floor beside the wardrobe.

I thought I didn't have much time left. Why was she wasting it?

"No, no, no. Ah! This." She unpinned the harmony bob and let it hang from her thumb and forefinger. "Why, Shield Mallorough, I didn't know you had it in you."

"Jus' jewelry," I slurred.

"Not at all. It's so much more than that. Expertly crafted, expertly enspelled. And worn next to your heart ever since. This might be the saving of you."

Wonderful. My life depended on a trinket. This would end well.

"Here, hold this." She put the bob in my right hand. "Don't change hands," she ordered as she saw that I was about to do just that.

Cree stripped down to her skin, then pulled from her trunk a garment of dark green with white designs embroidered down both lapels. It looked like some sort of robe, but made only of linen, the sleeves deep and wide, the bodice of the garment falling freely from the shoulders except where Cree fastened it down her front with hooks and eyes. It fell just to the top of her bare feet. Next she unpinned her hair, shaking it out so it hung loosely about her shoulders. Finally, she took off her rings, earrings and necklace.

Then she bent over her trunk again, throwing into another black bag another collection of bottles and vials and some sticklike things. Once she had everything she needed, she closed and locked the trunk.

I could hear the irregular thuds of Taro destroying the table in the basement. He'd done his share of chopping wood while we'd been on Flatwell, but that had been a while ago, and chopping something like a table had to be trickier than chopping logs. I just hoped he didn't lose a foot or something.

There was something kind of comforting about hearing the thud and the clatter. Homey.

And then: "What the hell is going on here?"

Ah. LaMonte. Always a pleasure.

"Who is that?" Cree asked, going into the suite to lock the door to the hall.

"LaMonte," I answered. "Source. Old. Thinks he's in charge."

"And he's not in charge?"

"No. No one is." That didn't mean he couldn't cause problems for us if he wanted.

The sound of Taro chopping wood halted. Clearly, LaMonte had gone down to the cellar. After only a few moments, the sound of chopping resumed, and a few moments after that I could hear him coming up the stairs to the second story. Then a pounding on the door to my suite. "Dunleavy! What's going on?"

"You can't come in," said Cree. "Dunleavy has become extremely contagious. You must leave this residence."

The snort I heard even through a door and across two rooms made me smile. "Nonsense. She was fine yesterday."

"She is now extremely ill. And contagious."

"I've never heard such tripe. Open up at once."

"Please, Source LaMonte," I said, and it took enormous effort to make my voice loud enough to reach him. "It came on suddenly. Healer Cree was the only healer willing to come to see me, and she really knows what she's doing. She had to send Ben away, too."

"And what about Shintaro? How is he immune?"

"He's not," said Cree. "I have no doubt he's already infected, so I need his help for as long as he can give it, before he succumbs to his symptoms. I would ask you to leave before you risk infection, and make sure none of the others come into the house. Consider it under quarantine."

There was a long pause. "This seems highly irregular," he said eventually.

And LaMonte did hate the irregular. Not that I blamed him. I hated the irregular, too.

"So is her illness," Cree responded tartly. "Are you going to force me to risk infecting you and who knows how many others just so I can find a Runner to enforce my quarantine on this residence?"

"You can't have me ejected from my own home."

"I am a healer. Believe me, I can."

I had no idea whether that was true or not. If LaMonte's silence meant anything, neither did he.

I did think it would be hysterical if the two imposing figures met under more normal circumstances. I would have to introduce them. If I survived.

"I will be looking into this," LaMonte threatened.

"You do that." In a much lower voice, too low to be heard by LaMonte, she added, "As long as you look into it somewhere else."

We listened to LaMonte retreat from the door and go down the stairs. I didn't hear the outer door open and close, but that didn't mean LaMonte hadn't actually exited the building. I wouldn't hear that door unless it was wrenched open and slammed shut.

So there was no way to know, one way or the other.

In time, the thud and clatter from the basement ceased, and we heard footsteps on the stairs again. There was a knock on the door. "It's me," said Taro.

"Has that other person left?" Cree asked.

"Chris? Aye."

"Are you sure?"

"There's no reason for him to hide from me," Taro said impatiently. "Aren't we running short on time?"

Cree sighed with impatience, and she went to the sitting room to unlock the door. "Please assist Dunleavy down to the cellar."

"Need to get dressed," I said.

"No, you need to remain as you are."

Wonderful.

Taro came into the room, strands of hair flying free of the tie at the base of his skull, sweat plastering his cream-colored shirt against his chest and back. I wished I had an artist's skill, that I could make renderings of him in all his states of beauty. He would never want to look at them, or even know about them. I would just like them for myself. Maybe he would want to see them when he was much older, and beautiful in a different way.

# Chapter Twenty-five

Helping me down to the cellar meant carrying me down to the cellar, as my legs were useless. It was horribly embarrassing, though I couldn't say why. Both Taro and Cree had seen me naked, and no one else was there. That there was a serious danger of being dropped only increased my discomfort. Taro had exercised a lot of stamina in destroying the table, and I wasn't light.

I knew where the cellar was. I'd been there once or twice. There was something about the cellar that made me uneasy. It was completely underground. The air smelled heavy and unpleasantly musty. And I never felt I could move about freely.

Right then, lit only by a lantern set on the floor by the door, casting distorted shadows everywhere, the cellar looked unfamiliar and bizarre, the table gone and replaced by four piles of wood, one in each corner. Taro had dug a sort of trench around each pile in an attempt to prevent any spreading of fire once the piles were lit.

It struck me just how incredibly bad an idea this was.

"Lay her on the floor," Cree said. "Head facing this way, feet facing there."

"Directly on the dirt?" Taro objected.

"Now."

Wonderful. So I lay down on the floor, and despite the weird calm that had descended upon my mind, I had images of all the insects crawling in the dirt and possibly into exposed parts of my body.

Cree lit each of the bundles of wood, having poured some kind of oil over them. The warmth was immediately apparent. From her bag she took a black-handled knife, which she dug into the dirt near my feet. Shuffling backward, she cut a wide circle around me, ending back at my feet. Small sticks—rods, I supposed—were thrust into the ground, one at my head, one at the tip of each hand and each foot. From a bottle she poured a clear liquid from one rod to the next, connecting them all. This line was then frosted with salt.

"Take off your clothes, Shintaro," Cree ordered. "And step inside the circle, but stay outside the salt line." In a few moments, Taro was seated on the dirt beside me on my left.

Cree took my left hand and sliced a small cut into the palm. She took Taro's left hand and cut his palm, too. She took the bob from my right hand and put it in my left. She clasped my left hand and Taro's left hand together. "Don't let go until I give you leave."

Cree opened more bottles, and at various places within the circle poured out the contents. Sometimes the contents were a liquid, sometimes a powder. They were being poured to create patterns, but I couldn't see the patterns against the dirt.

A strange scent was developing in the air. It smelled like wet hay.

Once Cree was finished dumping stuff on the floor, she stepped outside the circle, standing near my feet. She plunged the knife deep into the soil. Then from her bag she took out another knife, this one with a white handle. "It is time for me to begin. Once I begin, I can't stop, or the fires will break loose and kill us all."

I was very displeased to be learning that death was a possibility this late in the proceedings.

"Dunleavy, you must not move from within the circle of salt. Shintaro, you must not cross the salt line nor leave the circle. Dunleavy, this will hurt. A lot. Shintaro, you must keep her from moving over the salt line, but you can't touch her with anything other than your left hand. Neither of you must try to get my attention. This is very important. I can't lose my concentration." She looked at me then. "Trust me, Dunleavy, as I am trusting you."

"Aye," I said. Apparently, I had no choice.

I was going to die. I wasn't ready to die. There were things I hadn't done. Gone to my parents' home. I'd never been. Gone back to talk to Professor McAuley. And I'd really wanted to see how Aryne was going to turn out. I had no doubt she was terrorizing the Source Academy, and more power to her.

Poor Taro. It wasn't fair.

Cree held the knife in both hands, at chest level, the tip of the blade pointed down. She looked ridiculous. What the hell was I doing?

"I call on the power of the earth," Cree intoned. "Source of all which heals. Source of the poison which defiles the blood of this subject. I call on you to draw this poison out, and take back that which should have never been drawn from you. Reclaim your essence."

The chants I'd read in the book had rhymed.

"I give to you blood. Blood of the half, who is strong and clean. Blood of the caller, who is wise and clean." She sliced her own right palm, then held her hand over the floor, palm facing down so the blood could drip from it. "Reclaim your essence."

Nothing happened, of course. Except the room was warming up and the smell of wet hay grew heavier, almost suffocating. Was this what her patients paid good money for?

"Reclaim your essence."

It was going to be so embarrassing. When I died, and Taro died with me, Cree would clear out her props and leave. She wasn't stupid enough to be found with a dead Pair and tools Runners would recognize as being connected to casting. And

what would people think, what would my family think, of
how we would be discovered? Naked in the cellar. And how
people would talk, how the Stallion of the Triple S and his Shield
had ended up. I hated the thought that I cared; it was stupid to
worry about what people would think after I was dead. Still,
what would my parents hear? What would my father think?

"Reclaim your essence!"

The circle flared into flame, low and blue, and Taro jerked
in surprise. Damn it, the fire was spreading. How stupid were
we, lighting fires in this small space? The temperature rose
uncomfortably, while the scent of wet hay seemed to coat my
nostrils and throat. It was foul.

I felt that jittery sensation again, piercing through all my
discomforts and the general assault on my senses. And I realized something. It wasn't the ashes that gave me that feeling.
It was the power of the spell itself. I could feel it when a spell
was being used. My gods.

"Reclaim your essence!"

And the fire leapt closer, and this time the flames were dark
green, tracing along the patterns on the floor.

That was it. I wasn't going to let myself be burned alive.
But when I shifted to move, Taro's grip on my hand became
painfully tight. I looked up at him, and he was glaring down
at me. I opened my mouth to tell him not to be ridiculous, and
he squeezed my hand so hard I thought a bone was going to
break.

I was stunned. Despite appearances to the contrary, Taro
was not a foolish person. How could he think we were doing
something sane?

It was more likely that he thought there was nothing else
we could do. And maybe he was right. I was hot and nauseous
and so tired. No one else knew what the hell to do.

I figured if Cree was still in the cellar, and she was, we
couldn't be in imminent danger of being fried.

Maybe Ben was out looking for a real healer.

"Reclaim your essence!"

Pain flared through every vein I had, sharp and icy and splintering, so severe I couldn't even scream. Gods.

"Reclaim your essence!"

I couldn't move. I wanted to. I needed to try to curl away from the pain, which didn't make sense, because the pain was everywhere. Except one spot that I couldn't really define, a location that didn't have the ice but instead some odd sucking sensation. It wasn't pleasant, but in comparison to the rest of my body it was a haven of comfort. I wanted more of it. But I couldn't move.

"Reclaim your essence!"

The shards of ice grew larger, tearing at my skin from the inside. For Zaire's sake.

"Reclaim your essence!"

I must have screamed then. How could I not? But I couldn't hear anything and I couldn't feel anything other than the icy, shredding pain tearing through every part of me, slicing at the bottom of my feet, ripping jagged holes into my stomach and chest, sending jolts of ice through my limbs. My left hand was hot, burning hot, and the focus of the strange sucking sensation. Gods, gods, gods.

"Reclaim your essence!"

The words pierced my ears and struck my brain. And then I felt nothing, a sublime relief.

When I opened my eyes, the fires within the circle were all gone, though the scent of wet hay lingered. It was dark and smokey and I felt filthy.

Taro was shouting. "There's blood all over her!"

Was there? It took far too much effort to move either head or limb to look.

"The poison is bleeding out of her." Cree was chillingly calm.

"Or maybe she's bleeding to death!"

"Keep your hold on her hand. She is taking blood from you."

There was something wrong with mixing blood from different people. I knew that. I just couldn't remember what the danger was, or what it meant.

"Don't touch anything," Cree said. "Don't move from your positions. This isn't finished yet." She went to each corner of the cellar, dousing the flames with a handful of powder. I didn't understand how that worked, a dash of powder putting out fire.

"Thank you," Cree said, and I knew she wasn't talking to either of us.

The salt she had lined around me she dug up with one of the rods she had sunk into the ground. She mixed it up in the soil, then poured more salt over it. "Thank you."

She plucked up the remaining rods, and when she had the last one in her hands, she said again, "Thank you."

"For what?" Taro asked her.

She didn't answer. From her bag she took out shorter, slimmer rods and she stuck them into the dirt in roughly the same locations as the first set. She lit them, and though none of them held a flame, they immediately began to smoke, thin white lines curving up from the tips. The smoke smelled nice, clean and refreshing, a little like mint.

All this smoke. I wondered if any of the food in the cellar was still fit for eating.

Cree knelt beside Taro, her hands clasped on her knees, her head bowed.

"Can't I—"

Cree shushed Taro sharply. He shut up.

So we just waited, in silence. I didn't know for what. I wished I could sleep. I was too tired to sleep. And too filthy.

And then, in time, she reached out and separated my hand from Taro's. The fact that both of our hands were smeared with unexpected amounts of blood should have probably been alarming to me, but I was beyond strong emotions. Cree plucked out the bob and placed it in a handkerchief, which she tied around Taro's neck.

Another bottle appeared from her bag, and in this was a liquid, clear and just a little thicker than water. This Cree slowly poured over me, over my forehead, temple to temple, hairline to eyebrows, and then my face, throat, torso and limbs, all very thorough, with the same intimacy she'd shown during my earlier examination.

That should have bothered me more than it did. I just didn't care. I was just happy the pain was gone, and the nausea.

"Thank you," Cree said once she'd finished with my feet. She untied the handkerchief from Taro's neck and tied it around my own. It was awkward, because I couldn't shift my head to help her.

Once the new rods had burned down to small stubs, she removed them from the dirt and threw them into her bag. Then she put her hands flat on the dirt, bowing until her forehead touched the floor. "Thank you," she said, and the difference in her tone told me this whole thing was over.

So. That was casting. It was real.

I would panic about that later. When I wasn't so exhausted.

"You can get dressed, Shintaro," she said, rising to her feet and shaking dirt from her robe.

Taro tried to stand, only to flop over on the floor.

"Don't worry. It's natural to be weak. Dunleavy has taken a great deal from you."

"How am I going to get her back upstairs?"

I laughed. For some reason that question struck me as hilarious.

"I will assist you."

And, oh, wasn't that an exercise in graceless danger? Carrying me was beyond Taro at that point, which meant he and Cree sort of dragged me up the stairs between them, each with one of my arms around their shoulders. There were several moments when someone nearly lost their balance. It was hysterical.

And of course, I was still naked. Later I would be pathetically relieved that there was no one else there to see me.

Cree directed us to Taro's suite rather than my own, though I balked at being laid on his clean sheets. "Filthy," I mumbled as they sat me down on the side of the bed, and I let myself fall back. I didn't think I could sit up unassisted if I tried.

"Yes, and you'll remain filthy until I come back to see you tomorrow. Neither of you will wash anything, not even your hands or face."

"You can't be serious." Taro's lip curled in disgust.

"Lie down." She left the room without waiting to see if she was obeyed.

Taro shifted me so I was properly stretched out on the bed. "How do you feel?"

"Don't know."

"Think any of what she did down there did any good?"

"Don't know."

And I didn't want to think about it. At least, not yet. The very idea of casting spells, that something so powerful and limitless existed for anyone who could read a book, was appalling. People were too stupid to be trusted with that sort of thing. People were too avaricious. And too vengeful. The possibilities were terrifying, and I was too tired to be terrified. I would be terrified later.

Taro sat on the other side of the bed. He was shaking, and his eyes seemed a little unfocused. "You all right?" I asked.

"Don't know," he answered with the tiniest smile.

In time, Cree came back into the room, carrying a tray with a jug and two mugs. "This is water," she explained, filling the mugs. "This is all you are to consume between now and my return. Neither of you will be able to tolerate anything else in your stomach, and vomiting when you're this drained can be dangerous." She gave Taro one mug and put a strong arm under my shoulders to lift me up and have me drink the water, whether I wanted it or not.

"You both need to sleep," said Cree. "Shintaro, I want you to lock the door behind me. I'll be leaving a note for your colleagues, instructing them not to disturb you. Should you somehow end up speaking with any of them before I return, you are to tell them I took you downstairs to sweat the illness out. No mention of casting to anyone. Understood?"

She gave each of us a hard look, and I was sure it would have been most effective had I not been so desperate for sleep.

"Sure," I muttered.

"Of course," said Taro.

She nodded and moved away from the bed, and I had no idea whether Taro followed her to lock the door, because I fell asleep.

I woke to pounding on the door, my heart leaping into triple time, because pounding on the door was never a good thing. I heard Taro swearing, and there was movement, and then I heard him shout out an inquiry, but I didn't hear an answer.

It turned out to be Cree. "What's wrong?" I asked, feeling confused and dizzy.

She was clean again, her hair tightly coiled at the back, her dress of simple clean lines and a delicate fabric unsuited to any kind of labor. She looked completely respectable. No one would think she'd been chanting in the basement with multi-colored fire dancing around her.

"Nothing," she said. "I told you I would be back."

It was morning already? I rubbed at my eyes, which felt gritty. So did my fingers, and I looked at my hand, which, to my surprise, was streaked with some kind of orange reddish sub-stance. And suddenly I felt just disgusting.

Cree put me through another examination, involving more little strips, and at the end of it declared all the niyacin had been cleared from my system.

And, really, I couldn't believe it. It was all so unlikely, to be so throughly sick so quickly, and to be cured so quickly.

Though I said nothing, Cree seemed to know what I was thinking. "How is your stomach?"

I'd been trying not to think about it. Now that I did, it cramped painfully. "Empty."

"You're hungry."

"That adjective seems somehow inadequate."

"Shintaro, how does she feel?"

"Excuse me?"

"Is she fevered or clammy?"

He put a hand to my forehead, my cheek, and then my throat. "No. She feels good. Normal."

"And her eyes?"

"They've lost their glaze."

My eyes were glazed? "But I'm so tired," I complained.

"Of course you are." You idiot. "You were poisoned, or as good as, and you lost a lot of blood last night. You won't be back to full health for weeks. But you will be back to full health. Provided you don't do anything stupid." She looked at Taro, who was leaning against the wall looking awful, the disarray of his hair crazed as opposed to sexy, his white shirt and black trousers wrinkled and encrusted with various stains. His face, pale with wrinkles about the eyes, had dabs of the same orange red that was streaked all over my hands and arms. "She needs lots of broth, and tea with high amounts of sugar and cream. No coffee, nothing with alcohol. Tomorrow, add fruit and greens, fresh. Nothing dried. The next day, you can add cheese and small amounts of meat. Don't touch that bread. I want you to bring it to me. If there's as much niyacin in it as I suspect, it isn't safe for anyone, whether they're sensitive to the powder or not."

It couldn't be the bread. I refused to believe Ben had baked niyacin powder, which he knew I reacted badly to, into bread that he had then calmly watched me eat. That was unbelievably cold-blooded. And why would he do it? He had never shown anything but reverence for Sources and Shields.

There had to be another explanation.

Cree was packing the last of her things. "I am having a dinner," she said. "All of the guests are people you know. I expect your attendance as payment for my services."

Really, we didn't have to pay her, but I tried not to be an ungrateful wench when I could help it. "Be honored," I said.

"Thank you so much for all you've done," Taro added. "We're aware of the significance."

"Are you?" she asked.

"We are."

She had either cast a spell, or had pretended to cast a spell. Which it was wouldn't matter to the law. She had put an enormous amount of trust in us, trust we hadn't earned.

"Good. I will write to you about the details. And Shintaro, while I understand your desire to attend to Dunleavy, your body experienced something traumatic last night. You need rest, too. Share the burden. Understood?"

"Yes, ma'am."

"Good. Let me know if there are any further problems."

"Thank you," I called out as she left, not sure if she heard me, my voice was so weak.

I pushed the blankets aside and dragged my legs over the side of the bed. They were heavy and barely felt like they were attached to me, just dead loads I needed to shift around with other parts of my body.

"Where do you think you're going?" Taro demanded.

"Bath."

"You need sleep."

"Bath first." And then something to eat, and then sleep. I was disgusting, filthy, in every crack and crevice. If I weren't so tired, my state of filthiness would have been making me crazy. I felt like I hadn't been clean in months.

"Lee."

"Bath," I insisted.

"Fine, then." He took me by the shoulders to pull me from the bed.

It was Taro's bedroom. I wouldn't call Taro a vain lad, unless I was trying to wind him up, but he did have more mirrors than I did. So I got a good look at myself that I could have done without.

Those orange streaks were all over my face and throat, all over my body bizarre patterns with no regularity. There were cleaner bits around my eyes, cleaner strips down my cheeks. And the substance, whatever it was, had gotten into my hair, creating clumps and patches all around my face. I looked demonic. "What is it?"

"You were bleeding, Lee. It was coming out through your

skin." Taro shuddered. "I'd never seen anything like it. I thought you were bleeding to death right in front of me." He took a few slow breaths. "Then Cree poured that stuff all over you, and I guess it turned the blood orange."

How thoroughly disgusting. I could have done just fine without knowing any of that.

I hated mirrors.

# Chapter Twenty-six

Bathing turned out to be an unanticipated exercise in brute force, the garbage on my skin proving to be somewhat resistant to soap and water. The water, being cold, was little help until Firth, bless her, brought up two kettles full of hot water. That made shifting the orange sludge a little easier. And then Taro washed my hair, which felt almost luxurious. All the effort was worth it—it was wonderful to finally be clean—but it was exhausting, and by the time we were done I was too tired to eat.

When we moved back to Taro's bed, the linens had been changed, and Taro curled around me. I felt comfortable and safe. I slept.

It was night again when I woke, and I was ravenous. Taro was still asleep beside me, and I was tempted to rejoin him, but at this point my hunger was almost overpowering.

My exit from the bed was not graceful, but Taro didn't stir. Lords, I was so tired, feeling weighed down just everywhere. But hunger could provide great motivation.

The residence wasn't as quiet as it usually was. When I reached the bottom of the stairs, I heard a gaggle of voices from the parlor, and it was so rare to have so many of the Pairs in the house at the same time that I was drawn away from the kitchen.

Beatrice and Benedict weren't there. On watch at the Stall, no doubt. But all the others were, talking about the disaster that had happened the day before. Apparently more people had died than the collapse of the bridge had really warranted, simply because of the lack of organization in the rescue and relief efforts.

Maybe if Cree had been there, she'd have been able to do some real good.

I wasn't going to think about that yet.

"Dunleavy!" Firth cried out, putting aside a cup of tea. "You look awful."

Her Shield gave an amused eye roll at that. "Have a seat, Mallorough. We have some soup on the stove. I'll get you a bowl."

What was going on with those two? Wasn't I still a sexual deviant? Or had my trials of the day before cleansed away the perversion from my activities?

Manners prodded me to object. I didn't. The walk to the kitchen, after the trek down the stairs, seemed an impossible journey to make right then, so I collapsed in the chair closest to the entrance to the room.

"Where is Shintaro?" Wilberforce asked.

"Asleep."

Wilberforce, on the other hand, hadn't changed at all. It was refreshing. "Is he all right?" Wilberforce stood. "Maybe I should check on him."

"Don't you dare wake him," I ordered with less heat than I liked. "He needs sleep."

"But really, I should just make sure he—"

"Sit down, Franklin!" LaMonte barked.

Wilberforce sat.

I pressed my hand against my lips to hold down the insane urge to giggle.

"Now that you're up and about, Dunleavy," said LaMonte, leaning back on the settee with legs crossed and hands laced together, "you can tell us what went on here yesterday." The fact that I didn't know what he was talking about showed on my face. "When that woman was here."

I still hadn't had a chance to properly think things through. I didn't want to talk about it yet. Or ever, really, but certainly not yet.

But LaMonte had been there that day, had been there long enough to know something odd was going on, and if I didn't keep him happy, he had the power to make things really difficult for Taro and me. Possibly Cree as well. And really, if someone was casting spells in the residence, didn't LaMonte and the others have a right to know? Even though I resented being ambushed as soon as I stuck my head in the door?

So, start at the beginning. "I became very ill. The only healer we could get, because of the bridge collapsing, was someone Taro and I met through a friend. Soon after getting here, she realized I was having a bad reaction to the niyacin powder Ben had been putting in the poultices for my hand." I didn't want to reveal that Cree had also thought it was in the bread. That was a serious allegation, and I wasn't going to speak about it without some kind of proof. "Where is Ben?" I wanted to talk to him and get this cleared up.

LaMonte frowned. "I haven't seen him since the other day. He left a note saying he needed to be with his daughter."

All right, that looked bad, but I still couldn't start throwing accusations about. "Does the note say when he's coming back?"

"No," said Wilberforce.

"He's been treating your hand for weeks," said LaMonte. "You just suddenly got ill with no warning?"

"You were taken off the roster ages ago," said Stone, handing me a mug of broth. "I thought that was because of your reaction to niyacin."

I'd forgotten I'd told her that. "It was."

"Did you not tell Ben you couldn't have niyacin powder?" LaMonte demanded.

"I did." This was going to come out whether I wanted it to or not.

"And he kept giving it to you?"

"We don't know what happened. That's why I want to talk to Ben." My conscience prodded me on, even though it was a little late. "Has anyone, over the past couple of days, eaten bread that Ben baked that had a lot of nuts in it?"

"What a bizarre question," LaMonte said dryly.

"The healer thinks I actually consumed the powder, and the bread was all I'd had to eat that day. She said it wouldn't be safe for anyone to eat."

"Why the hell would Ben put niyacin in bread?" Firth asked.

"I have no idea."

"For Zaire's sake, Dunleavy!" LaMonte threw up his hands. "Don't be so naive. He was trying to harm you."

"But why would he? It doesn't make sense. And it's a stupid way to kill someone. Everyone would suspect him."

"They would have a hard time determining what had killed you once you were dead," said Stone. "And even if someone did, Ben might be able to get away with claiming it was some kind of accident."

"I haven't seen the bread you're speaking of," said Firth. "I went out myself to get some because we were out." The others echoed her.

"So he must have disposed of it," said LaMonte. "And given this latest development, I think it's time we revealed the other piece of information we have about Ben."

I knew what he was talking about. "I don't think it's any more appropriate now than it was then."

"Then you're a fool," he snapped. "Everyone, Ben's daughter has been arrested for the murder of Mayor Izen."

And cue the outrage, the demands as to why we hadn't told them, and the assertions that they knew there had been something strange about Ben. I let LaMonte handle the bulk of the questions. He had the energy for it.

"All right, that's enough," LaMonte ordered. "We did what we did, right or wrong. What's important now is how we proceed. Franklin, I think you need to find a Runner. They need to know what's going on."

"We're jumping to conclusions," I objected.

"That's for a Runner to decide. Please, Franklin."

Wilberforce was torn. I could see it on his face. He was delighted to be singled out by LaMonte. He was offended to be sent on an errand. I guessed which impulse would win and was proven right when Wilberforce went scurrying out of the room.

I thought calling in a Runner was too hasty, and I couldn't believe Ben had been poisoning me deliberately. It just didn't make sense. I knew I wasn't beloved by all, but surely I'd never aggravated anyone to the point that they would seriously go to the effort of killing me. Aside from Creol, that is, and he'd been crazy. And I'd always treated Ben well, hadn't I? And he knew as well as anyone that killing me would kill Taro. Surely Ben didn't hate me enough to kill Taro.

I couldn't believe anyone could hate me that much.

"Why did that Cree woman say you were contagious?" LaMonte asked.

Ah, hell. I'd forgotten that. It didn't work with the truth that I'd been poisoned. "She said the treatment was . . . unorthodox. It would be dangerous to have it interrupted in the middle, and I guess she figured telling you I was contagious was the best way to avoid interference."

"Unorthodox?" That was Hammad, LaMonte's Shield, who rarely spoke, so it always surprised me a little whenever he did. "What does that mean?"

"That I sat in the cellar for hours while the table burned." Naked, but no one needed to know that. "It was quite disgusting."

"I heard—" said LaMonte, and he cut himself off.

What the hell did he hear? He was supposed to have been out of the damned house before anything was done. If he got Cree arrested, oh what a bastard.

"You just seemed in considerable distress," said LaMonte, his expression virtually unreadable.

That wasn't what he'd planned on saying.

"I was. She needed to do something kind of extreme, to get all the niyacin out."

"This is why we no longer have a dicing table?" Stone asked. "And the cellar smells something like what I imagined a bordello smells like?"

Williams's bordello hadn't smelled anything like the cellar did once Cree was done with it. Maybe cheaper bordellos did.

"Not to mention the cuts on your arms and on your face," Firth added.

"It was all about getting the niyacin out," I said. "The cuts to let the niyacin out, the burning stuff to draw the niyacin out."

"And this all worked?" Hammad asked, looking dubious.

I shrugged. "It seems to have. I'm dead tired, but I feel cleaner, somehow. She says, though, that it'll be weeks before I'm completely back to normal."

"Whatever that means," Firth said with a smirk.

It was close to an hour before Wilberforce returned with a Runner, an extremely young man who didn't normally work in our neighborhood. He introduced himself as Runner Calvin and explained that most of the Runners were still dealing with the many repercussions of the collapsed bridge.

LaMonte wanted to oversee my interview with the Runner. The Runner politely refused to allow it. I almost liked him for that. We went to the private dining room and the young man— really, did he even shave?—sat across the table from me.

"The excitable fellow who brought me here," he began, and I was even more impressed with him, "said you'd been poisoned. You look well for it."

"The healer said I'd been given niyacin, which I reacted to badly."

"Who is this healer?"

I almost answered, realizing just in time that Cree was unlikely to appreciate having a Runner showing up at her premises demanding answers that may lead to further uncomfortable questions. "I will suggest to her that she should speak with you."

"How about you just give me her name?"

"How about I just have her contact you?"

He scowled. "Are you wasting my time?"

"I might be," I admitted. "I don't really know what happened. The healer said I was given niyacin. I have no reason to doubt her, but I don't know anything about it."

"The excitable fellow said your servant poisoned you on purpose."

"He is not our servant." I knew my precision irritated him, but saying Ben was our servant had a host of inappropriate implications. He was a servant of the Triple S, not its individual members.

"Do you think he gave this niyacin to you on purpose, knowing it could kill you?"

It looked like he had. I didn't want to believe it. Or admit it. "I don't know."

"What has he said about all this?"

"I haven't seen him since I got ill." I told him about the note. I told him I hadn't seen it myself, and I didn't know whether Ben had more than one daughter, though I assumed he was with Sara. Calvin continued to press me for Cree's name, and I refused to tell him. Then he insisted on going into Ben's room, ignoring my objections.

"He's done a runner," he announced from inside the room.

I was waiting by the door, torn between respecting Ben's privacy and wanting to make sure the Runner didn't do anything to his stuff. Torn between my duty to watch this stranger in our home and my desperation to sit down. Leaning against the threshold wasn't going to be good enough for long. "He's what?"

And out of nowhere, LaMonte appeared. "What's going on?"

"Your servant has packed everything up," said Calvin, and I could hear him opening and closing drawers in quick succession. "Unless someone else has been in here and cleared everything out."

"We wouldn't dream of intruding into Ben's personal space," LaMonte chided.

"Clearly you should have," Calvin retorted. "Where's the note he left?"

The note had been thrown away. No one was able to find it.

Calvin felt all this needed to be reported. He ordered us to stay out of Ben's room and to look for anything that might be Ben's throughout the residence, though not to touch anything we found. Then he left.

Taro had risen by this time and was demanding to know what was going on. I was ready to crawl back into bed, my brain clouding with exhaustion. I asked LaMonte to fill Taro in and went back to bed.

It was dark when I woke again. A candle was lit on the table by the bed, and in that light I could see the steam rising from the mug of broth, also on the table and beside a glass of water. Taro was seated by the bed, watching me.

I drained down the water first, then started on the broth. Its heat was soothing and it filled my stomach pleasantly.

"I could demand an explanation as to why you came to this bed instead of mine," Taro commented.

A quick glance about told me, yes, I was in my own bed. I was surprised. I'd made no conscious decision about where to sleep; I'd just gone where my feet took me.

"I imagine, though," Taro continued, "that you're not up to much of an argument right now, so how about I do all the talking?"

Uh, all right. And it was the least he could do, since he had evidently decided to start an uncomfortable conversation while I was trapped in bed.

"I've been trying to understand why you were wearing the harmony bob on your underclothes the other day."

Oh lords. I didn't want to talk about that. But then, he'd just said I didn't have to, didn't he? So maybe the timing was actually excellent. Maybe.

"You would have no expectation that I would see it. Not that I think you would wear it just to please me. You don't do anything just to please me."

Prat. I did, too.

"So that means you have been wearing it all along, and I have to wonder why. And why you would wear the bob in secret, obviously with some effort of hiding that fact from me, as I haven't seen it on you during prior opportunities. It's made me very curious."

I took another sip of soup.

"Why do you think I've always worn the harmony bob?" he asked.

Hey, he'd just said I didn't have to talk in this conversation. I just raised my eyebrows and drank my soup.

"It did amuse me, of course. People wrapping up so many expectations in these little trinkets. But I was also making a public gesture. Except, clearly, you never perceived that. You know"—he smiled with just one corner of his mouth—"you can be quite clever in some ways but astoundingly oblivious in others."

People could stop calling me stupid anytime now.

"I shouldn't have to do this, I know," he went on. "It's embarrassing, and unmanly, and the very idea of it threatens to send me into a full-body cringe. But you'll never clue into it on your own, and sometimes you just have to do something flat out humiliating in order to get what you want. You taught me that, on that damned island."

Bastard.

"So here it is. It was a public gesture of my fealty, if you will, to you. An announcement that I love you, and will do so forever."

I choked on my soup.

"And so you laugh," he said with disgust. "That's what you do. Strip all the finer attributes out of everything."

"I wasn't laughing," I protested. "I was surprised."

"Why should you be surprised? What have I done to make you doubt that I love you?"

Nothing. Nothing at all. Nor had he done anything to make me believe he loved me. Not that way.

Unless he had been expecting me to take seriously all those off-the-cuff comments he'd made about what would be happening in the future.

This was a horribly uncomfortable conversation, even without having to contribute to it.

"I take it back," said Taro. "You're not clever at all." He leaned forward, so far forward that he could rest his forehead against mine. "I love you. I plan to continue loving you for the foreseeable future. And I would really appreciate it if you sent Doran packing."

I suddenly had trouble breathing. This was nothing like what I'd been expecting.

"Poor girl," he said. "I've thrown you into a panic."

Not a panic. Of course not. There was nothing to panic about. But the very idea of the Stallion of the Triple S telling me he loved me, and that he wanted to have it demonstrated as something more than a passing fancy, it was something out of a farce. The handsome lord did not fall in love with the merchant's daughter, not in real life.

Not that I doubted his sincerity. Taro was never cruel, and he didn't take things as lightly as many would believe. But this was just unnatural. And really, no one swore lifelong love outside of poetry and music. Because people couldn't know how they would feel about things ten or more years in the future.

"Do you love me?" he asked.

"Of course."

A small quirk of a smile. "Of course," he mocked. "And do you wish to do so permanently?"

Permanently? That seemed like an awful long time. Unrealistic, too. But Taro and I did ridiculous things all the time, usually forced into it by circumstances. Why not do something crazy purely for the hell of it? "Yes."

"And you'll send Doran packing."

"Yes." That wasn't working anyway. And I felt like a skeevy wench for ever entertaining the idea of keeping Doran hanging on until things with Taro settled down.

This was not what I'd ever contemplated for myself whenever I thought about who a long-term partner might be. Taro was not calm. He drew everyone's eye whenever he walked down the street. We liked none of the same things.

And maybe none of that mattered. I'd have to think about that. When I wasn't so tired.

Taro kissed me on the forehead, the chin, and each cheek. It felt strangely ritualistic, and although I'd never been fond of ritual, there was something calming about his gestures.

"Drink the rest of your soup," he said. "Then I'll let you get back to sleep."

Seriously, this whole thing deserved a joke or three, but I was too tired to come up with anything good. I sipped at the broth, until the mug was empty. Taro took the mug and blew out the candle before kissing me on the forehead again and leaving.

I snuggled back into bed, feeling relaxed and full and content.

# Chapter Twenty-seven

The next morning, I woke aching and tired, filthy and thirsty. Taro ordered me to stay in bed and of course I ignored him. I was tired of lying down. And I wanted to be in a public part of the house. I felt like I'd been hidden away from the other Pairs for far too long. They had all seemed genuinely concerned about my illness, and I felt I hadn't given them enough credit for the basic decency they all habitually displayed despite their annoying quirks. So I decided to go to the kitchen, easily the most frequented room in the residence, with Taro trailing me anxiously.

And, of course, the only person there was LaMonte.

"Has anyone seen Ben?" I asked him.

"No," he answered bluntly. "I'd like to speak to you, Dunleavy." He glanced at Taro. "Alone."

Taro didn't leave. He did cross his arms and glare at LaMonte, though.

And LaMonte smiled, which was not an expression I was used to seeing on his face. "Has the definition of 'alone' changed and no one told me?"

Taro bristled, and I said, "Whatever you want to say to me can be said in front of Taro."

"Really? My dear, I had no idea you'd developed the ability to read minds."

All right. I deserved that.

"The misunderstanding is my fault, of course. People do have the unfortunate tendency to say 'talking to' when they mean 'talking with.' I'd like you to participate in this conversation, and whenever you and Shintaro are together, you have the distressing habit of letting him do all the talking. You are the one I want to speak with."

Well, what if I didn't want a conversation with him?

LaMonte sighed with impatience when Taro didn't move. "Do you really think you need to protect her from me?" he asked the younger Source.

"She has had a very hard time. She does not need a lecture."

"I'm not going to lecture her. Don't be ridiculous."

"You never think you're lecturing," Taro retorted. "Talk about ridiculous."

We were all getting ridiculous. We'd be here all day. "I don't feel as bad as I look," I said to Taro.

Taro scowled. I waved a hand toward the door. Taro huffed as he left.

LaMonte looked at the closed door for a moment. "Might he be listening at the door?"

Obnoxious creature. "Taro does not lurk about eavesdropping on people."

He held up his hands in a gesture meant to be placating. "He seems to be crowding you at times."

Not that I'd noticed, but we could continue trading insults or I could hear what he had to say and move on to something more restful. "What's on your mind?"

LaMonte sat on the stool next to the one I was occupying. I noticed with a shock that his hair was rapidly thinning. When had that started happening? "I understand it's been confirmed that Ben had been trying to . . . well, to kill you."

"Nothing's been confirmed," I objected.

"He moved out without telling us."

I wasn't denying that it looked bad, only that it actually proved anything.

"And his daughter has been arrested for killing Izen for his ashes, for the use in casting spells."

"Apparently."

"It is possible that he might have been killing you for the same reason."

"No one has suggested that." It never even occurred to me.

"It is a logical assumption, given Ben's circumstances."

I didn't want to agree. There was a certain logic to it, I supposed, but why would anyone want my ashes? I was privileged, but not particularly lucky. No more so than the other Shields in the residence, who had never been put in the position of having to kill someone, or sent off to a place where Shields and Sources weren't respected.

"And that woman who was here, that healer, she cast a spell to heal you."

Now I was panicking. "Oh, no. Nothing like that. As if I'd—"

He put up a hand and I stopped talking. My automatic response to his gesture annoyed me, and I wanted to go on talking just to demonstrate that I knew he had no authority over me, but I had no convincing lies to say about Cree's use of spells anyway.

"There is something going on," he said. "Something monumental. This belief in casting, it's not just in High Scape. I've been writing to Sources at other sites, Shidonee's Gap, Seldom Go By, everywhere that I know someone. It's not as prevalent everywhere else as it is here, but there are incidents happening all over, indicating that there are more and more people believing in casting. That is the alarming thing to me, that it is happening in places outside of High Scape. There are reasons why people would want something to believe in here. It has been explained to me that the Harsh Summer shattered people's understanding of how the world works, and they need something they feel they have some control over."

I wondered who had been talking to LaMonte, because it was clearly someone who had made a considerable impression on him. But perhaps that person wasn't as knowledgeable as LaMonte thought. Because people had been believing in casting for a long time, for generations. How did anyone explain that?

I wasn't going to tell him that, though. He'd ask how I knew. I'd have to tell him about the illegal books I had. I didn't really think he'd report me to any authorities for it, but there was no telling who else he'd tell, and that could result in nasty repercussions. If I told no one, no one would ever know.

"Many are embracing these beliefs," LaMonte continued. "Others, including the Crown Prince, oppose it, loudly and publicly. Yet the Triple S is doing nothing about any of it. The council doesn't react to questions and hasn't given any public statements. One gets the feeling they are trying to ignore the whole issue."

Well, why wouldn't they? It had nothing to do with them, as far as I knew.

"I was thinking this was just a temporary foolishness. Like that harmony bob Shintaro insists on wearing. I thought people would become bored with it all, and move on to some other fashion. But this isn't like other fashions I've seen. So pervasive, with followers in every class. And there are equal numbers, including the Crown Prince, who are violently opposed to the idea of casting spells. It's becoming a serious criminal offense. And I've been hearing of episodes in schools, like in Far Flung, where a teacher was teaching spells from a book. She was released from her position and dragged out of the school for an immediate flogging that nearly killed her."

Good hell, what was wrong with people?

"Everyone, everyone, is dealing with this in some way, to support it or deny it or criminalize it. Except the Triple S. I've sent them a whole series of letters. They refuse to answer in any way. There has been no guidance as to how we, as individual members of the Triple S, are to react to all this."

Why did he have to be told how to react to the trend? He was so quick to behave as though he were the authority in all things, yet he was equally quick to subjugate his opinion to that of the Triple S. Such an interesting contradiction.

"It isn't wise to ignore something so powerful."

I would have never expected to hear from LaMonte any criticism of the Triple S, no matter how oblique.

"Whether casting is actually real or not, the belief in it and the reactions to it are having a significant impact on people, and this impact shows no sign of abating. On the contrary, the influence is growing."

He had a point. People did seem to be going crazy over this thing.

"So I am going to ask you a question. And I want your honest answer. I want the truth. I believe you owe me that."

I wondered where he got the idea that I owed him anything in particular.

"Do you believe that people can cast actual, effective spells?"

Ah, hell. The last question I'd expected, and the question I'd least wanted to answer. I'd been happy enough continuing to avoid thinking about it.

I could ignore what was going on right in front of my face with the best of them, but really, I wasn't stupid. And I had been thinking about things, remembering things, whether I liked it or not. The whole time the Reanists were killing aristocrats in a bid to stop natural disasters from striking High Scape, there were no natural events, and since the Reanists were stopped, the natural events had returned, though at a greatly reduced rate.

The people of Flatwell had been great believers in ritual. I'd thought it all superstitious nonsense, the bad luck the troupe had believed in greatly assisted by a dangerous lifestyle and the deliberate interference of Atara's murderous son. But the fact was that a member of the troupe died every time they lingered at a place for too long, and unless Yesit had spent all of his life trailing the troupe with no one noticing, it seemed the belief that Yesit's curse was the cause of all their difficulties might have had some merit.

And then there were more recent events, the bizarre nature of the fire during which I'd burned my hand, and Cree's ritual in the cellar. I was better. That hadn't been a medical treatment. At least, no kind of medical treatment I had ever heard of.

No one had ever told me spells were nothing more than a figment of imagination. No one had ever talked to me about spells at all, not while I was growing up. When I'd seen them in plays or read about them in books, I had dismissed them as fantasy. It was an assumption I'd made. Most of my assumptions were disastrous.

I didn't want to say it. I hated the very idea of it. The possibility that spells could influence the natural order undermined everything I had learned about everything. How did I know what to believe in?

"Dunleavy." LaMonte put the tips of his fingers on the back of my uninjured hand. "Stop."

I was breathing too fast. And hard. I was close to hyperventilating. I forced myself to pull in a long, deep breath and released it slowly. I was humiliated over losing control in front of LaMonte.

How dare he ask me, anyway? There was no good reason for him to do so, except to find yet another reason to sneer at me.

"I suppose that's my answer, then," said LaMonte.

"It's not that simple," I responded. "I don't feel comfortable giving a solid affirmative. I don't know enough about it, and part of me is waiting for the announcement that this is all a big hoax. But I've seen enough to know that it's definitely possible that there is real power behind it all."

Let the derision come.

LaMonte sighed. "I was afraid of that."

Why? Because it was now his duty to report me to the Triple S for being insane?

"I was hoping I could continue to dismiss this all as some form of temporary madness."

"You and me both," I muttered.

He actually smiled again. That had to be his quota for the year. "You will be well again?" he asked.

"Yes, I believe I will."

"Good," he said, and he cleared his throat before leaning forward to tap the back of my good hand. "I'll go tell Shintaro he can come back in."

"Wait."

He paused.

Really, I was so stupid. "Stone and Firth, they've said Taro and I are perverted, that the relationship we have is wrong." I wasn't going to say "sex" to LaMonte. I'd eat my boots first.

"So they've said."

I really didn't need the confirmation that they'd been talking about us when we weren't there. "What do you think?" Why the hell was I asking him? Why was I asking for more abuse? What was wrong with me?

"Why, Dunleavy, you've never cared whether I approved of you or not before. Why the change now?"

The weevil was playing with me, damn it. So I didn't answer. I was very good at not answering.

Finally, he got tired of waiting. "Like everything else, there will be those who believe it is a vile defilement of the natural order, those who think it is the most natural and the purest relationship in life, and those who fall somewhere between the two points."

"Where do you fall?"

"Dunleavy, it has nothing to do with me."

I was clenching my teeth to prevent myself from bursting out with something inappropriate. Was this really LaMonte? Where had this LaMonte been all the other times he appeared to be commenting on matters that had nothing to do with him?

"This is about you and Shintaro. It's not about a Shield and a Source. Only the two of you can decide what's right for you."

Well, as answers go, that was about as useful as wheels on a horse, but I supposed it was a little reassuring. I'd really expected him to castigate me brutally.

"Now, can I get Shintaro?"

"Yes, thank you very much."

I should have expected Risa to show up later that day. Whenever I was involved with Runners in any way, she came around. I couldn't believe that her superiors really felt it necessary to soothe my feelings by having her act as some kind of liaison for me. I thought it far more likely that she learned of my involvement and came around just to make sure I was all right and that the information the Runners were getting was correct. It was the sort of thing she would do.

My interpretation of her actions was confirmed when she showed up bearing a bundle of items meant to soothe me during my recovery. A berry wine meant to quiet the mind, a cream soap to soften the skin, a tea smelling of sandalwood to sooth the stomach—and chocolate for, well, chocolate.

All of these items were presented in beautiful jars and boxes. All of them cost more money than Risa should be spending. In my current state of exhaustion I was almost moved to tears that Risa would be so generous with me when she couldn't afford it. It infuriated me that there was nothing I could do to ease Risa's financial straits.

Well, nothing ethical, anyway.

After hearing about my poisoning and Ben's possible involvement in it, Risa sent Taro away. "Business is done. I want to enjoy myself now."

Taro scowled. It was cute.

"Stop hovering like a crow. I'll see to anything she needs."

"What is with everyone today?" he grumbled. He kissed me on the cheek before leaving.

Risa waited until she was sure Taro was gone before saying, "He's been acting strange since you two got back."

"I hadn't noticed." Of course I had, but I wasn't going to talk about that to outsiders.

"That's not surprising," she smirked. "You don't seem to notice a lot."

I sighed. I was getting very tired of having my flaws thrust in my face. What was it about me that invited people to speak to me that way?

Risa sobered. "All right, fine. What I have to say now is important, and I want you to promise not to tell anyone else about it, all right? Not even Shintaro."

"I can't promise not to tell until I know what it is." I tried to avoid making blind promises. That way led to idiocy and melodrama.

"Damn it, Dunleavy, this is serious. You don't have any idea how visible you are. As a Shield, I mean. People watch you, they talk about you, and sometimes information gets to the wrong ears."

I stared at her. People watched me? What the hell for? Didn't they have things to do? "You're not clarifying things."

She rolled her eyes. "Fine. You were seen buying—or requisitioning, whatever you people call it—a book of spells in the market. And the person who saw you reported you to Headquarters." What a dirty thing to do, watching and eaves-dropping and tattling. "I said there was no way you'd have done anything like that, that you thought it was all bunk and you were above such lunacy, but I would talk to you about it to make sure." She held up a hand when she saw me opening my mouth to speak. "I am sure, having been away so long and then so busy what with fewer Pairs in High Scape, you would not recognize a spell book for what it was had you inadver-tently picked one up. Shields and Sources pick up so many things without thought."

Hey, that made us sound like thieves.

"And then, when you actually did read it, you would prob-ably think it was fiction. Badly written fiction. So you would throw it out. Or even burn it." She put heavy emphasis on the word "burn." "And you would never dream of picking up any-thing so trashy again."

*All right, all right, you don't have to club me in the face with it.* "I promise not to say anything. To anyone."

She nodded. "Good. And it would be great if your Source didn't go so far out of his way to start rumors about having an unnatural ability to heal."

I rubbed my face with my left hand. So much for their promise to keep it quiet. There really was no point in doing anything for anyone anymore. "He can't heal people. He told them that."

"Too bad he can't. There are too many idiots claiming the riverfront areas are cursed, and that's why they're getting sick."

"You said you thought the water was making them sick." I was so tempted to tell her what Taro and I thought we knew, but we had nothing to back it up. In all of our nights of surveillance of the hub, we hadn't once seen a woman come to do anything to the drains with ashes.

"Aye, but no one can figure out how. We can't really prove it. And now people are trying to move into the other areas. Only no one else will take them in. Because they're sick. It's getting nasty."

Really, sometimes it felt like this city was really falling apart. Had it always been so chaotic, and that never made it into the textbooks? Or was I merely living in interesting times?

"You don't want them all landing on your doorstep looking for a miracle."

Too late. "No, I don't." I held the package of tea to my nose and breathed in the scent. It was calming.

"Do you understand what I'm telling you?" Risa prodded.

"Yes." I understood that she suspected we'd been engaging in illegal activities, and she was warning me to stop it and get rid of the evidence. That had to be against the rules of being a Runner. "Thank you."

Risa left shortly thereafter, once more warning me that Ben had not yet been apprehended. I promptly went up to my suite, lit my fireplace and threw all the books and pamphlets in. It irked me to do it. I should never have to destroy books just because I was afraid someone would learn I had them. But people were acting crazy. And anything I did, Taro would share the repercussions.

Besides, I'd already read all the books.

Taro wandered in while I was poking the burning books into ashes. "Am I allowed to be around you now?"

I slanted a look up at him. "I've often been the one sent out of the room."

"Not that often. What are you doing?"

"Taking Risa's advice."

"She advised you to burn your possessions?"

I told him of the warnings Risa had given me.

He sighed as he sat beside me on the floor. "I'm sorry."

"What for? You've done nothing wrong."

"I shouldn't have tried to heal those people. It brought too much attention to us."

Taro, unfortunately, couldn't help bringing attention on himself, the poor lad. "Aye, but what if it had worked? That would have been wonderful."

He seemed to be squirming a little. "That wasn't the real reason I tried."

I waited.

"I just feel so bloody useless here," he confessed heatedly. "No events all this time. There's no point to me being here."

"We're all in the same position when it comes to that," I reminded him. "All the Sources and Shields. That's why they've been transferring Pairs to other sites."

"Aye, but unlike me, channeling isn't the only tool in your kit bag, is it?" he said bitterly. "That damned island proved that."

Ah, that. Damned Flatwell, convincing Taro he was inferior. I wished we'd never gone. I wished he could forget about it. "I'm sorry you feel that way. I don't feel that way about you. I doubt anyone who matters feels that way about you. But you feel that way, and I wish I had the words that would prove to you that you're wrong."

He smirked. "I think that's the longest string of words you've given me in months."

I slapped him up the back of the head. But gently.

And then his inner protections went up.

"No," I said, knowing it was too late. "I'm not strong enough."

"I can't help it!"

He couldn't help it? Of course he could help it. Nothing could force a trained Source to begin to channel.

But he was channeling, so I had to Shield. And the images and tastes and sounds of cliffs and sea tore through me. They flooded my mind and swirled behind my eyes, filling my throat and mouth until I felt I couldn't breathe.

And I couldn't do it. I just wasn't strong enough. I could practically see my Shields shaking from the pounding of the forces. I was going to get us both killed. "I need a Shield!" I shouted as loudly as I could. "Help! Stone! Ladin! Benedict! Hammad! Help!" Please, please, let there be someone within earshot. Someone with the skill to Shield someone else's Source. Please.

"No!" Taro roared. And there was a huge wrenching sensation, painful in its violence. The rise of his protections scraped like a serrated blade across my mind.

What the hell was that? I looked at Taro to ask just that. He was pale and sweaty and shaking. "Are you all right? What happened?"

"I stopped channeling before the disaster was finished."

That was supposed to be impossible. When had he started being able to do that?

I didn't know how he could claim to feel useless when he was developing a new ability every time he turned around.

Then he fainted, and I had other things to worry about.

# Chapter Twenty-eight

Several days later, Taro had gone in search of chocolate, having eaten all of mine. He was pale and complained of a piercing headache. He was also impatient and restless and seemed unable to remain in the residence. So he left. To find chocolate.

After several hours, he still hadn't returned. And now I was the one who was impatient and restless.

He was late, but that meant nothing, I was sure. He had met up with some friends, that was all. He was having a few drinks at a tavern. He had been dancing attendance on me for a while, and then had been laid low with a headache that had taxed him ever since he collapsed from wrenching himself out of a channeling. Of course he needed some time away.

But he had left late in the morning, and now the sun was setting. I was starting to worry.

As I wouldn't have, had we not been sleeping together. Did that mean I had been a heartless, thoughtless wench before, or that I was a nagging, paranoid wench now?

Really, it only made sense that he was lengthening the leash a little. I slept like the dead for long hours at a stretch. When I was awake, I was usually no good for anything more than dragging my sorry posterior from the bed to a chair in the kitchen to a settee in the parlor. I was pretty much confined to the residence.

Maybe that was why I was so restless about Taro. I wasn't worried about him; I envied him. Maybe it was time I ventured out a little, put some muscles back on my legs.

Or maybe not. Just because he said he loved me didn't mean he wanted to spend every waking moment with me. It would be so humiliating if I were to show up and all he felt was exasperation because I would never leave him alone. I would hate to turn into a clinging weed, wrapping around everything in his life.

This was why it was so bad to fall in love. It turned a person into an idiot.

I was in the kitchen brewing coffee—doing it myself as Ben had not yet returned, and no, that didn't prove anything— when I felt Taro's protections lowering. I raised my Shields, of course—I would never do otherwise—but I was furious. He was getting way too cocky with his off-duty channeling, and we'd be having a nice little argument about that when I saw him next.

I quickly realized, however, that Taro wasn't channeling an event that was not in our jurisdiction, or attempting to soothe pain or heal an injury. He was creating an event. He only did that when something was wrong.

I didn't know what to do. I had no idea what kind of difficulty Taro might be in. He might be merely trying to stop someone else from doing something he considered wrong, or he might be in danger. The mere possibility that he might be in jeopardy meant I had to try to find him.

Only there was no way I could channel and search for Taro simultaneously, not properly. I needed help. Risa would have been my first choice, but I didn't know where to find her. I couldn't go out and find her while channeling, either.

I would need to get help from someone in the house. I hated that idea. I would have to ask for a favor from one of my colleagues. Worse, I would have to tell someone how I knew Taro was in trouble. We didn't want people to know he could create disasters. Telling another member of the Triple S would all too likely lead to questions from the Triple S council, something Taro was desperate to avoid.

But it couldn't be avoided. I needed help. So whom should I ask?

The name that first leapt to mind surprised me. Moving as carefully as I could while Shielding, I left the parlor and checked the kitchen and the private dining room before heading up the stairs to LaMonte's suite.

Taro was still channeling. What was going on with him? It was difficult, holding up the Shields so long while climbing up stairs.

I didn't know what I was going to do if LaMonte wasn't in. Panic, I supposed.

I pounded on LaMonte's door. I was so relieved when it opened that I almost couldn't breathe for a moment. I couldn't see his expression all that well—I wasn't really able to focus on that kind of detail—but he was probably annoyed at being interrupted. I didn't care.

"Taro's in trouble," I blurted out.

"What's wrong?"

"I don't know."

"Well, where is he?"

"I don't know."

He probably still looked annoyed.

"Are you Shielding right now?"

"Aye."

"Come in." He took me by the elbow, and the next thing I knew, I was sitting on a settee.

LaMonte surprised me by kneeling before me as opposed to sitting beside me. "What's happening?"

"Taro is in trouble. I need to find him." Why was he making me repeat myself?

"Taro is channeling right now?"

"Aye."

"You're not on duty. Why is he channeling?"

"I don't know. Can you find him?"

"How would I be able to find him?"

"You can feel where the event is." He would have felt the event, like all the other Sources in High Scape, but would have ignored it as he wasn't on duty. Apparently, only my Source felt the need to channel absolutely everything.

"I can't determine its exact location."

Oh, how disappointing. Now what was I going to do?

"Derek might be able to, depending on the nature of the event. He has a knack that way."

Oh, thank gods. Where was Beatrice?

"But why would that information assist you?"

"Does it really matter?"

"If you're going to ask me to do something unorthodox, yes, it does."

I supposed that was fair. Annoying, but fair. "That's where Taro will be."

"And you know this how?"

"He's creating the event. It means he's in trouble."

And that was when I learned that LaMonte was truly a beautiful person. He didn't imply I was lying. He didn't demand to know how Taro could possibly create an event. He merely said, "Wait here. I'll find Derek. Oh." He paused before leaving. "Never tell anyone else what you just told me."

Later, I would need to think more carefully on his words.

Then I had to wait while LaMonte tracked down Beatrice, convinced him we weren't crazy and brought him back. The whole time, Taro was channeling and I was Shielding. Taro was keeping all of the forces moving slowly, which meant he was causing tremors instead of a full-out earthquake. So we had some time. No one was killing him yet.

It was difficult to hold on so long. Luckily, I'd had some practice with that recently.

It was Beatrice who came back to me. "Chris is flagging down a carriage," he told me. It was the first time in my memory that he didn't sound at least slightly petulant. "We're going to find Shintaro."

Oh, thank gods. "You know where Taro is?"

"I can't just pinpoint the location from here."

Then what good was he?

"We'll have to track him down. I can do that."

I supposed it was better than nothing. It was certainly more that I could do. Would it be enough?

"Come with me. Let me guide you. I'll see you get to Shintaro. You just concentrate on Shielding. Don't worry about anything else." He took my wrists and gently urged me to my feet.

It was sweet of him to suggest I just put myself in his hands that way. It wasn't something I could do with anyone other than Taro. It wasn't as though I thought Beatrice would do me any harm. I just didn't know him. Which was a sad thing to admit after living in the same residence so long.

LaMonte had a carriage waiting by the time Beatrice and I reached the front door of the residence. LaMonte climbed into the carriage with me and Beatrice joined the driver up top. The carriage jolted into movement, pressing me hard against the back of my seat, the hooves of the horses clattering loudly against the surface of the street.

I couldn't recall traveling so quickly in a carriage before.

"Get out of the way!" I heard Beatrice bellow. "Move, move, move!"

It appeared Beatrice was taking this seriously. Who would have thought?

People out in the street shouted back. Some of the words were foul.

We took a sharp corner, and I was thrown against LaMonte. We seemed to take another quick corner, and I was forced back against the wall of the carriage. I clenched my fists in an effort to hold on to my Shields.

It was only a few moments later that I realized my left hand was actually digging my nails into LaMonte's thigh. That was embarrassing.

I could swear the next corner the carriage took, a couple of wheels left the ground.

"Don't kill us before we get there!" LaMonte shouted.

"Are we in a hurry or not?"

"All right, then, how about you try not to kill anyone else?"
Another sharp swerve had me tumbling to the floor.

"Don't let go of Shintaro," LaMonte ordered. "Maybe you
should stay down there."

That actually seemed like a good idea, what little thought I
could spare to it. So I stayed on the dirty floor.

There were more curves and corners and people swearing
at us. Then, finally, we began to slow down.

"We're entering the riverfront district," LaMonte commented shortly thereafter.

Huh. There was a reason that was significant. I couldn't
recall it right then.

The carriage slowed down. "Can you see him?" I asked
LaMonte, meaning Taro.

"No. We're not stopping. I believe we're slowing down because Derek has narrowed the search to a particular area. He
has to slow down to determine Shintaro's exact location."

I really hadn't heard much past the word "no." I hated that
we had slowed down, even if that meant no longer getting
thrown about the carriage. We had already taken too long.

And then the forces flowing through Taro intensified.
"Something's happening," I hissed at LaMonte. "We have to go
faster."

"He's going as fast as he can."

That wasn't good enough. I pounded on the side of the carriage. "Hey!" I shouted. "You have to go faster!" I reached for
the window so I could shout through it.

LaMonte grabbed me by a handful of hair and pulled me
back into my seat. "Derek knows how to do this. You do not.
Let him work. Your sole task is to Shield Shintaro. You can't
properly do that if you're worrying about what everyone else
is doing. Settle down."

Bastard. Damn him for being right.

Street after street after street. And despite the fact that we
were going slower, the ride was much bumpier. A couple of

times I was sure we'd lost a wheel and I'd have to swallow down a spurt of panic.

Finally, we stopped. Finally. "Are we there?" Wherever there was. LaMonte was between me and the carriage door. Why wasn't he moving? Was he really going to make me climb over him?

The door opened, and LaMonte still didn't move. Beatrice was standing in the way. "There's something strange going on," he announced. "There's a group, about six, I'd guess. They've got fires lit, and that's never a good thing. Shintaro's there, and I think he's alive. I couldn't see too well, but he seems to be tied up."

"They're doing this out in the open?" LaMonte asked in disbelief.

Beatrice shrugged. "They don't seem to be worried about being seen."

"Good," I said, frustrated with the chatter. "So let's go."

"That's a bad idea," Beatrice objected. "We should bring the Runners here. These people obviously mean harm and they outnumber us. We could just end up tied like Shintaro."

"I don't care," I said. "I'm not wasting more time looking for Runners. They'll kill him before we can get back. Or move him." And if I had to bite and pull hair to get out of that carriage, I would.

LaMonte spared me that humiliation by saying, "I agree with Dunleavy, Derek. We should at least keep watch while you get the Runners."

Beatrice sighed gustily. "Fine. We circled around after we spotted them so we wouldn't be noticed. You take this street up two blocks and then you go left. Follow that street until it ends. They're all gathered up against where the rivers meet, down by the wall. It shields them from the river traffic."

They were at the hub.

And we were, at long last, getting out of the carriage. I let LaMonte lead me down the proper streets. The ground was shaking, but not enough to do significant damage. Taro was developing a delicate touch with that.

There were no hiding places to allow us to stand and watch. The buildings just stopped suddenly and there were no trees, just dead, flattened grass between the last rickety building and the solid stone wall that stood where the three rivers met. Moving any farther would bring us out in the open.

I didn't care. Nor was I concerned about the lack of cover. I didn't need to hide. I knew what Taro could do.

So I started running toward the group. That was surprisingly difficult, running while Shielding Taro, and I couldn't run as fast as I normally could.

"Dunleavy!" LaMonte hissed in horror.

I ignored him. He'd have to run and tackle me if he wanted to stop me, and that would get everyone's attention as easily as anything else.

I didn't want to take the chance he'd try, though. "We're here, Taro!" I shouted. "Bury 'em!" I could barely see him, between the thickening darkness and my focus on my Shielding, but there was his form huddled against the wall.

The forces grew stronger, just for a few moments. There were varying shouts of alarm. But there were also people running around. Whatever Taro was doing, he wasn't burying people. That was something he had done before, and it was the easiest way, I thought, of dealing with these people. But maybe he couldn't bury more than one at a time.

I was hit from behind and struck the ground with a painful pounding. That hurt a hell of a lot, and I got a mouthful of dirt out of it. The weight was heavy on my back. I kicked out and connected with nothing.

"Stop channeling," I called out. I couldn't think while I was Shielding.

The tremors stopped.

That seemed to surprise the person on top of me, who gasped. I pushed at him, and his shock enabled me to wiggle out from under him. He grabbed at my legs and I kicked him in the face. I thought I heard a crunch.

I scrambled free, but I was merely tackled again, by two people. And when we were all on the ground, I heard a voice say, "How fortunate. You were the one we wanted anyway."

That made no sense.

The two pulled me to my feet and then dragged me to the wall next to Taro. And then I saw the problem. Taro was blindfolded. He couldn't see to bury people.

I had little strength left, but I saw a rope in someone's grip. I kicked and I scratched and I bit, and I was able to reach out and pull the cloth from Taro's eyes.

His protections went down, my Shields went up, and the ground began to heave, sharply. Everyone fell, and that was all Taro needed to sink each person far enough into the ground that they couldn't easily escape.

"What the hell was that?"

Heh. We made LaMonte swear.

Six people. Three men, three women. One of them was Ben Veritas.

He really had been trying to kill me.

There were two bonfires going. A table had been knocked over, dumping books and rods and bowls of powder on the ground. Taro was naked except for the ropes that bound him. That wasn't as shocking as the bruises on his face and body. Had he acquired those in the course of his abduction or after his capture?

I thought about suggesting he bury his captors all the way.

Then LaMonte was beside us, and apparently he was one of those people who was always prepared, because he was draping a cloak over Taro's lower half while I worked on the bloodied ropes binding his wrists.

"They wanted to kill me for my ashes," he said. "You were the preferred target, and when that didn't work they went after me."

How could they be so stupid as to try to murder a Pair? Was the alleged power they received from the ashes supposed to prevent them from getting caught? Had that worked for anyone yet? My attack could be explained away as a freak illness, maybe, but how could they disguise this much more blunt assault?

I looked at Ben, who was sunk to the ground up to his knees. He appeared to be wearing some kind of robelike garment of a deep blue. I would have expected him to be angry, glaring at us and shouting. At the very least, he should be trying to free himself as his collaborators were, digging up the soil with fingernails. Instead, he stared down at the ground silently, his shoulders hunched, sort of collapsing in on himself. He seemed pale. I noticed he was trembling.

"It was for my daughter," he said suddenly. "For Sara. She is going to trial. She is going to be hanged."

Only if she was found guilty. And how the hell were our ashes going to influence that? Was there honestly some spell out there that could determine the outcome of a trial?

"Are you claiming she didn't kill the mayor?" Taro demanded.

"What difference does that make?" Ben demanded in return with a flash of heated anger. "She's nothing but a servant. She has no money and no one to speak for her."

In another flash, the anger disappeared, and to my horror, Ben started crying. Loud, hacking sobs that had to hurt. It was painful to watch. It was difficult to believe that he was acting purely to garner our sympathy.

"It's not right," he blubbered. "You have everything, easy lives and food and clothes and everything you ever wanted, just because you're born what you are. You don't even have to work, if you don't want to. And you're not even needed here. High Scape's gone cold and isn't getting any more events. You've all said it. So where's the harm?"

"For gods' sake, man, shut up!" one of the women hissed. Ben didn't even glance at her.

Where's the harm? Was he crazy? "So you used me to get to Taro."

Gasping, Ben raised wet eyes to me. "I didn't need Source Karish," he said. "His death would merely be an unfortunate consequence of yours."

"I thought you needed the ashes from someone lucky."

"A woman of no birth, beauty or exceptional talent," he

said, "Paired with a highly skilled, noble Source. Who is more fortunate than you?"

It was unfathomable that a man who had been trying to kill me had the power to make me feel insulted.

It wasn't that what he said didn't make sense. I was the lucky one, wasn't I? Maybe not for the reasons so many people thought. Family connections didn't matter to me. I didn't care what family Taro came from. In fact, I could really do without his mother, and I thought he could, too. And while I admired his abilities, I didn't think skill in anything made anyone a superior or inferior person. But he was a good man. He was someone I could trust and rely on and feel comfortable with. And those were the qualities that made him a superior Source, partner, friend and lover.

So maybe I should just appreciate all that, instead of worrying about the fact that I didn't deserve it. So I didn't deserve it. I was lucky. There were worse things.

It was made clear to me how very stupid I'd been by believing in Ben's innocence for so long. But Ben had worked for the Triple S for decades. He had always treated me so kindly. So what if he'd made me uncomfortable? That had just been my own foolishness. So what if his daughter was suspected of murder? Why did that mean I was supposed to suspect him, too? There was no sense in that.

Every time I'd assumed the worst of someone, I'd been embarrassingly wrong. And a lot of times when I'd trusted someone from the start, I'd been dangerously wrong. There was just no winning. Understanding people should have been part of the formal curriculum at the Academy.

People had planned to kill me before, and I'd never imagined having to say that about myself. But with Ben it felt so much worse than the others. Because we lived in the same house, and he acted like he thought well of me. Really, what was wrong with me that people were prepared to do such things to me?

LaMonte called out when he saw the Runners approaching, and Taro unearthed all the crazy people. They immediately began gathering up all their casting gadgetry in the hopes of running away. All except Ben, who sat on the ground and stared into space. There were a solid twelve Runners galloping through the shoddy streets, because Taro had always been considered an important person. Ben's group was easily rounded up.

They claimed they had been buried by Taro. Taro claimed he saw them all snorting something. Taro was believed.

We took Taro home, where he was pampered and spoiled. Everyone was outraged that a man of criminal tendencies had been living among us, going so far as to attack two of us. The fact that no one else had suspected Ben didn't make my oblivion any easier to accept. Would I ever reach a point where I could see what was right in front of my face?

# Chapter Twenty-nine

The Cree residence was located in the North Quad, on a long winding road with very few other houses. It was small, but the wood used for its construction had a deep dark red tint that I hadn't seen before, and I assumed it was rare and expensive. The door was opened by a very pretty young man, and the first thing I saw beyond him was a silver sun set into the opposing wall, its rays stretching out to touch every edge of the wall. And like the house of Trader Fines, there were similar suns over every window we passed as we were led straight to the dining room.

Again, everyone else was already there. Gamut, Ahmad, Fines and Williams. They were all enjoying some comment made just before Taro and I entered the room. I was pretty sure they weren't laughing at us. Still, I felt awkward. I didn't like being the last to arrive at a party any more than I liked being the first.

I felt the muscles in Taro's forearm tighten under my hand.

"Dunleavy, Shintaro," said Cree, rising gracefully from her chair. "I'm so pleased you could join us. Dunleavy, you are looking hale."

"Thanks to you," I replied. Cree took my hand and led me to the empty seat beside Fines. That left the seat beside Gamut, at the opposite end of the table, for Taro. The table was set in the same manner as Fines's had been, but the food had not yet been placed. The clay pots were there, though.

"We understand Ayana has made a convert of you," Fines commented.

"Convert." I'd never liked that word. To me it had always suggested coercion and a weakness of mind. "Even I can't deny the evidence of my own eyes."

For some reason Taro found that funny, if his snicker was any indication.

Fines smirked. "Perhaps it is our definition of evidence which differs."

Smug bastard.

We were still rubbing the paste into our hands when the door to the dining room opened and several servants entered the room, two of them pushing trays piled with covered dishes. A bottle was placed before Taro while I was given a tall, narrow pot. "It is not wise for you to drink alcohol so soon after your treatment," Cree explained.

Well, I had been drinking wine with no noticeable effects, and it was a little annoying to be dictated to like a child, but the woman had saved my life, and she was my hostess. Besides, the tea smelled wonderful, fresh and clean, and was light in color as it was poured from the pot.

The other servants placed covered plates all around us and withdrew. Clearly, we were once more to rotate the dishes about the table. It kind of reminded me of the Academy, only much, much quieter. And the food was better.

"We heard that distressing news about Ben Veritas," said Ahmad.

It was, I thought, an odd sentence to speak and just leave out there, hanging entirely on its own. The logical assumption was that she was commiserating with us on the fact that Ben Veritas had tried to kill us. But it could be an expression of sorrow over the fact that he had been caught, for all I knew.

"It is certain, then, that he gave you the niyacin powder after learning of its effect on you?" Cree asked. "That he was doing it deliberately?"

"He's all but admitted it," Taro answered, rather shortly, I thought.

Trader Fines made a sound of disapproval in his throat. "To engage in such behavior toward a member of one's own household is highly inappropriate."

I put a spoonful of soup in my mouth to make sure I didn't ask if he thought it was less inappropriate to engage in such behavior with a person not a member of one's household. I was in a snarky mood that evening, for some reason.

"Is he being charged with attempted murder or purveying ashes or both?"

"I haven't been told," I said. "Wait a moment, a purveyor of ashes? We know that was his plan, ultimately, but I don't know that they could accuse him of selling ashes. He didn't get a chance to do that."

"Actually," said Fines, "he's well-known as a supplier of ashes."

There was no way to respond to that without sounding like an idiot. He sold ashes? He was well-known? Who was this person who had lived in our home and seen to our every need? How blind was I?

"How could he be well-known?" Taro asked. "People haven't been doing it for so very long."

"People have always done it."

"I thought it was only for the last half year," I said.

"It only became so very popular in the last year, but trust me, it's always been done."

How did he know that? "Always since when?"

"Always since the Landing. Before that, I have no way of knowing."

"But more and more people started doing it recently," Cree added. "And that enabled the Runners to decipher the pattern."

"It doesn't make sense that Ben has been doing this for

years," said Taro. "He doesn't have any money. He wouldn't still be working for the Triple S if he was making a lot of money selling ashes."

"I don't know how much the ashes garner for the diggers," said Fines.

"They're the ones who do the digging, who risk getting caught." And here I was arguing the economic unfairness of a criminal activity that nearly resulted in my death. It was ridiculous.

Fines shrugged. "Suppliers often get the least of any profit. It is the way of things."

I thought about what had been said as I, following the example of the others, placed my empty soup bowl in a sort of repository in the center of the table. "You knew Ben Veritas before he was arrested?"

"Knew of him. I've never met him."

"But you knew him as a source of ashes."

"Yes. He was well-known as being able to supply good ashes."

Good ashes. From the luckiest people? Was that what that meant?

"I don't know that anyone realized he was stepping into killing anyone, though," said Williams.

"Of course not," said Gamut. "It's ridiculous to think effective ashes can be harvested from a murder victim. Being murdered eliminates any luck the person enjoyed previously."

I kept my eyes on my plate, which had to be less rude than staring at Gamut. What kind of language was that to be using about the lives and the remains of human beings?

Maybe it was easier to speak that way when one wasn't a potential victim. Though why the others at the table were not potential victims was a bit of a puzzle. They all appeared to be enormously successful in their respective fields.

"How do you know about all this?" Taro demanded.

"Ashes are an important part of casting, Shintaro," said Fines. "This is what we do."

I didn't know why that surprised me. Cree obviously used

spells. I supposed I just never considered whether the others did, too.

"You're a trader," said Taro.

"That is merely how I make money," Fines responded. "It is not what I am."

"And your interest in spells, that is what you are?"

"Not quite, but it is an important part." Fines smiled. "Being a Source is an important part of what you are, wouldn't you say?"

I didn't understand what Fines was suggesting. Surely he wasn't claiming his interest in casting was as important to him as being a Source was to Taro. Fines playing with spells was just a hobby.

"It is not all that I am," said Taro. "I wouldn't even say it's the most important part of what I am."

I looked up at him, surprised. Was that what he really thought?

"You don't agree, Dunleavy?" Cree asked me.

Damn it, no one was supposed to be looking at me. "I wouldn't presume to tell Taro what he is."

Her eyes did that slight shift that suggested she really wanted to roll her eyes but felt herself too well mannered. "I am asking for your opinion of yourself."

I liked that question even less. Because I did think being a Shield was the largest part of what I was. From birth it had made me different from everyone in my family, though they didn't recognize my true nature until I was four. It shaped everything about me, not just my education and my occupation. My very personality was influenced—perhaps a better word would be "controlled"—by the fact that I was a Shield.

Yet I didn't want to admit that, not before these people. I wasn't sure of the reason for my reluctance. It wasn't as though I was ashamed of being a Shield and all it meant. But these people were disturbing me right then, and I didn't like the idea of thinking like they did. "I doubt there are many who would enjoy being reduced to nothing more than a personification of a single talent."

"Then you don't know a great many people all that well," said Cree. "There are many who consider a talent they deem worthy to be their defining characteristic, and many more who wish for a talent by which to be defined. Perhaps, surrounded as you have been all your life by unusually gifted people, you have difficulty understanding what it is like to lack such gifts."

"You're a healer," Taro said to Cree. "Why would you need to use spells to feel special?"

The silence that followed was tense, and Cree's face stiffened.

"None of us need spells for anything in particular," Fines said quickly. "Understanding magic is much greater than any one particular activity or desired outcome. It gives us a connection to the ground and the air and to the animal world and each other in a way nothing else can. It is something anyone can learn and embrace, with diligence and discipline. It's bigger than any one person, spanning any distance, and it has the power to last forever. Why else do you think the Crown Prince is outlawing the use of it?"

I thought it was because people were dabbling in things they couldn't control and burning their houses down. "Why would people want to be bound to everyone else for an eternity?" I asked. It seemed suffocating to me.

"To belong to something greater than themselves."

"You don't need to use spells for that."

"You belong to the Triple S," said Fines. "You have a Source who is bound to you for the rest of your life. Most of us don't have such things."

"But you have families, friends, your community."

"And what if you have none of those things?"

"How could anyone have none of those things?"

"It is possible. There are orphans. There are those who are isolated and outcast for one reason or another."

"And casting will somehow make them feel better about all that?"

"It gives them a connection."

"Enough of a connection to replace all positive human contact?" I'd be worried about someone so thoroughly unfortunate having access to magic. What would they do with it?

"Mere human contact is too fragile, too easily disrupted by inconsequential things. An understanding of magic and how it connects us to each other and the world, that is stronger and more powerful than any human relationship."

"And nothing about human relationships will tell you how the natural world works," Williams said. "The power of fire. Air. Water."

He put a heavy emphasis on "water" that made me look at him. He was trying to tell us something.

Gamut thought so, too, and he didn't like it. "Shut it, Morgan."

"No. I'm sick of this dancing around. If they're going to join us—"

Join them? For what?

"It's too soon, Morgan," Fines chided.

"It became too late once Ayana used a spell to heal the Shield. They already know what we are."

"It's certainly too late now, Morgan, thanks to you," Fines snapped. Williams communicated his lack of concern with a shrug. "Our Dunleavy has a reputation for not leaving things alone."

I did? When did that happen? Why were people talking about me so much? And why did they get everything wrong?

"Good." Williams crossed his arms. "So lets get things moving."

The tension in the air became stronger, which was all we needed. I really didn't want to hear what they had to say. I didn't want to be part of whatever weird club they had running. But I also didn't have the spine to interrupt them all with a "No, thanks" and "Where's my carriage?"

"This little group formed through our businesses," said Fines with a wave of the hand that took in everyone at the table. "In many ways our interests and our clients intersect. We began to work together, and we learned that each of us is more successful working together than as an individual. I learned of Cree's ability to use spells in a way similar to yours, Dunleavy. At one point, while overseeing some loading of inventory at the docks, I was badly cut. The vein was one of those that bleed out in less than a third of an hour. One of my servants fetched Ayana, and she used a spell that saved my life. In time, she introduced all of us to the practice. We owe her a great deal."

I didn't want to hear about it. I really, really didn't.

"How do you expect us to assist you?" Taro asked. "We can't help you with your businesses."

"It is true that you have no business interests to complement ours. But that isn't your most valuable asset."

"Our most valuable assets are our skills as a Source and Shield," I said sharply. And they had better not be thinking about asserting any control over those. We didn't channel, or not, according to anyone else's wishes.

"It is not those assets, strictly speaking, that appeal to us."

"Quit dragging this out, Richard," Gamut grumbled.

"As you are no doubt aware," said Fines, "ashes are a powerful component in many spells. And ashes are relatively easy to procure. But blood is even more potent."

I stared at him, appalled. "You want our blood?" I squeaked.

"As far as we know, no one's done any real experimentation with the blood of Sources and Shields, but it is only logical to assume the blood of magical creatures has all sorts of useful properties. Ayana has told us the spell she used to heal Dunleavy was unusually quick."

That had been quick? I guess I wouldn't have survived the usual spell.

"We are not magical creatures," Taro declared with noticeable impatience.

"My dear Shintaro," said Williams, "what do you call what you do when you protect the city?"

"Not magic," Taro retorted. "And, by the way, not illegal."

"Only the latter is true, and only because the lawmakers

made a random distinction about what magic is. What do you think those same lawmakers would call what you do when you heal people?"

Damn it, could no one in this city keep their mouths shut?

"It's not a talent traditional to a Source," Williams continued. "Would not most people think it magic?"

"We are not giving you our blood!" I said. "That's disgusting. And ridiculous." What were they thinking? That every week or so we'd let them bleed us?

"You can't make the usual contributions to our group," said Fines. "Blood would be an acceptable substitute."

Taro was shaking his head. "We have no reason to want to be part of your group."

"I saved Dunleavy's life," Cree reminded him bluntly. "There is no other healer in this city who could have done so. You would not have known to come to me, had it not been for this group."

She didn't add that she probably wouldn't have risked using a spell on me if she hadn't known me. It was still alarming to me that if it weren't for her, I would be dead. I hated feeling indebted to her.

"You would have access to everything we have, now and in the future," Ahmad said.

"There is no predicting how we could all benefit in the long term," said Fines. "And remember, you don't have just the two of you to consider. A merchant's fortune is a very fragile thing. Things can be done to assist it, or to destroy it. All it takes is a ship to sink and there begins a downward spiral to destitution."

I glared at him. "Are you threatening my family?" I demanded.

"Not at all. I am merely pointing out that people's affairs are more entwined than you might imagine."

Of course he was threatening them. Did he really have the ability to hurt my family? Was he somehow able to sink a ship?

"And, of course, most estates rely heavily on the goods

they produce. Were an estate to fall into disfavor, it could quickly fall to ruin. Your family's estate, Shintaro, don't they sell a great deal of whale oil?"

Taro forced a small laugh. "You're aiming for air if you try to use my family against me."

"Lord Shintaro, you abjured your title but kept your name. Do not try to convince us you have no family feeling."

"Why are you trying to blackmail us into joining you?" I asked. "From the looks of it, you are enormously successful. You don't need us."

"All things must move forward or they die," Cree told us. "Now that more and more people are using spells, more people will become proficient at casting, and our advantages will diminish. We must always be ready to act on new opportunities."

"Or be ready to create them," Williams added.

"And it represents a brilliant opportunity to acquire knowledge," Ahmad added. "Knowledge of how the world works."

"How the mind works," Gamut said.

"How water works." Williams stared at me.

I had no idea what he was trying to tell me.

"Shut up, Morgan!" Gamut ordered.

"My gods," Taro breathed, his eyes widening. "You're the ones who have been poisoning the water in the riverfront areas."

Certain pieces of my memory slotted into a new pattern. By gods, he was right. I looked at Cree. She must have been the one who had gone to the hub to perform some spell.

"Ben didn't guard his tongue much when they captured me," Taro explained. "He was very enthusiastic about all the people leaving the riverfront areas. He was going to use our ashes to create for himself ownership of that area where the rivers meet, because it's supposed to be so powerful. Or something like that. He was rambling a bit."

"You're killing people to have control of the riverfront?" I demanded, horrified.

"Don't be ridiculous," Cree answered sharply. "None of them have died."

"That's not what they're saying."

"People have a higher mortality rate in the riverfront area than those who live in other parts of the city. Those that died while ill from our tampering died of other causes."

She couldn't know that for sure. She was just making assumptions.

"It sounds far worse than it is, Dunleavy," Fines said in a soft voice, as though by mere tone he could somehow soothe me. Wasn't going to happen, friend. "All we are doing is encouraging these people to leave."

"But they have nowhere to go. If they did, they probably wouldn't be living there in the first place."

"This is a big city. And there are other cities."

So heartless.

"The whole area is a cesspool," Gamut muttered. "It's needed to be shaken up for decades. It could have used an earthquake or two if you lot would have just let it happen."

I covered my mouth with my hand, the only way I could hold in my shock.

"What do you plan to do with this riverfront area?" Taro asked.

No one jumped in to answer that question. I noticed a lot of glances being exchanged.

"I think we've said enough for now, Shintaro," said Fines. "I think it's time for the two of you to do some talking."

We were not spilling any of our secrets. I hadn't wanted to know their secrets. I shouldn't have to pay for things I had neither wanted nor asked for. I said nothing. Neither did Taro. There was a bit of a waiting game.

Which we won. They spoke first.

"All we ask is that you continue to join us for our meals and honestly participate in our discussions on a committed basis."

Oh, and our blood. Don't forget that.

"Thank you for your kind invitation," Taro said in delightfully chilly tones. "But I fear we'll have to decline."

The others ate in silence for a few moments. I'd lost my appetite. So had Taro, from the looks of it.

"To your knowledge, has any member of the Triple S been found violating the prohibition against casting?" Williams asked.

Taro glanced at me for confirmation before indicating he knew of no such instances.

"I imagine that Sources and Shields will be protected from things such as incarceration and flogging, should any of them be found to be engaging in magical practices, but I do believe members of the Triple S are punished if the crime is considered serious enough."

"Aye," said Taro.

"Pairs who are found guilty of serious crimes are sent to remote areas that have no need for their skills, is that not so?"

"Aye," said Taro.

"It's a shameful thing. Something Pairs don't recover from. Such a Pair would never be assigned to somewhere they considered reputable, is that not so?"

"Correct."

By the exaggerated roll of his *r*'s, I could tell Taro was getting as irritated by this line of questioning as I.

So after threatening our families, they were threatening us. That was infuriating. "You were the ones to cast spells," I said.

"There are five of us."

And only two of us. "People believe Sources don't lie."

"But we have impeccable reputations. Yours, you must admit, are a little dodgy. Long, unexplained absences from your duties. Healing people. You were both seen acting strangely at the hub in the middle of the night."

Damn it, they had seen us. That must have been why nothing had happened during our long nights of surveillance. Cree saw us or something, and stayed away.

"And then there are those strange stories about how the

Reanists were brought down at Lord Yellows's dinner. Definitely sounds like there were spells involved in that."

"And then, of course, there's this." Fines pointed at one of the clay pots. "Made from the best ashes."

My knife and fork fell to the plate with a harsh clatter as I gagged. We had been spreading human ashes on our hands?

My gods, my gods. I shook my hands, not that I thought that would accomplish anything.

"It's perfectly sanitary," Cree asserted.

"Are you crazy?" I demanded.

"I believe using this paste helped you survive the first use of niyacin powder on your burn."

"There is no way you can know that," I objected.

"I am a healer and I am proficient at using spells," she pointed out. "What expertise do you have to bear?"

Taro was scrubbing at his hands. He poured wine into his palm and rubbed it into his skin.

"You buy ashes." I couldn't believe it. Risa and her colleagues were running around trying to stop the trade in ashes, and we'd been eating with people who bought them. Who used them. We'd used them.

"Yes," said Cree.

"You buy ashes from Ben Veritas."

"Not directly, of course," said Fines, though I didn't understand what was so "of course" about it. "And we had no idea he was killing people."

I was curious about whether his killing people was a problem for Fines because killing people was wrong, or because murder tainted the ashes.

"We had not planned to introduce you to our practices in this way," said Fines. "However, Cree put herself, and by extension all of us, in great danger by her actions at your home. We needed to be sure of your silence. And your loyalty."

"You've made it impossible for us to give you either," I said.

"Don't answer tonight," Fines suggested. "Think about it for a few days."

"We don't need to think about it."

"Think of your families," Fines persisted.

They were really irritating me. "My family wouldn't want me being bled for spells to spare them trouble."

"And my family can go hang," Taro added in a sharp tone.

"We'll see if you feel the same way when you start getting their letters of misfortune."

Bastard. "Do you really expect us to join people who would blackmail us?"

"You're not approaching this with an open mind."

"I'm content in my close-mindedness." They had been collecting information on us. They had induced us to use illegal human ashes. Cree had saved my life, and I owed her for that. My blood was too much to ask. "If you do anything to our families, we will tell everyone, including Prince Gifford, what you are doing, and let things happen as they will."

Fines's frown was pinched. "It is disappointing to learn you have so little family loyalty."

"Blame it on my upbringing. We're done here."

No one said anything as Taro and I left the table and left the room. My heart was pounding in my throat. The people I had eaten with tonight had not been the people I had met before. There had been no playfulness, no humor. They had been grim and ruthless. Which was the truth?

I felt tainted. I had no idea what it would take to feel clean again. For some reason I felt water and soap wouldn't be enough.

Could they really hurt my family?

I didn't know what was the best thing to do. To submit to blackmail rankled. But when it came to my family's well-being, maybe blood and time weren't so much to lose.

Then again, that might not be all that they asked for. Once successful at getting blood from us, they might demand more. And they were hardly honorable, getting us to use human ashes without our knowledge. Something within me screamed that entering into any kind of agreement with those people would be a horrible idea.

"We're not going to do what they want, are we?" Taro asked.

"Certainly not."

He nodded. "Good."

I would just have to think of a way to warn my parents of possible problems without giving them any facts.

# Chapter Thirty

I had an unpleasant duty to perform. I had to end things with Doran. No more delay. No more games. The thought of the conversation we would have to have made my stomach clench, but it had to be done. So I went to his boardinghouse wearing the plainest gown I owned, my hair loosely tied at the nape of my neck, a particularly unattractive style on me.

He was in. He looked pleased to see me. I wondered why. Every interaction we'd had recently had been negative. Why did he think this would be a positive meeting?

He escorted me to the boardinghouse's parlor and kissed my cheek before settling into the chair next to mine. "You look wonderful," he said without the slightest trace of sarcasm in his voice.

Because of that, I merely said, "Thank you. You are very kind."

"It's good to see you looking so hale. I have to admit, I was worried the last time I saw you."

Oh, that made sense. I'd probably looked half dead the last time we saw each other. Anything would be an improvement on that.

"I'm so sorry to have caused you concern." Well, that was chilling and polite. I felt uncomfortable parroting meaningless phrases in the face of his sincerity. "Thank you for agreeing to see me on such short notice."

He frowned then. "Why wouldn't I?"

Um, well, yes, that had been a really stupid thing to say, hadn't it? As though he were some sort of stranger. "Well, it wouldn't be unexpected for you to have already made plans."

He shrugged. "Are you up to much yet? Because Weller is holding a small concert in his home the day after tomorrow, and from what I've heard of the repertoire, it's perfectly safe for you to hear it."

I didn't usually trust a regular's definition of safe. They often had no idea. And while I was tempted to delay things by talking about music and what kind I usually liked to listen to, I knew I had to get things over with. "I'm not good at saying important things delicately," I confessed. "So I'm just going to say it. You are truly a wonderful person, smart and witty and kind. But I can't see you anymore. In any capacity. I am sorry." There. That wasn't bad, was it?

His eyebrows rose. He was shocked. He hadn't considered this possibility.

How could he not, after our last meeting?

He rose abruptly, circling his chair, rubbing his nose. I got the feeling he didn't know how to react.

I felt compelled to say something more, but I had no idea what would be the appropriate words. Repeating sentiments with different wording would only weaken my original state-ment, and ran the risk of stumbling into a logistical frailty or emotional quagmire.

"I mean no disrespect to Shintaro," Doran said finally. "But he is not the sort of person to which one should attach aspira-tions of longevity."

I was offended even though I agreed with him. I had the right to think that way. He didn't have the right to say it. And it annoyed me that the first response he had about something that was relevant to the two of us, was a negative comment about Taro. "I really don't have a choice about that," I said. Doran once more looked surprised. "I'm bonded to him," I reminded him. "I hope that will enjoy a certain amount of longevity." As the alternative was an early death.

"That's different," he said with impatience. "You're being difficult."

I was being difficult? I wasn't the one trying to create a debate. There had been plenty of warnings that this was my mind-set. He was behaving as though it was coming out of nowhere.

I wished he would sit down. I didn't like having to look up at him.

"You are looking for someone to settle down with. For permanence. Aren't you?"

I frowned. "I wouldn't say that. I haven't been looking for anyone." For one thing, my life had been too chaotic since I left the Academy. For another, well, the logical side of my nature kept telling me that forever was a long time, and it was a little unrealistic for people to fall in love with the expectation that it would last for the rest of their lives.

Certainly, I had spoken of permanence with Taro, but I knew that really just meant for as long as we were both interested. That wasn't the same thing as forever.

"Shintaro will never be the sort of person to remain faithful to one person."

Really, how the hell would he know? He'd met Taro only a handful of times. "He has so far."

"You can't know that."

"Taro doesn't lie." Not to me.

"You can't know that," Doran insisted.

"Maybe not, but I can believe it."

"You'd be a fool to do so."

I found it fascinating how many people thought insults were an effective means of persuasion.

"I mean it when I say I admire him. I do. But in some ways he's like a child."

I opened my mouth to deny that and found nothing sprang

immediately to mind, I was that shocked. A child? That was a new one. There was nothing childlike about Taro.

"I've known many like him, Lee. They're spoiled. Not mean-spirited, but thoughtless, because all their lives they've been given everything they've ever wanted, with little effort expended. And people like that are too easily bored, because they don't understand the effort it takes to build something, and the value there is in creating something with their own labor."

I wasn't going to explain that Taro had spent much of his life being anything but spoiled. That was Taro's story to tell, and none of Doran's business. "I knew someone else who said something similar about Taro. He was crazy." And I'd killed him, though not because he hadn't liked Taro.

Doran snorted. "Only one?"

"Crazy person?" Unfortunately, no. The Academy hadn't warned me about all the crazy people I would encounter out in the real world.

"Person who agreed Taro's a—"

I cut him off. "I don't want to hear it!" I wasn't going to sit there and listen to him denigrate Taro. If he was going to say such things, he could say them to Taro's face.

"Don't want to hear the truth?"

"The truth? Rumors spread by a bunch of people who don't even know him?"

"Oh, and you do?"

Was he serious? "I'd wager that I've spent more time in Taro's company over the last few years than everyone else in High Scape combined."

"And you think that means you know him better?"

Of course. What else could it mean? "Yes."

"You're being naive."

Certainly. If I didn't agree with him, it had to be because I didn't know what I was talking about. "And you're being obnoxious. What do you think you're going to accomplish here?"

"I don't know," he admitted. "I wasn't expecting this, and everything is coming out all wrong."

Well, I knew how that could happen. "I'm sorry, Doran." And I really was. I liked Doran. I wanted to want him. It would make so much more sense. "But nothing you say now can possibly come out right."

He sighed. "I'm worried about you. I can't see this ending well."

Neither could I, but I was going to give it my best effort. And I couldn't give it my best effort if I kept Doran waiting in the wings. Besides, Doran should be marrying someone with money, as he had none of his own. And that reminded me of something. "That bundle of yellow flowers with the cake and the earrings, someone told me that was a token indicating an intention to open marital negotiations." I took his silence for assent. "What was that about? You don't truly wish to marry me."

He flushed and said nothing.

"Please tell me," I prompted. I wanted to be able to tell Taro the answer.

"Can I assume Shintaro saw it?" Doran asked.

"He told me what it meant."

"I assume the delivery created a great deal of"—he hesitated in his word selection—"discussion between you."

I felt my eyes narrow. He'd sent a token he probably knew I'd send back in order to cause arguments between Taro and me. "I underestimated you Doran," I said flatly. "I had no idea you were so devious."

"It's for your own good, Lee. It's all going to fall apart. You know that. And I can be there to help you through it if you want."

Unbelievable. Doran, not Taro, was the man I didn't know, and I was so sick of being manipulated by people. "My name is Shield Mallorough," I reminded him. "And it's past time I left."

"I'll be here when Shintaro grows tired of you," Doran said spitefully.

"I won't."

Well, I had predicted that one correctly. That had been

really unpleasant. Not to mention disappointing. Just because I had to stop seeing Doran didn't mean I wanted to think less of him. I headed home, feeling more weary than the slight physical exertion warranted.

Taro was waiting for me. As soon as I closed the door at the entrance of the Triple S residence, I heard clattering down the stairs. "Lee!" Taro called, a certain urgency to his voice. "Come up to my suite. Right now."

That didn't sound good. And he had called the suite his. He had been calling it ours. Something had rattled him. I wasn't up to jogging up the stairs right then, but I pushed myself a little harder than usual. I didn't know why I was trying to be quick. The bad news would be there whenever I got there.

Taro's hair was a tangled mess. That was another bad sign. "Close the door," he ordered when I reached his suite. So I closed the door. "We've been ordered to attend the coronation."

"Gifford's coronation? Ordered?"

"Technically it's an invitation, but it's not like we could refuse. It was dropped off by members of the Imperial Guard. They've offered to escort us to Erstwhile."

To make sure we actually went, no doubt. And sure, that was annoying. We'd just gotten back on the roster. I had no interest in going to Erstwhile and even less, if that were possible, in seeing Gifford crowned. It wasn't a disaster, though. "Why the panic?"

"He doesn't like us," Taro said. "Why is he summoning us?"

I took the letter and looked at it. "The only thing personal about the summons is our names. It's a copy of thousands of others, I'm sure. He calls us because he can. It's an inconvenience, but nothing to get excited about."

"Gifford isn't like the Empress," Taro said. "He's more likely to let his feelings rule him, and he feels he has something to prove."

"What do you think he's trying to prove with this?"

"I don't know, but it can't be good."

"It could be nothing more than that he can snap his fingers and we have to come running."

"It could be."

"But you don't think so."

"No."

"But we're of no use to him."

"I would have said the same about his mother, and look what she had us do."

I couldn't tolerate another journey like the one to Flatwell. I would go insane. But the Empress had had particular reasons to choose Taro for that task. Weird reasons, but she had clearly liked Taro. As Taro had said, Gifford didn't.

Maybe there were more family secrets that we were going to be exposed to.

Or maybe, upon the Empress's death, Gifford had learned about Aryne, and that Taro and I had been the ones to find her. He would be furious that his mother had sought another heir. And he would be furious with us for assisting her, whether we had had the option of refusing or not.

Now I was starting to panic. I went down to the kitchen for some wine to help me stop thinking. There was no point worrying about it until we were there.

# Chapter Thirty-one

So Taro and I were in Erstwhile yet again. Erstwhile was a cold site, which meant we should have never had to visit the city at all, as far as I was concerned. Most Pairs never did. It was just because the monarchs liked playing games that we were ever there at all.

At least this time we weren't expected to stay at the palace. For the past few days we had been enjoying the relative privacy of an expensive boardinghouse. It gave me hope that we would escape the personal attention of Gifford altogether.

The city had been enjoying a week of celebration. There was a variety of competitions, running and jumping and fighting and bench dancing. There was free food and drink. There were plays and musical performances. There had been a series of breakfasts, dinners and balls at the palace, to none of which Taro and I, thank gods, had been invited.

This was to be the final day, marked by a massive parade leading to Gifford finally having the crown placed on his head. I was curious as to how the Crown Prince felt about that moment. Was he excited or merely impatient?

The only contact we received from the palace once we were

in Erstwhile was the personal invitation to witness the coronation. That meant we had reserved seating immediately in front
of the platform on which the Prince would be crowned. This
was a highly privileged position, as thousands would be forced
to stand. I would have preferred to be lost in a crowd.

All the other people milling about the collection of seats
were the highest of titleholders, politicians and guild masters.
No one like us. I'd met a couple of them before, during my
other visits to Erstwhile, and we exchanged distant greetings.
And through it all, I was aware of a woman, tall and buxom and
blond and wearing a duchess's coronet, watching us closely.

When I finally looked directly at her, she approached
us. "Excuse me," she said to Taro. "Are you Source Shintaro
Karish?"

He smiled at her. "I am."

"My gods," she said. "You look so much like your mother."

His expression chilled. It was true—he and his mother
looked freakishly alike—but he didn't like to be reminded of
it. "How may I help you?" he asked coolly.

"I'm Fiona," she announced.

Taro grinned widely. "Cousin!"

"How are you?" She threw her arms around him.

I realized who she was. The current Duchess of Westsea.
The woman who wrote the hilarious letters and stood up to the
grasping Prince.

Taro seemed comfortable hugging her back. "It's wonderful to finally meet you," he said before drawing away. "This is
Dunleavy Mallorough, my Shield."

The Duchess of Westsea turned her warm smile to me
and offered her forearm for me to take. "A joy to meet you," I
said.

"Shintaro has written about you," she told me.

"That's unfortunate," I responded.

"So what do you think of this idiot getting the Crown?"

I almost choked on that. "You might want to keep your
voice down," Taro advised her in a mild tone.

She snickered. "I'm no politician."

I didn't think the titleholder of an estate as large and powerful as Westsea could afford not to be a politician. I agreed with her sentiment, though. I was very uneasy with the idea of Gifford being our ruler. I didn't trust him.

"Maybe you can give me some information, though," Fiona was saying. "I've applied to the Source and Shield Service for a Pair."

Taro frowned. "Flown Raven doesn't have natural disasters."

"It does now. There was a horrific earthquake a couple of months ago, and a few smaller ones since."

Taro gasped, his eyes wide.

"If everyone would take their seats!" some official called out.

"It's a delight to meet you both," Fiona said, squeezing our hands. "Maybe we can talk some more after the deed is done." She headed to the front row.

"What's wrong?" I asked Taro as we took our seats at the back.

"That's where those events were coming from," he said. "The ones from a distance. That's why they felt like something familiar."

I slapped his arm. "You're not supposed to channel events at your birthplace!" Weird things happened when Sources tried to channel events from the place where they had been born. In the past, the Pairs had died. More often, the events got away from them. There was a theory that the familiarity of their home made it difficult for a Source to decipher which forces needed to be channeled and which should be left alone. That was why Sources were never posted in the area in which they were born. Or raised.

It was why, probably, Taro had let so many forces flow through him, and why I'd had such difficulty Shielding him.

"I didn't know," he protested.

"Don't do it anymore."

"I haven't been."

And soon there would be a Pair at Flown Raven who would

channel the events, and Taro wouldn't feel tempted to do so. That was one danger avoided, so I could stop thinking about it.

I could feel the racket of the parade approaching. When I learned of the parade that was to introduce the Prince's coronation, I'd thought nothing more of it than another event on a day that was already too long. And yet I had never seen a parade quite like this. The sheer number of participants, for one thing, all in matching and highly tailored clothing that wasn't quite warm enough in the autumn air. There was dancing and tumbling, all in time to expertly played music that really had me wanting to jump and dance around, too. I had to sink my nails hard into Taro's arm to resist that impulse.

The floats were unbelievable. One was a huge horse, about four men high, black with blazing red eyes, pulled by four enormous live black horses. Visually stunning and a little menacing. I wondered what kind of message the Prince was trying to give with that float. Maybe I was reading too much into it. It wasn't likely that the Prince had made any of those decisions.

The next float was of the sun rising, a huge ball of metallic yellow—that wasn't gold, was it?—rising over waves of purple and dark blue, surrounded by creeping white smoke released by the various people walking around the float, dressed in frothy gowns of light blue.

It reminded me of the tacky decorations in the homes of Fines and Cree. And lords, I didn't need to be reminded of them. Taro and I had received several more invitations from them and the others of their group. We had turned all of them down. I hoped they would lose interest in us soon. I didn't know what I was going to do if they didn't.

At least I hadn't yet received news from my family describing business difficulties.

The next float was a large three-dimensional replica of the royal seal, a gaudy thing of red, purple and blue ribbons surrounding a round black shield, topped by a thick book, on which stood a white horse wearing a gold crown at a jaunty angle. I'd always thought that a hideous emblem, and learning what it all meant in history class didn't improve my opinion.

The ribbons represented royal blood and the seas, the two being mastered by the monarch. The shield represented military might; the horse represented wealth. The crown represented wisdom, and the book represented law and, therefore, in theory, justice.

Ben Veritas had had his trial. He had been convicted of attempted murder and a string of magic-related offenses. That pleased me, at least as far as attempted murder was concerned. He was sentenced to one hundred and twenty lashes followed by death by hanging, which disgusted me. There had to be a better way to punish people. As a victim, I'd been offered a reserved seat to witness the execution of the sentence, but I'd turned it down. A large part of me felt morally obligated to watch the results of my actions, but I knew I wouldn't last through the flogging. It was such a cruel form of punishment, and totally unnecessary.

Veritas hadn't survived the flogging, but his body had been hanged anyway, because that was what the sentence had dictated.

Ben Veritas was dead, as was his daughter, Sara Copper, who had also been found guilty at her trial. And from what Risa told me, people were still digging up ashes. I assumed people were still buying them. I certainly had no reason to believe Fines and his group weren't still using them.

A loud crash shocked me from my thoughts. Cymbals. Cymbals were too popular in parades as far as I was concerned.

The musicians were followed by a troupe of acrobats determined to kill themselves, if the way they flung themselves off high surfaces was any indication. And then another float followed, this one an elaborate throne propped high on a dais of gold. I was surprised the Prince wasn't sitting on it. For him to do so before being crowned would be a horrible violation of etiquette, but I'd never known that to stop him before. The float was pulled by dozens of men, marching in time to the music, which brought a disquieting uniformity to the display.

And following the float was the man himself, the Crown

Prince, a space maintained between him and everything else by a perfect square of his personal guard marching around him, marred only by the two pretty young men who carried the trail of his long red cape. Aside from the cape, he was dressed entirely in black. He had small brooches or the like pinned to his chest. I knew they were symbols related to the military and the justice system, but I didn't know exactly what they signified.

The parade was progressing up the center street of Erstwhile, which was wide and white and led straight up to the steps of the palace. I thought it a rather stupid setup, allowing invaders a direct path to a vulnerable part of the palace despite the tall iron gates that had been pushed open for the occasion. But I didn't know anything about such things, except that there hadn't been a large-scale attack on the palace in centuries.

The participants of the parade didn't cross into the palace grounds, instead splitting off into the crowds. The Prince and his attendants did cross over, heading toward the small stage set up in front of the steps to the palace. On the stage was an elderly man who I'd been informed was the solicitor to the royal family. The solicitor formally held the title of ruler between monarchs and kept the secret code that identified the next sovereign. A series of spectacularly brutal executions had made clear the fate of solicitors who attempted to abuse the trust placed on them by trying to claim the title for the long term.

The solicitor stood beside a table. From where I sat, I couldn't see the articles on them, but I knew what they were.

Once the Prince stood before the stage, the music stopped and all the murmured conversations were cut short. In silence, the Prince ascended the steps to the stage. The solicitor bowed to him, the Prince offering no gesture of his own, which I thought rude.

I could hear Taro's teeth chattering beside me, and I glanced at him. He was trying to keep his teeth still, but his shivering was noticeable. His stiff black garments stood out among the colored finery of the others, and they weren't suitable for the weather. I wasn't going to remind him that I'd warned him to wear a cloak. I didn't want to turn into a nag.

The Prince faced the masses.

"State your name," the solicitor ordered.

The Prince didn't seem to react to the tone. "Gifford William Hiroshi Madas," the Prince announced, loudly enough to be heard by everyone seated and, I was sure, a good many who were standing. I wondered if he'd practiced.

"State your lineage."

"Son of Constia Alexandra Fiona Madas, who was daughter of Kemmeth Elisia Yuuki Madas, who was daughter of Aneck Randolf Emery Madas, who was son of Benik Chapry James Madas, and stretching back into the mists of time."

It was Benik who stole the throne from Emperor Koitchi through means both legitimate and not. I supposed it wasn't regal to admit to that.

"How have you proven your right to the position of high commander of the legions of the empire?"

"Through tests of strength and strategy."

Test of strength could mean anything. Lifting a weighty object. And perhaps he'd won a game of chess or two. I was fairly sure the Prince had never been in any kind of combat.

"How have you proven your right to the position of high justice of the empire?"

"Through study and reflection."

Fortunately, the Emperor didn't actually hear cases. The monarch used to, ages ago, and apparently it was a nightmare. The title, like that of high commander, was purely ceremonial. In theory, people who actually knew what they were doing ran the military and the judiciary.

"Who will attest to your character?"

A man in the front row rose. "I do," he said in a voice I could hear even though the man was facing in the other direction. These people must have been chosen for their ability to bellow.

"And you are?"

"Lord Gray, the Duke of Conrad."

"And what say you, my lord?"

"I attest that the Crown Prince is a man of honor, of honesty, of valor and of sound mind."

Well, to be strictly honest, I couldn't dispute any of that, not really. Just because I didn't like what he did didn't mean it wasn't all aboveboard. His mother was just sneakier about what she did. I wondered why I had liked her better.

"Why should you be our Emperor?" the solicitor asked.

"I have been born and bred in the knowledge of my responsibility to the people, and tutored in the honor to be found in the service of others. I am prepared to spend my life in the service of others. Always will I know that every decision I make must be made with the best interests of the people in mind, that their needs come before my own, that I am merely the most visible of servants to the people."

I wondered how hard that last phrase made him want to choke.

"I have been privileged to have had before me, my entire life, the best example of what a ruler should be. A ruler who never took a single action without first thinking how that action would affect her people, who put the needs of her people before her own, whose every action was one of compassion, of mercy, of justice. She was the model of all that was good and strong and right."

It alarmed me that he could lie so convincingly. At least, his praise of his mother sharply contradicted all the rumors I'd heard about how much he'd despised her. Maybe he'd really admired her and no one knew about it. Or maybe he just wished he'd been able to admire her.

"With this understanding of the needs of the people, I will dedicate myself to the peace and prosperity of all. This shall be my guiding principle for the rest of my life."

From the table beside him, the solicitor picked up the monarch's sword, said to have been carried by the first emperor and never used again. I wasn't sure if that story was true or not. Certainly it was a very shiny sword, thinner than the ones I sometimes saw the Runners wear, and it was reputed to be stronger than any sword any contemporary blacksmith could make. "Do you affirm," the solicitor asked, "on your name, your life and your lineage, that you will keep the position of high commander of the empire with all honor, putting aside personal connection and favor where it may conflict with duty, for as long as you shall live?"

"I so affirm," said the Prince.

The solicitor presented the sword to the Prince over his forearm, hilt first. "I bestow upon you the rank of high commander."

The Prince took the sword in his right hand, holding it rather awkwardly and making sure no part of it touched anything else.

The solicitor then picked up the staff, standing as high as the average man's shoulder and as wide as a thumb, a slim, plain rod made of gold that was, for some reason, the symbol of the justice system. "Do you affirm on your name, your life and your lineage that you will keep the position of high justice with all honor, putting aside personal connection and favor where it may conflict with duty, for as long as you shall live?"

"I so affirm."

Like the sword, the solicitor presented the staff over his forearm. "I bestow upon you the rank of high justice."

Due to the length of the staff and the lack of natural grace in either man, the transfer of the staff looked cumbersome, and the Prince held it at an unwieldy angle.

Finally, the solicitor held up the crown, a band of gold with no decoration or finesse. I'd never seen it before. It looked bulky and heavy and was probably uncomfortable to wear.

"Do you affirm on your name, your life and your lineage that you will keep the position of emperor with all honor, putting aside personal connection and favor when it may conflict with duty, for as long as you shall live?"

"I so affirm."

And standing behind him, the solicitor carefully placed the crown on the Prince's head. I imagined if he got the angle wrong, the thing would have slid off and hit the floor with a clang. That would have been fun to see. "I bestow upon you the rank of emperor."

May the gods save us all.

The crowd roared. I wondered how they could. Perhaps they had no idea what the Prince was like and what his new position would mean for them. Perhaps his ascension really did mean nothing to them, one ruler being pretty much the same as another. Perhaps they were just happy they hadn't had to work for the past few days.

The Prince, now Emperor, wearing the crown and holding the sword and the staff, looked unfortunately impressive, awkwardness notwithstanding. Clothing could lie so well. Anyone would look regal with such costumes and props.

"Troubling influences have been creeping into our great cities," he announced once the cheering faded away. "Our beloved Empress stood firm against all that was divisive and destructive, yet over the course of her failing health a darkness has begun to poison the land, attacking our traditions and our laws, endangering the peace and prosperity of all. To restore the world to its proper path will be Our first and most important task. To return glory to the people will be Our just reward."

The crowd cheered again. I hoped they understood what the Emperor had just said, because it had sounded like nothing more than gibberish to me. Ominous gibberish.

Lord Gray stood and climbed the few steps to the stage, lowering with some difficulty to one knee and bowing his head. "I, Lord Gray, Duke of Conrad, offer to the Emperor and his heirs my eternal faithfulness, and that of my descendants. I offer the best portion of my land and stock, the might of my servants, and the enforcement of the laws of the land."

"We, Emperor Gifford, accept the offers of Lord Gray and give in return protection against danger and want." That, I knew, was the traditional oath of the monarch to one of his vassals, meaning not a whole lot since the powers of the monarch were given boundaries by the Council. The following words were not traditional. "In honor of your recent services to the Crown, it is Our duty and Our honor to grant to you the lands of Vast Greens, yours and your heirs' in perpetuity."

That caused some gasps. I'd never heard of the place myself. Gray's expression as he returned to his seat was blank, so I couldn't tell if the boon was expected or not, an advantage or not.

Gray was only the first of many titled landowners to swear their fealty. The second was the new Duchess of Westsea, Taro's cousin, Fiona. She swore her oath in the flattest voice I'd ever heard in a regular, which made me think I might really like her.

The titleholders were followed by the heads of the guilds, a judge, a representative from the Runners of Erstwhile, and various other important people. Most of them merely gave their oaths and returned to their seats. A few were granted boons as Gray had been. It was all excruciatingly boring.

And as time wore on, I felt that distinctive jittery sensation. Someone was casting a spell. Right then and there. Who was it? I looked around, but no one and nothing seemed out of place. Certainly no one was waving any symbols around.

Except for the Emperor. Holy hell.

Aye, the Emperor's lips moved at times other than when he was responding to the oaths. And he was looking around a lot. My gods. The Emperor was performing a spell. He who had increased the sanctions against spell books and the tools of casting. What a hypocrite.

I couldn't figure out what the spell was meant to do. I couldn't see anything happening. Was it a spell to bind people, the people swearing the oaths, to him? That would be horrible. It had to be wrong.

So what was all that about increasing the sanctions against people casting spells? Or, excuse me, pretending to cast spells. Did he really find it a dark poison? Or did he just want to keep all that potential to himself?

What else had he accomplished by casting spells?

Hell.

And then I was horrified to hear the Emperor say, "Source Karish may approach."

I looked at Taro. His shock was clear to see. And the Emperor was looking right at him, perhaps having been aware of his location throughout the entire ceremony.

Taro recovered himself, easing out from the chairs before striding up to the stage, looking all dark and gorgeous. If he was feeling frantic and out of his depth, no one would know it by looking at him.

I really never wanted to be him.

He bowed, which I supposed was correct, instead of kneeling. I couldn't imagine Taro ever being incorrect. Yet the Emperor frowned. "You may kneel."

I clenched my teeth. It was unreasonable, I knew, to be offended on Taro's behalf, that the Emperor would make him kneel when he had no oath to give. We were all required to show deference to the Emperor. It was just that Taro was by far the worthier man.

Taro knelt, as demanded.

"There is an oath We would have from you," the Emperor announced.

Taro couldn't speak for the Triple S, who were not required to give fealty to any monarch. Nor could he speak for the duchy of Westsea. He could speak only for himself.

"We are aware you have not come prepared to speak," said the Emperor. "And indeed, why would you? A mere Source, at an occasion of this magnitude. But We are aware of your loyalty to Our Honored Mother, and We would enjoy the comfort of sharing such a worthy gift. Solicitor Tarin, if you will."

The solicitor stepped forward, and if Taro wasn't panicking, I was. He couldn't swear an oath of loyalty as Source Shintaro Karish. It was essential that a Source remained above and beyond influence. If people thought a Source's skills could be controlled by anyone outside the Triple S, the results would be . . . well, unimaginable by me right then, but definitely neg-

ative. One of the reasons everyone was expected to help support members of the Triple S was to avoid the perception that
anyone owned us.

"If you would repeat after me, Source Karish . . ."

And yet, Taro could hardly refuse to give whatever oath the
Emperor might demand, especially in front of all these people.
Those repercussions would be highly negative as well. No
doubt that was one of the reasons the Emperor chose to do it
at this time. And damn him for doing this. What was he playing at?

"I, Shintaro Ivor Cear Karish"—and the solicitor thought
Taro was an idiot, because he paused there so Taro could repeat his own name—"do swear personal loyalty to you, the
Emperor." Taro hesitated just long enough to be noticeable to
everyone, and when he did speak the words, it was in a voice
so low I couldn't hear them. But I didn't doubt they had been
said. I was sure the Emperor wouldn't feel too ashamed to
berate Taro, loudly and at length, should my Source fail to give
the oath.

"Putting my services to the use of the Emperor . . ."

That got a reaction from the crowd, those that understood the significance of what was going on. Damn it, damn it,
damn it.

". . . and his heirs in perpetuity . . ."

Once Taro was allowed to stop talking, the Emperor gave
no responding oath of protection. Wonderful. So Taro was
expected to serve the Emperor in some way and would be left
hanging when things went wrong. He did say this: "As a
reward for the loyalty you have demonstrated before these
great people, We grant you the comfort of your true home.
Flown Raven has been enduring earthquakes recently and is in
need of a Pair. Henceforth, your post shall be Flown Raven.
You are dismissed."

Son of a bitch!